1

LUV, BAJAN STYLE

For Audrey (SBB)

"If it feels good, do it."

Alphonse Mattia, Tonyville,
Mt. Standfast, St. James, Barbados
Circa 1986

One

Barbados 1986

Brian McKenzie motored the fifty-five-foot black hull sloop MY CANADIAN MISTRESS, into Carlisle Bay, and turned the engine key to the off position. The two and a half day sail from the island of Antigua was both exhilarating and exhausting, but he was pleased with his purchase of the Mystic 55, since it had handled superbly on the open sea, despite the frequent need to tack, and with Susan able to spell him in the cockpit. The English built boat had been sailed down to Antigua two months earlier to allow for any changes that might be needed, but most of the acceptable conveniences were standard and already in place. Brian however was specific regarding the placement of the name and did ask for a photo to be taken and emailed to him in New York.

Susan McKenzie came up the ladder from below, already changed from her bikini to a halter-top and matching blue shorts. "What's up Love?" She asked as the anchor hit bottom and bit deeply into the sand.

Brian watched her moved seductively toward him. She was as beautiful as ever after eighteen years, her daily workouts keeping her in excellent shape.

"There is a launch approaching. Possibly their Coast Guard to check out our papers. Honey, make certain our passports are topside, and give a yell to the kids to come up on deck." Brian had earlier changed into tan slacks and a yellow golf shirt.

As Susan disappeared below, he observed that the launch bore no official insignia, other than the artistically painted face of a leering pirate on both sides of its bow. He smiled wondering if Blackbeard himself was here to escort them ashore. David was the first to come topside, followed by Meghan a few years younger, and the image of her mother as she ran to the bow, waving to the approaching vessel.

Brian was able to make out printing on its port side as it came about. 'PIRATE ADVENTURES', it read with a local phone number printed below. "Ahoy!" A voice called out. "We have come to bring you ashore. May we come aboard to assist you?"

"Sure," Brian called out. "Are you the Barbadian water taxi welcome? What a great service." The two men, who introduced themselves as Joey and Jollybuns, boarded the sloop and then helped the four Americans onto their launch.

Meghan laughed and when she asked the taller of the two why he was called Jollybuns, he turned around and wiggled his rear as Susan blushed. "How come you have a normal name?" David asked of the man at the tiller.

"You know," Joey, said, "most of us Bajans have nicknames since childhood, but I guess no one ever got around to giving me one." Their patois was more understandable, the McKenzies having spent time in Antigua.

It took no time to reach the dock, where a tall, tanned man, sporting a black mustache and matching goatee waited. "That be Mr. Geoffrey Townsand. He sent us out to fetch you all." Joey said.

Susan smiled as the launch touched the rubber tires protecting the dock. "How did he know that we had to be fetched?" She remarked as she accepted Geoffrey's hand. David and Brian stepped up on the dock as Jollybuns lifted Meghan, and handed her to Joey. Once the passengers had disembarked, Joey climbed back into the launch, started the engine and motored off as Jollybuns did an exaggerated wiggle much to Meghan's delight.

Geoffrey Townsand introduced himself and while, Brian thought that he held Susan's hand for an extraordinary period of time, she did not seem to mind.

"Actually one of my catamarans passed you at sea and, the captain radioed that they had seen your sail. They also said that there were two beautiful women aboard, so I came down to the pier to see for myself. I trust that I have offended no one." Susan blushed again. "Tell me, what does that magnificent hull draw? Not too much I should imagine." Geoffrey inquired.

"Draws about eight feet or so according to specs," Brian responded.

"I just fancy all boats, particularly such gorgeous sloops as yours. If you plan to spend some time on my island, I can offer you a slip in the Deep Water Harbor next to my two cats." Townsend said.

"That would be very nice," Susan said. "But we should be just fine in the bay. What do you think Brian?"

"Probably safer closer in." He responded.

"Good. The only time ship are moored out in deep water is when we expect rough seas, so they do not rock onto the dock and do damage." Townsand said. "So, it is done. Although they work for Miles, I am certain either Joey or Jollybuns would bring in your boat later. What ever might be your pleasure? Tell me. What do you call her?

"She is called 'My Canadian Mistress'", Brian replied

"Really?" Geoffrey said as he addressed Susan. "Are you then Canadian?"

"Actually, no. I am a born and bred New Yorker, but Brian is from Canada. However, he was born here in Barbados, you know."

Brian smiled. "Yes, both my mother and father are Bajan but they moved to Ontario when I was but four, and sadly I remember nothing about the island."

"Fantastic! Listen you two, I should be quite rude if I did not offer you a drink to welcome you all to Barbados. Come. One of our best bistros is just a short drive from here, so we can sit and talk." It was difficult to refuse Geoffrey's offer so they all settled into his Mercedes and drove to the Careenage. Susan still had not become accustomed to driving on what she considered the wrong side of the road.

He sat them at a table under an umbrella that advertised a local beer called Banks.

David and Meghan drank limeade, but Geoffrey order an amber colored rum that he taught Brian and Susan to shoot, followed by an ice water chaser. Then he asked if either of them smoked, and finding neither did, Geoffrey admitted that he had happily given up the habit a few years back.

"So," Geoffrey said, "You sail quite an expensive boat. What may I ask do you do for a living?"

Brian looked at Susan and then to Geoffrey. " Susan is an attorney and I work for a brokerage firm. What do you do here on the island Geoffrey?"

Geoffrey looked at Susan. "I lease two cats that take guests on day trips, but my full time occupation is in Villa rentals. My office is not far from here in Fontabelle."

He handed each a business card, drained his glass and gulped some ice water, wiping away any liquid that had dripped on his mustache. "And sometimes I captain an Adventure cruise. So, what brings you to Barbados?"

"We all have roots. I wanted to find mine. When I purchased the sloop, it seemed that sailing from one island to another would be just ideal, and since I may have descendants on Barbados, David thought it would be exceptional to write an essay, and actually those were the terms under which his school would permit him a holiday. They have become quite strict you know." Brian said. "Both Susan and I have worked hard at our professions and fortunately are able to take extended vacations."

"A moment. McKenzie, I seem to recall that name but the only McKenzies I know are blacks, and one happens to be employed by me. Brian, I believe that I can be of help to you finding family. We shall go to the Barbados Museum where I shall speak to people who will assist David in gaining access to the Archives at the University in Black Rock. "

Geoffrey thought for a moment. " I know it can be done since a while back, a friend, was allowed to do just that. Trust me young man."

"We really must not take you away from your own work." Susan said. "I am certain that your time is very valuable."

"Not a problem and I shall insist." Geoffrey said.

As they returned to the Mercedes, a man in a red and white striped shirt approached Geoffrey, and briefly spoke to him. Geoffrey opened the front door of the Mercedes for Susan and indicated that Brian and the children occupy the rear seats.

"I must admit, I did not understand one word you said to that man." Susan said.

"Every once in a while I do lapse into Bajan which is easier for me when I speak to the locals. That man works the sails on one of my ships and also fills in as kitchen help when lunch is served. Actually, we most likely spoke of nothing that might interest you." Townsand replied, "and it would please me if you would call me Geoffrey, as in Rush, the actor."

As he gunned the engine of the Mercedes and spun about a turnabout, David asked. "Geoffrey, does everyone drive as fast as that in Barbados?"

"Only when one desires to get somewhere," Townsand replied with a smile.

They soon arrived at the Barbados Museum and found it filled with tourists from a Norwegian cruise. David was attracted to a glass case that held what appeared to be very old documents, while Meghan found shells more interesting.

Geoffrey continued to chat up Susan while Brian stared at an old map of Barbados that clearly outlined all of the parishes.

"East Coast looks interesting." Brian said.

"Our Atlantic Coast is absolutely marvelous." Geoffrey said. "I must take you all there. Wait, now. I have an idea. We shall settle David at the Archives, and then drive up to St. James and collect my wife, and then pass over to the East Coast Road. You shall love the scenery and a roar of the ocean, so loud that we all must shout in order to be heard. Very often we have Sunday picnics there and you must join us with our friends. I shall teach David, here how to handle a cricket bat, which is a bit different than what you Americans use to strike a baseball." Geoffrey then took a deep breath.

True to Geoffrey's word, the staff at the Archives of the University of the West Indies made every effort to provide David with the material he needed. With all of this history at his fingertips, David thought it might be fun to research his father's family tree, as he undertook to document an adventure that began sometime during the early 1600s and would lead him to an old plantation called Simonton, where he would eventually come across the name of a man called David Thomas McKenzie.

After Joey retrieved their baggage from the McKenzie boat, Geoffrey drove them to Simonton, where a very surprised Rachel Townsand graciously accepted her husband's explanation that he had opened their home to his new friends. Geoffrey brought out a bottle of rum, and the four talked for hours, just getting to know each other.

Two

Barbados 1986

On their second day on the island, Brian, Susan and Meghan spent the morning at Mullin's, a local St. Peter's parish beach between Highway One and the sea. They swam, rented sea scooters from local beach boys, and had the use of the beach bar, its refreshments and showers. On her way to the Fontabelle office, Rachel dropped David off at the Archives in Black Rock where he could continue his research.

Since Geoffrey had left a car at his disposal, Brian, who able to obtain a local driver's license, the previous day in Holetown, drove to Black Rock around noon to pick up David at the University. When they arrived back at the beach bar, they found Susan and Meghan well into their lunch of flying fish on a bun with fries. "Order what we got, Daddy. It's really yummy." Meghan suggested, so Brian did just that, while David opted for a Jamaican patty and a Coke.

"So. How's your research coming along?" Susan asked.

"This stuff is really interesting," David said with a mouthful of patty, and then washed it down with some cola.

"The people there let me have a go at everything. Sometimes it's a bit hard to understand them when they talk fast, but if I listen hard I get the gist of what they are saying."

"Problem is when they ask a question I don't understand and can't come up with a quick response. Now, some of the material is in Old English and hard to read, particularly the ship manifests, but I found lists of people who were transported here as slaves by Oliver Cromwell, who was England's Protector after King Charles was executed. One of the lists contained the name of a Robert Townsand, a Cavalier who supported the King. Do you suppose Geoffrey is a relative?"

Brian finished the last bite of his sandwich and started on the fries. "Why don't you ask him this evening?"

Susan said. "Do you suppose the question might offend him, being related to a criminal?"

"No, Mom, these people were not necessarily criminals although, a bunch of those types were sent here as well. Apparently their only crimes had to do with their support of the King, or they might have been captured in battle."

"I don't see it as a problem and it did occur almost five hundred years ago." Brian said.

After lunch, David changed into a bathing suit and he and Meghan went for a swim, while Susan and Brian found lounges and read about the island from books they found at the house. Susan kept looking to see where Meghan was, but David always was there to protect her from the local beach boys who wanted to take her for what they called a 'free ride' on their water scooters.

After a number of hours in the sun, they showered and changed into shorts and drove down into Holetown, a small community with private homes, a police station, a supermarket and a bakery. There were also a few restaurants and shops that catered to the tourist trade. On the way they passed Miramar Beach as well a number of other beach side hotels. Just before they reached their destination, they observed a school where uniformed children were playing cricket, a game unfamiliar to both David and Meghan.

The Super Center was a rather compact supermarket whose rows were so narrow, that one could barely maneuver the small shopping cart around people coming toward you. The prices were in Barbadian dollars approximately twice the value of American paper. They first did a perusal of the store in an attempt to see what was available. The Cadbury chocolates were the first things into the cart as both David and Susan had a sweet tooth, but Susan was careful to read the labels to make sure that they were made in England.

They walked around to the rear of the market where they found bins of tropical fruits such as papayas and mangos, bags of raw peanuts and slightly bruised bananas. None of the scrawny, blemished, vegetables, appeared to have been cultivated. Behind an ancient glass case, a man in a wide brimmed straw hat and a dirty apron carved meat and was obviously the butcher. As they walked the aisles, they heard the chatter of the local patois, some of which they understood. Susan was particularly interested in the dairy section where a variety of butters and cheeses from New Zealand and Ireland were displayed, but she was immediately turned off by the blue color of the frozen meat, some of which was labeled clog. Finally, they came across, the alcoholic beverage section, which was relatively small, and were able to select from many bottles of local rums, placed along side of expensive wines and imported liquor, that they could have been purchased at duty free for half the price.

"I'll spring for a bottle of Dewar's," Brian said. "I noticed one almost empty at the house."

"At that price, you are insane," Susan said. "Find something cheaper or just drink local rum which is certainly more reasonable."

"No. The Townsands have been more than accommodating. It shall be well received." Brian responded, placing a bottle into the cart.

"Well, all right, but do get some rum. I believe Mount Gay is a good one." Susan said. "We have not bought all that much."

After they paid for their purchases and locked them in the boot of the car, Meghan suggested that it might be fun to check out the shops. "Please we have enough hats and tee shirts." Susan advised.

"Let them have their fun." Brian said. In a shop that sold records and small tapes, they came across an album featuring a group called the Merrymen. After reading the information on the cover, David found out that they were a local group of musicians, and bought a tape. Having completed their excursion, they headed back to Simonton on a road that was now clogged with yellow and blue busses and people just taking a walk. Susan constantly reminded Brian to keep to the left, but he said he understood the traffic rules on the island, having driven in Antigua.

When they reached the plantation house, they found Rachel and Geoffrey on the spacious stoned patio that overlooked a garden in the rear of the house.

Large casuarina trees around a good size pool provided swimmers some protection from the strong rays of the midday sun. Since it was already late afternoon, the air felt cool as the sun neared the horizon to the west.

"As you can see, we started without you", Geoffrey said as he showed them his half filled glass. He offered them seats and asked what they would all prefer to drink. Brian presented the bottles of rum and Scotch. When Geoffrey saw the latter, he said, "Scotch is too dear on the island. We Bajans do not drink our friend's expensive liquor as such."

"Our gift for your graciousness," Susan said, winking at Brian.

"Right, Geoffrey said, "now who is drinking what?" He poured two shots of rum an offered them to Susan and Brian. Rachel sat and nursed a glass of Scotch whiskey and soda. "There is ice and water at the wet bar, and if you wish cocoanut water or what we Bajans call nature's chaser, feel free. Meghan and David, having already changed into bathing suits, took their cups of lime squash down to the pool.

Geoffrey refilled his glass and did the same for Susan and Brian. "I trust that David had no issues at the University."

"He said all was good and he found everybody more than helpful." Brian responded.

"And he has a question or two for you." Susan added.

"Not a problem," Geoffrey said. He walked to the edge of the patio and stared at the grounds. "You realize that this plantation holds an amazing amount of history, and some of its relic windmills and old building are still standing. Feel free to explore the property and make certain you visit the old sugar mill, a fantastic bit of engineering for its time. That is where the cane was processed. Now, whatever cane is grown, is cut by day laborers and then loaded onto trucks to be taken to the new factories on the top road."

If you are interested in nostalgia, there is an old cemetery where Simonton families are interred, still protected by an ancient tamarind tree. From there, the view of the Caribbean is spectacular." He turned to his guests. "Refills all around?" No one refused. He looked at Brian. "I must thank you both for your generous gift of Scotch whiskey, although it was not at all necessary."

Rachel, who had been chatting up Susan, looked at her watch. "It is getting late, and I am certain you all wish to shower before dinner. Anna has prepared a delectable pork roast with local vegetables. It smells just gorgeous. She has turned out to be a remarkable find for us."

"You both have gone to so much trouble to make us comfortable in your home and after all, we are strangers. You both have to work and we are on holiday." Susan said.

Geoffrey refilled the glasses again. "I must tell you both something. From the first time we met down at the Careenage, I knew we all would be friends. You are in no so sense strangers. Believe me."

Susan called David and Meghan up from the pool to shower and change for dinner. As Geoffrey met them at the patio steps with towels, Meghan said, "David found your ancestors or something."

"What is this I hear?" Geoffrey asked.

"I found the name of a Robert Townsand among a list of indentured servants sent by Cromwell to Barbados." David said, looking scornfully at his sister.

"Do you mean to infer that I am related to convicts, and common criminals?" Geoffrey asked. "You are inferring that great-great-great grandfather was a thief?"

"Oh! No, Sir." David responded embarrassed. "They were really not criminals. They just sided with the King."

"I know." Geoffrey said with a twinkle in his eye. "I was just skylarking with you. I know that some of the family was transported here as slaves, but I never took the time to check it out. Perhaps, in the course of your research, you might look up my family tree and find a branch for each of them."

"I would be honored to do so." David said proudly. "After all, you are really a good guy, and skylarking is a new word for me. I shall have to remember it."

"Thank you for that, young man." Geoffrey said. "It means, let see, joshing or lazing, perhaps not the right choice but I believe you get my meaning. We Bajans have a language of our own, and a word for everything even if we alone understand its meaning. Rachel, I believe we have a book in the bedroom on Bajan dialect that David might like."

"I know exactly where you left it." Rachel said. "Everyone. Time to shower."

Susan and Brian showered together in a bathroom that adjoined their bedroom, toweled off and dressed for dinner. Susan selected a red strapless dress that came to just below her knees.

Brian decided on a flowered shirt and white pants and put on a pair of sandals ,while she opted for a dressier pair of black pumps.

Dinner was delicious or as Rachel referred to it as simply gorgeous. Meghan was exhausted, but decided to fight sleep and watch an old Lucy sit-com on television, while David said he would write up some of the information he had collected.

Susan and Brian had gone back to the room when there was a rap on their door, and Geoffrey entered. "Party time. We are going to the Coach House for after dinner drinks and to meet some very good friends of ours.

Brian came down wearing a jacket, but Rachel took it from him and placed it on the back of a chair. "Quite informal, you know. Comfortable shirt and trousers and those flip-flops are just fine. You shall meet no people putting on airs, except perhaps some British tourists whom Geoffrey and I call four-fours, because of the way their mouths are shaped, and the sounds they make. I do believe it is because of their large upper teeth."

Geoffrey smiled. "This is Barbados where there is a time for proper formality, but tonight is not one of those."

As it turned out, the Coach House was a local watering spot where the Bajans came to unwind. It consisted of a thirty foot bar that curved around to the left where there were a few tables already occupied by people having fun. Three bartenders poured rum and assorted other liquids from large bottles suspended upside down from shelves behind the bar. Taps connected to hidden kegs advertised Banks beer, the local brewery product.

Susan ordered a sugar cane brandy and soda as recommended by Geoffrey, and began to examine the old pictures that covered walls of the bar that was once part of a grand estate. Brian and Rachel were deep in conversation with a large man whom Rachel introduced as the chef at the Miramar Beach Hotel. He was rather friendly and jovial and Brian took to him immediately. Susan went outside to escape the smoke from the Dunhill and 3Fives cigarettes that polluted her air space, and found a bench by an old horse carriage that long ago been left on the lawn and forgotten.

Geoffrey caught up with her in the car park and handed her a drink. "Could not take the smoke? I do not blame you at all, at all."

He gazed up at the dark sky, filled with an uncountable number of stars. "We have been blessed with a cool, rainless evening, and look at the stars," he said. "A beautiful Bajan night, and I am with a beautiful woman."

Susan smiled. "Truly magnificent. So much light where we live, you cannot appreciate the vastness of the universe." Susan said sipping her drink.

"We Bajans would reply True, True. So if you want to be included among us you must say it as well." Geoffrey said taking her hand. "Go ahead."

Susan looked at him. "It is definitely a True, True night.

Geoffrey smiled and squeezed her hand. "Now I shall teach you something else." He made a noise with his tongue and lips that had a squeaky clipping sound. "That is chip sing," he said.

"We make that sound for a number of reasons. It could be used for doubting something, or showing slight annoyance, but we use it for more reasons than I can think of."

Susan attempted to make the sound and succeeded on the first try. "Now," he said, "You are a true, true Bajan. Ah, let me refresh your drink," He said taking her glass.

"I'll go with you. We'd best see what Brian and Rachel are about." Susan said as she slid her hand from his grasp, and followed him back into the noisy bar.

Geoffrey introduced Susan to Sandy the bartender, who refilled their glasses. "Now, we have not yet made a toast. To what should we toast?" He said raising his glass. "I know to your maiden visit to our island and many more, I hope."

"I shall readily drink to that, but it is also my birthday, and do not ask what year, since you will not get a true, true answer." Susan said as their glasses clicked.

"Well, since asking the age of the celebrant is a Bajan custom, I shall defer to the second rule that states, if age is not forthcoming, a kiss is required." Without waiting for a response, he brushed his lips against hers.

Susan put her arms around his neck and forced her lips against his. "I know you can do better than that." She said. "This is a more acceptable birthday kiss."

"True. True" He said as he kissed her again.

Susan laughed and downed the rest of her drink. "Bajan custom my ass. You made all of that up." The bar was so crowded, that no one seemed to notice as he kissed her again

Geoffrey looked at his watch. "Best we find our spouses, My Luv. It is getting close to the witching hour and we locals do have to go to work in the morning." Rachel and Brian were in the car park waiting for them.

"Rachel introduced me to the nicest people." Brian said. " I have to thank you for a great evening and am beginning to understand why Barbados is such a fantastic place." The four got into the Mercedes and Geoffrey started the engine.

"Air or Bajan air?" He asked, and the other three responded by opening their windows. "So you all like our island. You have not seen anything yet," he said as he moved the car slowly out onto the road. "Tell me, do you switch?" Susan squeezed Brian's hand tightly but neither uttered a word. "Oh, well then. Do you play bridge? If so, we could spend an evening playing bridge instead of frequenting any of our many drinking venues. Or to quote Leonard Bernstein's Candide, we can enjoy the best of all possible worlds."

Brian held on to Susan's hand as she answered, "True, True."

Three

Simonton Plantation, Barbados

The Townsands had completely renovated Simonton Great House when they purchased the plantation, and with the help of old records and diagrams, began to bring back the grandeur that the old place once enjoyed. The great staircase had been replaced with a replica. Most of the original paintings were in bad repair and would require the services of an art restorer. The upper floor had been divided into two wings, each with two bedrooms suites and full baths. Iron gates secured both areas in the evening for the protection of its occupants. The McKenzie bedroom was just across the hall from the master bedroom. Meghan and David were already asleep in the Townsand children's beds, since both of the girls were away in school in Canada.

Brian undressed and lay down on the soft bed. He watched Susan apply assorted creams to her face, as she frowned at new lines that had formed around her mouth and eyes. Alarmed at the thought of growing old, she took time and effort in the care of her skin. Her muscle tone had become taut ever since she joined the health club, and she jogged regularly along the East River, as time allowed.

Brian marveled at how beautiful his wife still looked, and believed that Susan would always be the exciting young woman he met on a blind date he almost never made.

Susan moved under the covers, wearing a short pink nightgown, and nestled next to her husband. She moved her hand to his abdomen and exclaimed, "My goodness! It doesn't take much to get you aroused." She thought for a moment. "So, what is the source of this arousal?"

"With someone as beautiful and sensuous as you lying next to me, why are you surprised?" He said.

"Look, either before or after we make love, we must talk." Susan murmured.

"Wow! Gone in sixty seconds," Brian said dejected. "So much for before. What's on your mind?" He said sheepishly.

"You apparently have forgotten something said in the car on our way back." She said. "If you recall, Geoffrey mentioned something about switching."

"I don't remember ever doing it. Do you?" Brian stammered.

"Well, in any event. I believe it was idle conversation and harmless." Susan added.

Brian looked at her as he reached to turn out the lamp. "So, why the need to discuss it?" He asked.

Susan moved her hand between his legs. "Brian, are you attracted to Rachel?" She asked, stroking his penis.

Brian thought for a moment as he began to respond to her caress. "Rachel is a beautiful woman. I am certain many man on this island has desired her. Hold on now. Where is this going?"

"You have not answered my question, and while I believe the entire matter to be moot, let's explore the possibility." She continued to stroke him gently.

"Susan! We are not discussing the purchase of a new washer and dryer." He exclaimed.

"I understand, but let's pursue this conversation." Susan responded. "We can discuss the pros and cons."

"Okay. While I am not comfortable with where this is going, how about discussing contracting a disease as a strong con." Brian retorted.

"There are always condoms." Susan said.

"You know condoms are not foolproof. You recall the angst when we had one tear before we were married. We have two great kids and since not wishing for more, I had a vasectomy and you had your tubes tied. I always thought it was overkill, but that's what you wanted." Brian said.

"Well, I just wanted to be certain. Vasectomies have been known to fail." She offered.

"Okay, then, so what's your point?" He asked.

"Well, we have never done anything like this before and I have concerns that, if we do, we might like it. Do you suppose Geoffrey was serious or just skylarking?" Susan asked.

Brian sat up in bed and turned the bedside lamp back on. "Now that I think more about this, I saw how he looked at you, and you both were away from the bar for a while. I would say he was serious. Very serious."

Susan leaned back on her pillow. "If we did it, do you think that it would screw up our marriage?" You know I love you as much today as when we first met, and I hope you feel the same."

Brian thought for a moment about the potential consequences of switching partners. "Susan, if we go into this, we must agree that it will be a brief lark. But right now I am getting hard with every word you speak

"I can both see and feel it," She said as his hand moved between her legs. She was very wet. Susan swiftly lifted off her nightgown and moved toward Brian. "Darling, get those pjs off. I cannot decide whether to make love tonight or just, plain fuck!"

Four

Barbados 1986

Geoffrey and Rachel had left for their office in Fontabelle at 6 a.m., after advising Anna to allow their guests to sleep late. Brian, awakened at about eight, went down to the patio where David and Meghan were having breakfast. Allowing Susan some extra sleep, he drove David to the Archives, and told Meghan that he would meet them at Mullin's beach. Upon his return, he found Susan in a small kiosk, bargaining with a woman selling beach attire. After changing into swim trunks, Brian took Meghan on a banana boat ride that she thought was rather silly. By two in the afternoon, they had tired of the sun and sand, and all three drove to the University to collect David. Once back at Simonton, and finding the house to themselves, Brian chose to swim laps, Susan read a book she found in the den, and David went off to explore the plantation. Meghan ran upstairs to shower off the sand she had acquired at the beach.

Dinner that evening consisted of broiled steak fish with potatoes, and a dessert of pecan pie. As Anna cleared the dishes, Geoffrey made an announcement. "People," he declared, "I have an idea, and he momentarily left the patio, returning with an acoustic guitar.

"Cool!" David said. "I can play bass guitar."

"You, my young man, are in luck. I have one of those as well. One moment please." He returned with another guitar and handed it to David. "Follow me, if you can. I shall play in the key of C The only key I know." Geoffrey began to play some local songs such as 'Beautiful Barbados' and 'Island Woman', and David had no difficulty following. Susan and Brian enjoyed the music as Rachel sang along. They played and sang for another two hours. Since his sister had long ago gone to bed, David excused himself citing a need to go over his notes from the Archives.

Assured that her son had gone upstairs, Susan announced that she felt hot, and needed to go for a swim in the pool. She hesitated for a moment, disrobed and then dove into the tepid water.

Brian and Geoffrey looked at each other and shrugged. "If it feels good, and it certainly appears so, let's do it!" Geoffrey said, and the two men raced to the pool, removed their clothes, dove in and caught up with Susan who was treading water in the deep end. It occurred to Brian that they might be in big trouble, but the feeling disappeared as Rachel joined them, after depositing four robes on a chair. They swam for a while seemingly attempting to avoid physical contact with each other.

As Geoffrey swam next to her, Susan looked to Brian who seemed nervous. Rachel on the other hand was perfectly comfortable being naked next to Brian, who had difficulty keeping his eyes from her breasts.

Once the four had enough pool play, they exited, and put on the robes Rachel had provided. "We shall play poker." Geoffrey announced. "And clearly only one hand shall afford the big winner. No ante required, but the loss of a hand shall require an article of clothing."

"But, Geoffrey, we have only our robes," Susan said coyly.

"True, True," Geoffrey said, "so perhaps we should dispense with the ice breaker and get on with what we all want to do." Geoffrey took Susan's hand. "Come with me." He said, leading her back onto the patio, into the house and up the stairs to the bedroom he shared with Rachel, as Brian watched nervously.

Rachel, sensing Brian's discomfort pulled him down to the lounge chair, they now occupied and forced her tongue between his lips. Afterwards she placed his hand on her breast, and as her robe parted, she kissed him again. "We had better go into the house," she said. "We are well protected from the neighbors but it would not be a good idea for the children to find us as such."

Rachel led him back into the house and up to the bedroom that he and Susan shared. As she removed her robe, she felt his growing erection pressing into her thigh.

"What do you suppose they are up to?" He asked meekly.

"What do you think," she responded. "Neither of you have ever done this before, have you?" Brian started to answer, but she placed two fingers on his lips. He said no more as she dropped to her knees and took him into her mouth, as all thoughts of what Susan and Geoffrey might be doing with and to each other disappeared, temporarily from his mind.

It was after midnight when Rachel left the room and Susan returned. Both women had passed each other silently in the hallway. Brian lay naked on a bed, whose sheets and covers had fallen to the floor in disarray. He became, again, aroused when Susan removed her robe, watched her fold it neatly over a chair, and then lay down beside him, amazed what they all had done, and with their children in the house. Susan rolled over on top of him, and helped him enter her. Brian's desires had to be met. What had occurred earlier in the evening had stimulated both of them to a height of passion unequaled to that night when they made love for the first time.

Brian slept fitfully and within a few hours, he awakened to find himself fully aroused. He looked at Susan who was in deep sleep, and reached over to cup her breast. Susan yawned and stretched. "It cannot possibly be time to get up." Her eyes remained closed, and as she softly moaned, Brian fondled her nipple.

"I lie here wondering what the two of you did." He said, staring up at the dark ceiling.

"I don't think that it would be good to compare." She said, finally opened her eyes.

"It is just that I found the thought of the two of you together exciting," He said as she placed her hand between his legs.

"Any more exciting than that is called priapism." Susan laughed. "Look, if we must discuss this. Don't try to make me tell you if he is better than you, because it was different, and I just can't do that. Suppose we start this way. Would you like to make love with Rachel again?"

"How about you with Geoffrey?" He asked.

"No, don't answer my question with another question. It calls for a simple yes or no." She said.

"Yes, I think I would, but that depends upon Geoffrey and Rachel doesn't it. I so hope I satisfied her." Brian said wistfully.

"We had finished and were lying there in bed talking, when we heard Rachel scream for the third time. Certainly I was glad that the children were sleeping off in the other wing of the house. Geoffrey seemed impressed with Rachel's response. I doubt if there is an issue. But I do have some concerns that we should talk about." Susan said as she stroked his penis.

"We won't be talking much if you continue to do that." Brian said as he rolled partially to his side facing her.

"Point well taken." Susan said. "I would very much like to do it with Geoffrey again, and he told me that he wishes that as well, but I explained to him that it would not happen if you did not agree. If this relationship has a chance to continue as such, you must have the same desire for Rachel and she for you. He also asked me about an ménage de trois, but I told him that if you were not one of the three, you might not agree to it. But that is beside the point. It was so exciting, but if we never do it again, I can, reluctantly, live with that decision."

"I have a concern that you might want him more than me." Brian said. "And I would not like to think you might sleep with him without my knowledge."

"That, Luv, shall never happen," She said as she pushed him on his back and rolled over on top of him. "I am awake, so what the hell!"

The next morning, they greeted each other as if nothing had ever happened, and Brian wondered if it all had been a dream.

Both Meghan and David were up at dawn and were already in the pool doing laps. After a breakfast of yogurt, papaya and small sweet bananas called figs, they planned their day. It was decided that Geoffrey would drop David off at the Archives, and asked Brian if he would like to accompany him down to the Careenage, where he planned to check provisioning for the catamarans.

Then he planned to return to St. James to spend the day doing whatever every one wished to do. Brian suggested that he rent a car, but Geoffrey would hear none of that. The traffic was unusually light despite the fact that the 'dig we must or men not working' road crews had broken up portions of the macadam and seemed in no hurry to lay down new road. "That shall look the same for about a week." Geoffrey said. "Our answer to that is, this is Barbados."

They dropped David off on the road in Black Rock since he said he could walk up to the Archives. Once he left the car, Geoffrey turned to Brian and asked if he enjoyed himself the night before. Brian nervously replied in the affirmative.

"Rachel said she would like to do it again, that is if it is good with you, but you realize that it might not become a regular occurrence every night during your stay on the island." Geoffrey said, passing a large blue bus, while avoiding a confrontation with a mini-moke in the on coming lane.

"I understand, and you have a very sensuous wife." Brian stammered. "Susan and I discussed things last night afterwards. Whatever we choose to do we must be cognizant of the children, and not let anything happen that might interfere with our friendship."

Geoffrey smiled as he pulled into the car park. "Tonight we shall go dancing."

Geoffrey and Brian were back by eleven in the morning, and everyone agreed to spend the day at Mullins, but by noon, Rachel having had enough sun, volunteered to collect David, since she had some shopping to do in Holetown. Geoffrey arranged for the remaining four to go out on the glass-bottomed boat and for Meghan to ride on one of the new sea scooters once she had a few lessons. When Rachel returned with David, they drove back to Simonton where, reading, swimming and doing very little seemed what most desired.

The decisions regarding dinner were quickly resolved when Meghan announced that she missed having pizza. "Well, while we have a Pizza House of sorts in Holetown, Barbadians have not figured out that it might be best to be Italian. They have strange toppings such as pineapple," Geoffrey said.

"However, a Kentucky Fried just opened in Black Rock, so I propose we order and I shall go and collect a bucket or two of their best, and I must tell you that at one time, everyone on the island believed that the chickens were obtained by virtue of road kill, but none of that was true. What do you all think of that?" Completely reassured, everyone agreed that KFC would be a great idea.

They finished three buckets of fried chicken that David admitted was as good as that he had ever had at home and demolished the pecan pie, Rachel had purchased in Holetown. Brian decided that he was too full to even think about going dancing, and the other adults agreed much to the chagrin of Meghan who thought it would have been the best idea. The kids found a chess set and became engrossed in that, while, Rachel, who had given Anna the night off, was happy that there were no dishes left to clean. Geoffrey brought out the rum bottle and some ice water and re-taught Susan and Brian the fine art of drinking Bajan quickies.

With the kids already in bed, Brian announced he was exhausted and both he and Susan returned to their room, when it was evident that nothing more exciting was to happen this evening.

"You don't suppose there is a problem?" Brian asked.

"Why?" Susan snickered. "Everyone needs a night off, don't you think?"

"I know, I guess I was just anticipating something exciting." He said as he felt her hand moving between his legs.

"I can feel that you were, and we have had sex so many times, I have lost count. I really don't know how many times. You remember you kept me up half the night." She said. "I doubt if you have been denied."

"Oh, you really were not just an innocent bystander." He replied. "You do not suppose this is a test of some kind?"

"Hey, you are an educated, sophisticated person. It is nothing. Leave it alone." She said.

"Maybe it was too much Kentucky Fried." He said as she glared at him.

"I feel that it was a positive influence on our sex life, which was becoming much too routine," he said. "What happened to make this so important?"

"I don't know but I do agree with that sex has become exceedingly stale, but if this works, who cares. Maybe we just became too predictable, and the fact that someone else desires us has made our own sex life less routine and considerably more exciting. We just must handle it properly." Susan said.

"Okay, so if for argument sake we do not ever switch with the Townsands again, why can't you tell me what the two of you did? Brian asked.

"Are you just so upset that you did not screw Rachel tonight?" Susan asked.

"Perhaps I am just angry with myself for agreeing to be a participant in the first place." He said.

"All right, if it is so important to you, here are the dirty details. When we got up to the bedroom, we took our robes off and frankly I did not know what to do, but Geoffrey quickly relieved me of that responsibility, and laid me down on the bed, where he kissed me and I responded to his kisses. I felt him grow against me and had the scary feeling that he was going to be too big to get inside me. Are you getting all of this?"

She looked at Brian who waited for her to continue. "He kissed and then alternately sucked my nipples and it felt wonderful, and then he asked if I liked to be eaten and I said yes. He put his tongue between my legs and thought I that I would cum, but he knew when to stop. It gets better, Brian."

She looked for a reaction, but he said nothing. "I took it upon myself without him asking to put his penis in my mouth and I sucked it until he pushed me on my back. I swear that it was as big as large salami, and he put it in me. Neither of us uttered a dirty word and we both came together and it was wonderful. Now tell me how it was to fuck Rachel? We did not use condoms, did you?"

"I am not certain how I can top that, but why would you think it was as big as a salami." He asked.

"Give me a break!" Susan replied. "I'm going to sleep."

Five

Barbados 1986

Brian had begun to doze off at the pool when he heard Rachel drive her car between the iron gates. It was Thursday, and he and Susan, having had enough of the beach, had decided to stay at Simonton. Susan had already gone back in to find something for lunch.

"Hey everyone. I would fancy a rum and coke. How about you two?" Rachel called out from the kitchen. Susan went out to the patio to see what he wanted to drink, and asked him to call Meghan to have something to eat.

Drinks were poured, and the three adults settled down on the patio as Meghan announced she was going to take a shower. "Tonight, we go on a Pirate Cruise which is lots of fun." Rachel said. "The children shall go as well, so collect some clothes and a bathing suit for David. We shall pick him up on the way." David had decided to spend the entire day in the Archives. She explained that Geoffrey would captain the ship for the evening, as a favor to the owner, adding that it was a rare occurrence for him to do so. "Lots of Canadians from Quebec booked for tonight, and they are a strange lot, but fun since few speak but a smattering of English. They shall drink lots of beer, and get sloshed, while consuming the rest of the keg in the few minutes is takes to return to the Careenage, but they are very faithful and pay well.

It was a full boat and of course, Geoffrey would not let Brian pay for anything. "Watch out for the rum punch. It is eighty proof and needs lots of ice." He wore a Tee Shirt with a picture of a bearded pirate across its front with the initials P.A. in its center. Geoffrey explained that the usual band had been booked for another occasion so a new group called the Oistin Five would be playing on the upper deck this evening. David and Meghan loved the rope swing, and had to be pried away for a dinner consisting of stewed chicken and rice, with a macaroni salad. David particularly liked what Geoffrey referred to as the sexy garlic bread.

The band energized the crowd as they sang some of their own songs as well as some that the Merrymen had made popular. The boat lay at anchor off Austins Bay, a last minute choice since the sea to the north closer to Mullins Beach, was reported not to be its usual calm. As Rachel had advised earlier, the French Canadians were a happy, drunk group of grocers who enjoyed rum and lots of Bajan beer. David and Meghan made friends with two people their age and the language barrier that initially stood between them was quickly forgotten, as they danced to the beat of the calypso music.

After dinner, Susan followed Geoffrey back to the helm, where he was to perform the perfunctory scripted tourist marriage.

When Brian observed Rachel being hassled by an inebriated guest, he placed himself between the two, and put his arm around her. She responded by taking his hand, and as their eyes met, he knew that their first night together had meaning for both of them. The crew weighed anchor, a huge metal claw that was winched up from the sea by motor power, and with a strong wind that took the sails, Geoffrey steered the boat back toward Carlisle Bay.

As the boat approached its slip in the Careenage, people waiting on the dock, danced to the song 'Hot, Hot, Hot and the Canadians rushed for the beer keg. When the last of the guests were loaded on their buses for the return trip to their respective hotels, Geoffrey met Rachel and the McKenzies back at the Pirate Adventure office where he was selling tee shirts.

"The night is young, people. What ever is your pleasure?" He asked. Both David and Meghan said they were tired, so Geoffrey called Jollybuns who had been helping him sell tees, and asked him to take the two back in Rachel's car, and to stay at the house until they returned. "Not sure what time, Mon, but make yourself at home."

They drove down to St. Lawrence Gap, where they drank, chatted up people at the Yellow Bird Hotel, and then bar hopped back toward Holetown where they brought their glass from one pub and refilled it at the next. While Geoffrey and Susan's relationship seemed to have been established, it took Brian's protective action on the boat to convince Rachel that she could take a lover that her husband had perhaps not chosen for her. The four had become so comfortable, that Brian and Rachel now occupied the rear seats of the Mercedes that sped down the dark empty road back toward the plantation.

Considering all that they had to drink, all four were relatively sober. "Too bad the hour is late." Geoffrey said, as Brian noted that it was two in the morning on the console clock. "If it were earlier and we were hungry, we could have gone to Enid's, a local chicken place on Baxter's Road. Phenomenal fried chicken." He added.

They found the house secure and the gates to the wing where the children slept, locked. Except for the sounds of the trade wind as it passed over, the house was silent. Rachel wakened Jollybuns who had dozed on the living room couch and let him out. He had only a short walk to his home down the road. The four, still energized by the evening sat on the dark patio and despite the lateness of the hour, chose to chat.

Geoffrey leaned back in his chair and looked up at the star filled sky. "For all of my experiences on this island, and Lord knows, as well as Rachel, there have been many, I believe that the four of us have developed something of an unbreakable pact, and we both wish you to understand, that Rachel and I shall always be at the ready if needed, and Susan, I know this shall be true of you and Brian." He walked over to Brian and hugged him, and then turned to Susan to kiss her. "We have a very unique love story," he whispered into her ear, and she was pleased that Brian seemed not threatened by it all.

"Don't even ask about another rum quickie," Brian said with a laugh. "I am just about sobering up." Rachel took his hand and was willingly led back to the bedroom where they fumbled with each other's clothing, lay down on the bed and quietly made love. They dozed in each other's arms for a short while only to be awakened by the sound of Donna Summer's 'Love Me, Love, Me Baby coming from the master bedroom.

"Geoffrey just loves to do it to Donna Sommer. Actually, that did not come out right, but he probably would do her as well. You know I meant the song." She smiled and kissed Brian, rolled over him, collected her clothing and left. The wait for Susan seemed endless, and at least another half-hour passed before she quietly entered the room, her dress neatly folded over one arm. She was naked.

"Where you been, Luv? Rachel left a long time ago." Brian asked turning on the small table lamp.

"Just chatting and did not realize the time." She said.

"The three of you?" She nodded as she got into bed and pulled the sheet over her. "You were all lying naked, together, in the bed?"

Susan chip singed. "Only talking or would you rather I make up a story that we all had unbelievable steamy sex, particularly Rachel and myself?" She fluffed the pillow and tucked it under her head.

"You know that men get a charge out of seeing beautiful woman making love." He said as he turned toward her.

"What study is that you are quoting? Brian, you really are not mad at me for staying a bit with them are you?" She asked.

"I just think that it would have been fine if you all invited me in as well," he said as he cupped her breast in his hand. She moved away. "Why?" He asked.

"They are a bit sore. Geoffrey did a job on them, so a bit gentler fondling please. Tell me. Why do you suppose men would rather watch two women and not two men? Sex is sex."

"You are being facetious. Gay men would like to see two men, but most men are not gay. Let me ask you that question." He said.

"Would you be turned on by two men?" She said she would not and he breathed a sigh of relief.

"What was the sigh for?" She asked.

"Nothing," He answered. "So since you brought it up, would you consider having sex with Rachel?"

"Actually that was what the three of us talked about. Geoffrey wanted to explore the possibilities, so that if it happened, no one would be hurt." She responded.

"He's quite the conductor, isn't he? I am hurt because I was not included. When were you planning to tell me?" He asked.

Susan turned of the lamp and rolled over and mounted him. "Shut up and make love to me."

The next morning all four adults slept until nine, so Anna arranged for Jollybuns to drive David to Black Rock on his way to work. After a breakfast of flying fish and eggs with home fries and a few cups of caffeine, Geoffrey offered to drive Susan to Bridgetown, since she wanted to shop at Cave Shepherd, one of the island's major department stores.

Despite the late hour, many school and commuter busses clogged the road, and since taking the top road would put them out of their way, Geoffrey was content to sit in traffic, giving him a chance to talk further with Susan.

"Susan," he said without taking his eyes from the road ahead, behind one of the big blue buses that picked up and dropped off riders at every stop. "How would you feel about having sex with Rachel and myself?"

She thought for a moment. "Sounds like it could be very exciting, but what exactly would you expect from the two of us?"

"Well, it certainly would give the three of us an opportunity to explore our sexuality." He said.

"Goodness, Geoffrey it sounds too clinical for me. Sex is supposed to be fun. Right?" She said as an open yellow bus with riders standing precariously on a rear running board, passed both the Mercedes and the long blue bus, barely avoiding a collision with an overloaded truck hauling sugar cane.

"Look, Susan. We all seem so comfortable with each other and I would think that it might be healthy for you and Rachel to become closer." He said.

"You are speaking in the physical sense, Geoffrey. For starters, I, we, have never done anything like this before, and the two of us seem to be excluding Brian from the equation, which is something I am not at all comfortable with. Why is it that important to expand already acceptable horizons?" She asked.

"Because it would seem the natural transition." He said. "And because I crave excitement in my life."

"And what are Rachel's needs for excitement? Are they the same as yours?" She asked.

"Rachel has a very open mind." He responded.

"Geoffrey, you know that begs the question, and keep your eyes on the road, please." Susan said. "Is it your ultimate goal that Rachel and I have a physical relationship?"

"No, but it would be a hell of a kick for me, what ever the two of you might decide to do." He said.

"Of course, Brian would have to agree to all of this", Susan said, realizing that she might have lost the argument.

"Luv, he will surely want his turn at it." He said.

"I never asked you what Rachel's feelings are about this," Susan said.

"She cannot wait," Geoffrey said, turning the Mercedes into the car park. "And I cannot wait as well," He said as he turned off the ignition. "Call me at the office when you are ready to return and I shall come for you if I can, or send someone to take you back if it is clear that I will be detained."

Susan exited the car and laughed as she approached the walkway, and soon became lost amid the shoppers and tourists that crowded Broad Street.

Six

Barbados 1986

Rise and shine, everyone!" Geoffrey called out. It was Sunday and neither he nor Rachel had to go to work. Anna had been up early, preparing a picnic lunch of fried chicken with biscuits and sides of macaroni salad and slaw. "Bathing suits only and au natural for those more adventurous, and definitely some protection from the sun. Joey and his gang will tote the pop and collect some ice on the East Coast Road, and Jollybuns has strict orders to make an excellent rum punch. We shall all meet at Pico Tenerife for a day of food, drink and cricket, and, and I must tell you all that David has volunteered to explain American baseball to everyone." Sunday at the beach was a time for the families that worked all week, to meet and just unwind. Everyone looked forward to a good time on the Atlantic shore.

David was happy to have a day off from the dusty shelves of the Archives, but had collected a great deal of information and hoped to have time to start on his paper that night. Meghan was just excited about spending time with children her own age, and Rachel assured her that she would not lack for company.

"I had better collect your folks," he said to David as he approached Brian and Susan's bedroom. The door was partially open so he entered quietly and heard laughter from the shower. "Am I missing anything?" He called out.

Susan parted the shower curtain and laughed. "Just two people in love having fun. Would you mind closing the door?"

"The kids are helping load the boot with food. Time to towel off and get dressed." He said as entered the bathroom closing the door behind him.

As Brian and Susan exited the shower, Geoffrey picked up a towel and proceeded to dry her back. "How about some help for Brian?" She asked.

"Never mind," Brian answered as he quickly dried himself and donned a pair of blue bathing trunks.

"Brian, does this mean we are now even," She said referring to a previous conversation they had had.

"Not the same," he answered. "Geoffrey and I, we are not naked."

"All right," Geoffrey said. "Either I am lost or the two of you are communicating in code. Unimportant. This is our schedule for today. We shall spend the morning on the beach, playing cricket, whatever, and then lunch, and since I understand that both of you are divers, we shall dive the Stavronikita this afternoon, since I always dive that ship on my birthday."

"I see," Susan said as she approached Geoffrey. "Then I demand my right to extract a birthday kiss from you. Tit for tat or something." Brian stood silent watching Susan kiss Geoffrey.

"Stavronikita? What is that?" Brian asked.

"A few years ago, this Russian freighter caught fire out in open sea off the west coast, actually off Miramar Beach. We saw it burn, but there seemed not to be any effort made to extinguish the fire. What was left of the hull was towed in to a mile off shore not far from Payne's Bay and sunk with explosives. The wreck is about three hundred feet long and lies now in about one hundred feet of water. It is a short, but simply beautiful dive, but not for the kids unless they have been certified. I would think that they might like to snorkel with Rachel since she has an ear problem and cannot dive."

"Tell me," Brian asked. "How long shall we be down?" Both he and Susan were certified NAUI, but they had never been deeper than eighty feet.

"Maybe fifteen minutes at most. Most of the time involves the preparation and then decompression hang-time of about ten minutes, and that's pretty much all. The most important thing is that we all stay together, and each diver will have a buddy. Once we are off the dive launch, we can free dive or go down the anchor chain. It is critical that we all are cognizant of how much air is left in our tanks; here are the basic rules. Everyone waits on the launch until signaled to enter the water. No one shall spend more than a total of fifteen minutes on the deck of the ship and no one permits his air to be less than 1500 psi since we must allow for a reserve to decompress for ten minutes below the surface. Be assured we have a dive master who shall go over all of this before we go over the side. More than likely the three of us, and the dive master will comprise the dive team.

"One hundred and twenty feet, you say." Brian's stomach churned a bit.

"That is the depth on which the hull rests." Geoffrey advised. "The deck where we shall land is at eighty feet. Make sure you bring wet cameras if you have any with you. Look, we are almost at Pico Tenerife."

The pink white sand that made up the beach at Pico Tenerife seemed to go on forever, and the roaring surf was just as Geoffrey had described.

A number of people had already set up beach chairs, by the time they arrived, so Rachel and Geoffrey made the introductions. Most of the adults worked for Geoffrey or were in some phase of the tourist business. A cricket game began down near the water where the sand was cooler, and Meghan and David had soon collected another group who were keen to learn about American baseball.

Since the Atlantic Ocean was much too rough for swimming or body surfing, everyone had to settle for sitting in pools of sea water that had collected between the coral reef as the tide moved in and out.

The picnic lunches were washed down with cold bottles of Banks beer, except for Geoffrey, Susan and Brian who selected water or pop since they planned to dive the sunken wreck later in the day. Goodbyes came early for them as they left for Carlton Market car park on the west coast, where they were to meet Ray Stock, the dive master who would take them out to the Stavronikita. Ray was waiting on the beach, with eight bottles of air, that he personally filled and other gear that the divers may not have brought with them. Brian had gone back to their sloop to collect their own regulators, masks, booties and gauges, and Susan brought along a half wet suit since she tended to become cold when diving. Brian and Geoffrey said they would be fine in swim trunks and tees, but the dive master opted for a wet suit as well.

They met Alex, an exceptionally attractive woman, who would drive the dive boat and watch for their bubbles. Once they had boarded and stowed the dive gear, Alex backed the boat from the shallow strip of sand that served as the Carlton Park beach and Ray described the dive and what he would expect from the divers so that safety would be assured. He made specific reference to the need to adhere to the buddy system, and demonstrated the use of the octopus, reviewing the emergency system known as buddy breathing, that most likely would not be needed since there was an adequate air supply for the dive. Nevertheless, he said he would bring an extra bottle of air down with him.

Stock described the various ways one might prefer to enter the water, and the need to wait at the buoy chain until all divers were in the water. It was important that they all stay together, and not drift south with the current, and the only area that would be explored was to be around the ship's helm. Since this was a deep dive, they would not spend more than fifteen minutes, depending upon the remaining air supply and reserve which had to be checked regularly. Upon signal, they all were to ascend slowly to about ten feet below the surface, where they were to decompress for a period of ten minutes. Lastly, he informed the group that two resident barracudas might be circling around the top of the ships mast, but they never bothered with divers.

The divers put on their weight belts, vests, flippers and masks, and when Ray Stock was satisfied that the regulators had been properly attached to the air bottles, he went over the use of hand signals. Susan was the first to go over into the water and waited at the chain for the other three to drop in. The four divers descended slowly into crystal clear water to the deck that was a depth of about eighty-five feet, and then swam around the wheelhouse greeted by thousands of brightly colored fish. While sergeant majors seemed to be the most prevalent, they also saw schools of surgeonfish and gar.

To Brian's dismay, Susan would disappear over the side of the ship periodically. He enjoyed diving but had became more concerned with safety with each subsequent dive, having come to the conclusion that humans were never meant to be swimming around with fish at deep depths. Fortunately, he had brought his watertight camera, and by taking pictures, he concentrated on photography rather than his fears. He remained a cautious diver, checking his gauge often since both depth and over breathing could use up precious air.

The only sounds heard were those of the regulators, as the divers inhaled air and exhaled carbon dioxide.

Ray suddenly appeared with Geoffrey and waved the McKenzies to follow them over the side to see the gaping hole that explosives had made to sink the ship. Then they all swam into the dark hold and existed from a hole on the starboard side.

Brian checked his gauge and noticing that he was already down to 1500 psi, signaled to Ray who pointed upward, advising the start of a slow ascent. Since one of the divers had to descend, Ray indicated that they all would ascend despite the fact that Susan still had plenty of air. Looking upwards, the divers could barely make out the surface, but as they rose, they finally could clearly see the keel of the dive boat. They reunited with Brian at ten feet below the surface and remained for ten minutes to decompress. The barracudas were nowhere in sight, much to Brian's delight.

Alex had set a small ladder in the water where they could hold on and remove their weights first and then finally their flippers, and vest to which the air bottle was attached. Only after all were aboard and the gear secure, did they talk excitedly about what they had just experienced. Brian was amazed how clear the water had been at that depth and believed that his pictures would be exceptional. Geoffrey was so pleased with the dive that announced it was to be repeated every year on his birthday, and insisted that he would pay all expenses as a birthday gift to himself.

They thanked Ray for his assistance and waved as the dive boat moved up the beach toward Payne's Bay where he maintained a dive shop. They were grateful to use the shower in the park to wash off any residual sea salt. When they returned to the house, they found Rachel in the kitchen, and the kids were in the pool. Geoffrey disappeared for a moment and then reappeared with glasses, ice and a bottle of rum.

Susan and Rachel brought some lime squash down to the pool, and Brian remained on the patio with his drink while Geoffrey was speaking long distance to Canada.

Geoffrey refreshed his drink. "The children need more money for this or that, so I shall wire the bank tomorrow. Where are our gorgeous women?"

"They brought some drinks to the pool for the kids." Brian responded.

"They left their cocktails here on the table." Geoffrey said.

"They shall return." Brian advised as Geoffrey took a seat next to him. "Uh, Susan mentioned something about you suggesting a threesome. Perhaps we should discuss this."

Geoffrey downed his rum and finished with an ice water chaser. "I see. Then it is now a forgone conclusion. Good. Great fun we all shall have." He filled his and Brian's glass. "Cheers!" He said as they clinked glasses.

"I think that there better be ground rules." Brian said.

"But that shall take away all of the spontaneity, you know." Geoffrey responded.

"For argument sake, let's say that Rachel, Susan and I are placed in that situation." Brian suggested.

"Then, Cheers all around and more power to you. I say we drink on that as well. I shall get more Mount Gay since I do believe we have polished this one off."

"Wait, have you discussed this with Rachel?" Brian asked as he followed Geoffrey to the bar.

"Absolutely, and I can see that Susan has gotten you up to speed as well." Geoffrey found a full bottle and brought it and a bucket of ice back to the table.

"Actually, we spoke about it the other night but came to no decision, Geoffrey." Brian said.

"Really? I thought Susan was gung ho for it."

"Gung Ho? She told you that?" Brian asked.

"In so many words," Geoffrey responded as he refilled both glasses.

"Perhaps you would share some of the words with me." Brian said.

"I asked her if she would like to be made love to by two men at the same time, and she said she found the thought of it very exciting. Then I broached the subject of two woman and a man, and while Rachel did not say she was appalled by the suggestion, she did say she might consider it." Geoffrey said.

Brian drained his glass, poured another glassful, drained it and followed it with ice water. "You have just mastered the art of a Bajan quickie, at least the drinking kind." Geoffrey said with a laugh.

"Let me phrase it this way." Brian said. "What would you say to having sex with Rachel and me?"

"I do not plan to have sex with you, Brian."

"You are sporting with me. Did I not say it correctly? You know what I mean." Brian said.

"Yes, but you were to have chip singed as well. Look, Brian, make no plans. Just let things happen if they are meant to. What is wrong with exploring our sexuality?" Brian looked at him quizzically.

Susan and Rachel sat next to each other on lounges, watching David and Meghan swim laps in the pool.

They had already each drained two glasses of vodka and soda that Rachel had fixed at the poolside bar.

"We sort of discussed this the other night, but both Geoffrey and I would like to have a physical relationship with you, uh, at the same time." Rachel said, making certain that the kids were making to much noise in the pool to overhear.

"Having never had the experience before, exactly what would be my participation?" Susan asked.

"Your call." Rachel answered. "It could be great."

"My concern is that it has the potential to destroy our marriages." Susan said. "We have already taken a long walk on the dark side."

"Then again, this could help make them more exciting. It really depends if you are willing to take a chance." Rachel said.

"Hm, it could be just an extension of what we have already done, I suppose." Susan said, and leaned closer to whisper in Rachel's ear. "I must share this with you. The other night when you came naked in the room and lay down next to me, I felt aroused."

"I felt it as well. Good, we are half way there, and what else is there to say. I think we let nature take its course, Susan. Let me ask another question. Do you believe there is a difference between fucking and making love?"

"Very definitely, but I doubt if most men know what it is, or if they even believe it exists. While we are talking, how do you feel about the four of us in bed together?" Susan asked.

"It can be awkward, but certainly worth a try. I am going to fix me another drink. You?" Rachel asked.

"Sure. Why not."

"I must ask another question. Why do I have the feeling that you all have done this before?" Susan asked, but Rachel just smiled. "Let us hold the drinks for dinner. I shall check with Anna as to when it shall be ready." She got up from her lounge chair and touched Susan's hand gently.

"Hey guys! Tine to get out, shower and change for dinner." Susan called out and then ran after Rachel. "Wait up, before you go into the house." She caught up with her at the patio steps and saw Geoffrey and Brian deep in conversation. "I had a thought. Since I am still quite tentative about this entire matter, and do not wish to begin something I won't be able to finish, this is what I propose. See if you agree. Since we are attracted to each other, do you suppose we might…I am not sure how to phrase this." Susan stammered.

"Have sex with each other? Like a trial run before the big test?" Rachel whispered. "I think that would be great, but if they found out it would blow their minds. I tell you what, while David is busy in the Archives tomorrow, I can arrange for Joey to take Meghan on a morning cruise. I know Geoffrey will be busy at the office and I'll convince him I need a day off. Boat leaves about eleven."

"Yes, but what do we do with Brian?" Susan asked.

"I think that you must convince Brian that it would be terrific for him to spend what you Yanks call quality time with his daughter. Any way, the day cruises are fun and there will be lots for them to do." Rachel said. And Monday is Anna's day off."

"We are truly wicked." Susan said.

"Not as wicked as we are going to be." Rachel said. "We shall spend our time together, and in the evening, I propose we have a sexually stimulating nude dinner on the patio. How does that sound to you?"

"And the children?" Susan asked.

"I haven't worked that out yet. Of course the other option is to get the boys too drunk to perform. Doesn't ever seem to deter Geoffrey though."

"You know, we have done all right for now. While I think the nude dinner could be spectacular, let's put it on hold for now. But us, and Brian taking Meghan on the cruise is a go." Susan said.

Geoffrey looked up as Susan put two fingers to Rachel's lips. "Our secret."

Seven

Barbados 1986

Brian was on the phone with American Airlines confirming their flight back to New York. With Geoffrey's help, a crew was hired to sail MY CANADIAN MISTRESS back to Antigua, and with luck, it might be chartered often enough to pay for its expensive upkeep.

When Geoffrey came down to the kitchen he announced that neither he nor Rachel were going to work, since they planned to make the McKenzie's last day on the island a memorable one. "Not the last day, by any means," He said. "We want you to consider our island your home away from home and when you return, you shall always stay here with us. This morning, we shall embark on a road trip."

They drove north toward Speightstown, and then turned east passing small communities, each of which had its own grocery, church, petrol station and numerous rum shops. The Mercedes handled the hills without difficulty, and soon they reached the burned out relic of an estate that had once been used in the film 'Island In The Sun' and now Farley Hill had been established as a national treasure.

They continued up to Cherry Tree Hill and down a winding road, where children peddled peanuts, local candy, and stalks of sugar cane and showed their green monkey for a small fee. David was particularly interested in Morgan Lewis, one of the oldest operating windmills on the island, since he had come across its name in his research of the island. They had now reached the Scotland District, and after a ten minute drive came to a small town that consisted of two rum shops, a school, and a police station. Goats and chickens roamed freely along the road. Geoffrey powered the car down the East Coast Road again and to the Atlantic coast of Barbados, where they stopped at Barclay's Park for beer and soda and then continued on to Bathsheba and Three Boys Rocks. There they had lunch and cooled down in the surf. Sated, Geoffrey turned the Mercedes inland, past Coddrington College and up into the hills of St. John and St. Joseph until they reached the Crane Beach Hotel and its magnificent vistas. Passing Seawell Airport, a single story building Geoffrey remarked sadly. "There is where we all shall say goodbye tomorrow, if your plane is on time that is, and both Rachel and I hope for a long delay like an unrelenting ice storm in New York."

Now having made a complete circle, they were back on the top road that led them past the enormous gates of Bagatelle Great House, and Susan remarked how she would like some day to have dinner there.

Geoffrey took a turn past St. Thomas Church, and from the highest point on the road, they could see the Caribbean. Then back onto Highway One, he turned the car south and then up Holder's Hill for a quick look at a polo match, and then down to Sandy Lane for a drink, and another at the Miramar Beach Hotel, and one final drink at John Moore's rum shop where the McKenzie's were made to feel most welcome.

On the way to Simonton, Meghan said she had an important question. "Does everyone on the island drink as much rum as you all?"

Geoffrey responded with this is Barbados.

Brian just said. "We are on holiday."

Rachel said. "Cocktails on the patio when every one has freshened up." The kids said they were going for a swim.

Brian said. "More rum? You have got to be kidding." But was immediately convinced that since it was their final night, the McKenzies owed at least this much to the Townsands. "Oh, well what's the difference? Tomorrow we return to reality."

This time Susan brought two bottles of rum from the kitchen and poured generous drinks. "You cannot imagine how sad I shall feel leaving you all."

Geoffrey raised his glass. "Cheers to our best friends who will assuredly wish to return to this island."

"I have a toast," Susan said. "Well, it's not really a toast but some thing I want to share so you remember us. Okay, lift your glasses everyone and repeat. 'Over the teeth and past the gums, look out stomach here it comes'." With that she fell to the floor laughing.

Rachel suggested that David and Meghan might appreciate a pizza at the Barbados Pizza House in Holetown. The kids, who considered themselves connoisseurs, thought the pizza was pretty good. After dinner, they walked the short distance to the beach and watched the lights on ships moving toward Carlisle Bay.

David looked up into the brilliant sky ablaze with millions of stars. "This was the most fantastic vacation, and I have learned a lot. I also have come across a few surprises that I'll not yet share, but I just know that when I complete my paper, it shall be worth no less than an A plus. Please thank everyone who was so kind to me at the University and I shall send a note when I return to New York."

"I have something to say as well." Meghan offered. I have to thank Rachel and Geoffrey and Joey and Jollybuns and all of the crew on the Pirate Adventure. I will never forget this vacation, and I just don't want to leave." She began to sob.

They returned to Simonton at eleven, and both David and Meghan were finally convinced it was time for bed. After kissing their parents and Rachel and Geoffrey good night, the retired to their wing of the house.

"Well," said Geoffrey. "I am up for suggestions."

"Since I believe myself to be the most sober, I suggest that we pair off and then all four of us meet afterwards. What do you say?" Rachel took Brian by the arm and led him back to his bedroom, leaving Susan and Geoffrey in the den.

"What's your desire, Luv?" Geoffrey asked.

"Last night," she said. "Let's make a go of it."

An hour had passed and Rachel rested her head on Brian's chest. "I guess everyone has talked about a foursome. What do you say we join the two of them?" Brian said.

"Was I not enough for you, Brian? I do believe you just want to watch Susan and Geoffrey do it, don't you?"

"Well, let's just see what they are up to now." He said.

Opening the door to the master bedroom, they found Geoffrey and Susan deep in conversation. "We are here for another round," he announced. He lay down next to Susan, pulling Rachel along side.

"I tell you what and being a good sport. I am going to get myself a tot of rum for me and anyone else and then sit here in the chair and watch the three of you, get me all hot." Geoffrey said as he found a bottle and some glasses in a nearby cabinet.

Brian knew exactly what he wanted as he lay down between the two women, fondling their breasts and pinching their nipples until they began to respond. Rachel and Susan passed knowing glances. "I bet Brian would fancy a massage, Rachel so why don't we give him a good one." Susan and Rachel turned to their stomachs and moved down the bed until they faced Brian's enlarging penis. Suddenly they were upon him, both beautiful women taking turns sucking his balls and licking an erection a size of which Susan did not recall ever seeing.

He had completely forgotten that Geoffrey sat a few feet away. Brian turned Rachel and Susan so that they now faced each other, and moving down between their legs, he pushed their vaginas together so he could stimulate both clitori at the same time. So occupied, he didn't notice Susan take Rachel's nipples in her mouth, gently sucking on them, and Rachel responded by kissing Susan on the lips with an open mouth. Both women were now enjoying each other along with the sensation and stimulation of his tongue between their legs.

Still oblivious to what the two women were doing to each other, Brian turned onto his back, and whispered something to Susan who instructed Rachel to mount him as she guided his erect penis into Rachel's vagina. Susan then kissed Rachel and turned to Brian who while holding her buttocks positioned her vagina over his face. "When Rachel cums, you switch, he groaned." Rachel and Brian synchronized their thrusts as Susan moved in a circular fashion allowing Brian's tongue to explore and stimulate an already swollen clitoris.

When Rachel was no longer able to suppress, she had an explosive orgasm that impressed even Geoffrey. Then she tapped Susan on the shoulder and the two women switched positions, continuing, as each subsequent orgasm seemed to grow larger and longer.

Geoffrey sat mesmerized holding his own erection in his hand having witnessed an amazing sex act that Brian had both designed and was an avid participant.

"I am not certain that this what we all had in mind." Geoffrey said feeling somewhat disenfranchised.

"Geoffrey, thank you so much for suggesting we do this" It was marvelous. Now you chose to be a voyeur. Why I do not know. I enjoyed every fucking moment." Rachel said as she kissed first Brian and then Susan.

Susan looked at Geoffrey. "Next time it will be your turn."

Geoffrey looked at his watch. "Hell, no better time like the present, and it was now Brian's turn to sit and watch. He did not seem to mind at all. He did remember, however, that when Susan went down on Geoffrey, she muttered something about 'salami'.

The following day was a workday for Geoffrey and Rachel, but they insisted upon taking the McKenzies to the small airport, where a steel drum band said farewell to those leaving the island, while welcoming new visitors. As Susan boarded the plane she wondered if the Townsands might find another couple to take their place.

Bajan Properties Ltd.
Fontabelle, St Michael, Barbados

Geoffrey Townsand   President

Rachel Townsand   Vice President

246-6969

December 14, 1986

Dearest Susan,

I have needed to write to you ever since you left the island, but never quite got the nerve to do so until now. All remains well in Barbados, and our season has been exceptional with most bookings filled. I cannot begin to tell you how much I miss you both, but particularly you, Susan, who has awakened something in me that I thought I had lost a long time ago.

I would like to visit with you in the states, since I plan to be in New York in the next few weeks. I shall be staying at the Marriot in mid-town. Could we arrange to have dinner sometime during my visit, which may only last a few days? If this would at all be possible, let me know. It would make my stay so much more enjoyable. My most prudent address for your correspondence would be Main Post Office, Bridgetown, Box 862.

Luv, Geoffrey

Adams, Feinberg, McKenzie and Kent PA

Attorneys At Law

1223 W. 57[th]St. Suites 13-18

New York, NY 10001

12/24/86

Dear Geoffrey,

I only received your letter a few days ago. I would suppose that overseas mail is delayed due to the holiday. I am happy to hear from you and pleased that things are going well in Barbados. We miss Barbados and we miss both of you.

When I returned, I found my desk piled high with work and trials that had been postponed are now rescheduled. So, I am still trying to make up for the time away when we were on holiday. The good news is that we expect to hire at least two more attorneys.

I do look forward to your visit, but was the dinner invitation meant only for me? I do not think it would be fair to Brian.

I shall discuss it with him and get back to you as long as it is only dinner.

You may send all correspondence to the above address. It is my office, and while my staff will not open any letter marked personal, it would be best that what you write not be in any way suggestive. I shall get back to you soon.

Miss you. Love to Rachel,
Susan

Bajan Properties Ltd.
Fontabelle, St. Michael, Barbados

Geoffrey Townsand   President

Rachel Townsand Vice President

246-6969

January 18, 1987

Dearest Susan,

I received your letter today and if you could see how red my face is, you would understand my state of embarrassment. I never meant to offend either you or Brian, since I value and treasure our unique friendship. As you know, I can be glib and charming in person, but when I have to pen words on paper, I seem to be out of my element. Would I like an interlude alone with you? Of course since I know we have something special, but in no way would I jeopardize that. Let us just chalk it up to 'I tried and failed'. Absolutely include Brian in my invitation to dinner and please choose the finest restaurant. I nervously await your reply my Island woman.

Luv Geoffrey

Adams, Feinberg, McKenzie and Kent, PA
Attorneys at Law
1231 W. 57th Street   Suites 13-18
New York, NY 10001

1/30/87

Hey Mon

It is around 9 pm, and I am still in the office reviewing cases for tomorrow's court calendar. Brian got home early and just called to say that he has a bottle of Mt. Gay ready and I should hurry home. Geoffrey, all four of us have shared very special times that I shall guarantee 100% of our friends never had or never will experience. Brian plays his Merrymen album, "The Islands" constantly and we often speak of the wonderful times spent with you and Rachel. We look forward to more of them.

You have no reason to be embarrassed. There are a few things we must discuss. I am uncomfortable sending mail to postal box. I love Rachel as a friend and I should not discuss things with you that I would not share with her.

From now on, I shall post mail to Simonton Great House. Brian is in full accord with what I have decided and hope it meets with your approval.

In order to clear my calendar, could you give me specific dates for your visit? We both wish to spend as much time with you as possible. Additionally, cancel your Marriot reservation. We would not hear of you not staying with us at the apartment. No argument, please!

We wish that Rachel be aware of everything we all might engage in and if this makes her in any way uncomfortable, Brian and I shall respect her wishes. We are sorry that she will not accompany you this visit, but hope it shall be possible at a future date. I am looking forward to your reply. Geoffrey, perhaps it is time we used the phone since timely mail delivery has been unreliable. And we have decided to sell our sloop. Will tell you more when we see you.

Love,
Susan

Eight

Barbados 1987

About a month after returning from Barbados, Brian received a call from English Harbor, Antigua. There were no charters pending for the sloop, and slip rentals were to be increased twenty percent. The agent offered a number of suggestions that the McKenzies should entertain. They immediately rejected sailing the boat back to the New York area. Brian and Susan discussed the pros and cons of keeping the boat with the children, and ultimately they all agreed that it would be best to put it up for sale. Fortunately, the market was still strong and they were able to negotiate a reasonable price without having to pay the usual ten percent charge and it would be a cash sale.

The money from the sale of the boat proved to be enough for a down payment on an apartment in the Dakota, on Central Park West, three stories below the one occupied by John Lennon's widow. The board that reviewed new applicants immediately accepted their credentials, and since the suite had been freshly painted, they chose to take immediate occupancy, and leave the sale of their present quarters in the hands of a broker.

Susan was thrilled that they would be close to the Natural History Museum and the Metropolitan Museum of Art directly across the park. Both would provide excellent educational resources for David and Meghan. Susan maintained a busy law practice, and the stock market had flourished. Brian was an astute trader did well for both his clients and himself. Together, they made well over six figures, so it was no wonder that getting into the Dakota, proved to be a breeze.

Their new apartment had three large bedrooms, each with its own full bath and a Jacuzzi in the master bedroom. There was a library, a computer room and a state of the art home theater, which fulfilled a dream of Brian's. The kitchen was modern with new Sub Zero appliances and other amenities that would make a CIA graduate's mouth water. And best of all, they could well afford it.

Susan had been corresponding with Geoffrey, who was due in New York on business. Rachel had recently returned from a brief holiday in Trinidad, where she visited her sister. Their two girls had spent the holidays in Barbados but now were back in Canada. Susan and Brian had both cleared their calendars to spend time with Geoffrey. She was thrilled that they were able to now have adequate room where they could properly entertain him.

Geoffrey's flight to JFK had been on time and Brian found him at the luggage carousel, where they hugged and passed the usual amenities while waiting for the last piece of baggage to make its trip around.

After getting a porter to take the bags, Brian advised that he would meet him at Arrivals and he would be driving a red Beemer.

"I am truly impressed," Geoffrey said as he got in. "How is Susan?"

"Susan is just great. We all are. And we have moved into the Dakota." He looked at Geoffrey. "Right, you wouldn't know about that. It is an upscale building on Central park, and we lucked out. So, how long will you be in the city?"

"Actually only a few days since I must be in Connecticut on business." Geoffrey said.

"Tourist Board stuff?" Brian asked.

"No, Miles is building a new boat, a sister ship, since he has been overwhelmed with extraordinary business on the cruises, he asked me to oversee completion of construction of the boat. The ship is being built in Connecticut."

"Speaking of sailing vessels, we sold MY CANADIAN MISTRESS. Costs for upkeep were getting to be prohibitive and we weren't going to use it. It was a lark and we had fun." Brian said.

The doorman at the Dakota, whom Brian introduced as Francis, took Geoffrey's luggage from the car that was then driven to the garage by a valet. Geoffrey's eyes widened when he saw the suite he was to occupy during his stay. "Puts our little place to shame." He said.

"Are you kidding? I would give anything to live in Barbados." Brian remarked. "Say, how about a glass of rum. I've got Cockspur, Mount Gay, and lots of other good stuff. Even had some Banks beer shipped in. Would surely like to have gotten some flying fish, but I guess that shall have to wait."

"Cockspur would be just fine, and there is a frozen pack of flying fish and steak fish in the box I left in your palatial kitchen. Best to unpack it and place in the freezer for now."

"Fantastic!" Brian exclaimed.

Geoffrey looked around. "Where is the bar?"

Brian led him into the room that housed the home theater. "We have just VHS's but I hear some good stuff like movies on discs will be available in a few years." He went over to a consol and pushed a button and a wet bar appeared from the wall. "Ice, neat or Bajan quickie?"

Geoffrey looked at his watch. "Is Susan expected soon and how is she?"

"As gorgeous as ever. You can never tell with her that she is being overworked." Brian said.

"You clearly are in need of another vacation in Barbados," Geoffrey said taking a glass of rum. "Cheers and so good to be with you. I must ask a question if you will. In light of our previous interactions, are there any rules?"

"Obviously we are short one person." Brian said referring to Rachel. "We have been too busy to discuss anything, so may the chips lie where they fall." Noting that Geoffrey had drained his glass, Brian refilled it.

"How rude of me. David and Meghan. How are they?" Geoffrey inquired.

"David has almost completed his term paper on Barbados. He's on the school skiing team and presently is competing at Lake Placid. That's about a six-hour drive north of us. Do you ski?"

"You mean on snow or ice? One has to be young or crazy. You will not get me out in the cold with two pieces of wood strapped to my feet." Geoffrey said taking a seat in a soft leather chair, one of four that faced a darkened movie screen.

"Both Susan and I snow ski, and the technology has come a long way. The equipment is really sophisticated now. Meghan is an excellent down hill skier as well."

"Good for all of you. There are at least two things you won't get me on. The first is skis and the second is the back of a horse. When do you expect Susan?"

"She left a message that she'd be a bit late, but would bring supper. She also suggested that we not drink all of the rum." Brian said with a laugh."

"Never happen," Geoffrey said, "since I brought two full liters with me. In my large luggage bag."

"So we know where David is. How about Meghan?" He asked.

"Meghan is in New Jersey with Susan's sister. They promised to take her to the Paper Mill Play House where the Nutcracker is being performed. So, she will be home some time tomorrow."

"So, you have quite a faux theater here. Any blue movies?" Geoffrey asked as he took in the large screen television.

"I don't keep anything like that in the house. Susan says she'd rather do it than watch it, and we usually do not need a kick-start. Do you?" Brian asked. Geoffrey's face reddened, and did not respond. "How about bringing me up to speed on what's going on in Barbados. The phone rang in the kitchen and as Brian went to answer it, Geoffrey heard someone fumbling with keys at the apartment door.

He opened it and came face to face with Susan standing with two bags of groceries. "Hello Luv!" He said.

"You just do not know how I have longed to hear you say that again." She put the bags on a table and embraced him. "Hope you like sushi."

Geoffrey finally released her. "Hope you brought California roll and lots of wasabi. I hear tell it is an aphrodisiac."

"Yeah, sure," Susan said. "So your flight was good and on time I see."

"Any flight that brings me close to the two of you has had to have been spectacular. That reminds me." He went to his room and returned with two large bottles of rum. "Glad to see these babies came through unharmed."

"So it is Cockspur." Susan said. "What happened to Mount Gay?"

"Both very fine rums but, Cockspur is currently giving us a better deal for the pirate cruise, and we use so much for pirate rum punch."

"Right. I remember the spiel. 'This is not ordinary punch. This is pirate punch and eighty proof'." Brian said.

"Have the kids called yet?" Susan asked.

"David competes tomorrow in a slalom and Meghan is looking forward to the ballet." Brian responded.

"I see you to have already started. I am looking to catch up. Where's my drink?" Brian brought her a filled glass. "Okay...over the teeth or is it the gums?"

"Forget it Susan. I am famished." They consumed miso soup, a green salad and four different kinds of rolls and assorted sushi.

They sat and talked and sipped rum for hours until Brian noted that it was already eleven. Susan said it was time for the late news, and asked Geoffrey if he would like to watch TV with them in their bedroom. He said he would join them after he showered.

The local news had just ended when Geoffrey knocked and entered the bedroom, and by the glow emitted by the TV he saw that both Susan and Brian lay naked on top of the sheets.

"Hope the news was not too distressing for you." He said as he took off his pajamas and joined them on the bed.

Susan lay on her back in between Brian and Geoffrey, and grasping an erect penis in each hand, she began to stroke them.

Geoffrey stifled a laugh. "You must feel quite powerful right at this moment."

This was to be a new experience for Susan, since she had never been made love to by two men in this fashion. Although no pecking order had been established, Brian lay quietly as Susan released him, allowing Geoffrey to kiss her and caress her breasts.

As she became more aroused, Geoffrey slid his hand down between her legs and felt her wetness. Susan lifted her head and momentarily looked at Brian who smiled.

Assured that she had his approval, Susan turned and took Geoffrey's swollen penis into her mouth, moving it in and out and when he could no longer contain himself, he turned her onto her back and easily entered her. She responded to Geoffrey's thrusting, circular gyrations by moving her hips for deeper penetration. Brian attempted to become a participant, but when he tried to suck one of her nipples, she pushed him away and with one forceful motion, turned Geoffrey on his back and rolled on top without dislodging him.

Susan rode him until she began to experience that intense sense of physical excitement that precedes orgasm. She leaned forward, her nipples brushing her lovers lips. Then she came, and relaxed as he exploded inside of her, and then she came again.

Susan rolled of Geoffrey and turned to Brian offering her nipples that he eagerly began to suck. "I want you to eat me now," she said and Brian moved down between her legs. She turned to Geoffrey and kissed him passionately. "And I want you to stay and watch," She whispered. When she felt she was close to orgasm, she straddled Brian and forced her self down upon his erect penis, rhythmically moving her hips back and forth until she was ready. "Hold my ass and suck and bite my nipples now, I have to fuck your big cock." Geoffrey lay next to them and observed probably the most exquisite orgasm any one had ever experienced.

He was ready to have her again, but Susan said no. Before he went back to his room, he told them, "This has been one of the most exciting evenings I have ever experienced in bed. You too are truly sensuous human beings. I wish Rachel had been here with us."

Susan turned the TV to mute and put her arms around Brian. "Should we bother to change the sheets?" She asked.

"It can wait till tomorrow morning." Brian said. "Hey, you were extraordinary, sensational."

"It bothered you when I pushed you away didn't it?" She asked.

"I'd be a liar if I said no, but it turned out okay." He said.

Susan lay back down on her pillow with her hands folded behind her head. "Did you ever in your wildest dreams think that we would do the things we have done when we first decided to buy the boat and sail to Barbados?" He just shook his head.

"Tell me Brian. Do you regret any of this and that Rachel was not here?" She asked.

"I enjoyed being with Rachel, but probably not as much as you like being with Geoffrey. When, if we return to Barbados, I could easily make love to Rachel, but who know if she will feel the same." He said. "Do I regret any of it? No Luv."

"You did like our threesome. The time with me and Rachel." She asked.

"Honestly, it was fantastic honey, but I am running out of ideas." He said. "But I sure would like the chance of thinking up new ones."

"Check out the Karma Sutra." She said. "Brian, do you realize how lucky we are, having the best of all possible worlds?" She smiled warmly at him.

We are still married and very much in love. I would make an educated guess, that most people would long have gone their separate ways under similar circumstances. I'll be right back. Got to pee."

When she returned, he was still awake. "What do you think our friends would say if they found out about our double life?" Brian asked.

"My friends would be shocked and very jealous. Your friends would want to hear all the dirty details over and over again." She said. "Seriously, if Geoffrey should meet any of our gorgeous lady friends, we shall have to warn him that they are off limits."

"Perhaps we should warn your friends," Brian said. He can be quite a charmer. Look before we go to sleep, I am concerned that he might want a twosome and that would make me uncomfortable."

"It is 2:30 in the morning and both of us have to work tomorrow." She said. "I told Geoffrey when this all started that I would do nothing that might jeopardize our marriage or our relationship with Rachel and him. Nothing, Brian, will happen without your knowledge." He was about to ask her to clarify what she had just said when she began to fondle him.

He moaned, "I can go into work a bit later tomorrow. How about you?"

The next morning, Susan prepared breakfast of scrambled eggs, toast and bacon for the three of them, and after they each downed two cups of coffee, she and Brian left for their respective offices, allowing Geoffrey to go back and sleep as long as he wished. She arrived to find a message from Geoffrey that he had just received a call from Connecticut and would take a cab to Penn Station, and probably would be gone for a few days dealing with the new cruise ship.

When Susan finally returned home around seven, she found David eating the last of the sushi, and Meghan in the shower. Just as she began to open the mail, Brian announced he was home.

"Hey, guy, we didn't expect you back so soon. How'd you make out?" Susan said kissing her son on the forehead.

"We finished early when the other team's lead skier twisted his knee at the last gate, and had to hobble down the rest of the way. Tough way to win, but we'll take it. They were very competitive. Hey, I found a lot of dirty dishes and glasses in the sink so I put them in the dishwasher."

"Geoffrey is staying with us while he is here on business, but had to go to New England for a few days. He is involved with having a new ship built for Pirate Adventures." Susan said.

"I thought as much when I saw the luggage in the guest room and the one and a half bottles of rum on the wet bar. I put everything away." He said.

"How's the paper coming along? It is due soon isn't it?" Brian asked.

"Well, I have just about finished the family tree part and have some tentative ideas on expanding it. I, at first became stymied when I came across the name David Thomas McKenzie, a free coloured man who had inherited Simonton plantation. Now his father and grandfather were also freemen. Everything sort of got stuck there since there were only a few records.

But apparently England had instructed Barbados and for that matter all of the colonial possessions to register all slaves in the early 1800's, the planters were forced to keep records by law. When we were in Barbados, Geoffrey had some old dusty ledgers that had been hidden under the floorboards beneath his desk."

David remembered something else. "He also found an old black book that had been stashed away under some rotted flooring near the entranceway only remembering them when I asked him if he knew of any old slave logs that might have been left at the Great House. The original owners were meticulous with their record keeping and listed the slaves owned on the plantation long before formal registration had been required. The original owners were white people, but as I said, this David Thomas McKenzie was a mix or coloured. Therefore I have come to the conclusion that some of our relatives were black and coloured."

"Your grandmother will have a fit." Susan said.

"Wait, there's more," David said. "I also traced the Townsands and believe we are related. Isn't that great?"

Susan momentarily felt a sense of anguish, but then composed herself. Actually, even if they were distant cousins, it wasn't anything like incest. She thought for a moment and then relaxed. He would be Brian's relative and not hers anyway. "Perhaps we should keep this as our deep dark secret." Susan said.

"Why?" David asked. "I am going to tell Geoffrey when he returns. He will really get a charge out of finding out that we all are related somehow. In fact, I don't plan to stop with the paper for school, I was thinking about expanding it into a book, perhaps."

Geoffrey returned to New York after three days and brought news that the ship's hull was almost completed. It would be larger than its sister ship and hold more passengers, but he did not expect it to be finished until late fall.

The presence of the children at such close quarters prevented the three adults from any bedroom activities, and Susan told Brian that it was just as well since she thought she might be developing cystitis. They took Geoffrey to dinner at the Palm where he enjoyed an American steak.

The weather was not cooperating since it snowed on the last two days of his visit, but they did get to take him to a couple of shows on Broadway. He loved 'DREAM GIRLS'.

They both accompanied him to the airport where he caught a British Airways flight back to the island, and they promised that they would return to Barbados when they were able to schedule more vacation time.

Nine

Barbados 1988

Brian and Susan did not return to Barbados until the following February and this time, without David and Meghan who could not afford to miss additional days of school. Susan's younger sister, who was a graduate student at New York University, volunteered to stay with them. Since Brian insisted upon renting a car, Geoffrey arranged to have the vehicle, a bright green Land Rover, waiting at the airport when they arrived. The driver, who introduced himself, as Sam Bailey, was a bear of a man with a gentle disposition. He informed the McKenzies, that when he wasn't driving for Geoffrey, he operated a rum shop in Mellows, and Susan made a mental note to accept his invitation to come visit when they were settled. Sam suggested that it would be best for him to first take, or carry them, as he phrased it, to the Holetown police station, where they would be able to obtain local drivers permits.

Sam spoke with a Bajan patois that was clear and precise. "Weather, she been real good Mon. Not too much rain." He said as he drove on rural roads that led past Barbadian fields where cane was being cut and loaded onto trucks.

"Pass me already mon if you likes," He growled, looking in the rearview mirror at an impatient mini-moke that had pushed its nose out onto the narrow road behind them. Sam explained that he was taking a shortcut to bypass school and business traffic that was heavy at this time of day. Soon they were on the familiar top road better known as Highway 2, when Sam made a quick left turn that down past Porters, now an idle sugar cane factory. He stopped the Land Rover where the road intersected with Highway 1 waiting for traffic to pass so he could make a turn to the left. "Look to the big house on our left. Sir Alec Guinness once lived there." He said proudly.

Sam stopped before the Holetown police station where a man whose badge identified him as Sgt. L. Holders issued two driver's permits, stamping them with authority after methodically reviewing the McKenzie U.S. licenses.

He accepted the fee of ten "dolla" Barbados for each permit, smiled and wished their stay to be a pleasant one. Susan reminded Brian to drive on the left as he gingerly moved the car into late afternoon traffic. "Just carry me up the road." Sam said with amusement as he watched Brian maneuver in traffic. "I can catch my bus to Mellows." He had earlier told us that he lived there with his wife and daughter, whom he described as God's experiment, and again invited the McKenzie's to stop by his rum shop, as he exited from the Land Rover and waved goodbye.

Traffic had become heavier as school and commuter busses from Bridgetown clogged the road, but Brian skillfully maneuvered the Land Rover until they reached the Great House of Simonton plantation, where a radiant Rachel came out to greet them. It was already late in the day and the sky had begun to darken, but the rich orange hue forged by the sunset, hovered over the quiet Caribbean Sea.

Rachel hugged and kissed both of them. "You both look wonderful. It is great to see you. Geoffrey told me of his smashing visit and your palatial new home." Susan and Brian exchanged a quick glance as they followed Rachel into the house. Brian realized that he had missed Rachel, the moment she appeared at the gate. "Brian you can take up the luggage later. For now, let me look at both of you." She chip singed. "Geoffrey should be home shortly and then we shall go to dinner. I am certain you'd like to freshen up and dinner is, as usual, informal."

"All right," Brian said. "But dinner is on me. I insist."

"Absolutely," Susan agreed."

"That you shall have to settle with Geoffrey. You know how he is." Rachel said.

They did not have to wait long before Geoffrey arrived, elated to see both of them with hugs and kisses. "Ah. I do believe that it is five pm. somewhere in the world. Drinks, yes?"

"As if that ever mattered," Susan said with a laugh.

"Meghan and David, I trust are good." Rachel asked. "Shame they could not come as well." Both Susan and Brian chip singed and Geoffrey laughed.

"Excellent, you still have that wonderful Yankee sense of humor," Geoffrey said as he squeezed Susan's hand. "Now we have an absolutely gorgeous dinner planned at the Sandy Lane Club House, and no, you shall not pay for dinner since I have an account and they do not take cash."

"Fine," Brian said. I shall write you a check."

"And offend your hosts? Never." Geoffrey said.

Brian dressed causally, as suggested, in a black golf shirt, belt less white slacks and white shoes without socks, while Susan wore a short blue dress and a cotton blouse that began somewhere mid shoulder, exposing enough cleavage to keep Geoffrey and the other men in the restaurant visually occupied.

The restaurant was small with a dining area, seating possibly twenty people, and providing a vantage point that allowed them to watch lights from cruise ships moving toward Carlisle Bay. The waiter brought them glasses of sugar cane brandy and soda and took their dinner orders. Geoffrey chose local pork, which he said, had been excellent, and Rachel and Susan ordered poached dolphin, while Brian selected shrimp scampi. All chose the pumpkin soup for starters which they agreed was just gorgeous.

After dinner, Geoffrey ordered a bottle of cognac for the table and again asked how the children were. Susan told him that they had recently been skiing in Utah, one of the reasons that they could not take off more school time. "The thought of snow on a mountain just makes me shiver," He said, as he swirled the amber colored liquid before tasting it. " This is just grand." Rachel, who had been unusually quiet during dinner, ordered a glass of rum, neat with no chaser.

When they reached the house, Rachel announced that she was fatigued and left Geoffrey and the McKenzies chatting on the patio.

Brian was a bit disappointed having hoped to spend some time with Rachel. At around midnight, Geoffrey excused himself as well, after bringing nightcaps.

Left alone, Susan and Brian looked at each other. "Perhaps, she said, "We mistakenly assumed, we all would just continue where we left off. You know, I could do with a quickie, Brian. The drinking kind."

The next morning after flying fish omelets, Geoffrey announced that Rachel and he were taking the day to explore places that Brian and Susan had not yet visited. His only caveat was that Brian do the driving and in the Land Rover.

They drove north passing Heywards and a strip of beach that the locals called Miami Beach near Six Mans Bay, until the road, which appeared to support only one way traffic, become a rural path that Brian decided was non negotiable. They had reached the top of a long rocky incline that provided s magnificent view of the blue green sea, when Brian pulled the car to a halt.

"Wha you stop, Mon?" Geoffrey asked.

Brian got out of the Rover and looked down the steep, rugged, rut filled hill that was in part covered with tall grass. "Guess we have to walk the rest of the way." Brian said looking down at his flip-flops.

"Nonsense!" Geoffrey said. "Mon, you driving a Land Rover which shall get she any where down this road."

Brian reluctantly started up the engine and gingerly moved the truck down the steep incline over rocks that precipitously tilted the vehicle, tossing its occupants back and forth, finally coming to rest at an overgrown flat where the road seemed to end. He got out and looked back up from where they had come.

"Now what?" Susan asked.

"Through that path in the trees, lies Maycocks Bay, just beyond the cocoanut forest. Since access is difficult, most people come by sea." Geoffrey said. "It is quite secluded."

"No wonder," Susan said as she picked her way over sharp and slippery rocks that made up the path. Brian found walking in his flip-flops difficult, while Geoffrey and Rachel moved over the terrain with ease. They finally came to a clearing that led to a beach of white, glistening sand. "Not too secluded," Susan observed as she saw a number of local boys sitting naked in a circle on the sand. "Are they doing what I think they're doing?" She asked.

"You don't want to know," Brian said as he turned her away. "Let us leave them at play."

"I believe we have a winner," Geoffrey said as he followed along behind them, as Rachel and Susan looked back with curiosity. Geoffrey smiled and said. "Hey guys, maybe we should try that sometime."

Rachel punched her husband in the arm. "Shut up Geoffrey."

Upon reaching the end of the beach, they turned back toward a path that would lead back to the road. "Okay, we have seen Maycocks and it is time to go." Geoffrey said. When they reached the Land Rover, Brian made a quick K-turn and looked back to the top of the rocky hill. "Geoffrey, you have got to be kidding. You said it would be a piece of cake. No problem getting down the hill."

"True, true," Geoffrey replied. "You never inquired about getting back up. Just give it some petrol."

As Brian gave it gas, the Rover lurched forward and moved up the road at a forty-five degree angle, trying to get to the top as fast as possible. A local man herding some goats watched in disbelief as the Land Rover righted itself and finally moved on up the road to level ground.

"That was fun. Where to now, Geoffrey?" Brian said sarcastically.

"I am just now giving that some serious thought. Okay, turn about and head back toward Speightstown, but before we get into town, make a left at the flashing light. We shall head east."

Susan observed how specific the road signs marked the routes. The direction was always somewhere via some place. "We Bajans are very literal," Rachel said. "Geoffrey, we cannot possibly go everywhere today."

"We are doing just smashing," Geoffrey said. "When we get to the top road, swing a right until we reach Lascelles.

"Geoffrey, Luv, we could have reached the East Coast in a more direct way." Rachel said.

"This is how I have resolved this. We can do Cherry Tree and Nicholas Abbey another day. I thought that it would be nice to visit Welshman's Hall Gulley and then go over to the Kingsley Club for lunch." Geoffrey said.

"I take it back. You do plan well." Rachel said. "I have not been there for ever so long a time. Perhaps you should drive."

"On the contrary, our friend here is doing just fine." Geoffrey responded. Look, we are at Welshman's Hall now. Pull into the car park. There is a bit of a walk."

Geoffrey paid the nominal admission and they walked past a sign marked, National Trust Open since 1961. He led them down a steep path, and they were soon surrounded by groves of towering trees whose vines trailed to the ground, and whose lush foliage provided a most comfortable humidity

Susan was wide eyed. "This is absolutely gorgeous. Are those nutmegs?" As they wandered through beautiful ferns and many different species of flowering shrubs, Brian, who had studied some botany in college, tried to recall some of the things he had learned.

The path turned and ultimately led back toward the car park. "I trust you loved Welshman's Hall. It is a most unique part of this island." They were soon in the Rover driving toward the East Coast. "Driver, be sure to exit to the right and look for a road sign that indicates Bathsheba via Bloomsbury."

At the highest point at Bloomsbury, they had a great view of the Scotland district that overlooked the white sandy beaches bordering the Atlantic Ocean.

Even though it looked quite close, the circuitous nature of the road still left a half hour in which to reach the main East Coast Road. Brian drove tentatively down into Bloomsbury Gulley, hoping that he would not meet a car coming from the other direction.

"Outstanding job." Geoffrey said. "Now you must look for a sign stating Frizers via Mellowes."

"Didn't Sam Bailey, the man who picked us up at the airport say he came from Mellowes?" Susan asked.

"Believe he did that." Brian said without taking his eyes from the road.

They followed the sign, eventually arriving at an old estate that had seen better days. Geoffrey introduced them to Steve Painter, an American expatriate who was trying his hand at experimental farming. He explained that Barbados produced only a limited amount of vegetables for local consumption, and the majority of the hotels had their produce shipped in from the states. Painter said that it made little sense to grow something like onions and ship them out only to import them at much higher costs, so he was trying to cultivate crops that the soil would support, like tomatoes and peppers.

"In fact," he said, "I believe it would be a fabulous idea to start a canning industry, if I could convince rich folk, like Geoffrey to part with some seed money." He looked for a response. " I guess not." He added.

Painter, a portly man in his mid forties led them to the house that once served as quarters for the plantation overseers, and there they met his friend Connie, a slim young woman whose clothes and hair smelled of stale cigarettes. He went into the house and returned with a bottle of Mount Gay, six glasses and two cocoanuts. "Oh these, we call natures chasers." He said with a laugh. The glasses were of various sizes, and some of them in a previous life contained jelly or small pickles. Steve pierced the eyes of both cocoanuts and emptied their cloudy liquid into a tall glass.

Susan stood up. "This is my part folks. Over the teeth and past the gums, lookout stomach, here it comes." She laughed, downed the rum in her glass in one gulp and took a swig of cocoanut milk. "Ah, natures chaser," she said.

"You are definitely now Bajan." Geoffrey said as he sipped his rum and forsook the chaser.

They talked for a while and when Geoffrey saw it was getting late, thanked them for being so gracious. Taking their leave, they continued down a narrow rocky path that crossed overflowing creeks, until they reached the East Coast Road. "Over to your left down the hill is Cattlewash and Barkley's Park. We go right up the hill and then take your next left down the hill. There will be another left. I shall tell you when. I would like to show you a property that I am interested in."

Brian drove almost to the bottom of the hill, when Geoffrey indicated a left to a roadway, which led to a car park servicing an old hotel. "We have time. Actually, we could do lunch here if you like." Rachel made a face. The Ocean Cliff Hotel was situated on a bluff overlooking the beach and Atlantic Ocean, whose waves seemed endless. They approached the swimming pool where a few guests sat in lounge chairs watching their children splash water on each other. The doors to the main dining area opened out onto the pool.

Geoffrey made some small talk with a rather large man dressed in a chef's cap, and directed Rachel, Susan and Brian to a table that seemed to perch over a drop of a few hundred feet to the rocks below. A waiter appeared, took drink orders and advised that they could choose from the menu or opt for the fixed price buffet. Rachel and Susan left for the washroom.

"I am glad we have a few minutes to ourselves." Geoffrey said, as the waiter brought two Banks and ice tea for the ladies.

"Perhaps you all were wondering why nothing eventful occurred last evening."

"I have to admit, it was discussed." Brian said as he took a drag from the cool but not cold bottle of beer. "Cheers."

"If you recall at the get go, I said it might never occur again. It has nothing to do with the two of you. Uh, Rachel and I are having some difficulties." Geoffrey said.

"I shall not pry." Brian replied.

"I may share the story when I am prepared to do so." Geoffrey downed his beer and looked for the waiter.

"I hope it is all sorted out favorably and in no way disturbs our friendship." Brian said.

"True, true. Ah! Here are our beautiful ladies now. I have decided to forgo the buffet where one tends to take too much and instead have a flying fish on a bun with fries." The others agreed it was a good choice.

After lunch, Geoffrey walked Brian around the property, the back of which dipped down to a gulley over crowded with vegetation. "That is called Joe's River." Brian looked down and saw nothing but overgrown weeds. "Let's take a look at the rooms." They walked up a flight of stairs to a second story and through an open door way. "This is the bedroom suite, obviously unoccupied for repairs."

"My observation is that the whole place is one large repair. A big costly one. If you are contemplating a business venture, why not look into that canning prospec." Brian advised, and as he sat on a toilet seat in the master suite bathroom he slid to the floor with the seat still under him.

Geoffrey laughed. "Are you all right? Look, Steve's a nice guy to have a drink with, but you do not choose him for a business partner. It is truly a very long story. This place on the other hand has lots of potential. People love this coast. It is not as crowded, and you must look at the beauty of the landscape. Brick and wood can be replaced, and with an imaginative architect, we could do wonders with this place. I was considering a Club Med type atmosphere. For instance, I was in Jamaica one time at Sandals on business, and in my room, when there was a knock on the door. I opened it and there was this absolutely beautiful nubile young lady standing in the nude asking for a light. This is what I envision for this place."

"Your not including me in this venture are you?" Brian asked.

"Had not thought about it to be truthful." He smiled. "Look I am not contemplating a whore house. We have enough of those in Bridgetown. We have had this fantastic experience. Why shouldn't more young couples do the same?" Geoffrey said as he led the way back down.

"You just told me that there were issues between you and Rachel. Wouldn't this just fan the flames?" Brian asked.

"Ah! That is where you and Susan come in. A little positive effort on your parts to support my project, perhaps." Geoffrey said. Before Brian could respond the girls appeared.

"This is really a disgusting place Geoffrey. The toilets are an abomination." Rachel said. "I hope none of us get sick." Geoffrey frowned and looked to Brian for help. "The car park." She said,

"I'll drive from here on." Geoffrey said as he climbed into the driver's seat. They drove the short distance to a restaurant bar called the Round House. It was closer to the beach, but still high enough to provide a view of Bathsheba and Three Boys Rocks. They ordered rum and cokes and enjoyed the refreshing breeze, but when they returned to the Rover, it felt like an oven.

"Air conditioning please," Susan cried out. "I feel like my ass is on fire." The air came on quickly, and soon it was more comfortable in the cabin of the truck.

"Sorry Rachel," Geoffrey said but I wanted to show Brian the hotel. Do not say it. We should have had lunch at the Kingsley Club. I agree and will make it up to you all. He drove north and then turned toward the center of the island until they reached the top road and then back down toward St. James and Simonton. When they reached the plantation house, they were hot enough to go for swim. After an hour in the pool, Rachel and Geoffrey toweled off, and informed the McKenzies they would see them later for cocktails on the patio.

Susan, who had been reading on a lounge chair, tossed Brian a towel as he pulled himself from the pool. "Bit strange, all this. Don't you think?" He said.

"Did he tell you that they were having problems?" She asked.

"Yes, but you two came from the John before he could elaborate, and I am not convinced he was prepared to do so any way. So, what's the story?"

"I am not certain how much to share, but the argument is over Geoffrey trying to talk her into a switch party involving a number of couples." She said.

"You are talking about an orgy, aren't you?" He asked. "He said the issue was over purchasing this hotel."

"Don't lick you lips now." She said. "It is not going to happen. The argument led to her accusing him of never being satisfied just having her. His answer was that 'he's Bajan…etc…etc. Would you like the good news?"

"There's good news?" He asked.

"Rachel still wants to do it with you, and since I told her that I wanted Geoffrey again, I think we can, so to speak, get back into the swing of things." Susan said. "The hooker is that she hasn't told him yet. I wanted you to be assured that the vacation will not be wasted."

"I don't feel that way. This is our vacation." He sat next to her on the lounge, and pulled her to him. "How about us swimming naked in the pool?"

Susan looked around and saw that they were alone. She got into the water and stripped off her bikini, and as he kissed her, she felt him grow hard between her legs. The orgasm was quick and satisfying for both. "I hope they don't mind." He said.

"Would doubt that very much. Tell you what. I'll speak to Rachel and bet we have some fun tomorrow night. I'm hungry and I noticed pizzas in the freezer. Suppose you deal with them and I'll get a salad together. Probably better to eat in tonight. Tomorrow we dive the Stavronikita."

Brian picked up the bathing suits as Susan wrapped herself in a dry towel. "You planning to surprise Anna or something?"

"Oops," He said and put on his wet suit. Walking back to the patio, she heard him humming... "Stavronikita, Stavronikita, Stavronikita It's lots of fun." She unwrapped her towel, threw it at him and walked into the house stark naked.

Ten

New York 1988

Brian, can you take a call from Geoffrey Townsand in Barbados? I told him you were on a call with a client."

"Of course, Meg, but let me finish up with Awesome Enterprise. Take a number. I'll call him back." Brian said.

"He is very insistent." She said.

"It's all right. Tell him I promise to get back within a half hour, unless it is an emergency of course." Brian waited for a response.

"He said that would be fine, and that he liked my voice and wanted to know what I looked like." She said still standing in the doorway.

"Brian covered the mouth piece with his hand and smiled. "Tell him that you are fifty years old and weigh two hundred pounds, with your nice voice and I shall call him promptly as I said."

Within fifteen minutes he was on the phone with Geoffrey. "Everything okay?" He asked.

"We are just fine. I just returned from the airport after putting the girls on a plane back to Toronto. They had what they call an intersession. You and Susan should meet them. They are two wonderful people, I tell you. The sad thing is that they have lost the Bajan accent and now sound like the rest of the Canadians with oooot and abooot. How far can one stretch an o? That's not why I called."

"How are things with Rachel and you?" Brian asked.

"You guys did wonders when you were down here. Rachel is as loving as ever and although I have not gotten her to agree about my hotel idea, she is definitely listening. The way I figure it, it can be done in about four phases, but that's not why I called." He cleared his throat. "You met Miles DaCosta, the owner of Pirate Adventures on one of the cruises I captained. He has to sail one of the party boats down to Grenada, to set up pirate cruises there as he has done in Barbados, and has invited us to cruise the Grenadines with him. There are so many fantastic islands there. It shall be great fun. Would you and Susan be interested? Rachel wants to know before she accepts. I would call it a vacation of a lifetime."

"Sounds great, but we both would have to clear are calendars and make certain we have someone to stay with the kids." Brian said.

"Of course. Now I haven't been on one of these cruises, but those who have, told me that all kinds of stuff goes on." Geoffrey said.

"What kind of stuff? Nothing illegal? I hope." Brian said.

"Certainly not. Everyone will be of legal age. Ever hear of bare boating?" Geoffrey asked.

"I am becoming worried already. Who all is of legal age? Perhaps I should not share that part with Susan. What's Rachel's take?" Brian asked.

"Do not plan to discuss something that might not happen." He chip singed. "I shall get to the they, presently."

"How long is the trip?" Brian asked.

"Possibly, the most a fortnight, and the least a week to ten days. Then we fly back to Barbados." Geoffrey said. "I still envision a sexy sojourn at sea."

"And Miles and the rest of his people are cool with this?" Brian asked.

"Miles most likely will not join us. He's a bit pussy whipped. I believe he will send his Captains. You know Joey and Jollybuns now work for him full time." Geoffrey said.

"Let me run this by Susan. Give me the dates. I have a feeling it might be a hard sell, but, not for me. Sailing the Grenadines has been a dream of mine, however."

"Well, then let your dreams be a reality and tell Susan, Rachel and I would like to continue where we left off in February." Geoffrey said. "If that does not motivate her, nothing will."

That evening, while dining on poached salmon and lentils, Brian brought Susan up to speed on Geoffrey's invitation. She had him pour her another glass of Chablis, and suggested they sit and talk about it. After they had cleared the table and placed everything in the dishwasher, Susan savored the chilled wine and licked her lips. "So, what's this trip really all about?"

He discussed in detail, most of what Geoffrey said, including Rachel's wish that they accompanied them. "The Grenadines." She went to get the atlas from one of the shelves. "Here they are. Very tiny and in the middle of the sea." She said.

"Geoffrey said it could be the trip of our lifetime." Brian said.

"Did he now?" When is it to occur?" She asked.

"He knows we have to arrange our calendars and said he would call as soon as we made a decision. He also said something being naked for the entire trip."

"He did not say any such thing! Did he? Who else is on this trip, Brian?" Susan asked offering her glass for a refill. "I bet both you and Geoffrey would love to run around naked on the ship. Women are just different and more concerned about what other people think about their bodies."

"Why?" Brian asked as he ducked the atlas she tossed at him.

"I want to go." She said.

"Even if it's a nude voyage?" He asked.

"Knowing Rachel, it shall be none of the kind." She said. "I shall call her and get the real story. And if so it could be sweet sweet."

"Best not to mention the naked stuff since I made it up." He said.

Eleven

Barbados 1988

It was the second week in October, when Susan and Brian landed in Barbados, and rolled their carryon luggage down the long walkway that led to customs and that ominous red line no one dared to cross, unless asked to do so by the uniformed officer at the desk. Rachel and Geoffrey waved from the glass window high above the center hall, through which all visitors were obliged to pass. The customs inspector checked their passports, smiled when he saw they were frequent visitors, and welcomed them again to Barbados. Geoffrey and Rachel met them with hugs and kisses at the luggage carousel, and a red shirted porter recovered the two soft bags that Brian indicated were theirs.

"I trust that you have not brought a good deal of luggage, since I can truly assure you that you shall need very little on the trip." Geoffrey said. "We are going to be in swim wear or nothing if that's you thing. You have heard of bare boating, right?"

"Susan stared at Brian but said nothing."

"Just what you see, and that's it except for Susan's personal stuff and my cameras." Brian said smiling.

"Actually, we brought extra shorts and bathing wear in our carry on just in case the airline lost our luggage." Susan said.

"Goody. Did you bring video as well?" Geoffrey asked.

"Of course and lots of batteries." Brian said.

Since they had nothing to declare, and the fact that Geoffrey knew the man at the door, they were in the car park in minutes. Geoffrey stowed the luggage into the boot of the Mercedes, and they were soon on their way to the careenage, where the crew was preparing for departure. Brian noticed that a number of people had already boarded. He recognized both Joey and Jollybuns, but the rest were strangers.

"All of those women. Are they the part of the crew?" Susan asked sarcastically.

"Actually, no Geoffrey said. They are ten young women who had been on a Pirate Cruise, and Miles convinced them to make the trip. They are all airline attendants who have to use vacation time before the end of the year."

"Geoffrey, do you know if they are paying customers?" Rachel asked.

"Haven't a clue since it is not my party, and why should you care? On the other hand, we four are guests and can act as crew or not if we like. But I do know that these women will be arranging for their own return flights at their expense."

Geoffrey boarded first, and then assisted Rachel and Susan. Brian followed with their bags. "I see what you mean by bringing as little clothing as possible," Brian remarked upon noticing that some of the women were already topless on the upper deck.

He did the math quickly and counted twelve women, including Susan and Rachel and six men.

Rachel pulled Susan aside. "There will be hell to pay if they are seen like that. The Anglican Church frowns upon such nudity in public. They just should have waited until we were out of port."

"Right. We shall just have to keep our husbands busy all day and contained at night." Susan laughed. "Actually, I would not mind running around in the nude for a week, myself. Life is too short not to try everything."

"You think? Okay, I am game as well, and it will drive our two guys crazy. Don't worry about Joey, Jollybuns and the other men. They are all cool and in a few days, they shall pay no mind. I worked out the accommodations so we would have the cabins. The rest of them will probably sleep up on the deck, weather permitting." Rachel added.

Geoffrey had tapped the keg and brought four plastic cups filled with ice and rum punch. "Remember this is Pirate Punch," He warned.

The ship was about one hundred feet long and twenty-five feet at its widest beam. There were two masts, and an upper deck, that served as a lounge with a well stocked bar and adjoining kitchen. Below decks was a cabin that would serve as sleeping quarters for the Townsands and McKenzies, and additional bunks set along the wooden hull if needed. There were two heads and second narrow stairwell that led back to the deck above.

After stowing their gear in the cabin, Brian turned to leave. "Where are you going dear?" Susan asked.

"I thought I would find Geoffrey and get acquainted with the rest of the guests." Just then Geoffrey appeared in the companionway.

"I just bet you did." Susan said.

"Geoffrey gave her elbow a playful squeeze. "Chill out, Luv. I shall make it a point to keep him out of harm's way."

"Let them go and get it out of their systems now. We have at least a week ahead of us. On the other hand, it portends to be a beautiful trip. The Grenadines are nothing like anything you have ever seen." Rachel said.

"I believe we can handle ourselves." Susan said as she gave Rachel a peck on the cheek. "Why don't we change and join the party." They felt the boat shudder as it started to motor away from the dock. "I think we are underway." She said, as music streamed down from the speakers on the deck.

Six of the ten women lay naked on towels, while the other four had removed just their bikini tops. As Brian and Geoffrey approached, those who noticed smiled and then closed their eyes. "Hello ladies, my name is Geoffrey and this is Brian." A long limbed red head turned over onto her back and waved, as Brian's eyes almost popped out of their sockets.

She sat up and extended a hand. "I'm Jen," she said allowing Brian to help her to her feet. Jen was about 5ft. 10 and perfect in all respects. A small purple tattoo of an iris had been inked just above her cleanly shaved pubic area. "You're taking it all in Brian. What do you think?"

As Brian began to blush, Geoffrey came to his rescue, and asked if they could bring up drinks from the bar, but the red head leaned against Brian. "You guys are still dressed in slacks and shirts. What fun is that going to be?"

Brian moved away and said he would be glad to act as waiter and get a drink order. Jen introduced the rest of her friends, who she said worked for Caribbean Airlines with a hub in Norfolk, Virginia.

Brian tried to remember all nine names, but was happy when they all decided on rum punch. "We shall return," Geoffrey said as he accompanied Brian down the ladder. "What a candy store for adult men," He said. "Go easy on the ice."

"I would remind you that we are not stag. So let's not screw up this trip, on day one. How much do you suppose our wives will tolerate before they throw us overboard?" Brian asked.

"I think Rachel will be cool. What about Susan?" Geoffrey asked.

"Don't know, but she is full of surprises." Brian said as he found a tray and filled ten cups full of rum punch. Geoffrey filled four additional cups and they went back up the ladder.

The ship was well out into Carlisle Bay and heading south when Rachel and Susan joined them on the upper deck. Both wore bikini tops that could better be considered as nipple covers and thongs. "See what I mean about surprises?" Brian said.

Geoffrey passed around the cups of rum punch. "Come Brian, we are decidedly overdressed. It is time that we changed into swim trunks."

Brian drained his cup, observed Susan and Rachel as they proceeded to introduce themselves, and then he and Geoffrey went down to their cabin to change. Jollybuns at the helm, grinned as they passed him.

Rachel and Susan moved away from the other women and lay down on towels they had brought from below. The ship was passing the south coast of the island, and in the distance they could see planes landing and taking off at Grantley Adams.

"What do you say we give the girls some competition?" Susan said. "It shall blow our boy's minds."

When Geoffrey and Brian came back up to join them, they found Susan and Rachel, totally naked and comfortably conversing with Jen and two of the other women who Rachel introduced as Carmen and Donna, each of whom could have posed for Playmates of the month.

"The candy store just took in a few new items," Brian said. "Our girls could certainly give these younger ones a run for their money." Geoffrey nodded in agreement and too amazed by what he saw, to speak.

When he recovered some of his composure, he detailed information regarding the cruise as given to him by Joey, who said that they would stop at St. Vincent for stores and continue on down the Grenadines, taking as much time as they wanted, since Miles DaCosta said there was no rush to reach Grenada.

Jollybuns had turned up the stereo, and as the sound of calypso filled the air, the women on the top deck moved unconsciously to the beat.

"This is our itinerary," Geoffrey said, and from what I gather, not written in stone. Joey has checked the weather and it seems fine all the way down. He also informed me that Miles had just radioed in to make sure that you all consider this your ship for the week, and pending good weather, we can stop over wherever we all want. Now there is not much to see in St. Vincent, so the visit there shall be brief. Oh, and something else, Miles has arranged for a gourmet cook to board at St. Vincent, so we shall all be eating very well."

Rachel and Susan walked by as Geoffrey unfolded a map of the Grenadines and laid it out on the deck. "If you would like to see where we shall sail, come around."

Jen and two of the women got down on their knees next to Geoffrey, as Rachel turned around to watch. Brian touched Susan on her shoulder as she started to descend the ladder. "Where are you going?" He asked.

"We are on our way down for more rum punch, Luv," she said with a smile. "Our new friends are thirsty. Oh, by the way, they want to know why you two are overdressed. What shall we tell them?" Both women went down to the deck below as Brian's face reddened.

"After St. Vincent, we sail on to the island of Bequia which is pronounced Beckway. It is the largest of the islands." He paused as he felt Jen's left breast touch his elbow. "Uh, nice secluded beaches for however we all choose to utilize our time. The plan is to anchor at Admiralty Bay, here." He pointed to a spot on the map as Donna moved in on his other side. "Any way here at Admiralty Bay we shall overnight."

"What is there to do there, Geoffrey?" Donna asked in sultry voice, and he was certain that Rachel and Susan had put her up to this.

"You can snorkel." He said.

"I don't snorkel. Geoffrey." She responded.

"All right, you can take out one of the small cats. If you like. They are great fun."

Donna rubbed up against his thigh. "I don't cat either," she purred seductively.

"Okay, then," he went on. "The next island shall be Mustique and after it, Canouan and Mayreau, which we might skip."

Rachel arrived with a full tray of drinks, and Susan brought an unopened bottle of Mount Gay. "As I recall, not much to do there," Rachel said as she passed the tray around. "But there is great snorkeling."

"Donna does not snorkel or cat," Brian advised. "We have not polled the rest."

Geoffrey looked at Susan and Rachel. "Okay, you have made your point."

"Which is what?" Rachel said.

"With all of you naked women hovering around us, it sort of takes away the magic." He said.

"If I may," Brian said, "it shall take away the mystique of Mustique." He ducked as Jen and Donna tossed their empty cups at him.

Rachel whispered in Susan's ear. "Didn't I tell you they could not get it up surrounded by twelve naked women?"

The LORD JIM whose mainsails had been unfurled, moved out into the open sea, passing a Norwegian cruise ship, where passengers fought for rail space to observe twelve naked women gyrating on its upper deck, to the strains of 'Hot Hot Hot.

It was well on its way to the island of St. Vincent, where after taking on additional water, food and a cook they would begin the five-hour sail to Bequia and Admiralty Bay. Chantel joined the crew at St. Vincent as cook.

Jollybuns, whose name Susan finally found out was David, had trolled a line and was fortunate enough to catch a large dolphin that he filleted and had Chantel cook for dinner. Chantel was a thirty five year old exotic French national who had lived on Martinique for a number of years before finding employment at a small restaurant on Young Island, St. Vincent. There she mastered the art of Caribbean cooking, that essentially taught her to make do with whatever was available from the land and the sea. Now there were thirteen sensual women on the ship.

Everyone dressed for dinner, meaning that the women reluctantly put on some clothes.

Miles had provided more than adequate bottles of Chilean Merlots and Chablis, certainly enough to satisfy the palate of the guests and crew. Every one complimented Chantel on her dinner, and those who were neither drunk nor exhausted, remained to chat in the lounge. Geoffrey immediately found out how vulnerable Chantel was having just concluded a five year relationship, but he readily accepted Susan's invitation to dance to a Merrymen's rendition of 'Beautiful Barbados', that Rachel had found among a collection of tapes. That evening, the McKenzie's and Townsands slept soundly side-by-side, too tired and too drunk to pursue any more prurient objectives.

The next morning, both Geoffrey and Brian found that their wives were not in bed, hurriedly put on their bathing suits, and went to find coffee and to see what Rachel and Susan were up to. "Do you suppose that this is their way of getting even?" Brian asked.

"For what? We have done absolutely nothing at all to upset them." Geoffrey responded. Once back on deck, they found their women attired in different but yet, seductive bathing wear. Some of the flight attendants were still asleep.

At Bequia, Geoffrey decided that a good way to break the ice was to continue his travelogue as Susan and Rachel listened amused. "Okay, those who wish to go ashore, may take a motor launch to the main town of Port Elizabeth. Bequia was initially one the islands noted for boat building and as a whaling station."

Susan observed a number of upscale yachts moored in the bay, and Brian joked that some of the small launches that trailed after them might best be called Dingalacs. Jen, Donna and some of the others who went ashore came back with tee shirts they had purchased and bottles of wine they believed to be an exceptional buy. Once aboard, they resorted to their more comfortable attire of undress.

That evening they all dined on rock lobster generously dressed with a garlic butter sauce, and fried potatoes, accompanied by the wine Jen and Donna had purchased. Music from an on shore steel band accentuated the great mood all were feeling.

Later, the evening of dancing was complimented with music from Trinidad, by bands vying for Carnival.

Brian and Geoffrey felt an obligation to pick up dinner dishes and deliver them to Joey and Jollybuns who with Chantel washed and dried them. The two then joined the women on the upper deck wondering what to do next. Geoffrey began a conversation with a girl named Naomi, who kept on leaning on him. Oddly enough Rachel did not seem to notice.

Naomi, however, had observed the earlier interaction between Rachel, Susan and Brian. "Geoffrey," she said. "I would like a glass of Merlot."

"I shall fetch it immediately," He said.

"I'll go with you," she said. "That is if you do not mind."

Alone at the bar, she watched Geoffrey as he found and opened a fresh bottle. "The four of you seem very attracted to each other."

Geoffrey filed her glass. "We are very good friends."

"Actually," she said as she took a sip, "my entire group has developed an unusual relationship with each other, and Jen was concerned that the manner in which we party might send the wrong message."

"You are telling me that we are sailing with ten lesbians." Geoffrey said. "Those that shall be the most amused shall be Rachel and Susan."

"No, some are bisexual, but we have developed a friendship with Susan and Rachel and will not intrude upon your marriages," She said. "I thought it important to tell you."

"Bisexual?" He smiled. "Have you ever had a Barbadian quickie?" He asked.

"I have heard of the Big Bamboo." She said.

"Would you like a demonstration?" He asked as Rachel approached. "Hi, I was preparing to demonstrate a Barbadian quickie," he said, pouring rum into a cup.

"I can do that," Rachel said as she grabbed the glass of rum, drained it and followed with four ounces of ice water. "There it is in a nutshell. Naomi, please excuse us. My husband and I are going topside to dance.

They danced to Donna Summer singing 'Dim All The Lights' as the tide seemed to move the ship to the beat of the music.

Brian and Susan cut in and they exchanged partners as Naomi appeared with a full glass of rum and stood beside Jollybuns, watching them with interest. She moved over to Jen and put her arm around her. "What is your take on the four of them?"

Both Jollybuns and Jen said in unison. "Just very good friends."

"Hey Mon," Jen said. "Will this cruse get more interesting?"

She put her arm around Donna, her fingertips gently caressing her breast. "Some of us want to get laid."

Twelve

Bequia, the Grenadines 1988

By midnight, the wine and the rum had taken its toll, and both the Townsands and McKenzies fell fast asleep onto one bed. An hour later, Geoffrey returned from the head and quietly awakened Brian. "No action down here, and now I am stone sober. What do you say about taking a harmless stroll on the upper deck?" Now fully awake, Brian agreed to join him.

Despite the late hour, they found the flight attendants awake, still drinking rum, and enjoying the music that drifted in from the shore. Donna had introduced the concept of the Barbados rum quickie to the rest of the women. "Fantastic!" Geoffrey exclaimed. "My kind of party!"

Donna called them over to where she sat, cuddled with Jen and a girl she introduced as Anecka. "She is Swedish." Donna said. "And now we have two unescorted handsome men. Let's party!"

Brian pulled Geoffrey off to the side. "I think that we should think this out. At some point we should draw a line and that line excludes any of these women." Geoffrey looked perturbed.

"The point, well taken, is despite all of the available pussy, we have no further than look to our wives for sex. I believe that is the message they were sending. Getting back to that guy Voltaire, I think we both have the best of all possible worlds. Let's not fuck it up!"

"You know Brian, I believe you are correct. We love our wives totally. Why do any thing to disrupt what we all seem to enjoy?" Geoffrey said. "But, right at this moment, they are both asleep. Why shouldn't we just enjoy this night and have a few more drinks?"

"You have no argument from me as far as the drinks, but" Brian never got to finish what he had to say as Geoffrey gently cupped his hand over his mouth.

Rachel stirred in the bed, and found the space next to her empty. In the dim light, she saw that Susan was alone as well.

She removed her nightgown and slid under the covers beside Susan, who moaned as their hips met. "Rachel, your skin is deliciously cool," Susan said as their lips met and. Rachel slid down toward Susan's abdomen and in for mutual satisfaction. Afterwards, they lay back arms around each other. "What do you suppose the boys are doing?" Susan asked softly.

Susan hugged Rachel. "Absolutely nothing exciting, I would guess. I could use some more. How about you?"

At three in the morning, Rachel had to use the head, and after a moment's thought, decided to go up on deck to check upon Brian and Geoffrey whom she found sound asleep and still fully clothed.

She left them and quietly returned to bed. Susan asked where she had been. "Up checking on the boys."

"And?" Susan asked.

"They are safe and fast asleep. Forget them. I need some more of what we can give to each other. We have no time line. Let's just take our own needs to infinity."

"What a great idea. I love you Rachel."

"And I you, so very much. Susan. So are we now considered to be lesbians?" Rachel asked.

"Nah, we are just two of the coolest women in the Grenadines." Susan said.

Brian awakened by the sudden movement of the ship, checked his watch. It was four in the morning. A naked Naomi lay next to him, but he was still wearing the clothes he wore for dinner. He awakened Geoffrey who asked if he knew what if anything had happened.

"Nothing that I remember," he said. "Do you realize that we have the most loving, sexually stimulating women in the world down below, and both have been sleeping soundly ignorant of the fact that you and I, despite the enticements around us, have remained faithful to them."

"Geoffrey, you are correct. We owe it to them to go back to bed and inform them that absolutely nothing sordid occurred. Agree?"

"True, True," He responded.

"You guys are really boring," Naomi said, as she rolled to her side. The two men went below, undressed and lay down next to their sleeping wives, satisfied that nothing had occurred to adversely affect their relationship

As the heat of the morning sun warmed the naked bodies of the women on deck, they were awakened by Susan's announcement on the speakers that it was time for morning exercises. "Now, ladies and gentlemen, you are all, in order to earn breakfast, required to participate." The airline attendants just groaned and went back to sleep.

Geoffrey joined her at the helm and took the microphone. "All members of the cruise not engaged in preparing the Lord Jim for departure shall be expected to muster on the dancing deck." Susan brushed her hip against his and thanked him.

"Where were the two of you last night?" She asked. "The bed was suddenly devoid of husbands."

"As celibate as novice nun, I can assure you," He said as Susan thought about Rachel and just smiled.

"Can we find some time to talk, Geoffrey? It is important." She said.

He covered the microphone with his hand. "In lieu of a major broadcast, of course."

Eight of the ten women with the exception of Jen and Donna finally responded to the exercise muster and Brian, Geoffrey, Joey, Chantel and Jollybuns lined up along side the others.

After a half hour of exercise and a great deal of laughter, the group stopped for breakfast, tired but nevertheless energized.

Geoffrey joined Susan at the helm to share a plate of flying fish, bacon and eggs. "I think we should talk about you." She said.

"Me? In what respect?" He asked.

"Geoffrey, it is my sense that there is more to you than a half hour in bed with each other." She said.

"Only a half hour?" He responded.

"Whatever. You miss the point. I want to find out what excites you. I don't care if it is current events, or the arts, anything. I only know that you watch CNN for what is happening in the world and probably not the best source of truth."

"Susan, I am surprised. I have much more depth than that. When in London I spent as much time at cultural events as I did at local pubs. Well almost."

She grimaced. "I was an economics major with a minor in marketing. However, besides Re-deffusion, our only exposure, aside from tourism, to the world outside Barbados is CNN." He said.

"Please, Geoffrey, do not consider CNN as the totally unbiased source of world news, because that, it is not. It has as much credibility as does the New York Times. When I was in the eleventh grade, I faithfully read the Times and looked forward to the Sunday crossword puzzle that I pleasured in doing in ink, but as I matured as an adult I came to realize that the paper was doing a disservice to the public. Editorial comment should never have replaced front-page news, and I feel the same about the Washington Post. As you may have surmised I have become quite the conservative. And this comes from a person, so very liberal during my formative college years. I can go on and on about why I believe that the Liberals running for office have only their own personal gain in mind, but if you look at the mind set of any of the people who seek public office, their main thrust is not to make good on promises made, but only to prepare for another election with more false promises. Such is how I feel about any of the Democratic candidates, and most of the Republicans. Sadly, in this respect we have the worst of all possible worlds."

"Luv. I understand your passion, but I meant this cruise to be a less sophisticated and more animalistic and erotic. That said, I must inform you that I have more depth than you may think. However, as far as world politics is concerned, Barbados is so very dependent upon what the U.S does, and so am I." He said.

"Sorry, Geoffrey. I just wanted you to know that our friendship is about things other than sex. Oh, well, where are we bound for today?"

"I fully appreciate that and I can assure you that Brian feels similarly, and we both regret that we left you and Rachel alone last evening." He said.

"Please, Geoffrey, have no regrets." Susan smiled as she recalled how she and Rachel had spent the time in their husbands' absence.

After having aroused most of Bequia, Joey moved the Lord Jim out to open waters, and Geoffrey, again, sought out Susan who was engrossed in reading. "Tell me," he said. "What else do you wish to know of me?"

"For starters," she said as she put her book aside, "Do you like to read?"

"We Bajans must read technical material just to survive you know. One time when I was in the States, I looked through your Yellow Pages and had a good laugh. You had this endless list for plumbers, electricians, auto-mechanics and carpenters. In Barbados, that would be listed under one person. We Bajans do what is required, you know."

"I believe I get the point," She said. "But you said that you like to read other things. What specifically?"

"As you can see, I have little time for leisure pursuits such as reading, but I have taken a fancy to Jeffrey Archer,"

"Please do not use him for an example just because you fancy screwing an attorney." She said with a smile. "You know that Brian reads a great deal about the plight of our own Native Americans and the terrible things done to them under the name of progress by my own government."

"I have read the 'Trail of Tears' he said. "I had to read it twice, actually. I could not believe that humans could do such to other humans."

"I am now truly impressed," Susan said. "But how do you rationalize the island's reliance on slavery?" She did not wait for an answer. "Enough of that. So tell me. Have you had an unrelenting hard on with all of the available chicks on board?"

"I admire your amazing ability to drastically change subject. As much I would like not to admit it, I enjoyed having an assortment of naked women within arms length to stimulate me. But with regard to your reference to my physical response, it was much less than expected, and when Brian and I compared notes, he admitted to the same. Is that the answer you wanted?"

"Geoffrey, I am please non the less, and believe it or not we all shall be both strengthened and energized. Just wait and see." She said.

"I love you, Susan, for just being you," he said. "Just to change tack a bit, we shall reach Tobago Cays by lunch if the wind holds up. This is a place you shall adore. It is so pristine. I have a guide book I shall fetch, and in the mean time see where Rachel is."

Brian joined her just as Geoffrey went below. "I never realized, darling, that Geoffrey has a depth greater than we imagined."

Geoffrey returned shortly with a small book dog-eared on the section on Tobago Cays. Susan quickly reviewed the text and exclaimed, "We are all going to love this place. It is almost close enough to those small islands that we can cross over to them, if the tide allows. There are five different beaches we can explore." She handed the book to Brian.

"I hope there are no rules on nudity there," Jen exclaimed, since the rest of us plan to romp in the all together."

Geoffrey looked at Brian as Susan took Rachel's hand. "I agree with Jen. Why not?" Both of the women removed their skimpy bikinis and Brian and Geoffrey peeled off their bathing trunks. With all inhibitions now dissolved they joined Jen and Donna and the rest totally unconcerned that they were nude. It was amazing to Brian, that the fact that they were all naked was irrelevant, and more amazing to Susan that he accepted it. She hoped that he would be as accepting of her deep emotional link with Rachel.

Her dilemma revolved around the fact that Brian in no way could accept Geoffrey as she had accepted Rachel, and in no manner was it imperative for him to do so.

Rachel immediately exhorted the other fair skinned women to shade themselves from the sun, so as not to be as burned as the Red Legs would be.

"Red Legs?" Brian asked.

"True, True. "Rachel responded. "There were a group of Barbadians believed to be descended from Scots and Irish who lived above the cliffs of St. John and St. Joseph, back before the turn of the eighteenth century. Kept mostly to themselves, they did, and intermarried. Many of the progeny were not normal and some descendants are physically deprived, you know. We call them the Eckybecky. From what I have been told, one of the most industrious of them founded a dairy industry that we, actually still use today."

"I suppose if people are allowed to develop and grow without governments interference, they can achieve successes once believed unattainable." Brian said. He winked at Susan who acknowledged him with a high five.

Thirteen

Tobago Cays, The Grenadines

Susan found Tobago Cays exactly as described in the Grenadine guide book and so much more. Joey dropped the LORD JIM's anchor just beyond the two-mile long horseshoe shaped reef that protected the four islands encompassing the marine park. The depth of the water was about twelve feet and so crystal clear, that the pink sand and myriads of sea life were readily visible below water, that periodically changed color from emerald to turquoise. Jollybuns made a number of trips, dropping people at the beach, and then motoring back for the next group waiting their turn.

Naomi, Jen, and a stunning blonde named Ingrid, ran up the narrow beach and laid down towels before stripping off their bikinis and splashing into the surf. Rachel and Susan, who had arrived with the first group, decided to explore the small island, finding little, but an occasional crab scurrying from one hiding place to another in the hot sand.

Geoffrey, Brian, Jollybuns and the remainder of the women were the last to disembark, while Joey remained on board the ship.

Jollybuns decided to hang out with Jen and Naomi, while Geoffrey and Brian carried up large boxes containing the snorkeling gear. Brian fitted a pair of fins over his dive booties, picked up a snorkel and followed Geoffrey into the water. He found more colorful fish at a depth of six feet than he had seen during the deep dive of the Stravronikita. Brian remembered that at a depth of eighty feet, objects lose bright colors, and the deeper one might dive, objects reflected mainly browns and blacks. The two swam leisurely over large conch shells, most of which were intact, since the sea remained calm and was rarely intruded upon by motor launches.

Brian suddenly felt a bite on his right buttock and turned to protect himself only to find Susan, laughing and sputtering as she swallowed seawater. "What a simply extraordinary place," She said when she stopped coughing. "Virtually uninhabited and almost still pristine," she added. "Truly a tropical paradise."

"Why do you say, almost still pristine?" Geoffrey asked as he and Rachel joined them.

"Well, Luv," Rachel said grinning. "Susan and I had decided to explore a bit and found some of our fellow shipmates, screwing behind the dunes."

"More power to them," Geoffrey said. "Is it a private party? And may we participate?"

"Geoffrey," Susan advised. "It was only the stews." He responded by replacing his snorkel and diving under the water.

The four friends eventually found a secluded spot to lie down on the sand and doze off, later to be awakened by bells from the deck of the LORD JIM, announcing that lunch would soon be served.

"I say that we all could use some real exercise and swim to the boat rather than wait for Joey to fetch us." Brian said, as he became aroused watching Rachel struggle to put her fins back on. She looked back, smiled and then strode into the water.

"Wait for me," Geoffrey called out as he fumbled with his fins. Splashing into the water, he called out. "Why make Jollybuns row more than necessary, since he must be exhausted already." Rachel and Susan had decided not to tell their men how they spent the previous evening without them. Brian tossed the floatable equipment box toward the dingy as it neared them, and then joined the others as they swam toward the boat riding at anchor.

Swimming smoothly in the calm water, they soon reached Horseshoe reef, and the Lord Jim's mooring, as the aromas of cooking pleasantly greeted their nostrils. They savored the lunch of flying fish, fries and a green salad, washed down with bottles of Banks beer. From Tobago Cays they could see their next destinations, Palm and Union Islands.

Susan and Rachel sat on the so-called fun deck lunching with Jen, Naomi, Ingrid and Donna. "This is great!" Susan exclaimed.

Jen finished her second flying fish sandwich and wiped her mouth with a paper napkin. "You all could just have left us there, you know. I dig this life with no clothing, and no competition for best ass. I say screw dieting!" She said. "I hope we have not stressed out your guys with our love of just being bare ass naked."

"Not at the very least." Susan said. "Both of them just enjoy people who insist on freedom of self expression." Rachel laughed. "I wish that our culture did not frown upon it as much as it does." Susan said.

"Hey, we all thought you both cool when you stripped down the first day." Jen said.

"You know, Jen, it was the first time that I felt totally uninhibited, and wondered who makes the rules and why." Rachel said as Susan agreed. "If they only knew," She whispered to Susan, after Jen and the others left them to bring their empty dishes back down to the deck below.

"Rachel, I believe that I could really enjoy being naked forever." Susan said.

"Well, would the guys still want sex with two broads whose asses have dropped and breasts have sagged while running around in the all together?" Rachel said.

"I would venture a guess that Geoffrey and Brian would, no matter what, but you definitely have a point, Luv. Their motto would be 'have vacuum, will fill', but would it change how the two of us relate to each other?" Susan asked.

"Fear not. I believe we are solid." Rachel looked around and finding that they were still alone kissed Susan.

They first anchored off Palm Island, which was a short distance from Union Island, the larger of the two, and everyone came ashore, with plans to meet at the Casuarinas Beach Hotel bar that had been built of pink coral.

Susan ordered a banana daiquiri, and asked Raul, the barman if there were any shops that sold local art. He explained that while Palm Island had little to offer other than refreshments, they might stop at an island called Cariacou, which was actually a major island in the Grenadines. He made mention of a local artist named Canute Calliste who had paintings for sale, albeit very primitive.

When Susan asked Geoffrey about Cariacou, he frowned. "Oh my, that shall be our last island before Grenada and I do not wish all of this to end."

"Raul, a refill, please for everyone, before we become too saddened that all of this wonderment shall soon come to an end." Susan told the barman.

The group split up for a half hour. Brian and Geoffrey returned from unproductive shopping spree to rejoin the group at the bar. "We saw shops down the beach. Buy anything?" Brian asked.

"Rachel helped me pick this out. What do you think?" Susan pulled a thong from a white bag.

"You do have a most magnificent ass for that piece of beachwear." Geoffrey said, as both Susan and Rachel finished their drinks. "Come Rachel, I shall buy you a gift." When Geoffrey and Rachel returned, Susan was wearing her thong.

When everyone was on board, the ship motored to Union Island, where they would anchor over night. Union island, relatively desolate and consisting mainly of rocky tors, and mostly inhabited by goats, was the southern most port of entry into the Grenadines.

"Does not appear to have too much going on here," Brian said as he noted the narrow empty beaches.

"There actually is a small hotel here and an airport as well. People come for the desolation. If you like, we can go ashore before supper and explore a bit." Geoffrey said to Susan.

Brian said that he preferred to spend the afternoon reading, and Rachel told Geoffrey and Susan that she would remain on board the ship as well.

Geoffrey helped Susan down into the dingy and advised Joey that once he dropped them ashore, he could return to the boat.

They wandered over the beach to a forested area, where Susan shyly asked him to turn away while she relieved herself. "Just protect me from tourists." They continued over rocky terrain until reaching a clearing where animals quietly grazed. "Oh, my, sheep!" Susan called out.

"No, Luv, they are goats," He corrected. "Worry not. Most people make the same mistake."

They seemed to have walked for miles, when Geoffrey announced that they had reached the highest point of Union Island, about one thousand feet above sea level. "We are actually on the westerly side," He told her. They rested on a large outcropping enjoying a cool breeze, as Susan took off her sandals and rubbed the soles of her feet. Geoffrey reached over and kissed her.

"Don't expect much more. We agreed it would not happen, Geoffrey." She said. "But if you would massage my poor feet, I would be most appreciative."

Geoffrey gently rubbed the soles of her feet. "Why, we have been intimate on a number of occasions?" He asked.

"Because both Rachel and Brian trust that it shall not happen." She said.

"Agreed, but reluctantly," Geoffrey said.

"There are things that I wish to ask you, Geoffrey," Susan said.

"Ask away. I am at your disposal." He responded.

"How did you and Rachel meet?" She asked.

"Rachel, as you know is Canadian, born, schooled and raised in a non descript Ontario town by the name of Beeton, where the most exciting event celebrated, if you exclude mud wrestling in a local pub on Friday, is a yearly corn roast, what ever that might be. Doubt if you shall find it on any map." He said. "She was engaged to what she, herself described as a small town accountant, and questioning if this was the person with whom she wanted to spend the rest of her life, decided to take vacation in the Caribbean and chose Barbados. I happened to accept an invitation from Miles DaCosta to listen to a new group called the Merrymen whom he had auditioned to play on the Thursday night Pirate Adventure cruise and there was Rachel. We danced the entire evening, and when I suggested that she come back with me to my apartments, she accepted."

"I convinced her not to return to Canada, having fallen in love with her, and the rest is history. We married and our two darling daughters followed a year apart, and she has never regretted her decision. Now it is your turn." He said.

"Brian, although also raised in Canada as you know, came to the States with an interest in economics and landed a job at a company I had never heard of called Bear Sterns." She said. "I had just finished college and having decided to visit our American West, got on a bus that eventually took me to a real cowboy town called Cody, Wyoming, where I met Brian, sitting on the porch of the Irma Hotel with a group of wranglers who had recently come off a cattle drive. We just, as you would say, hit it off. Nothing intimate happened, and we just exchange telephone numbers. He called me when he returned to New York. We dated for about six months and realized that we were very much in love. In the meantime, I enrolled in Columbia Law School and here we all are." She said.

Susan brushed sand from her toes and slipped her sandals back, on as she saw dark clouds gathering over the distant horizon. "Are we due for a storm, Geoffrey?" She asked.

"I believe we might be in the way of a shower, but it would dry off with the heat as it is." He responded.

"Is this not hurricane season," She asked.

"In the Grenadines?" He asked. "A rarity all the way back to St. Vincent and even Barbados for that matter. I do not recall the last bad one that hit Barbados, but I can assure you that we most likely rode it out at some bar, the Bajan way."

"Really, Geoffrey. Does that mean that you all just fucked your way through the storm?" She laughed.

"Luv, let me educate you in the Bajan way. I doubt if you have ever heard me utter the word fuck, even during our most intimate bindings. We use the word foop since it is not as specific and possibly more delicate. Having deal with that, have you ever visited the Miramar Beach Hotel?"

"We did, when Brian first drove your wonderful roads, he needed a drink and we stopped at the hotel bar. Why, is that of some note?" She asked.

"Getting back to your query regarding how we Bajans ride out a hurricane, one time we decided to have a party at the Miramar Beach Hotel. There we all sat, in bathing suits, drinking rum and cokes, changing to Banks so as not to get too drunk. After all, what else was there to do?" He laughed.

"We just tossed the palm fronds driven into the bar by the winds, away, and watched waiters attempting to serve the few guests who valiantly showed up for their dinners. When one English gentleman, who required oxygen eventually came to dinner, our friends, including the chef, would sneak off to his room for hits from his oxygen tank."

Susan felt drop of rain. "What ever the point of the story, it is clearly absurd. True, True, Eh?"

"Now the rain was heavy, and the storm frightened the sheit out of everyone including the rats who ran back into the kitchen. That same bloke got out his twelve-gauge shotgun and took aim. Unfortunately, in doing so, he took out the water pipes. In the morning after the storm had passed, he had a tough time explaining the flooded kitchen. At any rate, we, who rode out the storm, did manage to almost drink the bar dry."

"Geoffrey, I am getting soaked." Susan exclaimed.

"But you have on a bathing suit." He responded.

"I was just curious how Bajans dealt with the anxiety of hurricanes when hurricane parties were not the sole answer to survival." She said. "Let's get back to the boat."

Fourteen

Union Island, The Grenadines

By the time Susan and Geoffrey reached the dock, the rain had ceased although dark clouds menaced overhead. Jollybuns sat waiting in the small boat as it rocked to the movements of the tide, while island music from the Lord Jim reached their ears. Geoffrey cast the mooring line back on the dock as Susan climbed down into the boat.

"You are the last to arrive," Jollybuns said, as he started up the small outboard and steered toward the black hulled two master, that rode majestically in the bay. "When the wind really became strong, we were concerned that you might have some trouble, but things just quieted down." Warm sun suddenly bathed the three as the dark clouds parted and then move off to the west.

"As you see, weather is totally predictable here in the Grenadines. Nothing bad stays around, at all, at all." Geoffrey said.

"I have to admit that I did have some concerns." Susan said.

Geoffrey moved closer to Susan and whispered in her ear. "I was thinking about something, you know. Perhaps we could go off sometime for a holiday."

Susan tried to talk over the drone of the engine. "I am not sure Brian can get away again this year."

Geoffrey cupped his hands over her ear. "I was not planning to ask Brian." He smiled, but Susan did not respond. "We shall talk more when conversation is less of a strain and we are alone."

The small boat was brought near the ship's ladder where Brian waited to help them aboard. "Hey, we blew the horn quite a while ago. We were worried about the two of you with the sudden change in the weather."

Susan kissed him. "Thank you for worrying, but we were fine. Geoffrey took me on a hike to the other side of the island and up to the promontory, when it became overcast and started to rain. Since there was no place to take cover, we just sat there getting soaked, chatting. As you can see, my clothes are almost dry."

"I am famished," Geoffrey said. "Did you leave any food for us? And what have you been doing with all of these horny women?" Brian whispered something in Geoffrey's ear and he almost choked on a glass of rum punch Rachel had given him.

"Buffet's still set up," Susan said, wondering what Brian had told Geoffrey.

"Actually, we all waited for you two, although, we have a head start on a very early happy hour." Brian said as he passed plates and plastic service wrapped in white napkins to Rachel, Susan and Geoffrey.

"Looks grand," Susan said as she observed the cooks selection of tropical fruits, luncheon meats and fried chicken. "What I don't see is hot sauce."

"Not to worry," Geoffrey said. "I shall be back with hot pepper sauce momentarily."

When he returned, they sat on the bulkhead, balancing their plates and drinks as the crew prepared to get the ship underway.

Rachel explained that she had been looking at a map and the next stop would be the island of Cariacou. "If someone would hold my lunch, I shall go put on the stereo." She said.

Brian took her plate, and went to the buffet declaring that he was ready for seconds on the fried chicken.

"Good food and definitely extraordinary company. Come let us dine on the upper deck. Much cooler up there, you know." Rachel said when she returned.

When they reached the top rung of the ladder, they found women, again in various states of undress. "Bloody hell!" Geoffrey mumbled under his breath, his face suddenly reddened. He quickly escorted Susan to a set of cushioned seats well away from the others. "Did you know that they are all lesbians and Brian joyfully shared that information with me?" He whispered.

"I had my suspicions but that was all." She said.

"Brian just informed me when we came aboard." He said.

"And pray tell, why is that such a big deal?" She asked.

"Susan, you know, he said. What I do not understand is that if Brian knew, it did not at all faze him." Geoffrey said.

"Did you mean get him aroused? Figure it out yourself," She retorted. "Perhaps my husband just has his priorities in the right place, and you know exactly what part of his anatomy I refer to."

"I just bet that Rachel has been laughing her head off," Geoffrey said.

"I cannot believe that it did not occur to you that those women seemed more interested in each other than any of the other men on this ship." Susan took a bite of her chicken.

"I have gotten the point fully." He said. "But an airline that hired lesbian or even bisexual stews? On the other hand they could be bi-sexual, you know. Enough of that, how about my offer of a holiday for two?"

"It is extremely enticing. What did you have in mind?" She asked.

"Something really off beat. There are two small islands just off St. Vincent yet to be developed. I had thought perhaps an island retreat catering to singles or young couples. Not unlike camping out in one of your National Parks, but a return to nature with small thatched villas on stilts with both a gourmet restaurant and a wee market stocked with lovely provisions. I believe that I could acquire it cheaply enough. I envisioned us spending a week checking it and ourselves out." He waited for her reply.

Susan looked at him with amusement. "Personally, I would rather fancy a sojourn in Cannes with stop over in Paris or London, or even a New Zealand vacation," she said. "What you call paradise sounds more like a European youth hostel. And what about Brian and Rachel?"

"They can select their own holiday, what ever suits them." Geoffrey said. "In that way, the score shall be even. Please think about it." He said.

Rachel and Brian, their plates piled with food, appeared on the deck and joined them. Brian had a bottle of rum tucked under his arm. "Since you left us with no drink order, we took it upon ourselves to choose." Brian said.

Geoffrey made room for Rachel to sit beside him. "Hey Geoffrey, Luv, " she said. "Gotten over the fact that the two of us are the only available lays on your 'dream vacation'?"

"Don't be too hard on him, " Susan offered. "He has not quite gotten over the news." She put her arm around Brian's neck and kissed him. "I am looking forward to Cariacou."

"Miles, that bastard knew. He set me up, you know. Well, we Bajans play tricks on each other for sport, but I must admit that this, so far was the best ever. So far, that is. And as far as getting laid, was I too drunk to remember? He looked at Jen and Ingrid, both of whom had rolled over on their stomachs, but deep in conversation "You do not suppose that they were all in on it, do you?"

"I would assume that they had or have neither a clue nor a care." Rachel said. "Poor darling. Consider that this voyage has just begun. Play your cards right and everything abooot it, as the Canadians say, might be unforgettable."

Rachel explained that Cariacou was the largest of the three islands that made up the Grenada Territory, the others being Petit Martinique and Grenada. When they came ashore and set foot on the narrow beach, most of the airline personnel opted to walk, while the McKenzies, the Townsands, Jen and Donna were willing to wait for any local transportation that might carry them into the islands largest town, Hillsborough.

"It is unbelievably hot. Perhaps we should have gone on with the rest." Jen said to Donna.

"Wait," Geoffrey advised. "I recall all kinds of transportation showing up when you would least expect it." Suddenly a large yellow school bus came down the road toward them, and he flagged it down. They boarded and sat amid cases of soda destined for delivery to town, since that was its function when not bringing children to and from school. As the bus move slowly over a rise, Brian spotted the group that had chosen to go by foot. They were closely watching a large un-tethered bull, standing by the road and intrigued by Naomi's red blouse.

Naomi was the first to climb aboard. And it was a close call, since the bull obviously knowing good stuff when he saw it, began to paw the ground. "I have never been so frightened. Teaches me to wear red in bull country." She exclaimed, taking a seat.

Susan recalled the barman from Palm Island's telling her that there was an eighty-nine year old local artist on the island of Cariacou. His name was Canute Calisste, but he took a nap directly after noon, and in no manner would allow being disturbed. As the group dispersed, Susan came upon some paintings in a shop whose doorway appeared to be blocked by a pail full of foul smelling slop. Holding their noses they entered the shop.

Most of the paintings were quite primitive with people represented as stick figures, the fish horizontal globules and the water, a blue and white mass of vertical slashes. The shop's proprietor explained that once the artist, Mr. Canute Calliste had been discovered, his work became greatly in demand. Only once had he ever agreed to leave Cariacou to visit a gallery opening, and was confused as to what the fuss was about. He painted for his own pleasure and required little upon which to subsist on this island of his birth.

Nevertheless, Susan seeing something compelling about his art, wished to purchase a painting, and was upset when told that the artist was asleep and could not be disturbed. Geoffrey placated her when he assured her that this was an island well traveled by friends, who would, if so instructed, purchase an original Calliste for her. Believing that they had already seen all that the town had to offer, they met for drinks at a local rum shop down the road, and Geoffrey made arrangements to transfer the entire group back to the dock by bus.

Brian savoring a rum and coke asked." What exactly does this island produce?"

"At one time, Cariacou was noted for the growth of huge limes and an abundant sugar crop. As to the present, it now offers an opportunity for tourists who enjoy privacy and like to wander beaches and explore the ruins of once exotic estates. Had you not noticed that Cariacou still uses the old Eastern Caribbean currency? More than likely they are now a collector's item for those of us who never exchanged their dollars for ours." Rachel said. They all boarded the old school cum soda bus that took them back to the harbor, and the Lord Jim, anchored a few hundred yards off shore.

Fifteen

Cariacou The Grenadines

The plan is to overnight here in the harbor and leave Cariacou promptly after breakfast." Geoffrey said. "I still cannot accept the fact that I have been duped by Miles in such a fashion."

"Geoffrey," Brian said. "Leave it already. Our women are tiring of it. I am certainly tiring of it."

"Nonsense, they are all the same." Geoffrey said. "They want instant gratification when the juices flow just like all of the others. It is true for us as well. We do lust you know, Brian. It is after all in our blood. Ready and able, when duty calls. I dearly hope it calls soon."

"What world do you live in?" Brian asked. "Women want their knights in shining armor, while vacationing on the Riviera, to guarantee that their man is making love to them and only to them at that sudden magnificent explosive moment."

"Speaking of that, what is going on between Rachel and Susan? Have you observed that they don't seem to require our physical company?" Geoffrey asked.

"The sleeping arrangements have not exactly been terrific you know, and we have spent more time on deck at night because of you." Brian said. He made a mental note to ask Susan as to what Geoffrey was inferring, and smiled.

"Right. I suggest, then, that we take turns." Geoffrey said, a huge grin on his face.

"Geoffrey. I have to talk to you about something that concerns all of us." Brian said. "As long as I have known you, you have been trying, hopefully unsuccessfully, to get a little something extra on the side. Both Susan and I are afraid of getting infected with AIDS, so if we are to continue our own personal swing, neither of us shall permit our health to be jeopardized. I need that assurance or all bets are off."

"Fear not, friend. Rachel would more than likely cut me off literally and anatomically unless Susan and she were the only ones." Geoffrey said.

"You are telling me that you are all talk and no action?" Brian asked with a laugh.

"My past sexual experience on Barbados would make you long to have been where and with whom I may have been. Nevertheless, Rachel never insisted that I promise not to hope or wish or desire. It is just that desire keeps me alive, you know." Geoffrey answered. Brian excused himself as Rachel approached.

"Brian appears truly vexed, Geoffrey. Is it something you wish to share?" She asked.

"We were having a frank discussion." He said. "Brian has an archaic view of monogamy."

"Really, I just left Susan after having a similar discussion." She said.

He frowned. "You realize that we have talked more about sex than actually having it?"

"To be serious for a moment, Geoffrey. Both Susan and I are concerned of catching a sexually transmitted disease, if we all do not confine our experiences to present company." She said.

"I have already received an earful from Brian on that very subject. We have been lucky so far." He said with a shrug.

"Well, I for one do not fancy our luck running out." Rachel said. You do recall the Canadian couples and the Americans from Indianapolis. "You have an answer for everything. Now I shall give you fair warning. Fool around and I shall cut you off as well."

"What does as well mean?" He asked.

"Susan," she answered.

"Wouldn't that be Susan's desire?" He asked.

"Who knows what Susan might desire?" Rachel responded.

They were happy reach Petit St. Vincent where hot showers allowed them to finally feel human. Those guilty of over using the showers and fresh water on the boat never owned up to it. Showering with a friend proved not a saving either so ever since leaving Cariacou, washing up with seawater pulled up by the bucket had become the norm. After a quick lunch on shore, everyone returned to The Lord Jim and the long sail to Grenada.

The trip took about five hours, and Brian and Susan made use of the more than adequate library, reading and staying out of the broiling sun. A few of the flight attendant, still interested only in a total tan, ignored Jollybuns warning, and would soon regret doing so.

The crew brought the seventy-three foot long ship along side with merely a tap and Jollybuns jumped to the dock to secure the lines. The women still sunning on the top deck, scrambled for their bathing suits, while a few rushed below to cover their burned skin with aloe.

Susan suggested that they have dinner in Georgetown. She, Brian and Rachel walked into town without Geoffrey, who later caught up with them at a restaurant called The Fisherman's Catch. Much to Susan's delight, the restaurant had lace curtains adorning its windows. They all ordered rum and cokes and selected starters that they agreed to share.

"Rachel, Luv, did we not drink the bar dry here one night?" He asked.

"Hard to say, Luv since there were many nights, and many bars that could fit that scenario." She answered.

"I see, you are still in a testy mood, which is too bad since I feel terrific, and envision a late evening of strong sex between the four of us. What do you think?" He asked.

"I think you should keep your voice down," Susan said.

Rachel was about to reply when she felt Susan's hand on her thigh. She looked at Susan who earlier had made it clear that she was game for anything. Brian's reassuring smile, allowed her to warm to the idea.

"I forgot to share with you that Miles had radioed that the girls should be shown a good time at his expense, so those not too badly sunburned will be entertained by Joey and the others." Geoffrey said. "And the ladies will be staying at a hotel."

"Well, unless any of them are also bi, good luck to the crew of the Lord Jim." Rachel said. "When do we have to take our bags off?"

"Ah, the good news is that we shall have the boat all to ourselves tonight. As I mentioned, the crew shall stay in town, so since it is all ours, let us make the most of it." He leaned over the table and whispered. "You ladies can orgasm and scream to your heart's delight." He ducked a slice of lime Susan had thrown at him, and then groaned as Rachel shoved a foot into his groin.

"Another round of Cuba Libras," Brian called out to the waitress passing by as he felt Rachel run her big toe up his leg.

After a dinner of steak fish, fried plantains and yams, the four refused dessert and decided to take a walk. As Rachel and Brian stopped to look in the window of a video store, Geoffrey caught up with Susan who was occupied by yet another shoe store. He took her hand and swung it playfully. "My dear, you look simply gorgeous, and you foop good too."

"How nice of you to remember," She said. Now stimulated by the alcohol and earlier talk of sex, she was looking forward to a little excitement. "Geoffrey, do you fancy a foursome or shall we pair off?"

"I am game for anything, Luv, and I might look forward to watching you and my daring wife have a go at it." He said.

"Does that mean that Rachel and I might be treated to something between you and Brian?" She asked.

"When hell freezes over as they say. Moi and Brian? Are you sporting with me?" Geoffrey responded. "After all of this stimulating talk, Susan, you a bit horny by now?"

"True. True, as we Bajan's say." She called back to Rachel and Brian who were a few paces behind them. "I am all window shopped out. "How do you feel about returning to the Lord Jim?"

Upon returning to the cabin, Susan put her arms around Brian's neck and kissed him. "I am ready for a night of hot sex. How about you?"

"You know, we will probably grow old and all of this will be just a memory." He said.

"Swell then, I suggest that we make the most of it, and do now what we may not be able to do when we do grow old." Susan removed her dress, revealing that she had spent the evening out without wearing a bra or panties.

"Aren't you just ready?" He said.

"Luv, I have been ready all day. "Our friends at home would believe none of this." She said and watched him undress. "I see you are just about ready."

"Think our friend, Geoffrey has reached salami stage yet?" Brian asked.

"You know, that only happened twice. I remember the first time and one time after that." Never could understand why not again." She said.

"Geoffrey said we should meet on the upper deck." Susan said moving toward the stairs.

"Climb up that ladder, naked?" I don't think so." He retorted.

Susan slapped him on his ass. "Don't be a party pooper," she said she running up the passageway stairs. "Come on hon! Show off those great buns!"

Geoffrey had already positioned some large soft cushions together on the upper deck, and had lit one small candle for affect. Rachel lying naked on one of the cushions extended her arms for Brian to join her. This part of the deck was otherwise darkened and obscured from anyone who might pass by on the dock. He lay down beside her as the Lord Jim gently rocked to the movement of the tide. Most of the inhabitants of Georgetown appeared to have retired for the evening,

"I have a suggestion," Geoffrey said. When he outlined his plan, the other three were willing to give it a go. One of them was to lie back and allow the other three to stimulate him or her in whatever manner was chosen.

Susan elected to be first, and as she lay on her back, Brian and Rachel each took one of her nipples in their mouths, while Geoffrey positioned himself between her legs and gently moved his tongue over and around her clitoris. Susan responded by moving her pelvis upwards to meet his probing. After a while Geoffrey took Rachel's position, and she moved down between Susan's legs. Susan knew the difference as she welcomed Rachel's tongue. It had, after all been there before. When tired of the foreplay, Geoffrey entered Susan who responded by wrapping her legs around his buttocks, moving upwards to met his forward thrusts. Rachel straddled Brian who allowed her to take complete control.

Once they had all climaxed, Brian and Geoffrey switched back to their own wives. Still not fully sated, they switched again until they all lay back satisfied and completely exhausted.

Susan looked up at the star filled sky, marveling at what had just occurred, hoping that it would be repeated over and over again. Brian fell asleep with an arm around each of the women who lay next to him, while Geoffrey still erect, thought about the women, he did not have during the voyage.

The warm Grenadian sun, bathed the upper deck, and wakened them. Realizing that they were still naked, they quietly slipped down to the cabin and dressed, just before the new owner arrived to take possession of the ship. Since the flight would not be until late afternoon, Geoffrey arranged for a tour of the island by cab. They were taken up into the rain forest, where they enjoyed a guided tour and explanation about the spices for which the island was so famous, and gifted samples of nutmeg and ginger. When they reached the small airport, their carry on bags were waiting for them at the gate.

Susan sat with Rachel on the flight back to Barbados, while Brian, Geoffrey, Joey and Jollybuns grouped with the airline hostesses.

Geoffrey whispered into Brian's ear making him laugh. "What a waste!"

The Arvo flight to Grantley Adams landed early, allowing Brian ample time to check on their flight back to New York. It would leave as scheduled in an hour. Rachel took Brian aside and thanked him.

"For what, Rachel? You make this seem so final."

"Brian, I really love Geoffrey and I love you as well, but in a different way." Brian began to reply but she pressed her fingertips to his lips. Then she kissed him, turned and walked away.

Geoffrey hugged and kissed Susan and whispered into her ear as Brian joined them. "Hope to see you soon, Bro," Geoffrey said, grasping Brian's hand. "Do stay in touch and come back to our island soon." Geoffrey caught up with Rachel, who waved to Brian and Susan, as they took the long walk to their waiting plane.

On board, Susan leafed through a book she had brought with her, as Brian tried to make conversation. "I believe they just said goodbye to us." He said.

"Of course, we just left them and got on a plane." She answered.

"No, it seemed more final than that." He said.

"Honey, we are friends, who have shared each other and great times with no strings attached." She said.

"I am not certain I can end it just like that." He said. "But it was a very special time."

"Perhaps we should relish the memory and what it can do for our own relationship." She said.

"What's the matter with our relationship?" He asked,

"Nothing that we can't improve upon and allow to grow," she said as she snuggled closer to him.

As Susan read through the travel book on Grenada, she learned that in 1983, it had undergone internal political turmoil, where a coup d'etat had installed a man named Maurice Bishop as Prime Minister, after ousting Eric Gairy. Fidel Castro supported the new government, that was short lived when Bishop was executed, and a man named Bernard Coward was installed. The organization of eastern Caribbean States, concerned that the island would serve as a place from which to transport arms and insurgents into Central America, appealed to the United States to intervene.

President Ronald Reagan had already made a decision to invade because the instability of a government so close in the Caribbean, threatened the safety of American medical students on Grenada.

The island was invaded on October 25, 1983 and after several days of fighting the Cuban supported army was overwhelmed by the superior American forces. Susan closed the book and relaxed back on the headrest. "I found that extremely interesting Brian. What was your sense?" She asked.   Brian, fast asleep, had heard nothing other than the subliminal whirr of the 747's engines.

Bajan Properties Ltd.

Fontabelle, St. Michael, Barbados

Geoffrey Townsend   President

Rachel   Townsend   Vice-President

246-6969

10/Sept/1989

My dearest Susan,

I think about you constantly. It is not just the sex, but to be honest it has meant so very much to me. That last night on the Lord Jim was spectacular. Rachel does not often speak of Brian, although I know she loves him. She misses our daughters who we only see during their vacation from school, and worries that they shall soon grow up and marry and make us grandparents. She does not feel that our flings are any longer appropriate. She tells me that 'we've done it, so enjoy the memory'.

Clearly we have issues.

She no longer accepts the fact that I am a healthy Bajan man and need sex. I have been monogamous except for you, since we had our talk, is it possible that we could continue without Rachel? It is not that she does not desire Brian, but is questioning why. We sleep in the same bed, but if I try to touch her, she pulls away. I have asked her to seek help, but she tells me that there is nothing wrong with her. I just felt I had to get this off my chest. Please write. I continue to need you.

Love
Geoffrey

Adams, Feinberg, McKenzie and Kent PA.

Attorneys At Law

1223 W. 57th St. Suites 13-18

New York, NY 10001

10/28/89

Dear Geoffrey,

I am concerned office staff might open a letter and misconstrue its meaning. More to the point, I do not wish them privy to any of this. Fortunately I intercepted your letter before someone in the secretarial pool opened it, since it would not bode well in my company for any of this is made public knowledge.

How can I respond to what you wrote? I do miss you and am disheartened by your dilemma.

While I am torn by my affection for you, I do not wish this to destroy either of our marriages. I could not even consider being intimate with you without Brian's knowledge and I would not even consider it unless Rachel was accepting and from what you write, that would not be the case. So we are at stalemate.

In all marriages, little quirky things come up and both partners become uncomfortable with confrontation. My suggestion is that you and Rachel seek counseling if you both agree. Find out what is really bothering her.

Miss you,
Love to you and Rachel
Susan

Bajan Properties Ltd.

Fontabelle, St. Michael, Barbados

Geoffrey Townsend   President

Rachel   Townsend   Vice-President

246-6969

15/Nov/1989

My dearest Susan,

I know that you asked me to call, but I have misplaced your number. I had considered purchasing that East Coast Hotel, but Rachel was adamantly against doing so. As usual her business sense prevailed, but I took it on as a client. As a result, I am now a member of the Barbados Tourist Board. This brings me to the purpose of this letter.

I shall be in New York the second week of December for meetings and would so much like to see you both. Oh, yes and our daughter Sophia shall be married at Simonton. I can discuss all of the particulars when we get together. Love you so much,

Geoffrey

Adams, Feinberg, McKenzie and Kent, PA.

Attorneys at Law

1231 W. 57th Street

Suites 13-18

New York, NY 10001

11/30/1989

Dearest Geoffrey,

We both are looking forward to your visit, and we shall be at your beck and call. You hardly mentioned Rachel in you letter. I hope she is good, and you can fill us in when we see you. Congratulation on Sophia's coming wedding, and of course if we are invited, we would love to attend. Let me know of your flight plans and date of arrival.

Love,

S

Sixteen

New York 1989

Susan did not arrive at the office until 10 a.m., and found her personal secretary standing at her desk. "Alarm never went off." She explained. "I know I am not scheduled for court, but could you get my calendar for the day, Sandy?"

"Right away. I have it on my desk." Sandy Richter had been her Girl Friday for five years and very dependable. She returned with a daybook that listed all of Susan's appointments. "I have confirmed your appointments and hopefully they shall be on time. Oh, Janis picked up a personal call for you. She had to be in at eight to find papers for a depo. I don't know what it was about, so you'll have to ask her."

"Where is she?" Susan asked.

"You'll find her in the lunch room, having coffee." Sandy said. "Your first is not due until two, so there is salad in the fridge if you are so inclined. I think it is buffalo chicken. From what I hear it is spicy but yummy. Will there be anything else?"

"Not right at the moment. I think I'll look for her, but I'll pass on the chicken." Susan said. In truth she would not mind passing on both. The youngest member of the firm had hired Janis Smith for her body not her brain. Although any type of fraternizing with the secretarial pool was frowned upon, he was after all the grandson of the founder and main partner.

Janis looked up from a jelly doughnut she was eating, when Susan entered the lunchroom. The young woman wore a tight fitting pink cashmere sweater, tight enough to be provocative for the male employees, and a short black skirt that barely made it to her knees. "You had a phone call early this morning, Susan." Susan wished to tell her that Mrs. McKenzie would be more appropriate, but held her tongue.

"Was there a message that you may have written down?" Susan asked.

"He just left a phone number. Real hot sounding guy with like an island accent." Janis said, and taking a piece of paper from her pocket, she pushed it toward Susan while continuing to chew. Susan took the paper and returned to her office.

As she passed her secretary's, she shrugged her shoulders. Sandy gave her a nod that said it all. "I'll be on the phone long distance for a bit, so hold any calls unless they are from Brian or my kids."

She sat at her desk and looked at the number, which began with a New York area code. Susan dialed and Geoffrey answered with 'Hello Luv'.

"Good morning or afternoon Geoffrey. How did you know it was me?" She asked.

"You were the only one with whom I left my number. Well with your secretary, Janis I believe she said her name was. Sultry sounding, young thing. We had quite a conversation. What does she look like?" He asked.

"Same old Geoffrey," she said. "Forget it. She is taken."

"So were you, Luv." He said.

"And how is Rachel?" Susan asked.

"She is just fine and actually in Canada to see the girls and check out dresses for the wedding." He answered.

"Yes, I read that in your letter. This must be a very exciting time for both of you." Susan said.

"Indeed. Have you had lunch?" He asked.

"As a matter fact not yet." Susan said. "But I have a full calendar this afternoon."

"Okay. How about meeting for drinks and dinner?" He persisted, and then I shall tell you why I have come. Oh, does Brian like this charmer?"

"What, Geoffrey, are you talking about?" She asked.

"This Janis person." He said. "I thought we might make it a foursome."

"Geoffrey do you wish to meet this evening or not? She is off limits." She agreed to meet him at the midtown Hyatt Bar at six.

Susan met with three clients during the course of the afternoon, trying to sort out their various legal problems, grateful that their issues did not require too much thought on her part. She was both excited and concerned about meeting with Geoffrey.

Susan always kept a change of clothing at the office, since there frequently, was a last minute dinner that she and Brian might have to attend.

When she approached Geoffrey at the bar, his back was to her. He was checking his watch concerned that she was a half hour late. "Hey Mon," she said, as he spun around on the barstool.

He liked what he saw. Susan wore a low cut black dress and heels that gave her an appearance of being two inches taller than she was. It was obvious that she had spent a great deal of time and trouble preparing for the evening.

Geoffrey was attired in tan pants, a blue blazer with the flag of Barbados pinned to his lapel, an open collar shirt and loafers without socks. His face smelled of Old Spice aftershave. "Goodness, how formal and beautiful you look." He said as he kissed her hand, and then tried for a French kiss, but she politely kissed him on both cheeks European style. "Ah, you are correct. Inappropriate. And Brian?"

"Brian is attending a meeting in Boston for a few days." She said and wondered why she volunteered the information. He smiled.

"Excellent," He said. "Pierre has assured me of a quiet table all to ourselves. So, drinks and dinner?" She nodded and followed him, as the maitre de led them into a dining room, which was still quite empty.

Geoffrey looked over the menu. "I was thinking like Kingfish, but alas it is not part of the fare." He said.

"Yum, or poached dolphin after that gorgeous pumpkin soup we had at Smugglers Cove." She responded. "Here, we have meat, fish or pasta."

"Since you know your city, I was remiss in asking you where you would have preferred to dine." He said.

"I assume you have booked here at the hotel?" She asked.

"Actually, yes." He answered as he put his nose back into the menu. "How do you suppose the grilled salmon might be?

"Probably very good," She said. "I should like a drink. How many did you have before I arrived?"

"None at all. I waited for you." He said, as a young female waitress approached the table.

"My name is Jeanine," She said. "And I shall be your server tonight. Would you like to hear our list of specials?" Susan nodded politely as the girl began to list a number of dishes that sounded more elegant than they probably were. Geoffrey asked her to repeat the fourth item on the list, but she hadn't memorized them that way and proceeded to go over them again.

Susan suggested that she take a drink order first. Geoffrey asked if the bar stocked something called Very Old Rum. Jeanine said she would check and returned moments later with a list of rums, but not the one Geoffrey requested, so he called Pierre over and inquired if there were any local package shops nearby. Taking a hundred dollar bill from Geoffrey, the maitre de promised to send someone out to fetch a bottle if it was available.

"So, what brings you to New York?" Susan asked.

He explained that he had come to New York as a member of the Barbados Tourism Board. He again explained that his interest in acquiring the East Coast hotel had hit a snag when Rachel nixed the deal. "However, what I accomplish here can help both my rental properties as well as the catamarans."

"That was that place up on the bluff on the east coast with the pool." She said. "Brian said something about it and that Rachel was not too keen on doing it."

"I tried convincing her of its great potential." He said. "I know it is isolated, but there are plans for new and larger roads connecting both coasts of the island, but alas not to be." Pierre returned with a bottle of dark rum and handed some bills to Geoffrey, who handed a twenty back to the maitre de.

"As you recall, this is sipping rum", Geoffrey said, as he poured two glasses. "Really smooth and no need for ice water chaser."

"How hungry are you Geoffrey?" She asked.

He looked at her. "Your are really one smashing looking lady." He said. "Hungry? Had a late lunch." He lied.

"Me as well," she lied.

"Tell you what. Why don't we take the bottle upstairs and if we choose, order room service?" He suggested.

"I am game, and a burger and fries could be enough for me." She said. Geoffrey informed Jeanine of their change in plans, left money on the table, and they headed for the elevator bank in the lobby.

As the doors closed, Susan said "This entire scenario, pre planned or not?"

"My darling, how could you think me so evil?" He answered pressing the number fifteen button.

She was impressed with the suite whose floor to ceiling windows opened onto a wide panorama of the city skyline. He led her down into a sunken living room equipped with a wet bar and multi-speaker stereo system and comfortable looking couches. "Business must be good." She said.

"I have to impress both realtors and the tourist industry, you see. I have other interesting news. A developer plans to build villas and a marina on Miami Beach. Ours, that is. You might recall our trip to Maycocks?" He said.

"Vividly," She replied. "Down a precipitous goat trail in time for the circle jerk." Geoffrey laughed. "I know. It's a Bajan thing." She took off her shoes and sat down on the soft couch, folding her legs under her.

"Miami Beach. It was named by your sailors stationed at the now defunct naval base in St. Lucy." He said. "It will be a financial boon for the island. if the project goes through as planned."

Geoffrey filled two four-ounce glasses with the dark liquor and handed one to Susan as he sat beside her. "Would you like to see the rest of the suite?" He asked.

Susan sipped her rum and licked her lips. "This shall do fine for now. If I might make a suggestion, instead of burgers, I'd rather shrimp cocktail and crab cakes if they have them."

"Perfect!" He called room service and placed the order adding to it a chilled bottle of Dom Perignon.

"Something to celebrate?" Susan paused. "Geoffrey, about Rachel. I have posted letters, and she only answered one." What is going on?"

"Rachel has just not been herself and I have contributed nothing positive to her state of mind, in her way of thinking. I know that she has a lot to do with the wedding, but that's a long way off." He said.

"Who is the groom?" Susan asked.

"Someone by the name of Bucket Fields, and a native of Toronto. He plays ice hockey for a Maple Leaf farm team and expects, actually hopes, to be called up soon. I understand he is very good, but I know and care little about hockey. Seems to be in love with Sophia, however." Geoffrey said.

"That is what is most important, I would think." Susan said.

"Rachel is uptight about the fact that she shall remain in Canada. She was so hoping for a local boy who would keep Sophia on the island, so she could spoil a grandchild. Not much chance of fielding a hockey team in Barbados, but I have to tell you that I did some research on what it would cost to build and freeze a rink on the island. The cost would be phenomenal." A knock on the door heralded the arrival of their food.

Susan's juices had begun to stir, and she wondered how much effort she would put forth to control her libido. She had promised Brian that something like this would not happen, and wondered if she should just put her shoes back on, thank Geoffrey for the shrimp cocktail, and escape.

Then she began a process of justification. After all, Brian had been an active participant, so why should this be much different. Worse scenario, she was under no obligation to tell him. She seductively placed a shrimp between her lips and allowed her tongue to play with it.

Geoffrey poured more rum. It went down so smoothly without even a burn. He moved closer to her and felt her warmth. Geoffrey had had enough experience to know when a woman was close to ready. He took her glass and put it on the table. "Susan, you cannot imagine how much I have looked forward to this moment, where it truly would be just the two of us. Just to experience whatever our bodies and minds wish to explore."

"I want to say no, and run off, but I can't." She said as she placed her hand below his abdomen, finding him as large and as hard as ever. "Hebrew National unquestionably." She murmured.

"What is that?" He asked.

"Forget it." They both got up from the couch and when he untied the straps that held her dress, she allowed it to fall to the carpet.

Geoffrey undid her bra, releasing her breasts that now pressed into his chest, and he stood back to marvel at how firm her nipples were. "You are exquisite as always," He said, as he stepped back continuing to admire her.

Susan reached down and wiggled out of her thong. "Now, Luv," she said. "The picture is complete. True. True."

He moved to the large window. "I'll just draw the curtain," he said.

Susan joined him. "Please don't close the drapes, Geoffrey. She stood in front of him and gently dropped to her knees, slowly undoing, his belt buckle, and pulling down his pants to his ankles. "Leave them open. I find it more exciting, and who will know it is us?"

He wore no underwear. Susan helped him step out of his pants, removed his shoes and socks, and took him in her mouth, and letting all inhibitions dissolve, she swallowed him to the hilt. Concerned that the seven seconds might end right their, she backed off. "Bedroom?"

Geoffrey grabbed the now half filled bottle of rum and led her inside, where she lay down on the bed. Gently spreading her legs, he dripped some of the dark rum, allowing it to pool in her vagina. Initially there was a burning sensation, but as she allowed his cool tongue to lick it away, she felt the rising sensation that would ultimately lead to orgasm. Susan held his head in place until she could no longer wait and then pulled him upward. "I want to be on top," She said and Geoffrey rolled over.

She allowed him to slip inside her, and then began to gyrate her hips sucking him deeper and deeper inside. Susan seemed insatiable, as she increased the speed of her movements. Then she cried out to him. "Suck and bite my nipples now. I'm going to fuck your big cock."

They came together and as Geoffrey filled her with his ejaculation, she continued to use her vaginal muscles to squeeze every last drop from him. Then she kissed him tenderly and rolled off. Exhausted, they both fell asleep.

Susan awoke early the next morning, not exactly certain where she was. She observed that the bed, the wall furnishings as well as the room were unfamiliar, and then checked her watch, which was the only thing she was wearing. Geoffrey and not Brian lay next to her, sound asleep. She had awakened him around two in the morning, so he must have been truly spent, having experienced many of the positions that the Karma Sutra suggested, but the downside of all that sexual wonderment was the irritation she felt in her vagina.

Susan slipped out of bed and quietly into the living room where she called the apartment to see if there were any messages. There were two and both from Brian that morning. She looked at her watch and dressed quickly.

Susan returned to his side of the bed and gently touched Geoffrey on the shoulder. He stirred, opened his eyes and pulled away the sheet. Apparently he still had a lot left. Susan chip singed and said she had to leave for home. She did not want to return Brian's call from the hotel.

"How about this evening?" Geoffrey asked.

"Depends upon why Brian is calling." She said.

"I must ask you something. How celibate have you been?" She asked.

"Beside you and Rachel?" No one," he answered. "And the last time I had myself tested, I was negative for HIV."

"Why did you do that?" She asked.

"Another time zone, Luv. Another time zone." He said. "Tonight? Dancing?"

"Any good rum left?" She asked.

"Champagne is still cold and I shall have our friend Pierre fetch another." He said.

"I shall call you to firm up." She said. "That is, if Brian is still in Boston."

"And I shall await you as firm as possible." Susan kissed him and left the suite. She was back at the apartment in about fifteen minutes, and called Brian at the number he left, then while it rang realized that she had not showered or removed what may have remained of Geoffrey's Old Spice lotion.

Brian answered, and was happy to hear from her. "Called you twice, but there was no answer." He said.

"Took a long shower," she lied, "guess I never heard the phone."

"Thought I might come home today, but it looks like negotiations will take another full day. I shall fill you in when I get back. What did you do last night?" He asked.

"Had some paper work to finish from the office. Watched a little TV and hit the sack. How about you?" She asked.

"Oh, got lined up with three hookers and got laid. Only kidding. I miss you." He said.

"Me too," she responded. Susan felt terrible that she had become embroiled in the lie, and decided it probably would be best not to see Geoffrey later this evening.

Susan had to be in court for the better part of the morning, but just to argue some motions before a judge she trusted to be fair. She stopped at a Sabret umbrella outside her office building and bought a dog with relish that she was still munching on when the elevator reached her floor. Susan found Janis sitting at Sandy's desk engrossed in a People magazine.

"Sandy took a personal day," she said. "Somebody's ill at home, so I have been fielding your calls. Messages are on your desk, and your friend called again. Today she wore a blouse with a bra that hardly contained breasts just dying to be freed. Susan made a mental note to discuss her with the senior partner.

She found a pile of notes on her desk, some of which were legible. One was from GT. Susan was glad Geoffrey did not leave his name, but knew Miss Hotpants would recognize the accent.

Susan saw three clients and buzzed a puzzled Janis to cancel the last two. She went back to the apartment to change, not knowing yet if she would call Geoffrey to tell him she was not going to show up. Shortly after she left the office Janis fielded a call from Brian asking for Susan.

"She left early?" He said. "Any idea where she was off to?" Janis said she did not. "Change of plans. Beep her. Please, and tell her that I'm taking the first plane out and will be home by nine in the morning tomorrow. I'll leave a message on our phone at home as well. Thanks."

When Susan got to the apartment, she checked the mail. Meghan had left a note pinned to the fridge, that she would be late since there would be a rehearsal for the school play she had to attend, but had a ride home and not to worry. She showered, dressed and left the apartment without noticing that the message light on the answer phone was blinking. When she changed pocketbooks, she forgot to retrieve her beeper.

Susan hailed a taxi and went to the Hyatt where she found Geoffrey sitting on the same bar stool, drink in hand. "How did you know I would come?" She asked.

"Just took a chance." He said. "Drink?"

"Not right now." She said. "I have a lot on my mind."

"All right." He said.

"Not here." She said. "Too public."

Back in his suite, Susan began to relate her misgivings about being with him the night before. "You are very upset." He said, taking her hand. "Vexed with me?"

"I am angry with myself, for just doing what I promised Brian I would not." She said, as Geoffrey held her to console her. "How can I make it up to him."

"I guess if you did not share this with him." She answered.

"You are a grown, independent woman. He must have had an idea that, after everything else we have done, you might do some explorations on your own." He said.

"That thought never entered my mind." She said emphatically. "And if true, only with you, Geoffrey."

"Luv," he said. "I know exactly what you need. I have arranged for massages for both of us here in the room. They should be here soon."

"They?" She asked.

"Yes. A lady for me and a gentleman for you."

"I don't know Geoffrey." She said.

"You have gone this far. When does Brian return?" He asked.

"I spoke to him last night. He said possible another day to complete." She answered.

"Then it shall be all right." He reassured. "There are two robes in the closet. We should be changed before they come."

"No," She said as she slid out of her dress. "Cancel the massage. "I just wish to spend the time with you since this is most likely the last time, and I could use a drink," She said as she allowed him to finish undressing her.

Their lovemaking was brief, and not as satisfying as it had been in the past. Geoffrey thought that she was just going through the motions.   Dressed and ready to leave by eight-thirty in the evening, she kissed him and without turning back, left the room.

Seventeen

New York 1989

Susan returned home to find Meghan nuking a hot dog she found in the freezer. "That all you want to eat?" She asked.

"Yes, Mom." Meghan replied. "Rehearsal went great. I think we are all ready for Friday's opening." They were doing South Pacific and she was in charge of lighting the stage. "Just get home from the office? Rather late, no? Oh and I found a message from Dad. He will be in tomorrow morning, and David called as well. My big brother has a girl friend, you know."

Susan was trying to process everything at once. She had made the correct move coming home early, but was uncertain how she would explain everything to Brian if she went that route at all. She scrubbed the makeup from her face, showered for a half hour, and then listened to the messages that Meghan had not erased. Brian sounded so upbeat, so she assumed his business meetings had gone well.

The next morning she awakened in time to prepare breakfast and shoo Meghan off to school. Two hours later she heard a key turn in the front door as Brian entered carrying two large bags and a gift-wrapped box.

She hugged and kissed him. "From the message you left, all went well," She guessed.

"Better than we expected. This really a big deal and after we merge with Harris and McCarrick, we might move into their offices in the Empire State building. Oh, this is for you."

Susan unwrapped the box and found a neatly folded pink nightgown. "From Filenes," she said. "I hear it's a neat place to shop."

"So, what have you been up to? I called your office yesterday but you had already left. That Janis is really a piece of work. If she popped her gum one more time into the phone I was going to hang up."

"Oh, I had some shopping to do and unfortunately I left my beeper in my other purse." She said.

"Shopping," He said. "Shoes I suppose. Buy anything?"

"No," she lied. "Nothing struck me."

"Say who is GT?" He asked as she swallowed hard.

"I'm sorry." She tried to act surprised.

"Ms. Dentine asked me about a GT who called with what she believed to be an island accent. The only one who came to mind was Geoffrey. He's not in the states is he?"

"Did she now." Susan said holding the nightgown up to see how it might look on her. "As a matter of fact, he is in town for business. We had an early dinner last night."

"Where did you go? How come he's not staying here with us?" He asked. "And, why the big secret?"

"So many questions at one time. Uh, we ate at the hotel restaurant, and it never came up in conversation as to why he chose not to stay here this time." She looked at her watch. "I'd better get going. I have to be in court at ten, and I know I have a full schedule this afternoon." She carefully folded the nightgown and placed it back in its box. Then she gave him a peck on the cheek, ignoring his last question.

"How long is he staying?" He asked.

"Geoffrey? He has probably already left on the eight o'clock flight. What does your day look like?"

"I am taking the day off, so suppose I stop by and pick you up when you're done. We'll go to dinner to celebrate our successful mergers."

Susan, momentarily taken aback by the words he chose to use, kissed him, and left after telling him that there was coffee brewed and he could find bagels in the fridge.

At four, Sandy buzzed Susan to tell her that Brian was waiting for her, that he was having a nice chat with Janis. "Find something for her to do, and ask Brian to wait for me in the law library. It shall only be a few minutes".

When Susan joined him in the library, Brian was thumbing through pages of a law journal and Janis was nowhere in sight. "That Janis is really something else. Don't you have a dress code here?" He asked.

"Come," she said, ignoring his remark. "We'll leave through my private exit."

"We have reservations at the Palm. I am in the mood for a good steak. How about yourself?" He asked, helping her on with her coat.

Susan was not yet hungry despite skipping lunch. When they got to the restaurant, she excused herself and went directly to the ladies room, where she chewed on three Rolaids.

It was still early and they were able to get a window table where they could watch the passing parade.

"So, tell me," he said, "what brought Geoffrey to New York?"

"I though I told you that he had written in his letter that he was on the Tourism Board and they were meeting here. He had some interest in buying the hotel we stopped at, but Rachel would not allow it. He is promoting tourism and his rentals." She said as the waiter stopped to take their drink order. "Just some club soda with lime," she said.

Brian looked at her and ordered a light beer for himself. "Steak?" he asked, and she nodded. "Two porterhouses. One rare and one should be medium." They told the waitress that whatever veggies came with the dinner would be fine.

"Actually, you never shared Geoffrey's letter with me. So, what did you two do last night after dinner?" He asked.

"I was home before nine," she said. "Meghan had just come in from a play rehearsal."

"I don't know what it is, but you are not yourself, and I just have a gnawing feeling in the pit of my stomach." He said.

"Brian. If Rachel had come to New York and called you, what would you have done?" She asked.

"Rachel more than likely would not just come to New York, and whether she would call is moot." He answered. "You know I doubt if Geoffrey made any promises to her, but you sure did to me." She lowered he eyes. "You slept with him didn't you?" The waitress almost dropped the tray she had just brought to the table.

"Please, Brian, lower your voice. "I met him for drinks and one thing led to another. It wasn't as if we had not done it before. We have both been so busy that we have had little time for each other yet alone even cultural events."

"I see," he said. "He took you to Carnegie Hall, the opera, the Metropolitan and then back to the hotel so you could fuck him. Right! We could call that a cultural fuck, couldn't we?"

"I beg you. This is a public place." She pleaded.

He set aside the beer, and asked the waitress to bring two Mount Gays neat. "Why?"

"I wanted to," She said. How can you forget Barbados with the four of us, as well as our little ménage at the apartment? It was difficult to draw a line."

Brian leaned over to her. "One draws a line when one has the ability to control oneself, so one does not upset the person who truly loves one." He whispered. "What else?"

"We talked." She said.

He drained half of the glass. Susan had not touched her drink. "About what?"

"He again asked if we could take a vacation together." She said, while playing with the stirrer.

"Sounds like fun. A fort-night of screwing on the Continent. How goshe!" He finished his drink and called for another.

"I told him that I wouldn't since I was too much in love with my husband." She said.

"Now that it has come out, would you do it again?" He asked.

"Geoffrey asked me the same question and I told him not without your knowledge." She replied.

Brian looked at Susan and dismissed her response. "We have been very, no exceedingly fortunate. I don't wish anything to interfere with us. It was a lark and a very stimulating one. Let me ask you this, would you be upset if I humped that seductive beauty, Janis?"

"That, Brian is disgusting. At least pick some one with class." She smiled for the first time. Their dinners were brought to the table. Brian asked if they any hot pepper sauce and the server said she would check.

They ate for the most part in silence, and then Brian pushed his plate away. "Excellent. Susan, do you regret ever going to Barbados and getting in so deep as we have?"

"Of course not," she replied, and yourself?"

"Despite it all, it was probably the most exciting time of our lives, even with Geoffrey, the cad leading the way. I do not believe I would have done anything differently."

"It was not all Geoffrey. A no from you would have ended it before it happened." She said. "I'm full. It was quite good. Would you like to go back to the island?"

He seemed to have forgotten all about the incident. "That is what I am getting at. One of the partners Al Mattson bought a villa in St. Peter, and offered it for the firm's use when he was not there, as long as we took care of the staff and restocked the bar. He is having some changes made, but I understand that it is lovely."

"I am not ready to go back, Brian. Besides we were just there." She said.

"No I am talking about next year or maybe the one after." He answered. "Why don't we see how everything shakes out? Susan, has Geoffrey really gone?"

"I really do not know how long he planned to stay in New York. Rachel was in Canada making wedding plans with Sophia. I don't know if she is still there. Last evening, I said goodbye and left without asking any further questions."

"Maybe I am just a dumb ass, but I am going to forget about this if you don't mind." He said. "So who is getting married?"

"Sophia. Brian why don't we go back home for dessert?" She asked as she pushed her chair back.

"Sounds good to me. I stopped in a record shop and picked up a Frank Sinatra tape. Dessert? Were you thinking something like an ice cream sundae?" He said signing the check.

"No, I was thinking me, and I'd rather Donna Summer."

Eighteen

New York   Barbados 1991

The ride down in the elevator from the 60th floor was tedious, endless and crowded with people who had obviously put in a full days effort at what ever they did. When he exited the building, he looked at the tower that seemed to go up and on forever. Years earlier, he had seen the movie "The Towering Inferno", and wondered how safe it was to work on a floor so high up in the business sky as he did. Brian shrugged off his concerns and hailed a cab. As usual he had to explain the exact designation and the best way to go. Yusef Patel seemed accommodating, but spoke little English, and had limited knowledge of Manhattan's geography. As the cab pulled away from the building on 34th street, Brian once again looked skyward.

Susan was already home when he arrived. She was checking the mail and then the answering machine that indicated that there were no messages.

"Excellent," she said. "No one needs us, and I could use a hot bath. The humidity has been simply exhausting. I hope you had something to eat."

"Couple of hot dogs at the Sabret umbrella was enough for me. Hot bath?" Brian asked. "For two?" He had begun to take off his tie.

"No, I really prefer to soak alone. Why don't you shower and then we can meet in the sauna. How sexy would that be?" Brian smiled as she did her Theda Bara impression of a vamp slinking seductively into her bathroom.

Brian showered and waited in the sauna until everything important had taken on the appearance of a prune. He shut down the system and went to their bedroom where he found Johnny Carson already half way through his monologue, but Susan had heard none of it since she had fallen asleep naked. He eased into the bed pulling the covers as not to disturb her, and lowered the volume on the TV.

"I was watching," she said as she moved next to him and yawned. This was an old argument that he had never won and was not prepared to do battle with now. "Why are you dressed for bed?" She asked.

Brian just looked at her as Carson began his reading of funny headlines. "I waited for you in the sauna. It is almost midnight."

"Sorry, but I can make it up to you." She moved her hand into his crotch. "Goodness, it takes nothing to make you hard."

"Compared to who?" He asked.

"No one," she said. "I want that in me and now!"

Brian was ambivalent about this new Susan, who had become a much more aggressive lover. It took only about fifteen minutes from start to finish. "Did you come?"

"Of course. More than once. How come you didn't notice?"

"I just like you to tell me." He said. "Susan, are you excited about using the villa. It will be available to us in October.

"It is Meghan's first year in college, and she will have been there only a month. First year can be tough." She thought for a moment. "Of course on the other hand, we desperately need vacation time. We haven't taken any in two years. How long can you get away for?"

"I can bring my laptop so that will be no sweat. They have fax machines on the island, so all in all, I should have less of problem than you." He said, as she got out of bed, returning moments later, wearing fresh pajamas.

When she got back under the covers, Brian reached over and touched her breast. "Why the bra now?" He asked.

"Feel free to remove it at any time. Just gives me a bit more support." She replied.

"I have been waiting to ask this question for a long time. More than two years to be exact. Sex with Geoffrey the last time. Was it as great as ever."

Susan turned toward him. "If I must. I don't know how to explain it. It was different. The passion was still there. Not as exciting as that first time in Barbados or some of the others."

"And sex with me?" He asked.

"Always satisfying, but we have again, become so predictable." She said as he moved next to her. "You men are simply amazing. I am on top this time. She opened her pajama top, removed her bra and helped him slip off his bottoms. Susan was well in command as she rode him with all of the strength she was able to muster.

"I am still very much in love with you," he said afterwards.

"This could be the most wonderful time of our life," she said. "Why don't we enjoy it to its maximum. I am looking forward to Barbados." Brian watched as she turned her back to him, and soon she was fast asleep.

They arrived at Grantley Adams the second week in October, welcomed by a steel band entertaining tourists just outside the inbound entrance. The unpredictable weather of hurricane season in New York, almost delayed the flight, but when a window of opportunity arose, their pilot had been given clearance for take off from JFK.

The downside was the fact that two British Airway Jumbos and one from Air Canada had just deplaned and Customs was chaotic with incoming passengers trying to find the appropriate line in which to stand. Despite it all the McKenzies were thrilled to be back to what they considered their second home.

Getting through Customs and locating their baggage took another three quarters of an hour, but with nothing to declare, they breezed through inspection and were soon, again outside in the oppressive island humidity, waiting at the queue for a taxi. Actually, they required a van considering what they had brought for what portended to be an extended stay.

Their driver took them through the familiar St. George cane fields, onto the upper road, passed Porters' abandoned cane factory and down into Holetown, where they stopped of at the Super Center for liquor and an assortment of meats and snacks.

After a brief stop at the police station, where they obtained new driver permits. Susan asked the driver to pass by the Coach House and saw it was noticeably quiet. She sighed. "That is where it all began," and leaning her head on Brian's shoulder, closed her eyes. "I can remember almost every detail as if it were yesterday."

"Did you write the Townsend's that we were returning, but were not staying with them?" Brian asked.

"I just did not know how to tell them. I was chicken. I have to admit it." She responded.

"Oh, they will get over it, and it could be a wonderful surprise." He said.

"You think? I believe that Geoffrey will be greatly pissed off." She said.

"Pissed off and not vexed? Which do suppose is the stronger of the two?" He asked.

"Personally Rhett…" She thought for a moment. "A change of venue might do us all some good."

The driver appeared to know exactly where he was going, and when he turned the taxi into the third driveway past Mullins, Susan gasped at the size of the villa. A sign on the stone entryway identified it as the Blue Heron.

"This is just for the two of us?" She asked as Brian paid the driver, who carried their luggage through the open front door depositing them on a floor made of ornate tile.

Brian grinned. "You have not seen anything yet. I saw some photos," he said, as they walked through a center courtyard and entered an archway opening onto a patio, from where they saw an expansive stone-lined path leading down to the beach. There was a library and home theater just off a main hall, that led to the kitchen and formal dining area. Continuing to explore, they went up the winding staircase that led to the upper floor and bedrooms. A neatly dressed black woman came out to greet them, and introduced herself as the housekeeper, Lozzie.

She advised them that Mr. Braithwaite would bring their luggage to their room. The master bedroom suite had a round king sized bed with an adjoining bathroom that boasted a round pink bathtub and spa. What intrigued them the most were the mirrored ceilings in both the bedroom and bathroom. Portraits of beautifully colored fish lined the bathroom walls, and a number of Jill Walker reproductions had been hung on the walls of the bedroom.

Floor to ceiling windows were shielded by bamboo blinds that when parted, revealed a magnificent view of the sparkling Caribbean.

"There are also tennis courts and a good size pool." Brian said. Susan looked down to the patio below and saw Lozzie beckoning.

"Mistress, please come down. I have prepared a nice lunch." She said.

"I have got to get out of these clothes and into shorts or a swim suit." A tall black man brought up some of the luggage, identified himself as Braithwaite, and said that he would return with the rest shortly. "Hey how about those ceilings?" Brian said seductively.

"Truly a play land for adults," Susan said laughing, "but at this stage of life, I am not certain I wish to see myself from all possible angles."

"It will be great fun." He said. "And you look fantastic!"

"Not now, I do not think that Lozzie is one to keep waiting."

The housekeeper was more than likely younger than she appeared, but a hard life had taken its toll. She had laid out a lunch that consisted of flying fish on a bun, pumpkin soup and fried potatoes that they thoroughly enjoyed. From speakers above, came the strains of 'Beautiful Barbados'.

Lozzie had a stern look about her that made Susan uncomfortable. "De bar she full up Mistress with rum and assorted other liquors. Braithwaite'll bring you whatever you needs. As they finished a plate, Lozzie would clear it from the table. When they were done, Brian thanked her and told her that they would go out on the patio to enjoy the cool breeze. His clothing was already sticking to him.

"What does Braithwaite do?" Susan asked.

"He your handy man. He gwan bring de car around. If you wants to drive, okay." She said.

Brian looked at Lozzie. "So what rums do we have in our full stocked bar?"

"Any ting you can imagine." She said.

"And what do you prefer?" He asked as Susan glared at him.

"I fancies Mount Gay for my colds in de foots." She answered with a big smile that revealed two gold lower incisors and many missing teeth. Among other facial issues was a mole on her chin from which sprouted a large black hair.

"You rub rum on your sore feet?" He asked. She did not answer, collected the remainder of the lunch dishes and wobbled off to the kitchen.

"I just bet she rubs rum on her. More likely she drinks a few and waits for it to reach her foots." He said. "I think I'll check out the bar myself."

Susan looked at Brian. "You remember what Geoffrey told us that a Bajan cold in the foot could be anywhere from the hip down, so stop badgering her, Brian. She is scary but guess we are stuck with her since we did not hire her. Just make the best of it." Susan said.

"Easier said than done." Brian said. "She looks like someone capable of sticking those pins in little dolls."

"She is Bajan and not Haitian." Susan said.

"Whatever. I'll bring drinks out on the patio. Looks like a nice evening."

Brian found glasses and filled them with dark rum that easily slipped down their throats without ever so much a burn, as Susan recalled the first time Geoffrey had introduced them to a quickie.

Darkness began to over take the patio whose soft lights now cast eerie shadows. "Just what I needed with her prowling about." He said.

"We must call Geoffrey and Rachel," Susan said dismissing his concerns.

Brian dialed the number that Susan had committed to memory, and after a few rings, they heard Anna's lilting singsong voice. She was delighted to hear from them. "No both Mr. and Mrs. Townsend," she said "went to St. Lucia and will be back in two days."

When Brian told her that they had just arrived, Anna apologized for not making up their room because Mr. Geoffrey had not told her to do so.

"Not to worry, Anna. This shall be surprise and a secret between the two of us. Susan and I have a place to stay." He gave Anna the house number and asked her to have the Townsends call when they returned.

"They shall be sorely vexed when de find out you staying else where." She said.

"Remember Anna, this shall be a surprise." Brian said, and placed the phone back into its cradle. He looked at Susan. "We are on our own. They are off the island." Susan appeared momentarily saddened. "Hey, Luv. Think of all that mirrored glass upstairs. My suggestion is that we go dancing in that new disco in Holetown. I saw it when we left the police station."

Susan finished her drink. "You are just full of ideas, and good ones at that. Let's shower and dress up." She said as she walked to the bottom of the staircase. "Race you up!"

Lozzie stared at them as they ran up the stairs, and shook her head. Then she went out onto the patio hoping that they had left some rum in their glasses. She smiled when she saw one glass half filled.

As Brian drove into the car park, they could hear music coming from an open doorway in a two-storied building lit up with flashing lights that changed color with the beat of the music. At the entrance, a tall dark man sporting a diamond in his left ear lobe, and a broad smile, took twenty dolla Barbados for each and stamped the back of their hands with a blue T. "Bars everywhere, Johns to your right and dancing straight ahead."

They found themselves easily moving to the calypso beat as they walked onto a dimly lit dance floor, and were quickly swept up into a crowd of sweating, swaying people of all ages. The two danced for a while until Susan announced that she had to pee. Brian pointed out a bar where he would wait for her. From that vantage point he could see that the entire room, had been painted white, with seats and tables built from free-formed white stucco.

Brian felt a tap on his shoulder and turned expecting to see Susan, but instead faced a well tanned shapely blonde woman whose green eyes shimmered in the glittering lights. "Buy me a drink and I shall buy you one in return." She said.

He had difficulty taking his eyes from the off the shoulder top that showed more than enough cleavage. And she was stunning. "My name is Melody." She said extending her hand.

"Brian. Brian McKenzie." He responded taking the hand offered.

"I know that you came with someone. I saw the beautiful lady that you were dancing with. My husband, Chris is around somewhere." She smiled and showed Brian a large diamond ring that lit up her left hand. "Chris and I just arrived on our boat. It is just moored off shore, Want to look?"

"I think I had better wait for Susan. One can easily get lost in such a large crowd." He spotted her coming towards them and Brian made the introductions. Susan stared at the diamond ring Melody sported, as a tall, deeply handsome man suddenly appeared at their side.

"Melody, I wondered where you had gone." He introduced himself as Chris Simpson and continued to stare at Susan while holding her hand.

"Your wife told me that you have come by boat. Susan and I did that a few years ago, actually our first time in Barbados. Can I buy a round of drinks?" Brian asked.

"Delighted to join you and that would be grand. Dark rum neat for both of us," he said. "We arrived not too long ago from Antigua, showered, dressed and here we are."

"Phenomenal trip," Brian said. "As I mentioned, it was our introduction to Barbados."

"Extraordinary. Was it a motor or sail?" Chris asked.

"A Mystic 55." Brian said. "Smooth handling."

"I know that boat. Where do you keep it?" Chris inquired.

"Sold it a few years ago. We both fell in love with the island, and felt that we could spend more time here since it is only a four-hour flight from New York. And you two are from?" Brian asked.

"We live in Alberta in Canada. Own property midway between Banff and Lake Louise. Have you ever been?"

"We love that area of Canada." Brian said. "I was born here on Barbados but moved young to Ontario. Met Susan and decided to become a U.S. citizen."

"What hotel are you staying at?" Melody asked.

"Actually, we are staying at a villa my firm bought. It is out of this world." Brian said. "You should visit." He looked at Melody who smiled. "It is called The Blue Heron and is up the west coast road in St. Peter." Where are you staying?"

"On the boat." Melody offered. "It is quite roomy and very comfortable."

"I have an idea." Susan said. "This place has really become quite crowded, and if the music gets any louder I shall not be able to think yet alone carry on a conversation. We can all go up to the villa for drinks. It is still early and I guarantee it shall be much cooler and quieter. Our car is just in the car park."

The Simpsons accepted the offer, and soon they were on their way to Blue Heron. "What do you do Brian?" Melody asked from the back seat. He looked at her reflection in the rear view mirror and wondered what this might lead to.

"I am a stock broker, actually an analyst now." Brian said. "And Susan is an attorney. And you?"

Chris spoke. "I own a pharmaceutical company based in Toronto and Melody owns her own upscale hair salon."

When they reached Blue Heron, they found that someone had dimmed the villa lights and chained the front gate. Brian honked the horn a number of times, and Lozzie finally appeared.

"Company this late, Mistress?" She asked, noting that the McKenzies were not alone.

"Please unbar the gate, Lozzie." Brian said. "These are our guests, the Simpsons." Lozzie opened the gate and followed them into the house and out to the patio, sizing up Melody Simpson. "We shall take drinks out here," Brian advised as he noticed the bottle of rum he had left on the table, seemed to be less full than when they left. "Tell me, Lozzie will you stay on all night?"

"I have my rooms here, unless you wants for me to go home." She said.

"Tell you what. I shall take care of drinks. You can go to bed." He said, and then added, "I trust that the cold in your foots is much better."

"If you would be so kind to show me the John," Chris Simpson said."

Susan showed Chris the downstairs bathroom, and turned on the stereo. Soon the melodic voices of the Merrymen reached the patio.

"I could use some refreshing as well," Melody said.

"Come," Susan said, as she directed Melody to the stairway leading to the upper floor. Go right up. You will find it just off the bedroom to your right. "Chris is in the downstairs bathroom." Susan returned to the patio, not even thinking that she had placed trust in a perfect stranger to be alone in their room. Melody reappeared a short time after, with a broad smile on her face, finding that drinks had been poured, and Brian and Chris deep in conversation. "That's nice. This is what I like about the islands, where friends are made so easily." She took her drink and leaned against a patio rail, the moonlight silhouetting her shapely form.

Brian wondered if she had done this on purpose and Susan was well aware that she did.

Melody looked at Susan. "Can I show Chris your bedroom? I think it very unique?" Susan said it would be all right, so Melody led him back up the stairs.

When they returned, Chris looked at Susan. "Love the mirrors, really a great touch. Your idea?" He asked.

"Came with the house." Susan remarked.

They sat and drank for a while longer, until Susan yawned. Chris advised that the hour was late and they should start back. Susan gave both a quick peck on the cheek, and Brian brought the car around to the front of the house. Susan elected not to accompany them, so Brian drove the Simpsons back to Holetown.

When they reached the disco car park, Melody asked if he might like another drink and a dance, since their hands were still stamped. "It is late." Brian said. "Another time."

"Let me have your local number," Chris said. "Would you like to join us on the boat for dinner tomorrow evening?"

"It sounds great, but I must make certain Susan has not made other plans." Brian wrote his phone number on a slip of paper and handed to Chris. Melody reached up and planted a kiss on his lips.

"Looking forward to it", Chris said, and Brian waved as he drove out of the car park.

Nineteen

Barbados 1991

After leaving the airport, Geoffrey and Rachel stopped at their office at Fontabelle, where they found one message waiting for them. Geoffrey was surprised to find that it was from David McKenzie, who had not been back to Barbados since the first time they had met in 1986. Geoffrey dialed an overseas number, and David answered it.

"Mr. Townsend, thank you for returning my call. I hope that you remember me." David said.

"Please call me Geoffrey, David. Of course I remember you." Townsend said. "How may I be of service?"

"Actually, a number of things are on my mind. "You know that Mom and Dad are on the island." David said.

"Certainly," Geoffrey lied and looked Rachel.

"Dad's firm bought a villa in St. Peter, I believe between Speigtstown and Mullins, so they are staying there. It's called Blue Heron. But I am sure you knew that." Geoffrey nodded into the phone.

"Let me get to the point. During my last year in college where I majored in anthropology and minored in geology, I had an opportunity to spend an internship at the Museum of Natural History, not far from the apartment. Okay, now as you recall, that year we sailed to Barbados and spent time with you, I was allowed to do so by my prep school, as long I researched and wrote a paper that ultimately developed into an introduction to our Barbadian roots. Now that got me more interested in Barbados so I have read, bought or borrowed anything that dealt with its history, past and present. Bottom line is I want to write a historical novel, that would encompass the geologic origins of the island, its people and its politics."

"It would appear to me that you have undertaken what could become a life's work and for this I commend, but in no way, envy you, David. I look forward to reading this massive achievement one day." Geoffrey said.

"I really intend to do this. I fell in love with Barbados and its people and its history, which brings me to my next request. I met and have fallen in love with someone. She is an artist whom I met when visiting the Metropolitan Museum of Art. She was doing a watercolor copy of Winslow Homer's 'Crack The Whip'."

"I know that painting. I have a book of his watercolors. However if it is counseling on matters of love or art for that matter, I am not certain I am the right person to advise you." Geoffrey said.

"No Sir. We love each other. What I would like to do is bring her here to Barbados and perhaps you, a Captain, could marry us." David said.

"Look, Son. I am the owner of two catamarans, partnered with Barclay's Bank. I am not a real Captain, nor can I perform marriage ceremonies that are legal. What you saw done on a Pirate Adventure cruise was a mock marriage, and those captains rarely even know if the two people they marry ever knew each other.

If you are serious about this venture, there are rules that exist on Barbados. You must first make application, and be on the island two weeks before the ceremony is to be performed, and that would be by a Justice of The Peace."

He thought for a moment. "Now what I can do for you, is talk to the owner of Pirate Adventures, my friend Miles, and arrange for everything to be done on one of his boats, and suggest a person who will perform the ceremony legally. What do you say to that?"

"Fantastic. I don't know how to thank you," David said. "What do I have to do?"

"Send me all of the particulars including her name and vital statistics, and I shall send back any papers you need to fill out. But time may be of the essence, so best be conducted via air mail or fax"

"Oh, and Geoffrey. This is all to be a surprise for my parents. They are unaware that I had made plans to come down. Oh, one thing more. I need to get back into the Archives while I am on the island, and I hope you can arrange it again."

"I shall do that and assure you that my lips are sealed. Now you said The Blue Heron. Ah yes, I remember now. Speak to you soon. Ciao."

"David McKenzie?" Rachel asked. "You seem so terribly vexed!"

"I am vexed. Susan and Brian are on the island, staying at a villa in St. Peter and not with us. There were always welcome to stay with us. And did you know they were returning now?"

"No. Listen, Geoffrey. They are adults and entitled to make decisions without our approval. After all, we were in St. Lucia. I do not recall you notifying them." Rachel said and he nodded. "I shall call Anna and see if she has heard from them."

Rachel made a call and looked at Geoffrey. "Anna says they called yesterday and wanted their visit to be a surprise. As far as the villa, you shall have to sort that out."

On their way back to Simonton, Geoffrey explained the reason for David's call. "Oh, my goodness. Finally someone who understands the meaning of romance, and I think it marvelous that he wants to write about the island."

"I tell you what." Geoffrey said. "It is almost supper time. Why don't we clean up, grab some bottles of rum and wine, and go over and surprise them. I know the villa. It sits directly on the beach."

When they finally got to the villa at around six thirty, they found that the McKenzies had gone out for the evening. Lozzie was not exactly friendly, and did not know when they might return. As he drove back out the gate, Rachel asked. "Did you know that woman, because she seemed to know you?"

"As I recall, her name is Lozzie, something or other. She is a syphilitic old whore who infected my father among many others on the island. She is sick and has a very sick brain." Geoffrey said.

"Shouldn't Susan and Brian be told?" She asked.

"I guess," he said, "when we see them. I wonder where they went."

"I tell you one thing, clear," Rachel said. "I am not perusing rum shops looking for them. We have had a long day. I am ready to return home."

The launch Chris had sent to pick them up on the beach was waiting when they arrived. Chris had suggested that they wear something that could get wet, and bring a change of clothes for dinner. Brian and Susan had dressed in tee shirts and shorts, carrying their other clothing in plastic bags. Upon reaching the yacht and tying alongside, Chris met and assisted them up the ladder, to a foredeck lounge paneled in rich dark mahogany.

He showed them to a stateroom where they could change for dinner. Susan re-appeared wearing a yellow dress and matching pumps, while Brian had on an open neck shirt and white slacks. Chris had changed into a pair of light brown slacks and navy blazer. He wore no shoes.

"Ah," he said, "you both look just elegant." He instructed a tuxedoed waiter to place a bottle of rum on a center table, as the boat drifted around to give them a full view of the island, now illuminated by the moon and millions of stars.

"Melody shall be up shortly, I love that color on you, Susan," Chris said. " Ah, here she is now."

Melody appeared in an off the shoulder white dress with a front partially cut down below the navel, leaving an ever so small bit of mystery. "Welcome to our home away from home." She said, as calypso music boomed from speakers set around the spacious yacht.

"Hope you both are just starved," Chris said as he took Susan's arm. Brian offered his hand to Melody, who kissed him on the cheek. "I trust you are meat eaters since we have steak as well as lobster on our table this evening."

The dining area was done in well-polished complimentary mahogany as well. Crystal chandeliers illuminated the elegant table service, which were clearly British, where utensils not being used would be removed and replaced with others by the steward. The steak was chateaubriand and done perfectly. Chris said he was pleased that the cook had brought large African lobster tails that overlapped the serving dish, instead of the rock lobster, which was the usual island fare. Both red and white wines were offered, and when the meal was concluded, Chris produced a bottle of delectable champagne that he said had come from the vineyard of a friend.

"All right, shall we retire back to the salon for after dinner drinks and coffee?" Melody asked. The sat and chatted for another hour, until Melody excused herself. She returned wearing only a thong, and announced she was going for a midnight swim. "Who will join me?" She asked, as she handed a white bikini to Susan. "I am certain this will fit you that is if you wish to wear it."

Susan just wished Brian would shove his eyes back into their sockets, when she returned wearing the suit which apparently did not come with a bra top. She looked around and started to cover her breasts with her hands.

"Worry not," Chris said. "I have sent the crew ashore and the wait staff was a rental. They cleaned up and are long gone." He advised.

"You do realize that sea predators such as manta rays do come close to shore at night." Brian said.

"Piece of cake. We light up the bottom down to thirty feet with powerful beams." Melody said as she pointed toward the aft ladder.

Now here were two women, wearing attire that now left absolutely nothing to the imagination.

Chris could not take his eyes from Susan who accepted a brandy and coffee. Melody wanted neither. She stood behind Brian and tousled his hair.

"Of course if you did not bring a suit with you, it will not be a problem. We often spend the day on the boat bare-assed." Brian wondered if the crew was able to properly steer the boat under such circumstance.

Brian took a gulp of brandy that burned the back of his throat and almost made him sneeze. "Honey, I went to a coed college and lived in a coed dorm. Seeing naked women in the hallways was never a problem. "We Canadians are a loose lot, Eh! Chris?"

"You follow hockey?" Chris asked. "I was always a Maple Leaf fan. You?"

"Living in New York, you have to root for the Rangers." Brian said.

Melody grabbed Susan's hand. "We don't give a crap about hockey do we? We two are going for a swim." She led Susan to the rear of the boat, where a platform had been lowered to meet the water. Moments later both women were swimming in the sea.

Chris refilled their glasses. "Drink up. We can't lead them to believe that we are sissies." He stripped off his shirt and pants. Chris wore no underwear. Brian followed suit and both dove off the platform into the clear water.

The bright underwater lights allowed Melody to observe, despite the coldness of the water, that he was already aroused. Brian dove down to the bottom, and swam under boat surfacing on its other side. When he returned to the platform, he found himself alone with Melody.

"They got cold and went back aboard." She said. "So how come that thing got so big all of a sudden. Isn't that the reason guys take cold showers?"

He looked down, embarrassed. "Not in my case I guess."

"You find me sexy, don't you?" She said. "Wanna fuck me? I get horny easily."

"Would you just suppose that this all might be moving a bit too fast?" Brian replied.

"Oh bullshit man! The minute I saw all of those ceiling and side wall mirrors in your bedroom, I just knew that it had to happen." She said.

He had become flaccid. "I guess this cold water has taken some of the starch out."

Melody put her hand on his penis and began to stroke it. She giggled. "Never you mind. I know what you have. See what I mean? Someone wants me, and it certainly looks like you're the man. Tell me something Brian. What do you suppose Susan and Chris might be doing? That should motivate you."

"They are more than likely toweling off and having a drink." Brian climbed back up on the platform, helping Melody aboard, and as her breasts pressed against his chest, she gave him an open mouth kiss and, now fully erect, Brian returned the favor.

"You are not going to refuse me Brian and you won't need a condom since Chris and I are both squeaky clean."

They returned to the salon where they found towels. Melody shivered and removed the wet thong. "Ooh, that feels better. Brian you look like you have something on your mind. A pressing engagement somewhere perhaps."

He was thinking of that first time with Rachel five year ago. "No," he replied as he took a towel and began to dry her back. Susan and Chris were nowhere in sight, so the two of them were alone.

"Your turn," She said pushing him back onto the plush leather couch, drying his chest with another towel, as Donna Summers' doleful 'Love Me, Love Me Baby' suddenly filled the boat. "Ready or not," She said, as she straddled and deftly slid him into her in one motion. Melody rocked back and forth expressing her approval of how big he had become, as one of her nipples sought his mouth.

Brian maintained his erection thinking about what Chris and Susan might be doing below. Her thrusts increased with the intensity of the music, and as freely as Rachel had given herself to him, Melody held nothing back. He was distracted by a loud moan from somewhere below, and knew Susan just had a strong orgasm. Even after he and Melody had come, she pushed herself off, and getting on her hands and knees on the soft carpet that covered the deck, she implored him to take her from behind. Still hard, he entered her again, and as she exhorted him to pound her buttocks, he felt the muscles of her vagina tighten.

Unable to control it any longer he came, just before she did. "That was great, but I would really like to do it in front of those mirrors in your bedroom, and I am a multiple orgasm girl." She said. " I could use a drink. How about you?"

Brian watched her move seductively to the wet bar, most happy with her state of undress, making no effort to cover her nudity. She brought two glasses and a fresh bottle of dark rum. "I only brought two glasses, because knowing Chris, they'll be busy for a while."

"You've switched before?" He said.

"You really didn't believe you were my first?" She asked. "Chris certainly wasn't when we met."

Brian looked at Melody. She sat next to him thigh-to-thigh, unconcerned that he was staring at her breasts, wondering if this entire thing had had been a bad mistake. But he realized it was nothing more than fulfilling a desire he most assuredly needed. He was not absolutely certain that this was also true of Susan. "How long do you plan to be in Barbados?" He inquired. "Susan and I plan to stay at least three weeks."

"Don't know," she answered. "Hadn't thought about it until we met you guys. We'll keep it open ended." Melody kissed him, grabbed a towel, and the next thing he heard was the hiss of a shower from somewhere down below.

He had just pulled up his pants when Susan appeared dressed again in t-shirt and shorts she had worn to the boat. Her dress was on a hanger covered with plastic. "Get your stuff Brian, Chris said he would drive us back in the launch."

Brian looked at Susan. "Drinks, and the company were excellent. I actually enjoyed the naked swim. How was sex with Chris?" He asked buttoning his shirt.

She looked at him. "Chris is waiting down the ladder in the launch. Suppose I hold the gooey details until we get back home. Oh, since Chris expressed a desire to get another look at our bedroom mirrors, I took the liberty of inviting them for dinner tomorrow night."

"That good, huh?" He asked.

"Get in the launch." She said as she pushed him forward.

Chris said goodbye at the beach, and the two headed back toward the car park. "I plan to give Lozzie the night off tomorrow. At least I can cook without an attitude. What do you say to fresh fish and local vegetables, and key lime pie?" Brian thought it would be a good idea. He wondered why she had not asked him about sex with Melody.

The gate to the villa was again chained. "I guess it must be a good idea to do this, but we must get an extra key." He said as he honked the horn. Lozzie came out in her nightgown, and perched on her head was a yellow straw hat. "We need a key so as not to wake you," Susan said.

"Master Townsend and his wife was here earlier. They some what vexed dat you off."

"Open the lock Lozzie and tomorrow you may leave at three in the afternoon. We shall not require your services until the day after tomorrow." Susan said.

Lozzie stood her ground her hands defiantly on her hips. "As long as you pays me my usual wage and government incentives." She said.

"And what might those incentives be? I was only told about salary for the time we were here." Brian asked.

"I'll have government person call or stop by to give the particulars. You wan Mr. Braithwaite here then still?" She asked.

"Without a doubt, you may retire. I'll lock up for the night." Brian said as he entered the house. The gates that blocked off the patio had already been secured.

As soon as Lozzie and Susan were inside he closed the door and moved the gate in place, secured the bolt and locked it. Brian wondered what had changed on the island to justify the need for so much security.

"I hated her the moment I met her." Brian said.

"True, True. I don't like her at all, at all. At least Mr. Braithwaite is a more friendly sort." Susan said.

"I agree, but perhaps we should discuss the local work rules with Geoffrey and Rachel. They certainly would know better. That Lozzie gives me the creeps. Remember what I said about the dolls with pins in them."

"How about securing the gate between our bedroom and the main hall?" Brian turned to do it. "And could you forgive me for not having more sex tonight? Chris was an animal. I am so very irritated."

"Another reason to hate them," he said. "Perhaps the mirrors will stimulate us in early morning." Brian got into bed and held her in his arms. "How could you possible escape from me in a round bed? Oh, and Melody was phenomenal. I thought she would never stop asking for more. How was Chris? Did he satisfy you?"

"He did and I did. Go to sleep my darling." She rolled over and turned out the night-light.

Twenty

Barbados 1991

"Oh, Rachel," Susan said, on the phone, "We were terribly sorry that we missed you last evening, and definitely must do something to make up for it."

"No trouble. I told Geoffrey to call, but you know how easily he gets vexed." Rachel said. "It must feel good to be back on the island."

"I know that you all are upset about our staying at this villa, but it is owned by one of the principles in Brian's company, and he is someone you just don't say no to. At any rate, the good news is that we are back home."

"I missed you both. So when shall we see you?" Rachel asked.

"Tonight, here for dinner." Susan said. "Time for a night at home. Yesterday, after cleaning up, we decided to go dancing, at the new disco in Holetown."

"The disco? I know it. Very crowded and very smoky. We used to go dancing, but Geoffrey has been so distracted lately." She smiled. "And before I forget., thank you for taking such good care of him on his trip to New York." Susan held her breath. She didn't know if Rachel knew what had occurred, or was on a fishing expedition.

"Look next time, you come with him, and no absolutely no hotels despite our bad manners this time." Susan said apologetically.

"I am not at all vexed with you. I have been overwrought, however myself, with Sophia's coming wedding. I went to Canada, and finally convinced her to be married in Barbados. And of course you must come, and David and Meghan as well. I have had to deal with a great amount of tension, but I'll tell you about when we see you." Rachel said.

"We would not miss it." Susan said. "Oh, I lost my train of thought. At the disco we met the nicest couple from Canada. That's where we were last night. We had dinner on their boat, and asked them to come to the villa tonight, and we want Geoffrey and you to join us."

"Of course, can I do or bring something?" Rachel asked.

"How about some of your terrific pumpkin soup? I have given Lozzie the night off, so we'll have Mr. Braithwaite serve." Susan said.

"I have some in the freezer. Geoffrey tells me that Lozzie is a witch. I'll fill you in later. Tell you what. Let's make this a joint venture. What else can I bring?" Susan explained that she wanted to serve simple local food, and Rachel suggested that she could help prepare something, but offered an alternative. "There is a small restaurant and bar on the road between you and us, that makes a fried chicken than could rival Enid's down on Baxter's Road. She also makes dolphin and steak fish prepared true Bajan way."

"What a great idea," Susan said. "How much should I order?"

"Six of us? I'll take care of it. What were you thinking for dessert?" Rachel asked.

"Key lime pie," Susan responded.

"You are in luck. I have two in my freezer as well. This is what we'll do. "I'll pick up the food and bring the pies. You prepare a salad. Most everything else you can get at Elmer's market in Speightstown, and then you can just be the hostess."

"You are a good friend and life saver, Rachel. When I made the plans and gave Lozzie the night off, I bit off more than I can chew, so to say."

"Tell me more about these Canadians you met, Susan." Rachel said.

"Their name is Simpson, Melody and Chris. She owns or manages a beauty salon in Toronto, and he runs a pharmaceutical company there. They are young and lots of fun." Susan said.

"You seem to have hit it off well with them. What was Brian's sense?" She asked.

"The same. The two men seemed to have a lot in common." Susan offered.

"So," Rachel said, "and how about you two women?"

"Uh, well. She is a bit different, but I am going to let you decide for yourself." Susan said. "Melody is a bit of an exhibitionist. Geoffrey will love her."

"Of that I am certain. Break out the rum, Luv," Rachel said. "Lots of it."

"I have so missed you, Rachel. I wrote frequently, but received only one letter back." Susan said.

"It is a very long story, Susan, but I have missed you terribly as well. Perhaps I can offer some explanation."

"Does it have anything to do with what the two of us did?" Susan asked.

"Of course. It has everything to do with what we did." She answered.

"Do you regret any of it?" Susan asked. "I do not."

"I am not certain, and that is my dilemma. We shall talk more when we are alone." Rachel said. "So looking forward to tonight. See you at six for drinks. Right?"

Promptly at six, Braithwaite escorted Rachel and Geoffrey to the patio, where Brian and Susan greeted them with hugs and kisses. "I asked Mr. Braithwaite, here to unload the food from the boot," Rachel said. "He is a very nice man."

"Salad has been prepared. Braithwaite insisted upon taking care of everything himself tonight. He said he had been a cook one time at the Holiday Inn in Bridgetown, but Lozzie never would let him in the kitchen. I told him what you were bringing, and he said he would make it look home cooked. You know I looked in the freezer and found some smoky links and little American hot-dogs what we call 'pigs in a blanket'. We gonna be jes fine. To quote Braithwaite."

Geoffrey walked back toward the entryway. "For some reason, I believe I have been in this villa before, while it was being built. Yes, a friend of mine, by the name of Fields was the contractor. You realize that everyone in Barbados is a plumber and auto mechanic and electrician. If you noticed I said and, not or. This is a funny, although rather stupid story." Braithwaite brought in three bottles of different rums and the little hot dogs.

"Go on Geoffrey. Continue your story." Brian said.

"They were completing construction of the all electric kitchen, but when my friend came to check, the local workmen had nailed all of the sheetrock, but had left no holes in the walls for wiring or outlets. There was nowhere to plug in the refrigerator etal. Had to tear down the entire thing and start from scratch." Geoffrey said.

"The contractor must surely have been super vexed. Susan laughed, overhearing their conversation.

Geoffrey raised his glass and smiled. "You do not know the half of it. But, this is Barbados. There is the usual excuse for the inexcusable. And wait there is something else I remember about this place." He thought for a moment. "Ah. The magnificent, sexy master bedroom," he laughed wickedly. "Those fantastic mirrored ceilings and walls." You, Brian, are a genius in getting this place."

"Rachel you have not touched your rum." Brian observed. Would you care for something else?"

"Yes, I would rather some club soda with lime if you have it?" She said.

"No problem". Brian said. "Come let us fetch it together."
Rachel followed Brian into the kitchen. "I could have gotten your
drink from the wet bar, but you appear so upset. I wanted to talk
to you, alone."

Rachel put her arm on Brian's shoulder. "I have so much on
my mind and do not know where to begin."

"Just start from the beginning." Brian said.

"I have been four times to Canada about this bloody wedding.
What bothers me the most is that I truly believe that Sophia is not
in love with this hockey player. I just feel that she refuses to
acknowledge the possibility that it is his potential and not love
that has drawn him to her. Sophia is so unbelievably stubborn. To
add to the problem, he has not been a prince, and his family has
been most difficult as well, refusing to pay for anything.

I have not discussed any of this with Geoffrey since I know
he would blame it on my hormones. If I do not want to have sex,
it is always my hormones, according to Dr. Townsend, that is."
She began to cry. "Why do I burden you with my problems?"

"Because we consider you and Geoffrey family, and Susan and I are here for you and love you both dearly. I know Susan feels the same way." Brian said.

Rachel took a deep breath. "Sophia has decided to take a leave of absence from university and come home. She called me this afternoon, and I expect her within the week. In one respect, I want her to marry a Bajan, and choose to live here on the island, so we can enjoy our grandchildren, but she deserves to do what she wishes. Oh, Brian. He is not the right husband for my daughter. I truly believe that."

"I don't even know Sophia or her man, so I can't really have an opinion." Brian said. "In the mean time we are here for you." He handed her a glass of rum and led her back to where Susan and Geoffrey seemed to be having a heated political discussion, based upon what he had recently seen on CNN. Susan had decided upon Sugar Cane Brandy, while Geoffrey nursed his Cockspur neat.

"Luv, it is really not brandy you know," he said. "It is a Mount Gay marketing device. Courvoisier is brandy and this shit. Hello where have the two of you been?" He said as Rachel and Brian returned.

"Deep in conversation, but not that deep," Brian said smiling. Rachel had seemed to compose herself. "Your trip to St. Lucia, profitable?"

"In a sense, yes," Geoffrey said. "I would like to develop a rental business there as I have here. Interested?"

"What happened to phase whatever at the old hotel on the east coast?" Brian asked.

"Don't sell that short. One day that could be a profitable venture, you know." Geoffrey retorted.

"Yeah, right!" Rachel responded.

Susan put her hand on Geoffrey's arm. "So I hear you know our housekeeper, Lozzie. What's the scoop?"

"I would rather not ruin a delightful evening," he said.

"I have to call the office about terminating her. For now we gave her the night and tomorrow off." Brian said.

"Beware of little black dolls with pins in them." Geoffrey said, as Brian raised his eyebrows with a 'told you so look'. "So and where are your other dinner guests?"

Braithwaite brought more little hot dogs and informed them that a taxi had just pulled before the gate. "I shall go out and open it for them." He said.

When the Simpsons made their appearance, Rachel thought Chris looked rather dashing with his dark tan and muscular build. He wore a blue blazer, open neck shirt, white slacks and white shoes without socks. On the other hand she thought Melody to be under dressed and over made up with a tight fitting, braless outfit that barely reached her mid thighs, and she was chewing gum.

Geoffrey was cordial as he introduced himself, shaking hands with Chris, while giving Melody a peck on both cheeks. "I took the liberty of bringing a few chilled bottle of Dom Perignon." Chris said, as his embrace of Susan did not go unnoticed. Brian placed the bottles in a cooler on the wet bar.

"Drinks?" Brian asked. "What is your pleasure, everyone?" Braithwaite brought two more glasses and Brian filled four glasses with dark rum.

"Can your butler make a Cosmo?" Melody asked.

Rachel looked at her. "Doubt it. Might be best to stick with the straight stuff." Melody shrugged and Geoffrey poured her a hefty glass of rum neat.

Chris looked out at the darkened sea. "This is truly a beautiful island. We certainly plan to return here often." He looked at Geoffrey. "Truly an amazing villa. You should see the mirrored ceiling in the bedroom."

Geoffrey chose not to ask Chris how he knew about them. Susan rolled her eyes. "Oh," Geoffrey said. "I have seen them. Verily a work of art."

Chris had seen Susan react. "Melody, actually brought me upstairs to see them." He explained. Braithwaite came out and whispered in Susan's ear.

"Oh, that is wonderful, Braithwaite. He said his wife was able to leave her work early and had come to assist him with serving. I cannot keep calling you Braithwaite. What is your given name? You are a gem." Susan said.

"My given name is Samuel." He said. "Here on the island, most have an extra name, but Samuel would be fine, Mistress Susan."

"Then with your permission, Samuel it shall be. Certainly less formal." Susan said.

Dinner was as good as Rachel said it would be, and the Simpsons seemed to enjoy the combination of 'surf and cluck' as Geoffrey called it, and he had to admit privately that the chicken was almost as good as Enid's. Melody did show concern about eating dolphin but Rachel assured her that it was not taken from Flipper. Geoffrey stopped paying attention to Melody's cleavage when Rachel poked his leg with a fork. The bottles of champagne were quickly consumed.

"We can take dessert back out on the patio with after dinner drinks. There is key lime pie, coffee and brandy as you wish." Susan advised.

"Chris brought another kind of dessert," Melody said.

"Really?" Rachel asked. "What did you bring?"

"I am not certain." Chris stuttered.

"Not at all," Geoffrey said, suspiciously. Rachel relaxed. It was crystal clear that he had taken a dislike to Chris and she hoped he felt the same way about Melody.

Chris rose from his seat reluctantly. "I left it just outside." He said. He returned with a small square package tied with string that he proceeded to undo, after clearing an area on a glass table. After wiping the surface clean with his napkin, he looked around to make sure that Samuel and his wife were occupied elsewhere, and produced a hundred dollar bill and a small razor blade.

Geoffrey was furious. "Hold it right there. I understand from Brian that you are in the pharmaceutical business. Is this one of your products?"

"No, I got this in Jamaica, actually." He undid the package. In it was a small plastic bottle containing what appeared to be a white powder. "Primo quality." Chris offered.

"Close it up, now!" Geoffrey said.

"If that is what I think it is, we do not do drugs. How dare you bring that onto our island!" Rachel said, looking angrily at Susan and Brian for some response.

"We had no idea, Brian said. "Chris, Geoffrey is absolutely correct. Close it up."

"As a Barbadian, I shall give you an opportunity to pack it up, and take your drugs and this woman back to your boat immediately. In fact Brian and I shall see that you return to your boat, but not with that in your possession or in our car."

Geoffrey picked up the container and took it into the bathroom where he flushed the contents down the toilet.

"Melody, time to go. It is clear that we are no longer welcome." Chris said.

Geoffrey returned and handed him the now clean plastic container. "Tomorrow morning I shall check with our Coast Guard to make sure that you have exited Barbadian waters. Of course the other choice would be to spend time in one of our hot, stinking prison cells. Our judiciary is very unforgiving when it comes to illegal drugs."

Brian and Geoffrey drove the two back to Holetown, where from the beach, Chris signaled with a flashlight to the boat. Minutes later a launch came to a stop near the water's edge.

The Simpsons boarded without a word, and Geoffrey and Brian remained on the beach until they saw the launch reach the yacht. Brian breathed a sigh of relief.

When they returned to the villa, they all sat and discussed what had just happened. "Do you realize that we all would have been arrested if it were suspect enough to have police come here this evening?' Geoffrey said. "Now I need a good stiff drink."

"I believe we all do," Rachel said. " Are you as angry as we are.

"We had no idea. They just seemed like a nice couple." Susan said. "Neither of them let on that they had any interest in drugs."

Susan and Brian knew that pot and cocaine was available on the island having been at times, offered both by beach bums. The one time Susan smoked pot, she developed mood swings alternating between anger, crying, and unusual hunger. Brian had tried it, but it made him cough.

Geoffrey collapsed back into his chair. "The gall of those people. I knew I did not like them from the get go."

"Really?" Rachel said. "You could take your eyes from the gum chewer's tits all throughout dinner. You recall the fork? Susan, best you check under the table and see if that's where she deposited her chew."

Geoffrey smiled. "You must admit that her bossooms were eye popping. Where did you say you met these people?"

"Really!" She looked at Geoffrey. "At the disco, two nights ago." Susan said. "She came on to Brian. Honestly, we knew nothing of their surprise dessert."

"I trust there are no more question to ask." Geoffrey said quietly.

Susan rose abruptly. "No! And I do believe we all could use a refill."

"How long shall you be here?" Geoffrey asked after he calmed down.

"A few weeks," Brian answered. "Hey, there are tennis courts of to the side of the villa. How about knocking up a few in the morning?"

Geoffrey laughed. "Actually, I am considering taking up golf. "You do recall that time the three of us played tennis down in Holetown at the park? You have to admit that I was downright awful. I now use the racket to strain spaghetti."

Rachel got up from her chair. "It is late, but despite it all, the evening was wonderful up to that so called dessert. How about dinner out tomorrow evening, and we can decide what to do afterwards. The Merrymen still appear in a place they own down in St. Lawrence Gap. We could even have dinner at David's restaurant first."

"Super!" Geoffrey clapped his hands, as both Brian and Susan nodded in agreement. "And let's not find any more strange friends."

"Come Luv," Rachel said taking his arm. These two wish to go to bed."

"I guess we are not wanted." Geoffrey said feigning sadness. "Unless of course the McKenzies would desire company in bed."

"I think we all need some real sleep." Susan said.

"Jus makin lak fool." Geoffrey said.

"You can mak lak a fool out to de car, Luv." Rachel said with a laugh.

Brian and Susan waved as they drove away. "I hope the Simpsons leave the island. I do not want our yacht escapade to come back to haunt us." He said.

They thanked Samuel and his wife for putting the kitchen back in order before they left. Samuel said he would secure the front gate, and advised Brian to do the same to the one on the beach.

They lay in bed silently for a few minutes, when Brian rolled over to face her. "We have never talked about the evening on the boat." He said.

"You have got to be kidding, Brian, after what happened tonight. What time is it?" She asked.

"Eleven thirty and I am wide awake and alert." He said.

"All right, as long as you do not include erect in your description, I could give you a synopsis." She said. "Look we both made a bad mistake and were mucho foolish. And I have to be blamed for leaving you in the water with Melody. The whole thing was about him. He was very rough, but I wanted him. Sadly, it was anything but satisfying."

"As I think back, she was very aggressive, and it was all over in a flash. No warmth at all. We must promise each other that nothing like that will happen again." He kissed her as the phone rang.

"Hi David. What's up?" She asked. David told her of his plans to come to Barbados as Susan hit the speakerphone button. "Great! When do you expect to arrive?"

"I'll be there in a day or so, but Jen will arrive maybe next week." David said. "Let me tell you about the book."

"Hi David. It's Dad. Whose Jen?"

"I told you about her. She's an artist I met at the Metropolitan one evening six months ago." He responded.

"It's rather tight here but I am sure we can make room." Brian said.

Susan poked Brian in the shoulder and put two fingers to his lips. "We have plenty of room. This is a big house. You are writing a book?"

David briefly outlined his thoughts about the novel and both Brian and Susan thought it a grand idea. They talked for about a half hour and then hung up.

"He is writing a historical novel about Barbados." Brian said.

"How great it that." He added.

"What about the mirrored ceiling?" She asked.

"I think that they are a fantastic turn on. Let's try them out!" He said.

"That is not at all what I meant. What will the kids think of them?" She asked.

"Probably that we are nefarious island swingers, and they shall be right." He responded. "How would you feel about getting us some lime squash?" He asked.

"What about this Jen. What shall she think? After all we don't know her at all." She said as she started down to the kitchen.

Susan returned with the drinks, and laughed seeing Brian sprawled naked on the round bed looking at his reflection from the ceiling.

"You look terrific." He said, as she seductively removed her night dress." You are so young and desirable. I am looking at your beautiful reflection in the mirrors." Susan smiled and lay naked on the bed next to Brian. It was now her turn to observe her image from four reflected views, and she liked what she saw.

"Another issue," She said. "Might as well tackle it now. Will we allow them to sleep together?"

"Allow who to sleep together?" Brian asked.

"Why our son and his girlfriend, of course. Who did you think I meant?" Susan retorted. "He is apparently serious."

"What choice do we have? It seems so natural for kids to hook up as they call it these days. Perhaps it shall be her decision. Best not to do or say anything as yet. Maybe she would be offended." Brian said.

"Dream on my husband." Susan responded.

The next morning, they enjoyed a breakfast of yogurt, fig bananas and ripe papaya. Brian went to the beach for a swim and decided to take one of the water scooters out for a spin.

Susan called Rachel, but Anna told her that Rachel was on her way to Blue Heron to visit.

Susan brewed fresh coffee and when Rachel arrived, they sat out on the patio with coffee and fresh scones. Brian had not yet come back from the beach. "I need a good listener and a shoulder to cry on. Geoffrey is so difficult to talk to these days."

"Count on me," Susan said.

Rachel told her that Sophia was having doubts about marrying her hockey player, and was now on her way to Barbados for some R&R. "In her case it means re think and raise cane." Rachel said. "You'll soon find out what angst one goes through marrying off a child.

Susan raised her eyebrows. "What do you mean, Rachel?"

"Oh, I just did not think. It was supposed to be a surprise." Rachel said. "David called Geoffrey the day we returned, and wanted to know how they might go about getting married in Barbados." Susan put her hand to her mouth in amazement.

"We hardly know this girl. I certainly hope this is not a 'must do'." Susan said.

"Doubt that since they don't have to come down here for that. Besides, they have to fill out lots of paperwork, and be on the island a minimum of two weeks, before any Justice of the Peace would marry them."

"David called us last night and told us about his plans for the book and that Jen would be here next week. I cannot believe he would get married without Meghan being here. Brian and I were discussing sleeping arrangements for them. I guess we can forget that."

"Darling that was moot in any event. So we shall have both David and Sophia down here with all of us. How exciting." Rachel said. "Wouldn't it be just amazing if........"

"Do not forget this Jen person, Rachel."

"Right," she replied.

"Damn, I should keep my big mouth shut." Rachel said.

"No, it was right for you to tell me, but let's keep this all to ourselves about both of them, and see how it shakes out." Susan said. "We certainly have a lot of secrets, we two."

"Let's have dinner as planned tonight down at St. Lawrence Gap. If David comes in tomorrow we shall all go to a new restaurant called the Cliff near Payne's Bay." Rachel said. "It is quite elegant you know."

"My head is spinning. Two weeks to plan a wedding." Susan said.

"Perhaps not." Rachel responded.

Twenty-one

Barbados 1991

Geoffrey drove down to St. Lawrence Gap on the south coast to a restaurant called David's. Brian and Rachel ordered poached dolphin while Geoffrey and Susan chose steak fish Bajan style. After finishing bowls of hot spicy, pumpkin soup for starters, they agreed upon a bottle of red Chilean wine to complement their meals. "What a fine restaurant," Susan said. "And David, the owner seems to be a very fine gentleman."

"Great ambience. Fantastic view of the sea even at night." Brian added. "How wonderful this part of the island this is, and happily filled with tourists. Absolutely love it and I am surprised we have not spent more time here on the South Coast in the past."

Once dinner was over, they chose to forego dessert and go directly to the nearby Pepper Pot where the Merrymen were to play that evening. "I just love it." Brian said as his eyes took in the Pepper Pot, a rather large amphitheater filled with tables and people.

"What a great idea. An open air bar, theater and restaurant with class entertainment." Brian said as they made their way through the crowd.

"You would not think so, if it were raining," Rachel said as they found their seats. "There has been many a time when an unexpected downpour has rendered us sopping wet."

"Excuse me all. I shall be right back," Geoffrey said. "Order me a Mount gay and soda." The other three decided to start with Banks beer. He returned moments later with three members of the band. Emil Straker introduced himself first, and then Robin Hunte, and lastly the tallest of the group Chris Gibbs. Willy was absent, setting up the music, and Emil apologized for not sitting down with them, stating that they had to go on stage shortly. The three Merrymen passed pleasantries, and Emil made it a point to say that they all might get together again, perhaps at Bathsheba when the group returned from gigs in Canada and the States.

"Geoffrey, you really are something else." Susan said.

"I certainly hope so," he replied.

They drank and danced for the next two and a half hours. Brian found Rachel deliciously sensuous, as she moved her hips in perfect sync with her arms and shoulders. He watched Susan dance to the calypso beat, fitting her body to Geoffrey's as if they were one unit, blending into a crowd made up of local people moving seamlessly to the music. Every once in a while Geoffrey would turn her toward the stage, where she could see Emil Straker smiling, as he sang exclusively to her.

She danced to Beautiful Barbados with Brian and then the two couples switched partners again as the Merrymen finally sang a song that Brian had loved since he first heard it five years ago, Island Woman.

"Well", Geoffrey said, "where shall we go next? Coach House or perhaps John Moore? I am game, as you know for anything."

"I believe we all want to go back to the villa. Why waste the mirrored ceiling that I have heard about but have never seen." Rachel said as she smiled at Brian, and winked at Susan.

"Fantastic!" Geoffrey said. "Blue Heron it is."

When they arrived at the villa, they met Samuel Braithwaite, just at the gate as he was leaving for home. "If you need me I can stay later." He said. Since Brian had no further need for him, he thanked him, telling him to have pleasant evening. "Samuel, you have been an exceptional help. See you tomorrow."

"Oh," Samuel said. "Lozzie did call and inform me that she would not be available tomorrow since she had a cold in her foot."

"I see," Brian said. "You did not happen to check our rum stock did you?" Samuel laughed and said he believed it was all accounted for, possibly.

Brian padlocked the front and back gates, and the four went up the stairway to the upper floor, where they immediately disrobed and moved to the hot tub. Later, they lay down on the round bed and observed themselves in mirrors that seemed to continue on forever and ever, one reflection leading endlessly to another.

"We must look at this practically." Susan said. "In a day or two we shall have our children, who most likely shall not understand why and what we do."

"Spoil sport, Susan. But more importantly," Brian said as he took one of Rachel's nipples in his mouth and then looking to Susan, and continued finding Geoffrey's head already between her legs, "we do what we do because we have such a great love for each other and enjoy every bit of mutual satisfaction." Brian paused for a moment. "Hell, we all like a great orgy!"

"I am so fretful that I shall be distracted by all of the images of me, as well the rest of you as each of us does whatever to the other." Rachel said as she pulled Brian's face down between her legs.

"Close your eyes, Luv." Susan said, as the four seemed to fuse into a mass of arms and legs in perpetual slow motion.

David watched the island appear to grow larger, as the American Airline flight began its descent into Grantley Adams Airport. It took no time for the jumbo jet to land effortlessly. He was soon walking down the retractable metal staircase to the tarmac, ignoring the hot blast of Caribbean air that greeted him, so invigorated by the sound of the welcoming steel drums. David pulled his carryon luggage along the walkway until he encountered the sign that welcomed visitors to Barbados. Passengers from the jumbo from Toronto were still waiting at Customs.

He missed Jen. David thought his wait behind the orange customs line endless, but eventually was passed through without issue. The baggage area was filed with people, and luggage from previous flights that had not yet been claimed. He saw a young woman struggling to dislodge a heavy bag from the moving belt, and removed it for her. Then, David found both of his bags and was about to leave when he saw that the young woman still waited at the carousel. "Problem with another bag," he inquired.

"I seem to be missing one, and it's the one that I really need. This is just the icing on the cake," she grumbled.

"I have plenty of time. I can wait with you." David said.

"Oh no, I cannot inconvenience you. You are most likely on holiday" She replied. David insisted and she relented.

As it turned out, that piece of luggage never had been placed on the plane, and the next flight in from Toronto was not due until the following afternoon.

"I believe I have a ride. May I take you where ever you must go?" David asked.

"I took an earlier flight than intended and my parents probably are not waiting. Certainly, I can find a cab." She said.

"I then, am at your service." David said. "I am David, David McKenzie."

"And I am Sophia Townsend," She replied taking his hand.

David looked carefully at the young woman who stood before him. She was the image of her mother Rachel. She had auburn hair, green eyes and he thought her simply beautiful."

"It can't be," he said. "But I know your mother and father, albeit it was once five years ago that I met them, and they are very good friends with my parents. Actually, they all consider themselves family."

"I do believe that they have made mention of friends named McKenzie from New York, and I think that when my mother was in Toronto to help with wedding arrangements, my father was in New York on island business." She said.

David's heart sank when she mentioned her wedding plans, but he did not know why. He was after all, coming here to Barbados to arrange for his own wedding to Jennifer and as a surprise to his parents.

They passed through customs easily, and found Brian and Susan waiting across from the taxi queue. After embracing his parents, he introduced Sophia, whom they were delighted to meet. Brian suggested that they load the luggage into the boot and he would stop at Fontabelle first, to see if Geoffrey was still there.

Rachel, who had stayed late to work on the bookings, was overjoyed when Sophia alit from Brian's car. After all was explained, she said she could get in touch with Geoffrey before he went to the airport, hugged David, and said that they would pick them up at the villa that evening, and casual dress, as usual would be appropriate for dinner. David seemed reluctant to leave as Brian put an arm around his shoulder and led him out and to the car.

David was awed by Blue Heron. "This place is magnificent. More a playboys dream if nothing else." He said.

"Tell us about Jennifer," Susan said.

"Oh, she is one terrific person. We hit it off that first day we met at the Met." David said. "The decision was an easy one."

"And what decision was that?" Susan asked as Brian looked at her.

"Well, I guess you all should know that I plan to get married here on the island." David said. "I had meant it as a surprise for you."

"This is certainly a surprise. Should I guess that Jennifer might not also be in on the surprise?" Brian asked.

"Actually no" David blushed. "I had planned to spring it on her here on Barbados."

"Son, do you suppose I might ask you what if she said no?"

"To be honest I had not given that much thought." David said. I just assumed that because we love each other."

"David, dress casually, but nicely for dinner, Susan said. "We shall be picked up at six and I understand the restaurant is one of the best on the island."

"Can I ask you a question?" David asked after he had checked out the villa. "What's with the round bed and all of the mirrors in your bedroom?"

"Sorry, we had to make do since it came with the house." Brian said.

The Townsends were prompt, and chose to bring Rachel's Mercedes, which fit six more comfortably. For some reason David did not mind being squashed next to Sophia who was dressed to the nines. David who had worn a nice open collar short-sleeved shirt and jeans, wondered if his attire was appropriate, but it was clear that Sophia did not seemed to mind at all.

Geoffrey relinquished the keys to the valet, and was greeted by the maitre de of the Cliff, an old friend from school. They were immediately seated on the first tier where they had a clear view of the beach and sea beyond. Soft music came from number of sound speakers, placed along all three of the tiers.

Brian sat with Rachel and Susan on one side, leaving Sophia to sit between David and Geoffrey. When the server came for their drink orders, Geoffrey ordered four dark rums and looked to David and Sophia. "Hey," David said, "I am not driving. I shall have what they are having. Sophia?'

"She thought for a moment. "The only drink I know is a Cosmo."

"Then" David said, "a Cosmo it shall be."

All four chose varied portions of the menu, and declared that sharing would be tolerated. Once their plates were empty, they agreed that the meal had been exceptional. "Has anyone had the hot chocolate pudding cake?" David asked as he checked the dessert menu.

"David, that was my choice!" Sophia teased.

"Then we shall order it for the table," Geoffrey said, observing that Sophia had not taken her eyes from David.

When they reached Holetown, Sophia announced that they all should go dancing at the disco. Geoffrey agreed that it would be all right for a while, and if they got separated to meet at the car park at 11:30. David and Sophia danced all of the motion filled island dances, and then just enjoyed holding on to each other oblivious of the people around them, when a slow dance was played. As her head nestled into his shoulder, he lifted it and kissed her gently. "David, I don't know at this point what is right and what is wrong."

"A friend of the family once told me 'if it feels good, do it,'" He said.

She kissed him. "And did he do it? I don't know whether it is the island, the night or the music, but you have become a very special person to me in such a brief time. I would venture a guess that our old fogies of parents are waiting impatiently in the car park, so we had better go."

"I would suggest that you not think our parents old and not with it. Personally, I cannot sell them short after having seen the décor in their master bedroom." He murmured, and he held her tightly as they kissed again.

"David what on earth, are we doing?" Sophia asked.

"Do we really care?" She did not answer. "Then let's make some plans for tomorrow," He said. For the first time that evening he did not think about Jennifer.

They found both set of parents sitting on a stone wall that once had served as part of the Holetown fortification. "Sorry if we kept you up," Sophia said.

Rachel watched her daughter and thought she seemed happy for the first time in a long time. "You two have fun dancing?" She asked.

"Oh yes," Sophia responded and then looked at David.

"Everyone in the car." Geoffrey said. "The good news is that tomorrow is Sunday and we shall picnic on the East Coast. At Bathsheba."

When David exited the car at Blue Heron, he thanked the Townsends for a great evening. "Look forward to seeing you all tomorrow." It was clear that this was directed at Sophia who nodded.

Once inside the villa, David unlocked the beach gate and walked out to the patio, as Brian followed. "Not tired even after a full day that must have begun at four this morning in New York?" Brian noted. "Okay, you obviously have something on your mind. Hold what ever thought it is, I'll get us something to drink."

Susan found Brian at the wet bar. "More to drink? Please secure all of the gates before you come upstairs. A problem I should know about?" Brian shrugged. "See you upstairs, whenever."

Brian brought two glasses and the bottle out to the patio. "Rum?" He asked and David nodded. All right. What's going on?"

"It's about Jennifer. What do you think of her?" David asked.

"Know little of her," Brian said. "You brought her to the apartment once, and I did not get the impression that we hit off too well."

"That's only because you told your Museum of Modern Art story about how you don't get Jackson Pollack, and think a monkey with a brush could be just as creative." David said.

"Did I lie?" Brian asked. "The point I was trying to make is that if what I see is irritating to my eyes, why should I like it? I feel the same about certain music. What's the big deal? Frankly I thought she was a snob."

"I must agree that Pollack's paintings are loved by people with different taste and who, perhaps buy such art only for its prestige, but please do not share this with Jen. She would have a fit. Now, the big deal is that I came down here for two reasons. As I explained on the phone, to write a novel about Barbados." David said.

"And the other?"

"And the other was to make arrangements for the two of us, Jen and I, to be married here on this island. Geoffrey sent me all the information I needed." David said as he gulped some of the dark liquid.

"Sip. Don't gulp!" Brian said. "Okay, which you want to talk about first, book or marriage?"

"Jen and I seem to be very compatible. We like the same things and enjoy being with each other." David said.

"Seem to be. So, what's your problem?" Brian asked as he refilled both of their glasses.

"I met Sophia." David said.

"Let me ask you a question, David. Does Jennifer know about these wedding plans?"

"We have discussed living together and then getting married." David responded.

"So she has not a clue about a Bajan marriage then?"

"Not in so many words."

"She thinks she is coming down for a week of sun, sand and whatever. Right?" David lowered his head. "Then part of your problem is solved. I can see that meeting Sophia has had a real effect upon you, and you now regret having to share that news with your girl friend. Compounding your problem, is the fact that Sophia is engaged to some Canadian fellow?" Brian said.

"She did make mention of it."

"I think that the two of you should just step back and look at the big picture. First of all, Jennifer thinks she is coming down for holiday. You planned to make it a honeymoon. My advice is to leave it at the former. As far as living together, that seems to be the current name of the relationship game. We used to call it shacking up. While neither Rachel nor Geoffrey has said anything to me. My sense it that Sophia has real issues that made her leave school and the fiancé. My advice is that you not proceed with your plans for marriage here."

"We would have to be here for at least two weeks. Island rules." David said. "Lots of paper work."

"There's your out. Drag your feet. It does not matter since Jennifer doesn't know." Brian advised. "Think this out, Son. You have had some sort of relationship with this girl back home, and whamo, you meet Sophia on a tropical island and your head is spinning. Sounds a bit like a summer romance. Those usually take a summer to develop. You have known her for a day. But, it speaks for itself David. You have enough doubt to make no immediate decision about a marriage you might regret. Now, about this book."

"That's easier to talk about, Dad, and I really appreciate this. I have an idea to write a definitive historic novel about Barbados, ala Michener, and have not been able find one that has already been written."

"That's a good start." Brian said.

"My plan is to begin with the islands geologic beginning, and then develop a story about an Englishman who comes here as a pioneer. I did some research on the British political scene at the time so that shall be pertinent, but the main theme will center around how much slavery and sugar affected Barbados, and the families of the white and black people who's stories I shall tell. Obviously I haven't sorted it all out but I have a good idea as to the time line. I think, also that I have had too much rum since the words are not coming so easily."

Brian smiled. "Me as well, or as we Bajans say, True, true, true. Let's lock up and get some sleep. Tomorrow will be a fun day. Mom and I have been on Townsend picnics before. And you and Meghan have as well, if I recall correctly. And another thing, your sister would be very upset if you got married without her being here."

Twenty-two

Barbados 1991

David and Sophia searched the sand for shells that might have been deposited on the beach by the incoming tide. "Finding shells can be very difficult." He said. "You have to really concentrate hard. There are hundreds of shells just lying in front of us, but the sun and water makes it difficult to see them." Sophia grasped a handful of sand that, she suddenly let drop back to the beach "Sophia", he said. "You must be patient. Everything is here right in front of us. We just have to find it." Sophia smiled at David.

"You make it sound so easy." She said. "I am Bajan. I have been away from the island for a long time. Mommy taught me all of this years ago." She sighed. "Things we want are just here before us. Sometimes we just do not see them." Sophia reached down into the sand and came up with four small shells. "I would never have seen these." She said, "if, it were not for you, David."

"My father taught me how to find the shells the first time we came to Barbados." David said.

"I never asked you what brings you back now, David." She said.

David looked at Sophia. "Although I came here only once, there is something about this place and the people, that makes me love everything about this island. Also, I am planning to write a historic novel about Barbados," he said. "It was once a dream, but it has become an obsession."

"I must tell you something David," She said as she walked into one of the warm tidal pools. "I am engaged to a professional hockey player. He is in Canada and I have come home to decide if I miss him and love him."

"Sophia," David said, "Confession time. I came here also to arrange my marriage to a woman I really believed I loved, but after meeting you, I'm not sure. Is this strange or not?" He took her hand.

"Jennifer is expected next week, but she knows nothing about the marriage plans. It was my idea."

"Jennifer is a pretty name." She said.

"She is a beautiful girl." David responded, "but you, Sophia are more beautiful." He picked up a handful of sand and allowed it to sift through his fingers. "Is any of what I am thinking possible?" He asked.

"How long have you known Jennifer?" She asked.

"Not all that long." David answered. "What would you suppose our folks would think if we chose each other instead?"

"I know that they would like us to be happy. Mother has expressed her concern about me living so far away in Canada. She also believes that marrying a hockey player who might spend six months away from home would be a problem." She answered, as a Frisbee landed at David's feet. He tossed it back after looking at the 'Made in Canada' label. "They are telling us something, or that was an accident. We had better join the rest." She said. "Jennifer arrives when?"

"Next week." He said.

"Yes, you did tell me that already. And your plans are, were to get married on the island?" She asked.

"If indeed that was to become a reality, it was the plan. But by Barbados law, we must be here for two weeks before we could start the process." He said.

"And?" Sophia asked.

"I believe I shall drag my feet as my father suggested. I told him how I felt." David said.

"Your Dad does not really know me." Sophia said.

"Not to worry. He always seems to make the right decision." David said. "You have to meet my sister Meghan. You will just love her."

"Loving another member of the McKenzie family shall present no problem." Sophia said. "Lunch time and I am famished."

After lunch, Sophia watched David play in a cricket match where he was the bowler, and clapped excitedly when he hit the wicket. Rachel watched her daughter's expression of excitement and sat down next to her on the sand. "You are having second thoughts about your wedding aren't you? It is all right. You are entitled to make the right decision. It is, after all your life, isn't it?"

"Did you make the right decision, Mommy?" Sophia asked as she watched Geoffrey, playing the position of silly mid-off, race into the water to catch a ball."

Without question, darling. Without question." Rachel answered.

"And David's parents?" Sophia asked.

"I believe that both would answer the same." Rachel said.

"You know them very well, don't you?" Sophia asked.

"Darling, they are family." Rachel said as she hugged her daughter. "Follow your heart."

"You know about his Jennifer?" She asked.

"Yes. And he knows about the hockey player?" Rachel asked.

"Yes, David and I spoke of them." She sighed. "You are right, Mommy. He is just a hockey player. What's next?"

"How long had you planned to stay here on Barbados?" Rachel asked.

"As long as it takes." Sophia said.

Geoffrey announced that he was heading for Barclay Park, and asked if anyone wished to accompany him. Everything had been packed up, so the only evidence of people having occupied the area were footprints in the sand. Brian and Susan had observed David's preoccupation with Sophia. "What's going on with these two?" Susan asked.

"I would suggest we let nature take its course." Brian said.

"But," Susan tried to interject.

"David will make the right decision. Your little boy is a man, Darling. For whatever reason, I believe that he is on a better course now then he was when he arrived. I am thoroughly convinced that he will do the right thing." Susan looked at her husband not certain how to respond.

"Brian, it would be most unfair to have that girl fly all the way here, just to have her heart broken." Susan said. "We must speak with our son."

"We have had one spectacular picnic!" Geoffrey called out. "Let us be on our way, but it is Sunday. I propose that we get together at the Hippo Disco tonight at sevenish."

Joey, Jollybuns and their families drove north while Geoffrey took the Mercedes down the road toward Barclays Park, where rum punch and toilets awaited.

That evening, Susan and Brian after spending an hour in the pool, sat on their patio enjoying tea and scones, which the new housekeeper, had brewed and baked. "Compared to Lozzie, this one is a real find." Brian said, his mouth filled with what was left of his scone.

"She does have a name and it is Brenda," Susan said. "David has not yet returned from Simonton. We must talk to him about Jennifer, you know."

"As I said, I trust David to do the right thing, but if it shall make you more comfortable, we both should have a talk with him." Brian responded, as David came onto the patio.

"Hey, today at the beach was a blast. Geoffrey is something else playing cricket. I think I have convinced him to become a shortstop instead of a silly mid-off." David said. "Tea? You two are becoming old fogies? Although I doubt that, having seen your bedroom. Again. What is with those mirrors? Mind if I borrow those digs sometime?"

"Take a seat, and a rest, David," Brian advised. "Tea?"

"Thanks no, but I'll have some rum. I am old enough now." David said as he looked as his watch. "Oh, I am going to be late. Sophia and I are going down to the disco in Holetown."

"David, fill your glass with whatever and take a seat. Call Sophia and tell her you will be a bit late. Your Dad and I wish to speak with you." Susan said.

"Okay," David responded as he sat next to his mother. "I really don't need a drink, and we all do have to talk. I know, I am just trying to put off something that I am having difficulty dealing with. Everything just happened so fast. Sophia will understand if I am late."

"David," Susan asked as she put her arm around her son. "Do you love Jennifer?"

"I thought I did, but after meeting Sophia, I am not sure." David responded.

"You must think this out carefully before you have her come down to the island. I realize that she is not aware of your surprise, but she is also unaware of Sophia and your feelings for her. Best you call Jennifer and ask her not to come. Make up any reasonable excuse and tell her that you will discuss it when you return to New York. It must be face to face and not over the phone. Do you disagree?" Brian asked.

"I know you are right. But, what of Sophia? She has a similar problem being engaged to what's his name, the hockey player." David responded wearily.

"Sophia must make up her own mind, and we must stay out of that." Susan looked at Brian, who nodded his head in agreement. "It is you who must explain your feelings to Jennifer. Mind you, it is not essential to tell her about Sophia. But that will be your decision." Susan advised.

"I'll call her first thing in the morning, but now I must get to Simonton. Can I take the car? I am really going to be late." David said as he got up.

"We have no plans for the evening, so drive safely, David." Brian said. After David left, Brian turned to Susan. "I think it best that we speak to Rachel and Geoffrey." He slapped his forehead.

"You know, I never asked him if he had a local license. Wait a while before you make that call."

Geoffrey picked up the phone on the first ring. "Hello Luv." He said.

"Okay, now you have ESP or did you expect a call from another lover?" Susan said.

"No my darling. I have but two physical loves. Actually David and Sophia just left the house, and Rachel has already brought me up to speed, so I anticipated a call from you all."

"Do you suppose we adults should conclave on what might effect the lives of two of our children?" She asked.

"Rachel and I shall be over directly, since you have given up your transportation or wheels, as you Yanks say, for the evening. I would suggest that there be a goodly supply of alcohol. It portends to be a long evening."

"Geoffrey, does David have a driver's license?" She asked.

"I never thought to inquire." He said.

Twenty-three

Barbados

Geoffrey and Rachel, finding the front gate ajar drove through, and parked the Mercedes on the circular driveway, as Brian appeared in the doorway.

"Bloody foolish to leave the gate open. You never know what beach bum might pass through to do you harm looking for drug money." Geoffrey called out.

"You are correct as usual, Geoffrey, but look we are safe, quite whole but slightly, no exceptionally, inebriated." Brian replied.

"And we two as well." Rachel said, kissing Brian on his cheek. "And we too as well." Brian led them into the house and out onto the patio where Susan sat staring at the now black sea.

Geoffrey accepted a glass of Mount Gay from Brian and sat down next to Susan on the chaise. "I have found better reasons to get drunk, but this is surely a first." He said. "I would never have imagined that our children would marry." He thought for a minute and smiled. "Damn it all, we four have been committing bloody incest."

Rachel sipped her rum. "It does not quite work out that way, you know, Luv."

"But it sounds damn erotic," Geoffrey responded with a laugh. "Susan, you have been extremely quiet. You are troubled, aren't you?"

"Oh, it is not about Sophia. She is a wonderful person whom I would love to have as a daughter." Susan had tears in her eyes. "I am so concerned that both of our children really believe that they are in love with each other now and at this moment. You know they both have made vague commitments to others."

Brian put his hand on Rachel's shoulder. We as adults have made decisions that could have adversely impacted our marriages, but we seem to have weathered the storm." He said.

"The difference," Susan said, "is, that we are quote mature adults who do not take 'hooking up' lightly."

"Darling," Brian said, "there were times I had my doubts, particularly when you showed interest in going off with Geoffrey on vacation."

"Really!" Geoffrey said enthusiastically. "I!"

Rachel did not let him finish. "Cool down my dear. It was not going to happen, any more than your screwing the lovely flight attendants on the Grenadines trip."

"Oh! Rachel, stop spoiling the poor dear's desire. They were lesbians after all." Susan laughed. "Brian, I really need to get very, drunk so pour me another tot."

"Don't rub it in. Look, we are getting far a field. I believe that this meeting, so to speak, was to discuss the pros and cons of our children's melding." Brian said as he filled Susan's glass.

"Melding is it?" Geoffrey said with a leer. "Is that what you call it?"

Brian glared at him. "I was referring to their potential marriage and nothing sexual. Can we keep our discussion at a higher level?"

Rachel got up from her chair. "I have a great idea. I shall brew some coffee, and I suggest you drink up what you have in your glasses, since I am cutting you all off. We shall accomplish nothing being four sheets to the winds."

"True, True," Geoffrey said as he drained his glass, "but it would have been so much more fun, you know, with the hair of the dog upon us."

The McKenzies and Townsands sat around the kitchen table drinking coffee and munching on toast, that Rachel had generously slavered with peanut butter and jelly.

"I'll have you know that this is my favorite food." Geoffrey said. "I'm completely sober. How about you all?"

Susan rose to refill their cups. "How do we plan to handle this matter?" She asked.

"No more coffee," Brian pleaded. "Or I'll be up all night. Do you all realize that we are sitting around speaking of things that are basically none of our business? The children, our grown children, are the ones to make what ever decision, and it is up to the four of us to accept it or not. But, and that is a big but, we cannot interfere or make it go one-way or the other. Just leave the kids alone unless they ask for our opinion. After all David found Jennifer and Sophia found…" He paused. "I don't even know his name…the hockey player."

"Fret not. Don't bother to memorize his name unless you are a big fan of hockey. Who knows if he shall ever make it to the big time." Rachel said.

"It's called the National Hockey League." Susan said. "That much I do know."

"No matter," Geoffrey said as he savored his treat on toast. "It probably, will all be moot and what was that song sung by Doris Day?"

"Que sera, sera," Susan responded. "And I guess that could go for all of us." Brian and Geoffrey looked at her quizzically.

"Did you all know that hockey gloves and other sport equipment are made right here on the island? Speaking of gloves, I had a friend who had a factory here, and initially had all-purpose white cotton gloves cut and sewn here on Barbados, but some of the workers, poor ignorant souls, would too often cut and sew six fingered gloves more or less. Hard to give up the cheap labor here, but he resorted to cutting the gloves in New England and then shipping them down here to be sewn. Worked out for the better. He also had a hot looking wife." Geoffrey said avoiding Rachel's glare.

"Whom you almost screwed, while he was trying to make me go down on him. I never asked you. Why didn't you do her? She was naked and on top of you?" Rachel asked.

"She was just too scared for me. I did not have the nerve to take advantage." Geoffrey responded. "Asked and answered."

"So. What happened?" Brian asked as both Rachel and Geoffrey glared at him.

Susan raised her coffee cup. "Let us just drink to our children. It is, after all, their happiness that is most important. And, Que sera, sera to the rest of us as well."

"Geoffrey, we must let these good people get some rest and we as well. Lot's to do and consider in the morning." Rachel said.

"You, Luv, have always been the sobering influence in this family, but you are correct and we must take our leave, for the morrow is yet another day."

Brian walked over to Geoffrey and gave him a hug. "Okay Shakespeare, get a good night's rest. Perhaps the kids have fewer problems than we all think." Geoffrey smiled and releasing his grip, moved over to embrace Susan.

"Next time in bed, I shall think differently of you, Luv." He whispered. "We might be related, you know."

"And I you, " Susan responded, "and I you, my Luv, as well, but with no less enthusiasm, of that you can be assured." She smiled and kissed him.

David and Sophia had to huddle together in order to speak, the pounding music from surround sound loud speakers making conversation difficult. "I think, that I have had enough to drink and we danced up a storm, so how about getting some quiet air?" David said, taking Sophia's hand.

"You will get no argument from me." Sophia responded. " I am game to blow this place off." The two left the disco and walked to the sea wall, where they could still hear the music, but were able to comfortably talk to each other.

"Truth be told," David said. "I can get all of the rock I want at home. I come here just to listen to calypso and can take all the Merrymen wish to dish out."

"They are a wonderful group. Daddy has had them to the house so I know them quite well. I particularly adore Chris. He is the tall one with the deep voice."

Sophia smiled. "In fact, I saw them in Toronto and Emil invited me to watch from backstage when they performed there."

"I love their music, Sophia, but what are we going to do?" David asked, as he embraced her.

"I am prepared to call my fiancé and tell him that the wedding is off without giving him a specific reason." Sophia said. "And you, David?"

"I have to call Jen and tell her not to come down, but it is only fair that I see her to tell her the real truth. And that is I have fallen in love with someone else. I owe her that." David said as he kissed Sophia.

"David, I must tell you something. I have been intimate before. I love you and it is important that I be completely honest." Sophia said.

"With him?" David asked.

"No. There was someone else here on the island. He was the son of a hotel owner and had a choice of rooms whenever he wanted the use of them. I got drunk and it just happened that one time with him. Are you terribly vexed with me?" She asked.

"No Darling, because I must admit that I was not a virgin in college. After my first time, I just wanted to try is out as often as possible. But when AIDS became an issue, I just stopped." David replied. "We, Sophia are starting anew with no recriminations or regrets. Right?"

"I did not love him. It just happened, and he was my first. If I was supposed to experience something earth shaking, it did not happen. The one other time in Canada was not more memorable. Do you remember the times and the women you were with?" She asked.

"Actually, not, because none had any meaning. I was just satisfying my own needs." He said.

"That, David, is the problem with most men." Sophia said sadly.

"I will guarantee you this, my darling, it will be different with us, because for my part, your needs will always come first." David answered.

Sophia continued to stare at the passing ships in the distance. "David, we have no motels on Barbados and I have no friends willing to provide a bed, or who will not run to gossip with their friends. I can satisfy you in other ways, David if you wish."

David took Sophia in his arms and they kissed, exploring each other's mouth with their tongues. "We'll find a way. Don't you worry."

Sophia began to laugh. "What is so funny?" David asked.

"I was just thinking about a time here on the island when I was only fourteen. My friend Charles was a few years older.

Anyway, Charles' Dad was part of a group that owned this once beautiful old hotel right on the beach in St. James. It was truly gorgeous, but as time went on, became seedy, needing many costly repairs. Ownership decided to turn the rooms that were quite spacious into condominium suites, so that all had beachfront views. Well, one week, royalty magically descended upon Barbados and the former Queen of some Middle Eastern country chose the hotel for her stay. There was a problem, however. Along the walkway that led to the lower suites, there was a frog pond. It seems that the lady was vexed by the noise of the croaking frogs and insisted that the pond be drained." She paused.

"And they really drained it?" David asked.

"Without question. She was a big spender and had a large entourage. And, Darling this is Barbados. Now Queeny was extremely horny and wanted some action during her stay. Actually from what I was told, horny was a mild description. So this boy I knew, in that way," She blushed, "and his friend who worked in the kitchen, were prepared to satisfy all of her needs.

There were some completed suites on the second floor of the first section near the dining area. So, she obliged them and they provided whatever she wanted, etcetera…"

"They sound like fun people whom I might like to meet." David said.

"Really! Well! The next morning, the owner was showing some prospective buyers some of the suites and came upon not one but three almost totally destroyed. The chandelier on one was dislodged from the ceiling. Bed linens were scattered and some of the lanai furniture had been thrown out and on to the beach. Of course, his son being suspect was called into the office, where he denied any knowledge of what happened. And the Queen, having had the sexual time of her life would say nothing other than she was prepared to book an entire building on her next visit."

"And the kitchen guy? David asked.

"Oh, he is a wonderful friend and now a great chef. He was never called to task. He lives in Canada and Charles lives in the States somewhere. We never kept in touch." Sophia said. "And there were many more escapades, if you wish to hear of them." Brian nodded.

"Well, there was an elderly British gentlemen who always occupied room 101 near the dining room. Sadly he had a respiratory issue that required the use of oxygen, and when he was at dinner, Charles would take hits off his tank to get high." She said. "And there is much more."

"Sophia, we had better save them til another time. It is one in the morning. What is your pleasure?" David asked.

"If you are hungry, for now I can be satisfied with some fried chicken. How about you? We can go down to Baxter's Road and Enid's. She makes the best chicken in the entire world."

"The car awaits us, my dear." David said with a mock bow. Enid's chicken, it is then."

They drove out of the car park and headed south down Highway One toward Bridgetown. Traffic was light at that time of the night, and soon they were parked on a small side street just off Baxter's Road directly across from their destination.

Sophia led David up four steps and into a small restaurant that had about six tables filled with local people. Sophia embraced a small black lady who immediately found an empty table, by sending its seated occupants into the back of the restaurant.

David took a chair across from a glass counter filled with an array of food, none of which he could relate to. "Sophia, what is that awful looking stuff?"

She looked at the counter and smiled. "Here in Barbados nothing goes to waste. If it is a pig, the entire animal is consumed from feet to head. Those are livers and the locals will have it on some kind of bread. Feet are pickled and quite good if you acquire a taste."

"Please, tell me that if we are to be married, it shall not be on the menu." David begged.

"Fear not," She advised. "I understand and will sacrifice."

"You cannot be serious. You like this stuff?" He asked.

Sophia kissed him oblivious of anyone else in the room. "I hate it. Don't fret. We shall dine on Enid's glorious fried chicken. Legs, thigh or breast?"

"Can I have all?" He asked with a smile.

"In due time, my darling. In due time. I fancy a rum and coke. How about you?" She said.

David agreed and attempting to avoid looking at the samples in the case, agreed to an order of chicken breasts. The first rum and coke went down smoothly as well as the second. "You realize," he said, "that most people get drunk from the sugar in the coke, rather than the rum, everything being equal. I have heard that in the islands, one who has too many rum and cokes should switch temporarily to beer and that awful feeling of lack of control disappears."

"That's nice. Eating your chicken with your hands is cool here. Plenty of napkins." She said as Enid placed two large pan fried chicken breasts on the table."

"Hope you likes garlic, cause I use plenty of it." Enid said.

"Enid, if it tastes as great as it smells, all the garlic you have used shall be just fine." David responded as Enid smiled broadly, showing her two lower gold incisors, the only teeth she had in her mouth.

David and Sophia finished all of the meat down to the bone. "I must agree that this is the best chicken I have ever had. What's the chance of you getting the recipe?" He asked.

"Fear not." She said. "That I got a long time ago. Mommy and Daddy have been coming here for years and if you ask your folks, I am certain they have been here more than once as well."

"What more can I ask from the woman who shall be my wife?" David said using a napkin to wipe his mouth.

"David, you have not yet asked me to be your wife, you know." Sophia said.

"Sophia, I am asking you now." David responded taking her hand. Enid listening and observing that David had no ring, rushed toward the counter and returned with a cigar from which she removed the wrapper.

"Would this work for you mistress?" Enid asked as she handed David a small paper ring that she had removed from the cigar.

David smiled as he took the paper ring and slid it up onto the third finger of Sophia's left hand. "Again, Sophia, I ask that you marry me."

Sophia began to cry. "Yes, David. With all my heart, I do love and want to marry you."

"We'd better start back to the house," he said. "It is almost four and the folks will be worrying." "They know I am with you. No worries, my dear." Sophia responded. They paid Enid's bill, thanked her for everything and promised that they would soon return. David ignored a bit of hassling from a few of the locals asking for money, and turned the car back toward Broad Street and the roads that would take them back to the Parishes of St. James, St. Peter, and their respective homes.

Twenty-four

Barbados 1991

The next morning, Brian and Susan drove down to Mullins, where they breakfasted on flying fish omelets dribbled with Patsy's hot sauce, and then settled down on comfortable beach chairs for a few hours of reading and conversation. Sophia had picked up David earlier in the Mercedes, planning to spend the day at the Crane, after they dropped Rachel and Geoffrey at the office in Fontabelle. After two hours, of oppressive heat and feet burning sand, the McKenzies elected to return to their air-conditioned villa, where Brian found a note from Braithwaite, that he was to call the office in NY. He dialed the number and asked to be connected to the comptroller, Gretchen Weatherhead, who informed him that he was needed back in New York for an emergency meeting. Brian listened for a few moments while Susan waited patiently to find out what was going on.

"Important Brian," Susan asked.

He shrugged. "Seems there has been a problem, serious enough to let people go." He responded. Susan frowned.

"No," he said reassuringly. "My job is not on the line. That Gretchen did assure me of upfront. I will have to catch the first flight back. Do me a favor Luv. Call the airline and see what might be available, while I run upstairs and toss a few things into a carryon. Anything else I might need, I'll pick up at the apartment."

Brian was fortunate to get a seat in first class on a 4 pm. flight to JFK and as Susan walked him to the departure lounge, she asked, "When do you expect to be back? I could come with you, you know."

Brian hugged and kissed her. "It shouldn't take too long, and why should you have to give up your vacation." He made sure he had his boarding pass and ticket ready for the guard at the gate. "I'll call you tonight, but probably not before ten, if the plane is on time. Look, Don't."

Susan looked at her husband. "Don't what Darling?"

"Nothing important. I had better go. Will talk to you later." With that he squeezed her hand, and passed through the security gate. Brian watched her wave, and walk toward the car park. He was annoyed with himself. He had planned to suggest that she not do something he wouldn't do, but knowing that it would only antagonize her, never completed the sentence.

Brian ordered a rum and coke, and once the aircraft had left the tarmac, selected steak and mashed potatoes from the First Class menu. He was concerned that Susan, now left on her own would indeed become part of a ménage de trois with Geoffrey and Rachel. The thought, that initially was exciting, made him exceedingly jealous.

Susan sat in the Rover for a few minutes before starting the engine. This would be the first time she would be in Barbados with the heat, rum, sun and sex and without Brian. She found it all very stimulating. She carefully maneuvered the truck out on to the main road and headed towards Bridgetown.

Her car phone rang just as she moved onto Spring Gardens Highway. She heard David's voice. " Hi Dad, we have a bit of a problem."

"Are you all right? It's Mom. I just put your father on a plane back to New York on an emergency of some sort. What's wrong? Are you all right?" She asked again.

"We are fine. Both of us, but w had a problem with the car. No accident, I can assure you." He said. Susan could hear Sophia's voice in the background.

"What happened to the car?" Susan asked.

"We can give you all of the gory details later. Sorry for that poor choice of words. In a nutshell, we tired of the Crane and drive up to Bathsheba, parked the car and went shelling. After a while, a Canadian couple came up to us and asked if we drove a Mercedes that they said had been vandalized. All of the damage was on the passenger side where someone smashed the window with a piece of coral. Thankfully, my passport and other essentials were under the driver's seat and never found. I wanted to leave it alone but Sophia insisted that we report the matter to the Belleplaine police, and that is when the idiocy really began."

"As long as you both are all right, the window can be replaced." Susan said. "Was anything stolen?"

"Sophia lost a camera and a shawl. Nothing more." David responded. "And all are replaceable."

"I'll come at once to get you." Susan said.

"No, we are not the issue. The car drives fine, but would you please go to Fontabelle and bring Geoffrey and Rachel home. That was to be our chore, but we will be much too late by the time we finish with the crack Belleplaine police." David said.

"The car drives fine, but if you could possible drive over to the office and fetch Rachel and Geoffrey, it would be a big help." David said.

"Not a problem, since I am on Spring Garden as we speak. I'll hit the roundabout and fetch or collect them, as we say in Barbados. As long as you two are safe." Susan said.

"Sophia says thank you Mom. And you all will be in for treat when we relate the rest of the adventure, and it is the most inane one I have ever experienced. Oops! Sophia gently smacked me stating, 'this is Barbados'".

"As long as you both are all right." Susan repeated. "I am almost at the office at Fontabelle, and will see you both back home shortly."

Both Rachel and Geoffrey were surprised to see Susan enter the office. "What a lovely place." She said.

"It was a home, then actually a lovely restaurant that we frequented in the 70s." Rachel said. "The food was gorgeous and we became friendly with the young couple who owned it. The free form seating was designed by her husband who was an architect."

"You must tell Susan about the fantastic bed, Luv." Geoffrey added, as he stapled some papers and tossed them into an empty tray.

"You would remember that!" Rachel admonished, and then turned to Susan. "They had a smashing home in St. John. It is quite a primitive area. We were invited to come for drinks one evening and shown around this wonderfully designed home. In the bedroom, mind you, huge ropes or hawsers suspended the king-size bed. Quite difficult to get into, I would imagine, but it struck Geoffrey's fancy as you can see."

"The sex must have been fantastic," Geoffrey said. "Decidedly acrobatic, putting the Kama Sutra to shame. I would think. Preceded the waterbed, you know. I can imagine the thrusting."

"Enough Geoffrey," Rachel admonished. "Susan, what brings you here?"

Susan briefly explained the call from David, and told Rachel and Geoffrey that she had come to fetch them. Geoffrey locked the front door.

"Love being fetched by such a fetching beauty," Geoffrey said as he opened the car door for Rachel who proceeded to jump into the passenger seat.

"Have a seat in the back Luv. You can ride in style, being fetched, or might it be slightly tetched, that is." Rachel said laughing, as Susan directed the Rover slowly back onto the highway.

"So," Geoffrey said from the rear. "What mischief have the children gotten into?"

Susan watched the rear view mirror, making sure it was safe and remembering to pass on the right. In no time they were on Highway One where traffic was still light. "Something about the car being broken into and having to deal with the local police." She said. "Passing a restaurant on the right with the name "The Rose and Crown".

Susan asked if they had ever eaten there. Rachel stated that it was real Barbadian and the menu featured local lobsters and a great old bartender, named Joe.

"They are both all right, yes?" Geoffrey asked.

"David assured me of that." Susan replied. "Said they would see us back home."

"Susan, what did you do with Brian?" Rachel asked.

"Oh, he received an urgent message this morning that he must return to New York. I am just coming from bringing him to Grantley Adams". Susan said. "Not certain when he will return. That is up in the air. And depends upon when whatever he is called upon to do for his company."

"Really," Geoffrey said. "I would suppose you must make the best of it."

"I suppose you are right." Susan said, abruptly hitting the brake to avoid a small donkey cart ambling over the road towards Payne's Bay. Geoffrey was thrown forward against the back of the front seat.

"Not hurt are you darlin?" Rachel asked. Geoffrey sat himself back and smoothed out his hair, but said nothing.

Susan watched the wall surrounding the Coach House flash by and again, remembered that it was the start of it all, that night a few years back.

She wondered what escapades now lay ahead for her. After all, when Geoffrey came to New York, Brian did not object to their ménage. She drove past the old Miramar Beach Hotel which was now covered with pink stucco, and whose name had been changed to the Royal Pavilion.

With no significant traffic on the highway, they easily passed through Holetown . "My villa or your Great House?" She asked. "David did not indicate where he would go."

"Might as well go to yours," Geoffrey said. "Time for drinks, you know." Geoffrey smiled as he envisioned the three of them in the mirrored bedroom, as Susan observed him in the rear view mirror.

"The Blue Heron it is," Susan said as she passed Mullins, now filled with the early evening mix of tourists and locals. "Do you two fancy a stop here for an adult beverage?"

"No," Geoffrey said, having fashioned other plans in his head. "You have plenty of rum and what ever at home. Anyway, it looks too crowded here and more beach bums than I would like. Tell me, what plans do David and Sophia have for the evening?"

Reaching the gated Blue Heron, Susan said. "Have not a clue, Geoffrey, and be a Luv and get out and open our gate. It is just latched."

After he exited the Rover, Susan turned to Rachel and squeezed her hand. "What do you think our lover has planned?"

Rachel watched her husband move the gate. "We had better take it by the minute. Understand there is no obligation to succumb to his whims. That is, of course unless, you wish to. I worry, what Brian might think." She said.

"True. True. Let's deal with whatever, when we must. Brian is another story. Best I not go into much detail right now. Geoffrey, you have returned from your mission, so do get back in." Susan parked the car near the villa as Braithwaite greeted them at the door.

"Mr. Brian had to leave I see. I did set up some ice on the wet bar and have some as you call them "pigs in the blanket" in the freezer if you wish." Samuel Braithwaite said.

"What an exquisite idea. Why don't you nuke the pigs or whatever, and please a little hot sauce as well as mustard, and I shall tend to drinks for the ladies." Geoffrey clapped his hands and moved down the hall toward the back of the house.

Susan called after Braithwaite. "After you take care of that detail, you may leave for the night if you wish, and please leave the gate ajar for David. We expect him soon, and thank you."

The three settled down on the soft patio chairs. Geoffrey had poured two straight rums for Susan and himself, and a rum and coke for Rachel. They had not started on the second pouring when David and Sophia arrived.

"Started without us I see." David said in jest. Sophia laughed as she took a sip of Rachel's drink and made a face.

"Too sweet. Much too sweet Daddy, if I may I would rather some Sugar Cane Brandy and soda, that is if you have it Susan." Susan had not quite gotten used to a potential daughter-in-law calling her anything other than Mom, but did not object.

"There is soda in the fridge and I remember getting at least two bottles of Sugar Cane Brandy from the Super Centre." Susan said.

"She has acquired a taste for that." David said, looking at Sophia. "I can get it. You all just sit. Sophia why don't you begin to tell of our extraordinary experience and I'll fill in when I return."

Sophia settled back in her chair. "Well, we went first to the Crane, which was just beautiful and served a great lunch, but I could not feature walking all the way down those steps, there must have been a thousand of them, to the beach."

"We found a road that would lead us past Coddrington College and found our way quite near to Three Boys Rock in Bathsheba. The ocean was a bit rough, so I convinced David to drive up and around the Round House, then back onto the East Coast road where we found a place to park just above the beach. It was not too far from Barclay's Park, you know. We locked the car. No, Daddy, I forgot to put valuables in the boot, and went down to the beach, where we had just a wonderful time shelling, sitting in the small wading pools, and being with each other."

David returned with a fresh bottle of soda and prepared Sophia's drink. "Did you get to the good part yet, Luv?" He asked her.

"No, David. You will tell it so much better," She said.

"Not necessarily TRUE, TRUE as you have taught me my darling but I shall give it a go. Interrupt at any time to correct. Please." He said as he poured himself a glass of rum neat.

"Cheers!" David said as he took a swig of the amber liquid. "Okay, we parked, went down to the beach and just were so excited being with each other that time past quickly. We shelled, but Sophia probably has gone over that already."

This couple came up to us and asked if our car was parked up above near the road. They had parked alongside and noticed that the driver's side window had been exploded inward. Since we were the only people on the beach they surmised that it might be our car."

Geoffrey rose and offered to refill Rachel and Susan's glasses but they both declined. He shrugged, refilled his glass and resumed his seat.

Sophia sipped her drink. "So David and I went back to the car and found that it had been truly broken into. There was glass all over the inside, and the intruders took my bag and camera but did not look under the driver's seat where David had placed credit cards and all of the important stuff." She looked at David, who continued for her.

"I was willing to chalk it up to a robbery where nothing of real value was taken, but my darling here insisted we report it to the local police. That was our first mistake. What happened next should be on every 'how not to conduct a police investigation video.' I drove to the Belleplaine police station and attempted to make a report. The young clerk took down our information and when I asked for a copy, he said 'you means I have to write this down twice'? That was our first clue we were in trouble."

"Someone then with a police cap and baton, took me first to be interviewed. He wrote what I told him on the back of an envelope since that was all that was available. Then it was Sophia's turn. Constantly distracted by cars and roving chickens, he asked the same questions over and over again."

"Finally, he drove with both of us forced to sit in the back of the paddy wagon, to the crime scene, where I proved to be of more help when I found Sophia's bag in the bush along the road. It was empty."

"So typical of Barbados," Rachel said. "Then what?"

"We signed the complaint and went on our way." Sophia said.

"Then," David said. "Realizing that a broken window would not be too cool with sudden heavy downpours here, I drove down to Holetown, and found a mechanic in the petrol station across from the police station." David started to laugh. "I showed him the broken window and he scratched his head and told me to drive off and he would take care of it. Then I suggested that he might want to measure the window for size. Apparently he thought it a good idea since he took both hands without a ruler, and made some vague determination of window size appropriate for the Mercedes."

David laughed again, then went on with his story. "I no longer had any sense for arguing with these people, and after having the window covered with plastic, we returned to Blue Heron and here we are. I'll have another rum, neat, thank you, Geoffrey."

Geoffrey over walked to the wet bar. "That man is a bloody fool! And ignorant as well!"

"Mommy," Sophia said. "David has been absolutely grand." She looked at her watch. "I must have a shower and change. We are going down to the south coast for dinner. I hope no one is offended but we wish to spend more time together. David, seven is good for you? Yes?" David nodded.

"Let the kids do their thing." Geoffrey said. "I can go get dinner, or we can sup at some restaurant if you wish."

"I appreciate the offer of the former, but there will be clean up afterwards in any event. David and Sophia have made plans, so we should as well. Rachel, a suggestion?" Susan asked.

"A strange chap named Trevor Hunte, has a restaurant in Speightstown, called The Golden Apple that has good local food. How about that?" Rachel asked.

"I am game," Susan said, "as long as I don't have to do dishes."

"My treat. Never fear. And the food is quite good. Then this is the plan." Geoffrey said. "We have dinner there, and afterwards repair here to the Blue Heron for fun and games. I would doubt if the children would be back early, considering how they looked at each other. Like it or not, My Dears, we are about to be related in a much unexpected way."

"I am in desperate need of a shower." Susan said.

"What a wonderful idea," Geoffrey said. "May Rachel and I join you?"

"Hush yourself! Husband. The children." Rachel admonished. Fortunate for him, David and Sophia had gone into house out of earshot, and were busily picking through a pile of CDs.

"Geoffrey, we do not have a change of clothes. Why don't we take Sophia and the Mercedes home. Both have had a trying day. Right?" Rachel got up and motioned to Geoffrey to do as well.

Geoffrey went into the house and put his arm around Sophia. "You do, Darling, have plans for the evening? Right?" Sophia nodded and Geoffrey sighed with relief.

"Grand. We'll take you back home to bathe or whatever and David can pick you up in the Rover. It after all, has all of its windows intact. We will come back in the Mercedes. It's only a short drive to Speightstown."

Twenty-five

Barbados 1991

Sophia guided David down Broad Street in Bridgetown, across the modern replacement for the Old Indian Bridge and past the ancient building which still served as a movie theater. "Disgusting place!" Sophia said. "The low life think nothing of peeing in coke bottles and rolling them down the floor under the seats."

"That must smell horrific." David said, as he made the left turn onto the road that led to the south coast of the island.

"You won't ever find me there again. That smell will never go away." She looked out her window. "Look, David, your president Washington stayed here with his brother when the latter was recovering from tuberculosis. That building right there."

"Hey! Lots of activity in that place with the upstairs balcony all lit up." David said. "I hear music."

"It's the Belair jazz club. Used to be a hangout for locals Twenty-five and older, whores and musicians. My friend Charles, he would dress up as Jesus Christ himself, and sic whores on unsuspecting tourists, just for the fun of it. Daddy spent a lot of time there. I hope, just listening to the music."

"The building located just before it was Harry's Nitery. The Queen called Harry a man of ill repute. It was a whorehouse with a show. Now that I think about it I wonder if the Queen or Phillip had ever been there for a performance. A friend of Daddy's from the states, New York I believe, had the gall to commend Harry on a great show one time. I shall tell you more later of what I overheard Daddy tell Mommy one night when he attended a stag bachelor party there. People would spend time at Harry's, and then go next door to the Belair for drinks and the music."

They drove past a large one story building on the beach side, arrayed in multicolored lights. The sound of rock music shattered the quiet of the evening. "That looks like a rocking place. Why don't we go there?" Luv.

"That's the second time you called me that and I do like it. It is very Bajan. That is the CARLISLE disco. Lots of locals and tourists hang out. Mostly young people, too young to be sold liquor, but the police look the other way. This is Barbados, you know." Sophia snuggled close to David and he put his arm around her. "David, that scent your wearing smells like something Daddy has used."

"It is called Old Spice after shave. I found it in Dad's bathroom. Strange, that I never saw it before. Certainly not at home in New York. I like the smell." David said as Sophia kissed his cheek.

"I love it. And when Daddy wears it, and you are not right near me, it will always remind me of you and how I feel, David."

"Sophia, I shall always be either right near you, or not too far away." David said.

Sophia smiled. "That's the power and light building. The road just winds around it. Soon we will be at David's Restaurant. We must pass through Accra Beach area. Many tourists come here because hotels and rentals are much less expensive than on the west coast. Also true of the East Coast, but this area is far more the place to be. Mommy and Daddy's friends used have what we call fetes here, like for Valentines Day and such. Just another excuse to have a party and dance, mind you. I do like Bathsheba far better though."

"I would love to have a place on the Atlantic." David said.

"Oh, we had a home there at one time. It lay just at the base of the great chalk cliffs, but some crazed arsonist burned most of the homes along the road. I would think this is not the time to rebuild. But, it was just glorious to awaken in the morning, watch the sun rise over the Atlantic, and then walk down to the beach to allow the warm sand sift between our toes. When we returned, Grandma would have eggs and bacon cooking for breakfast. It smelled just gorgeous."

"Tell me about your Grandma and Grandpa." David said.

"Turn into the car park, David. We are across from the restaurant. We can talk more about family during dinner."

They crossed over the road and entered the restaurant via a short down flight of stairs, and were immediately met at the door, by a man who identified himself as the owner, David. "My name as well and a great one at that." David McKenzie said offering his hand.

Sophia made a point of telling him that Geoffrey was her father. "No matter, my dear. We shall treat you as royalty, never the less." The elder David responded with a smile. "Come. I shall offer you the best table in the house." He led them to a table that faced the expansive beach. It had one small candle for illumination. David McKenzie took pains to seat Sophia, who thanked him with a kiss on his cheek.

"Sweet. Sweet, my Luv," she said.

The tide was out, but the moonlight and neon lights from restaurants and discos along the road, lit up a beach that seemed to go on forever into the Caribbean. From their table, they had a wonderful view of St. Lawrence Gap and all of its bistros. "What's the Witch Doctor all about?" David asked, seeing a sign in the distance.

"Another night spot. I haven't been there in ages." Sophia said. There are all kinds of interesting places along the road. We have lots of time to explore."

"A life time, my darling." David said, as a waiter appeared to take their drink order.

"I would prefer some wine." Sophia said. David suggested a cooled pinot grigio. He had to admit that the year did not matter and explained to Sophia that wine was not his area of expertise.

"No matter. I never believed that fitting food to wine was any more than a hype from the wine industry." She said, taking his hand. "You cannot believe that I have not been more happy having met you, David." She said.

"It is absolutely amazing. I feel the same way." David responded, as the waiter had him check the bottle, and then poured a small amount in his glass.

David tasted the liquid and smiled with an acceptance that pleased the waiter, who half filled their glasses, and then placed the bottle in nearby ice bucket.

Their waiter returned to take their food order, and went through a memorized list of specials, but David asked Sophia to order for both of them.

"Let me see," she said scanning the menu. "We will have the pumpkin soup which I understand is gorgeous, and, I will have a green salad, and." She thought for a moment. "The dolphin, Bajan style. That shall do it for me."

David concentrated on the menu. "I was thinking of the steak," but when he saw Sophia shake her head, said, "Pumpkin soup, salad, steak fish and whatever veggies come with it. And I want the steak fish, bajan style." He looked at Sophia. What did I just order?"

"Not to worry," she said. "In New York you order steak. Here in Barbados, enjoy the fresh fish. The steak fish is probably a fantastic mackerel caught barely hours ago. You will love it and bajan style is the gorgeous spices it will absorb. The wine is perfect and you are perfect. You are my best of Barbados, and more than I anticipated when I decided to take a holiday from Canada."

"To you, Darling Sophia," Brian said as he clinked his glass with hers, "and to Barbados, a place that made all of this possible. "God, I love you!"

They were too full to even look at the dessert menu. David, the owner came by to make sure that everything had been to their satisfaction. Both David and Sophia assured him that it was one of the best dinners they had had on the island.

Despite the offer of an after dinner drink 'on the house' David thanked him, but declined. "We must have our wits about us and would like to take a walk, but thank you never the less for your kind offer.

David used a credit car to pay the bill, and they left the restaurant, and walked to the right down St. Laurence Gap, a long winding road that was packed with young men holding bottles of beer, trying to chat up any single women they found moving among the happy crowd.

"Sophia, I have to tell you that this scene is not for me. Why don't we drive back to the Carlisle and go dancing?" David said.

"I would really like that, David. I cannot relate to this scene at all either." She responded.

They walked back to the car and as he opened the door for her, David turned her and kissed her as hard as she would allow. "You cannot imagine what meeting and being with you means to me. You are so special to me." David said.

They drove back toward Bridgetown, silently. When David drove into the Carlisle car park, Sophia took his hand before he reached to open his door. "David. Could we just sit and talk for a bit?" She asked.

"Of course. We have all the time in the world." David responded. "You look troubled. What is it?"

"There is more about me that I must share with you. Before my fiancé and I met, I shared an apartment with a boy for a brief time. Money was tight and it made sense to do so. However, our relationship became more serious and we did sleep together. It did not work out and I moved out. And after getting job as a waitress, I earned enough for my own flat." David started to say something. "Wait, David and let me finish. Just leaving Barbados as a virgin is a great accomplishment for any young Bajan woman. I never told my fiancé about any of the men, and put him off time and time again, because I was ashamed and worried about what he would say. And now that I have told you absolutely everything, I am afraid about what you think of me."

"Come. I want to dance with my future bride." Sophia began to cry, "Look, if it will make you feel any better. Jennifer and I did have sex, but she didn't seem into it. I had great concerns that she never would, and intimacy, I feel is important in a marriage."

Sophia smiled. "Well, now that most of our secrets have been aired, let's dance and make the most of the evening. The music blared as the two walked, hand in hand toward the entrance.

The Golden Apple was not busy at all by Barbados standards. Since it was close to the beach you could hear the sounds of the waves and smell the brine from the dark Caribbean.

When Geoffrey, Rachel and Susan entered, a tall man who sported a small thin mustache met them at the door and seated them. He went over the list of specials on the menus and took drink orders. Rachel asked for her usual rum and coke while both Susan and Geoffrey opted for sugar cane brandy and soda.

"You know it is not real brandy, but I favor it at times never the less," Geoffrey offered.

"Geoffrey, we have heard that tale already. Give us something more recent, if you will." Rachel said.

"All right." Geoffrey drank half of his glass, "Rachel, my Luv, did you know that Trevor Hunte, here was just released from the prison or gaol as we used to call it?" He smiled and finished what was left in his glass.

"Really"" Susan said. "What had he been held there for?"

"Oh, something minor," He said as he gestured for Trevor to bring another round. "It seems he was accused of murdering his wife and chopping her up into little pieces."

"My God! Geoffrey!" Susan said. "Is this true?"

"From what I understand." Geoffrey said as Trevor returned with a tray of drinks. "Trevor my man, perhaps you should go over the specials again. Might you have charcuterie tonight?"

Just as Geoffrey spoke, Rachel kicked his shin, but the sound of things crashing down upon the tin roof above their heads drowned out his cry of pain.

"Those would be the golden apples. We have a tree just above the roof and when they fall they create quite a disturbance, and fall they will. Scares the life out of them that do not know." Trevor smiled. He was missing two upper teeth. "No charcuterie. Are you ready to order?"

Susan did not know what to say. Rachel ordered shrimp over pasta.

"Make a choice Luv the food is all good, and Trevor does not do any of the cooking. Right?" Trevor Hunte smiled as Susan ordered steak fish, bajan style and plantains. "Right! I shall have the same and bring lots of hot sauce."

The three ordered more drinks, found the food to be excellent, refused dessert, but allowed Geoffrey to order brandies all around.

When they left the restaurant, Susan asked Geoffrey. "You were skylarking about Trevor Hunte being a wife murderer. Right?"

"Actually not, and his defense was that she fell down a flight of stairs. He had an excellent barrister. Okay, it is early and the kids will be home late, I trust. What shall we do for fun?" He said.

"Probably nothing that would meet your expectations." Rachel said.

"It is a warm night." Susan said. "Come back to the house and we could go for a swim."

"That will only lead to trouble, Susan." Rachel said.

Geoffrey frowned, "What a wonderful idea, unless you two would rather go bar hopping. Why don't we drive down to the Coach House for drinks?" Susan wondered what Brian was up to in New York.

After an hour of dancing, David and Sophia decided to leave the disco. "Sophia," David exclaimed as he opened the car door for her, "You still move like a Bajan. I can never get all of the needed parts of my body to move sequentially."

Sophia sat back in the car seat. "David, I shall teach you all of the moves that you wish to be taught." David pulled her close to him and hugged her until she cried out for air. "Sequentially? Too words in your vocabulary. I come from a small Caribbean Island, after all.

"How about, I love you. No, I adore you and wish not to be separated from you for one moment. Translate that into Bajan if you can." David said.

"In any language, it means the same. How can I prove to you that I feel the same way?" Sophia responded.

"Well," David answered.

"David, I have had this conversation with myself over and over since I met you. What I wish, My Darling and what I do believe best is to hold off on intercourse. I am so afraid of cheapening our relationship."

Sophia thought for a moment. "Is it old fashioned, considering what I have told you? I suppose it may be just that. I so much wish to make a fresh start so what ever vows we would express at our wedding, will be me meaningful."

David turned the key in the ignition. "I shall do the best I can under the circumstances…" He said.

"But, my Luv, and you are my love. There are ways to keep both of us avoiding that frustration driving us to the point of insanity." Sophia said.

"Gotcha!" David said as he took her hand.

"And besides, there are no motels on this island, and we shall have to regard the feelings of our parents." She said.

"Right!" David said as he nosed the car out onto the roadway. "What was it that you wanted to tell me about that Harry place?" He said as he passed the building that once housed Harry's Nitery.

Geoffrey, Rachel and Susan spent a good hour at the Coach House, where they drank many rum and cokes with friends, and people they had met for the first time.

Geoffrey suddenly decided it was time to change venue. "Time to move on My Dears. There are more bars to be had and new friends to be made."

He paid the bar bill and ushered Rachel and Susan back to the car park. "I have a grand idea." He said. "Susan, you have yet to enjoy what the Bagatelle has to offer."

"Great idea. I just love the look of that old place." Rachel said. "Susan. You game for whatever?"

"I have come with you all so far. Why not?" She responded. All three of them had not surrendered their glasses back to the Coach House bar. "Oh Geoffrey, I do suppose I should return my glass."

"Utter nonsense!" He exclaimed. "In Barbados, we, well I, will have our glasses refilled at the next pub and so on and so forth. That is how we will do it."

"Is this history revisited?" Susan asked.

Rachel looked at Susan. "Trust me. He is making all of it up. But, to tell you the truth, I am game and you?"

"May the devil do all of us in," Susan said. "Carry on." She looked at her watch. The time in Barbados was one a.m., the same for New York and Brian.

The Bagatelle, a wonderful old manor that once served as the Governor's residence, was rather quiet. Geoffrey ordered straight rum for the three of them, left the empty glasses at the bar, and after paying the bill guided them out to the exit, each carrying a new glass of rum, and toward the car park where two enormous gates served as protection when the restaurant was closed.

"Once," he said, "Two of us closed those big gates and it took all of the strength we had. Just as a lark, mind you. We took our glasses to our next port of call, so to speak. Actually, we ran like the dickens because people could not get in or out."

The three made their final drink stop at John Moore's, a bar that catered to mostly local people. It was on the seaside in St. James, small but with a welcoming atmosphere from the proprietor and those that remained to drink despite the lateness of the hour.

Susan had enough to drink, and while feeling some guilt about her husband, wanted to know where David and Sophia might be.

"Hey! Guys! This has been terrific and I thank you for dinner, but I have go to get to bed." She said.

"Not to worry," Rachel answered. "We all have had a great time, and all good things must come to an end." She looked at a crestfallen Geoffrey. "That is with the understanding that tomorrow is another day."

Somewhat comforted, Geoffrey nodded in agreement and steered the Mercedes up Highway One toward St. Peters Parish and Blue Heron Villa. When Susan entered Blue Heron, she saw the clock flashing and knew that there had been a power outage. She went directly up to the bedroom, unaware of Brian's fax.

Dear Susan,

If you do not already know this, I do love you so much, but felt the need to again say it. I arrived from Barbados without incident, except for circling Boston for an hour or so due to congestion at JFK. I know, it might make me appear a fool, for saying over and over again how much I love you, but perhaps, there might be some justification in view of the fact that our recurrent behavior just amplifies my concerns. That is the question. What are my real concerns? Could they be guilt, remorse or just plain jealousy? We have both accepted the responsibility for forgoing our marriage vows when we chose sexual escapades with others, while hoping that they would not adversely affect our own relationship. We have called it a lark, something that would go no further but it has. You know that I had reservations from the beginning. I must confess that I am concerned that your relationship with Geoffrey might be more meaningful to you, than mine with Rachel, and this disturbs me. In any event, the bad news is that the possible misuse of funds by company executives could necessitate my remaining here for at best ten days, but I'll try not to let that happen. In the event, I might not be able to come back to the island, could you possibly return to NY earlier than planned? I feel that under the circumstances, we both must discuss what we expect of each other in regard to our marriage. Again, I hope all of the company issues are resolved quickly. Will fax this to the villa.

Luv you ,

B

Twenty-six

Barbados   1991

David eased the car up the long driveway that lead to Simonton Great House but stopped well before the entrance.

"So, My Luv," he said as he drew Sophia close to him. "You had a story to tell about that Harry place."

"You must promise never ever to tell anyone." She said.

"You have my word, and undivided attention." David said as he kissed her.

"Well," Sophia began, "One of Daddy's best friends, who was a chef at a hotel on the beach in St. James Parish." She paused. "I know of this because one night I was going down the stairs for some water, when Daddy came home quite drunk and Mommy was so vexed. She sat him down on the sofa and made him drink a beer, the local treatment for intoxication. I just sat on the upper steps where I could hear everything and waited until Daddy felt better."

David squeezed her hand." I understand, and your point is what?" He asked.

"Patience, My Luv." Sophia said. "It appear that Daddy and a group of his friends had arranged a stag party for Richard Weathers, who was to be married, and all of them went first to a place called the Zanzibar. You know of course they all had quite a bit to drink before they arrived and were three sheets to the wind. You do understand that, David?"

"Got the meaning, so what next?" David asked.

"One had to walk up about forty narrow steep steps to get to the bar which was located on the second floor." She said.

"Luv. How do you know how many steps there were?" David asked with a smile.

"So I have heard. Let me finish."

"We have many cousins on the island who are full of pranks. You must understand that the bar was a place where men of uh, need made connections with women willing to fulfill their need." She said. "They wanted to get laid."

"It was essentially a whore house?" David said.

"Not exactly." Sophia offered. "It was a meeting place. What one did and where one did it was another concern. I did tell you that we had nothing resembling a motel on the island."

"Sadly, you did," David responded. "Go on."

"Cousin Martin tried to sic this woman on Daddy but he thought better of it, and told her that another cousin had designs on her. Then he made his escape down the stairwell to the street where he met up with others who had escaped as well. Daddy said that the next venue was Harry's Nitery not far away, and the group marched in that direction."

"We passed that place earlier, but it was closed." David said.

"Definitely!" Sophia responded. "But that night it certainly was open to Daddy's exclusive party to commemorate Richard's last night of freedom."

"Is that how everyone on the island views marriage?" David asked.

"No! And I would certainly hope that would not be true of you." Sophia said. "One man and one woman. That is what I would expect and hope will never be changed."

"What happened at Harry's?" David asked.

Sophia started to laugh. "Daddy had sobered up. He said that all of the boys went up into Harry's and sat down in sort of a circle. And then some scantily clad women came out with a mattress that was placed on the floor. Drink orders were taken and about five new women appeared and moved seductively into the laps of my father and cousins willing to partake of what ever. Someone called for a volunteer and cousin Steven quickly removed his shirt and pants, standing only in a pair of briefs, encircled by a gun holster. This, he had to give up, which he did. But he gave the gun to another cousin whom Daddy knew was high on pot. Daddy quickly retrieved the weapon and the party continued. The whole thing lasted just minutes and cousin Steven did not score and had to pay for the rum and coke brought to him. Daddy said that he was so vexed, he refused to pay for it."

"Does not sound very sexual to me." David said.

"Apparently, it was not and no one really cared. They went on to Enid's. We went there earlier. You do remember?" Sophia asked.

"Sophia, I remember every moment I have spent with you." David said.

Sophia looked at David and smiled. "Well, at Enid's, it was crowded so Enid, bless her soul, showed the group to the back room to tables near the toilets. They were so drunk they did not even notice the smell, and Enid's chicken would overcome any adversity. The chairs were of metal and sort of concave. When one went to the John, someone would fill his seat with beer and what a surprise when that person returned and sat down. Apparently there was a fight with some locals and Daddy did pay that bill as well as many others. The good news is that the bride and groom did marry and still are together."

David looked at Sophia. "What I take from all of this is that your family would do any thing for each other protecting them from any harm. I do appreciate that."

"Mommy put Daddy to bed that night, made certain that all of the doors were secure and lay down beside him, happy that no harm had befallen him. That's just the way, we Bajan's are, David."

"Wonderful. There is no other way I can express my feelings." He said. "Now What?" He asked.

"Now, you be a good person and I shall be as well. Do drive carefully back to Blue Heron. I look forward to seeing you tomorrow." Sophia kissed David, exited the car and went into the Great House.

When David reached Blue Heron, he found that Susan had already gone to bed. Not ready to retire, he went out on the patio and poured himself a drink, and was ready to sit and enjoy the cool breeze blowing in from the sea when he noticed that papers had fallen to the floor from the fax machine. He took the fax back out to the patio and slumped down into a chair. David read and reread the letter from his father, unable to fully comprehend what he was reading. He walked down to the beach, tore the paper into shreds and threw them into the sea, not certain if he was ever going to tell them what he now knew. Complicating matters was the fact that his loving mother had a sexual relationship with the man who would be his father-in-law, not to mention Brian's relationship with Sophia's mother. He was determined to keep the matter a secret from Sophia, at least for the time being. However, he was prepared to confront both of his parents when the time seemed appropriate.

Twenty-seven

New York City, Barbados

Brian sat for three hours with the CEO, the CFO and the marketing manager; half listening to each of them as they droned on, while wondering what Susan might be doing in Barbados. He was startled when Warren Schultz, the CEO asked for his opinion, but quickly gathering his thoughts, he presented them clearly and concisely. It was determined on audit no fraud had been committed but some of the higher echelon had overspent on things that were not business related. It was ultimately decided that no heads would roll, but every employees' expense account would be carefully reviewed. Schultz thanked Brian for coming back to New York at such short notice, and told him to take another week in Barbados for his effort. Since it was already three in the afternoon, and too late to catch the afternoon plane to Barbados, Brian made plans to be on the morning American airline flight that would get him there by four in the afternoon.

The flight to Barbados left JFK and reached the island fifteen minutes ahead of schedule. Since he had only his carry-on, Brian breezed through customs, and while waiting in line for a taxi, heard a familiar voice calling his name.

Joey stood across the road in the parking lot, flashing his toothy smile and beckoning to him. As it turned out, Joey had just dropped off his latest girl friend, now en route to St. Lucia, and offered to drive Brian back to St. Peter parish and Blue Heron.

When he reached the villa, he found Samuel collecting ripe paw paws from a tree that had been planted just six months before. He told Brian that Susan and David had left early in the morning, and had not yet returned. Brian changed into swim trunks and headed for the beach. A strong swimmer, he quickly reached the float that had been set out a few hundred yards from shore, for guests of the nearby villas. He pulled himself up and found a bikini clad young woman sunning herself on one of the benches.

"Hi, sorry to intrude on your sun." He said as he cleared his eyes and his hair of salt water.

"Plenty enough for both of us," she said, pushing herself up to a half sitting position, removing her Foster Grants. "I'm Jessica, and who are you?"

Brian looked at her perfect body and blushed. "Brian, uh, that's me and I am staying at Blue Heron."

"Oh, I believe I saw a beautiful woman on the beach the other day sunning in front of the villa. Is she your wife?" Jessica asked.

"Yes. That would be Susan, and she is beautiful." Brian agreed. "And who are you visiting here in Barbados?"

"No one." She responded. "My parents own our villa, High Tide. I was able to take time off, and decided to spend it here in the Caribbean. This is my first time. How about you?"

Brian looked at the young woman, decided she was in her late 20's, and wondered why one so young and beautiful would have come alone to the island. "We have been coming here for a number of years and love this island. I notice that you have a healing scar on your leg. What happened?"

Jessica rubbed the area on her left leg, and frowned. "My boyfriend and I had decided to motorcycle to the Hamptons' a few weekends ago, and he had the bike at a speed not compatible with the sand we rode on, so we skidded and crashed. Fortunately, we both wore helmets and the worst thing that happened was the burn here on my leg. It's healing nicely, as you can see."

"And the boyfriend?" Brian asked.

"He was not hurt and is cooling his heels back in New Jersey, while I rethink the relationship. Hey! I have told you a lot for some one I just met." She blushed.

"It has always been said that I am easy to talk to." Brian responded.

"I see that you are." She stood, her bikini hiding little of her exquisite figure, and then suddenly dove into the turquoise water. Brian watched her swim back to shore and dived in after her. He reached the beach just as she exited, and started to walk toward her villa. Brian found himself with an erection that would have been much too obvious if he left the water. "Coming out, Brian?" Jessica asked as she turned back toward him.

He sputtered, having swallowed some water from a new wave. "I'll just swim for a bit." He gurgled.

"How about coming over for cocktails at six?" She called back as she moved seductively up the steps that led to her patio. "I don't take no for an answer, you know."

Brian moved effortlessly back out toward the wooden float, hung ten, and then swam back to shore. He repeated the process a number of times, aware that Jessica was watching him from her patio.

He was so worried about what Susan might be doing with Geoffrey, and here he was about to have drinks with a beautiful and amazingly seductive woman. That is unless, Susan returned from what ever she was doing early.

For the moment, Brian rationalized that what they had all done could be interpreted as an extention of sexual freedom for him, and Susan had no idea that he had returned to the island.

He remembered the fax he had sent to Susan, and regretted that he had sent it. Just another issue he would have to deal with, but he was now emotionally torn by a double standard. When he was able to leave the water and return to Blue Heron, he found that Samuel Braithwaite had already left. Brian removed his bathing suit in the bedroom and viewed his multiple images in the mirrors. He flexed his biceps and concluded that he was still a handsome, muscular, desirable man, and envisioned Jessica visually enjoying every possible sexual position by virtue of the mirrored ceiling.

He shaved, showered and dressed in white slacks, white shoes and a black linen shirt. After a quick spray of after-shave, he went out toward the beach and sprinted to the adjoining villa.

When he reached the patio, Brian found Jessica attired in white slacks and black low cut sheer blouse that showed her unencumbered breasts to their best advantage. Her straight blonde hair fell softly on deeply tanned shoulders.

"How interesting?" She said, noting his choice of colors. "Were you watching me dress, Brian, or is this just a coincidence?"

"Pure coincidence, but do not tempt me." He said. "We just like the same choice of costume for cocktail hour."

"Pick your poison," Jessica said as she pointed toward the wet bar.

"I would like Mount Gay rum, neat and sans ice." Brian said. "And what would be your preference, Jessica?"

"Ah, I will have the same, since you seem to know the island and its liquor." Jessica answered as she approached him. "Where is your wife this afternoon?"

"Susan apparently has not returned from what ever escapade she is enjoying. Nor has David, who more than likely is with Sophia. Actually, no one knows I am back." Brian answered.

"David? Who is David?" She asked.

"David is my son." Brian said.

"Ah and how old is David?" She asked.

"David is old enough to have a fiancé and her name is Sophia. She is the daughter of great friends, Bajans here on the island." He said.

"And you are old enough to have a wife, and," she paused, "and to be here with me having cocktails without her." Jessica smiled. "Fancy some music?"

She held her glass out to him for a refill. "The rum is rather strong, you know." He advised.

Jessica smiled. "I have been known to never had a problem holding my liquor." It sounded as if she pronounced it likker.

"I like the Merrymen if you have their music." Brian said as he gulped his drink. He wasn't sure of the meaning of her last comment.

Jessica looked though some tapes and held one up. "You are in luck," she said.

As the strains of Beautiful Barbados filled the patio, Jessica moved toward him. "Dance?"

Brian took her in his arms and the two moved gracefully across the smooth patio blocks. She pressed her breasts into his chest and he again felt stirring in his loins. Despite this he did not release his hold as the music moved on to Hot Hot Hot, where she moved away and swayed in a manner that suggested her legs were not attached to her upper torso.

"Where did you learn to dance like a Bajan?" He asked.

"From the disco in Holetown. It is amazing whom you can meet and what you can learn." The tape ended. "You now have lights on in your villa. Your family has returned." She smiled. "Perhaps it is best you do as well. I have enjoyed you Brian, and would like to enjoy you much more. I plan to stay at least for another week."

Brian kissed her softly on her lips. "I would like you to meet Susan. You would really like each other." He said. "We shall all have dinner together."

"I look forward to that, Brian. I really do. Best you go see what your family is about." She said, kissing him again.

Brian, reluctantly released Jessica, and moved down the steps toward Blue Heron and Susan. He wondered how she would greet him, considering the nature of the fax he had sent.

Brian found Susan pouring herself a drink. She was dressed in a bikini top that left little to the imagination and a thong bottom he had not seen since the Grenadine trip. "You are sexy as hell! I do remember that thong. Where have you been?"

Susan, startled, almost dropped her drink. "Brian, what are you doing here? And unexpectedly, at that?"

"Obviously," He said. "I have been here since five. And you?"

"David, Sophia and I have spent the day on the East Coast at Barclay's. We had lunch at the Kingsley Club and then just tooled around the island. Did all go well in New York?"

"Yes. About my fax," Brian said.

"I did not get a fax, Brian. What was it all about? You are dressed very nice, and smell wonderful. Where have you just come from?" She asked.

Brian thought for a moment, thinking the fax never reached the villa. "Dressed for you, my darling but I met our neighbor earlier and was invited over for cocktails. Since you were not at home."

Susan paused for a moment. "And what does our neighbor look like? I have not seen anyone occupying either villa."

"She is 20ish and apparently arrived not that long ago." Brian responded.

"Ah," Susan said. "And is she alone?"

"Apparently for the moment," Brian responded nervously. "She does have a boyfriend. We should all meet for dinner and whatever."

"Whatever would be whatever, Brian?" She asked with a smile.

"Oh, cocktails and dinner." He responded. "How are Rachel and Geoffrey?"

"Geoffrey has been busy so we have not seen much of him, but I have spent time getting to know Sophia. I really like her. Tell me my husband, why are you are really dressed to the nines? And by the way, I like it."

"I told you. I went for cocktails with Jessica, next door." He said.

"Jessica is it? I am sure she is very nice and would like very much to meet her." Susan said.

Relieved, Brian relaxed. "Pour me a straight rum if you will. You will like her."

"What does she do for a living?" Susan asked.

"I have not a clue." Brian said. He was envisioning Jessica and Susan in bed with him below the mirrored ceiling.

Susan offered Brian his drink but he seemed distracted. She snapped her fingers. "Earth to Brian, here's your drink."

Brian took the glass from his wife's hand. "Where is David?" he asked.

"David is upstairs changing. We will have dinner with Sophia, Rachel and Geoffrey at the Cliff this evening. I must tell you that our son has been acting strangely all day. I have not been able to hone in on the reason." Susan's affect brightened.

"Brian, I have a great idea. It would be so Bajan to invite your friend next door to join us. That is if she has not other plans. Why don't you run over and ask her?"

Jessica seemed happy to see Brian again and gladly accepted the invitation, saying she looked forward to meeting Brian's family and friends. Brian escorted Jessica over to Blue Heron where she met David and Susan. She immediately took a liking to Susan, who was absolutely gracious, but David seemed somewhat aloof, and she hoped she was not the cause of his discomfort. The four piled into the Range Rover, and Brian told Jessica that they would meet Geoffrey, Rachel and Sophia at the restaurant.

Upon their arrival at The Cliff, a valet took the Rover, and Brian and his party were immediately ushered to a table that would easily accommodate seven on the third tier.

The Townsands had not yet arrived. The restaurant was located on Highway One just past Payne's Bay, and close enough to the water to smell the sea. There was not another table available. Torches lit each tier and the sound of the surf pounding the shore could be heard despite the music and animated conversation from people at adjoining tables.

A waiter arrived, identified himself as their server and took drink orders. Brian and Susan ordered rum and coke, while David opted for a cold Banks beer. Jessica said she would have the same as Susan and Brian. The waiter had just left their table when Geoffrey, Rachel and Sophia arrived. Geoffrey hugged both Susan and Brian, as did Rachel. Sophia took a seat next to David and looked at Jessica, wondering whom she might be. After introductions were made, Susan watched Geoffrey take Jessica's hand and kiss it as only a Bajan gentleman might. Brian and Susan took it all in as did David and Sophia who seemed amused. Brian sensed a disconnect with David he could not comprehend. This was an uncomfortable feeling he had never before had experienced with his son.

Geoffrey called the server over and ordered rum for Rachel and scotch for himself. Sophia chose lime squash and squeezed David's hand.

Jessica smiled. "I am ever so grateful that you invited me to dinner and into your families. I was concerned about coming to a strange island without friends. May I consider you all my new friends?"

"Never fear, my Luv," Geoffrey said. "Anyone who comes to this island is our friend, now and forever. Let's drink to that." They drained their glasses and Geoffrey called for more.

"I shall order wine or champagne. No, upon consideration, we shall have both. Good friends call for good food and good drink." He snapped his fingers and the server took the order. "Now your dinners. Whatever you like, but if I might make a suggestion, the local pork is good and the US sirloin is phenomenal. For those of you who like fish, there is nothing more succulent than steak fish. Your choice." He looked at Jessica.

"I choose the steak fish with pumpkin soup as a starter." Jessica said.

"Excellent, my Luv, you are now a true Bajan, and I shall choose the same. If one has never had Bajan pumpkin soup one has not lived." Rachel stared at Geoffrey and opted for the same. Susan kicked him under the table and ordered the fish as well. David and Sophia decided upon pumpkin soup but chose a chicken dish, while Brian and Susan went for the steak.

The server opened a bottle of Dom Perignon and filled the glasses with the bubbly liquid. The group toasted each other, and once the glasses were emptied, Geoffrey selected a Chilean Merlot for those having steak and a Pinot Grigio for those who ordered fish. Rachel looked to Brian as if to momentarily question Geoffrey's fascination with the young, nubile, Jessica. She wondered if Brian felt emotionally connected to her as well.

Susan, on the other hand was amused by the fact that her husband could be attracted to a woman almost thirty years his junior. She was not certain she was willing to allow this attraction to persist if it at all existed.

Sophia was the only one who seemed to enjoy her dinner undistracted. David ate quietly, not certain if and when he should discuss with his parents what he had accidentally learned.

The diners enjoyed their meals that were ended with dishes of warm chocolate pudding whose recipe Susan cajoled from the owner. Geoffrey insisted upon after dinner cognac.

When it came time for the bill, Geoffrey informed Brian that it had already been taken care of. When Brian protested, Geoffrey said, "This is in honor of my daughter Sophia's engagement to David and our new friend, the absolutely gorgeous Jessica." David looked to Sophia who smiled, but who clearly was taken by surprise.

"Geoffrey," Brian said, "you must allow me to take care of the gratuity," but Geoffrey waved it off stating it was his pleasure. Jessica enjoyed the warm chocolate pudding as the men watched her spoon the dark, sweet delight, slowly and seductively into her mouth.

Twenty-eight

Barbados 1991

Brian insisted upon buying another cognac for everyone, but both David and Sophia declined, the latter stating, that she found its taste quite bitter. Brian offered a toast to their friendship and noticed that David did not raise his almost full glass of rum and coke.

"Well, then, I shall toast to David and Sophia, and to our new found friend Jessica." David raised his glass and clinked with Sophia's and then Jessica's. Brian looked quizzically at his son who looked away.

When the group made its way to the car park, Geoffrey handed the keys to the Mercedes to David, suggesting that, since it was still early, he might like to take Sophia and Jessica dancing. Jessica thanked him, but said she would prefer to return to the villa, so David and Sophia could spend time alone. The Townsands and Jessica got into the Range Rover with the McKenzies, and Brian turned the car north toward St. Peter.

When they reached Blue Heron, they all went to the patio where Brian poured rum shots and taught Jessica the Barbados quickie. She smiled, downed the shot and followed it with ice water as directed.

After three more drinks of the same, Jessica said she was ready to retire for the night.

"So early to bed?" Geoffrey said. "The night is still young, you are so beautiful, and we have hardly made a dent in the bottle. But, if you must. It was a delight meeting you young lady." He took her hand and kissed it. "Wait! You all remember I trust, that next Thursday is my birthday and the dive of the Stavronikita. Jessica, do you scuba?"

"I have snorkeled, but never scuba dived. What is the birthday thing you do?" Jessica asked.

"On my birthday, I and whom ever of my friends are willing, dive an old sunken Russian freighter, the Stavronkita. Its right out from Carlton market off Highway One. Not far from where we dined this evening. Great fun. Susan and Brian have dived with me in the past. How about you?"

"How deep is this sunken boat?" Jessica inquired, nervously.

"Now, I would guess with some expected settling, the deck sits at 118 feet below the surface of the sea. It is a beautiful dive. You cannot imagine the amazing sea life you will see." He offered. "Tell you what. I propose that you shall be taught by the best master diver on the island Edmund White. He will supervise your deep-water test, so you will have almost a week for preparation. And my Luv, I shall take care of everything."

"I don't know about that. That's deep, but my boy friend did convince me to sky dive, however." She added. "That was both a scary and phenomenal experience."

"Well, you are in luck," Geoffrey said. "That is clearly the opposite of what I propose. Fear not. If you or Edmund believe you are not ready, you shall not be pressed into it."

"How much will this cost? Jessica asked.

"As I said, it shall cost you nothing. Worry not." Geoffrey responded.

"I will sleep on it." She responded. "Right now I must get to bed."

Brian rose from his seat, and offered to escort her to her villa, but Geoffrey interceded. "Allow me to escort the young woman."

Rachel looked at Susan who shrugged. It appeared that their husbands were vying for Jessica's attention.

After fifteen minutes, Geoffrey returned to the raised eyebrows of his friends. "Took you long enough." Brian said.

"Okay, let's not carry this any further." Rachel said. "Brian, do take me, and my lothario home. I am tired." Susan kissed both of them good night and told Brian she would wait for him upstairs. Brian poured one last shot for Geoffrey and himself, as the wives looked on with disgust.

After the Townsands had left, he secured the entrances and went upstairs to find Susan already in bed. "She rose up on one elbow and looked at him. "What is it with you two and Jessica? Aren't we enough for you guys?"

Brian blushed. "It's nothing like that. Susan, are you certain you did not get a fax from me?"

"No. What is this fax?" She answered. "You asked me about that earlier."

"I sent a fax from the apartment the night I returned home." He said.

"Sorry, Luv. No fax. Get undressed." She said.

"I don't understand. There must have been a problem the first time it dialed. But then it continued to resend the fax, with a print out that it was finally received." He said.

"Okay," Susan said as Brian got into bed, and eased in next to her. "What was in this fax? You know, we did have a power out last night."

"I hope no one else saw the fax." Brian said nervously.

"Well, the only other person here with me was David." Susan said.

"Oh! God!" He exclaimed. "I was jealous of you being down here with Geoffrey and Rachel, I shared something that was meant only for you."

Susan sat up in shock. "Brian, you mentioned our relationship with the Townsands?"

"I am afraid so." Brian said.

"So, now you may have shared our secret with our son who plans to marry Sophia." Susan said angrily.

"I was upset. I didn't think. How would I know that David would intercept the fax"? Brian responded.

"Well, if he did, he did not speak to me about it. Wonder what happened to the fax. Oh, my, if he tells Sophia that might cause her to be angry with him for something he had nothing to do with."

"No wonder he would not toast with us. I sensed something was wrong." Brian said.

"This is what I suggest." Susan said. "We say nothing about it unless he brings it up."

"If he will remain angry with us, we will have to address it." Brian said.

"Right now, there will be no further sex with the Townsands." She said.

"How do we explain that to Rachel and Geoffrey?" Brian asked.

"We don't. Just leave it alone. I don't know why I ever got talked in to this in the first place." Susan sighed.

"Although, in the beginning it seemed harmless enough." Susan said as she looked up to the ceiling seeing their images reflecting back. "What were you thinking, Brian?"

"I am sorry that I ever agreed to switch." He said with remorse. "But, hold on. You did not put up much of a fight!"

"Let's not forget fucking the floozy and the drug runner," She said angrily, ignoring his retort.

"I regret that as well." He said.

"Why did we ever need to seek satisfaction beyond our own marriage?" She asked turning toward Brian, who continued to stare toward the ceiling. "Were we having a problem, that I am unaware of?" She touched his shoulder. "We were having problems, weren't we, Brian?"

Brian took a deep breath. "I tried to address this some years back. We had sex before we were married, and were really novices at it. After you gave birth to David, you seemed disinterested in sex, and after Meghan, it worsened." He said.

"But you never said anything." Susan responded.

"You were starting your law practice, and I thought that you were just too involved with that. I read nothing more into it. I was busy trying to support us in a market that was always in jeopardy. I initially chalked it up to the fact that we were just in the process of growing." Susan began to interrupt, when he indicated he had more to say. "You know I tried to be innovative with different positions. I suggested looking at some porno movies, but you seemed to reject them. I made you your own copies of porno movies that you could watch at your own leisure. You sort of were a good sport, but I don't know if you ever looked at any of them."

"I did look at them and told you that I would rather be a participant than an observer." Susan said. "You know that none of our friends at home ever switched."

"Actually, we do not know that for a fact. But that is not relevant. I wanted seduction. I wanted fantasy because I thought it might help us. We had rare arguments, so that was not a factor. We reached a point where sex was becoming just plain boring. If this was something that all women go through, there should be room for change, if desired." He said.

"Why do you assume it was just me with the problem? We have been through this before. Woman are not aroused as easily as men, and did it ever occur to you that I might have been exhausted or just plain angry with you? It upsets me that I never was able to satisfy you." Susan said tearfully.

"I was never certain that orgasm and satisfaction was in your calendar." He said.

"Brian, that is down right offensive. Look, you always did tell me that my satisfaction during sex was important to you and I apparently dismissed it." Susan said.

"I guess you did that." He said. "And when that night, we went to the Coach House with Geoffrey and Rachel, and he asked if we switched, despite being taken aback, I really believed that this could make our own relationship better, even though it required sharing you with another man. That is what one does when one switches."

"And you allowed it to continue even when Geoffrey came to New York and shared me as well as our bed." Susan said. "Even if you did not have the same with Rachel."

"I was not always happy about that. Don't get me wrong. Rachel was very satisfying. She did things to me that you never did." Brian said.

"I wonder if she had the need and desire to satisfy you in a way that I was never able to." Susan said.

"It was just different." Brian responded.

"In what way?" Susan asked.

"We had not the obligation to each other that I have to you. I think we became business as usual where sex was something that was obligatory. It was something that had to be done. You remember what your aunt told you." Brian said.

"Brian, you had a vasectomy. I might remind you of that," She said.

"So we did not have more children. And you had your tubes tied as well. Brian said

"That decision was made after we met Geoffrey and Rachel." Susan responded. Let's not rewrite history." Susan responded. "Brian, was I that bad in bed?"

"No, Susan. There were times you were just amazing. I just envisioned more, and when the opportunity arose, I just threw caution to the wind and went for it. Do I think we are better for it? Obviously I have my doubts."

"Brian, I have no regrets other than the fact that we have now been exposed. Do I love you more? I don't know. I certainly do not love you less. Do I love Geoffrey? Probably as much as you love Rachel." Susan said.

"I could not agree more." Brian responded.

"Brian, I am not going to worry about what our son thinks of us. Right now, I plan to remove my nightgown and ask you to make passionate love me in any and every way possible under those mirrors in the ceiling, and I plan to respond to your every thrust, touch and lick, until we both are so satisfied and exhausted, and we have not the energy left to continue."

Susan lifted her nightgown and helped Brian remove his pajamas. "What ever you wish to do, I am game."

Twenty-nine

Barbados 1991

The next morning, when Susan found that David had not slept in his bed, she began to worry. Then she heard a car engine sputter and suddenly stop in their driveway. When she opened the front door, she saw David speaking with a tall, deeply tanned, gray haired gentleman.

"This is Mr. White. He has come to teach Jessica about scuba." David said as he walked past his mother. "And I have decided to take a refresher course with him as well. As he went up the stairs, he suddenly stopped. "In case you are wondering, I stayed over at the Townsands last night."

Susan asked Edmund White in, and offered him a coffee that he readily accepted. White was very pleasant, smiled broadly at everything she said and spoke with the Bajan patois, to which Susan had become accustomed. Brian returned from his morning sea bath and offered to fetch Jessica, after shaking hands with Edmund White, who told them of the plans for the day. "Perhaps she is not up yet, Brian. Call ahead." Susan advised.

"When did Mr. Townsand get in touch with you? " Susan asked. "We spoke of this very late last evening."

Edmund White scratched his head. "He, actually rang me up quite early this morning." Susan thought 'I just bet he did.'

"I can't find a phone number for High Tide. I'll just take a chance and call out before I knock." Brian advised.

Within minutes, he returned with Jessica who wore a one-piece white bathing suit, that Susan thought most appropriate. Susan introduced her to Edmund White, who suggested they start to review some of the physics of diving. "Perhaps David should join us." White said.

Brian helped Susan prepare a breakfast of toast and eggs. Jessica asked if there was any yogurt, since that was her usual morning fare. Susan smiled and told her that she was in luck. David had changed into bathing trunks and a T-shirt, and asked about any equipment he might need. White told him that if he had his own regulator and fins that would be fine, and he had enough equipment for all of them. The plan was to go over the principles of scuba first, and then spend the remainder of the day in the pool.

Jessica learned the basics quickly, so the master diver thought it was time to enter the pool with tanks and regulators. He admitted that the eleven feet at the deep end was exceedingly shallow considering the depth that they would dive the following week.

Brian watched David and Jessica maneuver below the water's surface as they learned how to buddy breath. White had told him that every one would have the use of octopuses, or extra regulators. Edmund White had the two students sit for a while at the pool steps, while he went over the signals that would be essential for safety. Following this, David and Jessica them returned to the patio for a brief written test, that both did well on.

"You guys did just super, so I believe we can safely go for the deep water test tomorrow. We will start out from the beach and swim out to where the water is about thirty feet in depth. I shall explain much more before we start out. If you both do well, in the afternoon, we shall take the boat out over the shallow reef, and dive to a depth of about 60-80 ft. You must keep in mind to look at you gauge to see how much air you have left." He paused to clear his throat. "It seems like a great deal to digest, but safety is uppermost. If any one's gauge indicates 1500 psi he or she must surface slowly. Since you dive with a buddy, your buddy is obliged to accompany you to the surface. That is unless I am free to go up with you and return down."

White referred to a list of essentials he had written down. "As I said before I shall review the signals since they impact upon what your intent is. I am leaving these two books for your review. So, any questions?" Neither Jessica nor David had any, so Edmund thanked Susan and Brian for breakfast, and explained that since he had a dive charter later in the day, it would be best that he be on his way.

Jessica said she was going for a swim in the sea, and asked if any one else wished to go with her. David and Susan watched Brian run down the beach, where he caught up with Jessica as she dove into the water.

"Gee, Dad will chase anything, won't he? When do you suppose he'll start to act his age?" David said as he rose to leave.

"Sit down, David and talk to me. What are you so angry at?" She asked.

"What has been going on between you, Dad and Sophia's parents?" He asked. "I should have figured it out when I saw the mirrored ceiling. I read the fax."

"I am not certain that I wish to discuss this with you right now, but I must tell you that..........that. David, I don't know what I want to tell you. What exactly are you suggesting? All I ask is that you not speak of this with Sophia. Your happiness is more important. And the mirrored ceiling came with the house." David slumped back in his chair.

"I am not certain you should be judgmental. Let me ask you a question. Obviously, you don't have to answer if you have none." She took a deep breath. "Did you have sexual relations with Jennifer?"

David looked at her. "Yes, a number of times." He replied.

"Okay, then. Before Jennifer, how many girls were there?" Susan asked.

"Why is that important?" David asked as he got up from the chair."

"Sit back down, David, because everything is relative. Have you been intimate with Sophia?"

"No! She wants to wait." He stammered.

"That's fine. Now why is it okay for you do what you have done, while it is not okay for Dad and me?" She asked.

"Because you are my parents, and........." He continued to stammer.

"I see," Susan said. "And it is a known fact that parents don't have sex. In case you missed something, that's where you and your sister came from." David tried not to smile. "This, David, I will share with you as our secret." Susan took a deep breath and sat on the lounge next to her son. "There is a time in a marriage, when the flame begins to dim, no matter how torrid the romance at one time." She sighed and continued.

"For some women, having children does something to decrease the appetite for sex. This does not happen with men, who seem always to be ready, but I do not have to tell you that. I do not want suggest that Dad and I were becoming emotionally distant. Nor because we fell out of love, since we love each other very much. Then we met Geoffrey and Rachel and everything changed...for the better. By the way, Dad knew that his fax had been intercepted and because of the manner in which you have been acting, we assumed you had read it."

"I read it and tore it into pieces." He turned to Susan. "Mom, I do not plan to tell Sophia."

"And that goes for your sister as well. Yes?" She asked.

David leaned over to kiss and hug Susan. "Our secret, Mom. Although I don't completely understand or agree with what the four of you have done."

"Thank you David and don't be vexed with your father for chasing after a young chick. He will not know what to do if he catches her." Susan said with a laugh. Jessica will be just fine. Go to your Sophia." She sipped her coffee that had become cold, thinking about the conversation she had dared to have with her son.

Brian suddenly came running up onto the patio out of breath. "That girl can really swim. I could barely keep up." He said falling down on the lounge.

"Where is she now, Brian?" Susan asked.

"She stayed out on the float to tan. She is something else." He said.

"Really, Brian. Jessica is a lovely girl with great tits and a tight, amazing ass that I wish I had. Don't start anything you cannot finish. Listen. I had a long talk with David and believe I have straightened everything out. I don't think he will challenge you, but if he does, tell him the truth. I sort of went over some of the issues we discussed last night." Susan relaxed and put her arms around her husband. "Everything will be all right. Let the other chips fall where they may." She watched Jessica's body glisten from the brine that coated her skin as the young woman made her way back to her villa. Susan chip singed and followed it with a deep sigh.

Brian picked up the phone on the second ring. It was Geoffrey calling to find out how they had made out with Edmund White.

"Really a cool guy," Brian said. "I have full confidence in him."

"Bet you cannot tell me how old he is." Geoffrey said.

"Hadn't thought about it actually. Perhaps he is in his late fifties." Brian said.

"You are not even close. Edmund will be eighty come this summer. He is one amazing individual who takes great care of himself." Geoffrey said. "Hey, Brian, is Susan around?"

"She just went upstairs to get dressed. We plan to run down to Mullins."

"Brian. What do you make of Jessica? She's really hot. Right. Certainly well put together. How old is she?" Geoffrey asked.

"Said she was twenty nine, but looks younger. Why?" Brian replied.

"I was just thinking how it would be with her." Geoffrey responded. "I fancy her."

"Trust me on this. She has a boyfriend." Brian said.

"She going with you guys to Mullins?" Geoffrey asked.

"Haven't a clue." Brian said as Susan came back out on the patio dressed in a new but skimpy bikini. He whistled twice. "Hey let's continue this conversation later."

"I assume that Susan just came back. Look if you invite Jessica, I shall call in sick and meet you at Mullins." Geoffrey said.

"I'll see what I can do. Ciao." Brian placed the phone back in its cradle.

Susan turned to show off her suit. "Who was that and you shall see about doing what?"

"Your friend Geoffrey would like us to bring Jessica along with us and he'll take the day off." Brian said.

"And Rachel?" Susan inquired.

"Never entered in to the conversation." Brian answered.

"Hi!" Brian and Susan looked up as Jessica came up onto the patio. She had changed into a red bikini top that barely covered her ample breasts and a color coordinated thong.

"We were just talking about you. How about going up to Mullins with us. Good beach and great bar. Just a bit down the road." Susan said watching taking it all in.

"Great!" Jessica said. "But can I go like this?"

"Absolutely," Susan remarked. "You look just fine."

"I'll yell up to David and tell him where we are going. Perhaps he'd like to join us." Brian said.

"Why don't you call Geoffrey as well," Susan said. "I am sure he would come, just thinking about it."

Thirty

Barbados 1991

Geoffrey met Brian, Susan and Jessica at Mullins, explaining that Rachel had some errands to run, and might join them later. After giving Jessica a brief water scooter lesson, he called out to Brian and Susan that he would be taking Jessica up to Maycocks for a look.

"A look at what exactly?" Susan asked. "For her sake, I hope those over sexed adolescents are not up their exercising!" She watched as Geoffrey increased the scooter's speed, taking it well out over the reef, and then turning north in the direction of Maycocks. Susan continued to watch until the two became but specks in the distance.

Brian shook his blanket free of sand and told her he was going up to the bar for drinks. Susan thought for a moment. "Luv, fetch me a cold Banks please."

"Lots of luck if you expect the beer to be cold. Don't forget. This is Barbados." He responded with a shrug.

"Then have them chill it a bit. They can even toss in some ice in a glass." She looked back out to the point where the water scooter had disappeared from sight.

"Brian, I am concerned about Geoffrey and Jessica.

"Really," Brian responded. "Is this concern? Or could this be pure jealousy?" He ducked the sand, Susan kicked towards him.

"I should ask you the same, I suppose. Tell you what. Put the beer on hold. We can it with lunch." He started toward the water. "I'll race you into the sea. This sun is terrible today." Susan got up and started to run across the hot sand, joining Brian as he gingerly entered the water.

With Susan the stronger swimmer of the two, Brian had some difficulty keeping up with her. "Let's swim to the float." He gasped as he swam along side.

Susan turned over onto her back and began to tread water. "I don't think so. Looks fairly well occupied." She said.

Brian encircled her waist with his arms and the two floated together in the rather serene turquoise sea. A wave caused him to swallow some sea water that he coughed out and then began to laugh.

"What now Brian. What is so funny?"

"I just remembered the first time we came down to the island. You have not forgotten the fabulous Barbados suck off." He responded.

"Oh, Brian I was younger and could hold my breath longer under water. Don't tell me you have a hard on already." Susan reached down between his legs. "What the hell! She exclaimed. "We're on holiday." She dropped below the surface and pulled down Brian's swimsuit with her teeth, freeing his erection. Then opening her mouth, she allowed her lips to encircle it. The feeling a hand pulling on her hair, she surfaced, gasping, seawater spouting from her mouth. "What?" She cried out.

Brian nodded in the direction of the beach. David and Sophia had left the beach and were swimming toward them. "Pull up your suit." She said. "That is if you can. I have had enough sea bath for the moment." With that, she set off for shore passing David and Sophia who were on their way towards the float. "Hi kids. Make sure you say hello to Brian. He looks so lonely out there." With powerful strokes, she reached the beach and fell to the sand, unable to contain her laughter.

Brian was grateful that David and Sophia passed with a wave as they continued out to the now unoccupied float that had been anchored some one hundred and fifty yards out from shore. He tried to envision ways to get even with Susan, but for the time being, he would not be soon leaving the water in his present condition. He splashed around for the next twenty minutes, trying to think of anything other than sex, and believed he had made some headway, when a shout from Jessica reversed the process. She brought the water scooter along side and asked if he might like to go for a ride with her. Brian almost accepted so as to get even with his wife, when he saw Sophia and David swimming toward him.

"We are famished and are going up for lunch. How about you guys? We saw Jessica drop Geoffrey off at the beach and then spin back out." David said, treading water. "Thanks," Brian answered. "Why don't the three of you go in and get a table. I need to swim a bit more." Fifteen minutes later, Brian was able to comfortably exist the water.

When he reached the restaurant, Geoffrey and Susan were already into their second rum punch. David and Sophia were sharing an order of fries and Jessica had gone to shower.

"Brian, Darling. What took you ever so long?" You were out there long enough to resemble a prune." Susan laughed.

Brian just frowned. "Funny. Did anyone think to order me a drink?"

"Too be sure." Geoffrey said. "I ordered you a cold Banks, and Susan suggested I ask for extra ice. Sweet. Sweet!" He cupped his hand over his mouth to stifle a laugh.

"You didn't. Did you?" Brian glared at Susan who was pointing to a school of flying fish, moving three feet above the surface of the sea.

"It is my understanding that tomorrow, Jessica shall go for her deep water test and that David shall join her." He looked at his daughter. "Sophia, might you give it a go as well?"

"No, Daddy. You know I don't like to scuba. If you recall I almost drowned in the sea when you tried to teach me." Sophia said. "You all have fun, but stay safe. I'm not terribly excited about David going either."

David inserted a pair of fries into Sophia's mouth. "We'll be just fine. Mr. White is a good teacher, and very cautious."

After lunch, Susan suggested that they take a long walk down the beach. Jessica decided to find a lounge chair and read. Geoffrey and Brian, reluctantly agreed, while David and Sophia said they wanted to take one of the water scooters for a ride.

They had gone about a quarter of a mile, when David turned off the motor and allowed the scooter to roll with the waves. "Okay, David. We are not just here for the ride. Is there a problem?"

"Just wanted to get you alone for a talk." David responded.

"Well, considering where we are, you have my undivided attention." Sophia said.

"Better we were up to our cups in rum like the others most like are." David said wryly.

"Okay. What is really on your mind?" The scooter continued to turn lazily in the sea.

"I had this thought. Well, take Jessica for example. She is a young, beautiful, well-proportioned woman with a lot going for her. Yet, she appears to have come to Barbados just looking for sex." He said.

"David." She admonished. "You know nothing about her. What makes you think she is just looking for sex, and for that matter with whom."

"Hey, nothing about her has escaped our fathers. That is certainly evident." He said.

"And have you been seduced by her?" Sophia asked. "Look," Sophia continued. "She is a great looking chick who wears skimpy attire well. The thong between her cheeks has been most effective to draw attention. But I am not attracted to her, so who cares. What exactly is your point, David? Let's go back in. We have drifted far enough in many respects."

"It just seems to me that women of all ages come to Barbados, perhaps for what we in the States call a one night stand. What is the draw to Barbados that reeks sex and more sex?" He asked.

"David. This is not exclusive to women. Men come here to the island horny and with hopes to meet someone nice, who might agree to shack up for mutual satisfaction. Look around you at what Barbados has to offer. So many beautiful beaches, amazing food and music and our people with such inviting smiles are a huge enticement. And do not forget the rum and the weather. I would also suggest that so many of our tourists who have come from Canada and England, where young women, some not too terribly attractive, have labored all year in banks and assorted humdrum jobs, disembark from their aircraft to the sounds of the steel drums and the warm climate. So they now invigorated are hot to trot and horny enough to spread their legs for anyone."

"You know that for a fact?" David asked. "Pretty hard on the Commonwealth."

"Sorry, Luv. I do not. But I have loads of friends who have clued me in as to what the norm is on some of the Pirate Cruises. It seems that there always has been a challenge and reward for some of the captains who can screw the most females. It became so blatant that it became a great game and the individual who scored the most, laid the most tourists, was further acknowledged by having his name carved into one of the ship's bar stools." Brian could only look at her in amazement.

"I see I have gotten your attention." She said and then continued. "There have also been parties held in some of the residences in Holetown, where a pot of tomato sauce, without pasta or chile was the only thing on the menu, with the exception that is of what some of the women offered between their legs. Bon appetite! So, with ample rum to drink, people took cunnilingus for a Bajan spectator sport. Getting hot, yet, Luv? Daddy was at one of these with Mommy one evening, and would not leave her side when she fell asleep wasted in one of the bedrooms."

"Cunniligus!. That's a big word," he declared.

"Look it up," Sophia said.

"I know what it means." David remarked as he started up the engine and directed the water scooter back toward the beach. "So both Geoffrey and your mother were attendees." Sophia glared at him. "Look I am sorry I started this entire conversation. Some things I cannot comfortably discuss with you."

"We shall have no secrets. Right? David?" Sophia held him tightly around the waist. "No secrets."

David turned to kiss her as he beached the scooter. "No secrets." Noting that his parents and Geoffrey were still at the beach bar, he suggested that they find a shaded spot on the sand where they could lie down.

Sophia having no objection indicated a spot under a grouping of trees that afforded some protection from the direct sun. "I want to talk more about sex in Barbados." He said.

"Why? Might it be because I am not ready to have sex with you yet?" She asked.

"No. It is only indirectly related to us. It is m ore about the Bajan culture and the apparent sexual needs of people on this island." David responded.

"Still picking on the tourists?" She asked. "What are you just bursting to tell me? We have been over this. Barbados is a tropical island, no different from the many others in the Caribbean. I have to assume that in Hawaii, vacation, alcohol and a surplus of attractive women in all states of undress will lend itself to naughtiness. Everyone must make the best choice. What is it you want to tell me?"

"I love you Sophia, and don't want to, well vex you in any way. The folks are heading this way with Jessica. This will have to be continued later." David said.

That evening, Susan prepared a dinner of shrimp scampi, pumpkin soup, and then coffee and drinks back on the patio, where a welcome breeze cooled their skin. After a few Barbados quickies, Jessica yawned and asked to be excused, so Brian offered to walk her back to her villa. Rachel said she was tired and wanted to go back to Simonton, as Geoffrey reluctantly agreed. Susan said she was ready for bed, kissed everyone good night and went upstairs. David said he would stay for a while and drive Sophia home later.

Left alone, Sophia embraced David, kissing him. "My Luv, what troubles you so? We do have all the time in the world to deal with it. Right?"

"There is something, I know will upset you." He responded.

"You will never know if it will or not unless you share." She said.

David proceeded to tell Sophia about Brian's fax, and then explained sexual relationship both sets of parents enjoyed with each other.

Sophia sat quietly without interrupting, sighed and began to respond. "I am neither surprise nor angered, David. Who are we to judge our parents or whatever needs that had to be fulfilled. Perhaps, at some time, we should have a conversation with the four of them. Nothing will change my love for you, your parents or my parents. I hope that shall be true for you as well. What ever occurred between them has had no apparent ill effect upon their marriages. They continue to respond to each other's needs when called upon to do so.

"I always thought it strange that Rachel never accompanied him to New York when Geoffrey stayed with them." David said.

"Why?" She asked. "Mother had some need to stay on the island to take care of the house and their businesses as well. What might you be suggesting?"

"Just wondering about the nature of the rules of the game. Is it possible that my mother with or without my father's knowledge had something going on with Geoffrey?" He closed his eyes.

"And had that occurred without objection from my mother?" She asked. "Why does that trouble you?"

"Because it suggests that my Father participated in or was an observer while my darling sweet Mother fucked your father, to put it bluntly." He said, his eyes still closed. "What if it was Rachel?"

"David, despite what you believe, the island is more accepting of such a relationship than you might think. Most of the seemingly happily married men have one or more mistresses here or elsewhere. It works for them. I could name a number of our ministers, former prime ministers and lady ambassadors who have endorsed the idea as well."

"And I would assume that it would follow that wives have carte blanche to take a lover or lovers as well." David said as he looked at Sophia.

"No, my sweet. That would be a rarity. For some that might work well, and for others there is always divorce." Sophia explained. "I, on the other hand would expect my husband to be faithful, and I would be willing to provide whatever sexually he might wish without looking elsewhere. This island is a tough test for that, since there is an endless supply of willing men and women. As I said before, people will just have to make the right choice.

"Let me pose this." David said turning to her. "We marry and within months or even years, the opportunity in which our parents chose to participate suddenly becomes available to us. How might you feel about doing the same with another couple we both liked?"

"If that occurred early in our marriage, we would not be giving to each other what we need sexually or emotionally. If that could have been the case, we might just remain good friends and not marry.   Really David, how far do you wish to carry this conversation."

"Fair enough. Talking over. It's still early and I vote for going for a swim in the pool." David said.

"I don't know. Your Dad has not yet returned from his knightly errand, escorting the voluptuous Jessica home." She said as she got up.

"Not a problem. He passed by while we were deep in conversation and went in the side entrance. He and Mother are either fast asleep or enjoying the mirrored ceiling." He answered.

"I won't have a dry swim suit to change into after." Sophia said.

David smiled. "We will just have to improvise." He stripped off his shorts and shoes and dove into the warm pool. Sophia paused for a moment, removed her bikini and followed him in looking for him. He suddenly appeared beside her, his face illuminated by the bright Bajan moon.

"What do you think your Mother and Father are doing right now under that mirrored ceiling?" She asked coyly.

"I don't know if I should stimulate your libido." He said.

"Tell me everything you wish me to do and how you will make love to me." Sophia said as she place her hand on his penis. "Do Bajan women get horny?" She grinned. Absolutely. I would say particularly some who have spent too much time in Canada. Eh?"

He allowed her to stroke his now fully erect penis and push it between her legs. "You are so hard. I want every inch of you inside me." She purred.

"But what if, " he began as she placed a finger on his lips. Sophia parted her legs and allowed him to enter her.

"It is safe." She moaned. "I am not ready to be knocked up." She began to move against his thrusts.

David suddenly lifted her up by her buttocks and still securely inside of her, walked up the pool steps and positioned Sophia gently on a lounge. She suddenly moved upwards, dislodging him, but in a single movement brought his lips down between her legs, allowing him to freely explore her vaginal opening with his tongue. After three more thrusts of her buttocks, she came, and then she came again. Sophia got up on one elbow and positioned herself to take his erection in her mouth. Unable to control himself any longer, David allowed himself to come.

Later on lying on the night cooled grass she turned to David. "What else would you want or expect from me, at least the first time?" They went back into the pool and swam silently for a while.

Thirty-one

Barbados 1991

It was around 2 a.m. when David brought Sophia back to Simonton. Despite being utterly exhausted, she told him that she had no regrets for what they have done earlier. After a sustained kiss, she pushed him toward his car and watched wistfully as it disappeared around the bend still protected by the old royal palms that guarded the approach to the old house.

When David reached Blue Heron, he noticed no lights in his parent's bedroom. Brian left the main gate open but had securely hidden the key to the front door in a nearby planter. David unlocked the door and replaced the key, but too keyed up to go to sleep, he found a bottle of Mt. Gay on the wet bar, grabbed a legal pad and a glass of ice and went out onto the cool patio. He sat for a long time attempting to organize his thoughts.

David felt a hand touch his shoulder and turned to find Susan, in her robe, standing behind him holding an empty glass. "Since you are taking on some of our bad habits, perhaps you would like to allow your mother to join you. This is Barbados and this our rum, so pour me a tot."

She allowed him to fill her glass almost to the brim, sat down and drank drained half of liquid. "So, why are you up at this ungodly hour?"

"Dad asleep?" He asked.

"Soundly." Susan replied. "And noisily as well."

David took a swig of his rum and wiped his lips with his hand. "You recall, when we first came to Barbados, I had worked on a school paper about the island." Susan nodded. "I have given a great deal of thought to writing a book, actually a generational historical novel about Barbados. From geologic time to 1838 when the slaves here on the island were freed. With the world's current angle on civil rights, I think it could be well received. I still have all of my notes." He said.

"You do understand how difficult and costly it might be to have a book published. I have friends who have tried it for years." She remarked.

"I have already looked into the publishing angle and decided that I would write two books on Barbados. The first one I have already explained to you." He said after taking another drink.

"Well written, it could be a best seller and who knows what else. It will take a lot of good connections with people in publishing." She said and handed him her glass for a refill.

"I do realize that, but I found out after speaking to friends who self published at great expense and perhaps lackluster gain, I would need something sizzling in a second book to stimulate interest in me as an author. Novice authors are too often dismissed." He said.

"You are now losing me, David. Perhaps it is the lateness of the hour." She said.

"Perhaps it is also all the rum." He retorted. "Okay, this is gthe deal. With all of the so-called sex-capades that appear to occur regularly on the island, I thought a nice juicy, lust-filled novel about two married couples on a tropical island might be just the hook." He said as Susan collapsed back into her chair.

"David, you are not suggesting what I think you are suggesting. Are you?" She grabbed the half empty bottle and refilled her glass.

"It will obviously be fiction and as they say, 'any connection between living and dead is pure coincidental' or something like that. Setting it on Barbados seems ideal."

"But, David, this can be very hurtful, you know to a lot of people who care for you and Sophia." Susan said standing.

"Sit back down, please. I have dealt with everything discreetly, so as a teller of tales I will be no less discreet." He said

"You must hate us both very much." Susan said tearfully.

"When I stumbled over the fax and your indiscretions, I was confused, actually dumbfounded. How could I believe something like this of my mother and father? But after discussing it with Sophia, I have come to grips with it. Who am I to take issue with what you have done if it works for you all. Anyway, this is the conclusion we came to." He said.

"Oh, my, you shared this all with Sophia." Susan said remorsefully.

"She does not love you or Dad any less, and does n ot plan to tell her parents that she knows. Actually, it will be cool writing about all of this stuff. And could you fill me in on some details?"

Susan glared at her son. "Forget it. I am going to bed!"

"Just kidding. But I still believe that if this book sells, my historical novel, which is really my dream-work, will sell and sell and sell. The potential for Television and movies could be a financial boon for all of us. Look, don't tell Dad. Let's keep this our secret." David rose and hugged Susan whose attempt to control her tears proved unsuccessful. She then agreed not to tell Brian about the book at least for the time being and left him alone with his rum and legal pad. After a few moments, David began to write.

Brian awoke around eight in the morning, showered, shaved and went down to the kitchen to make coffee. He was particularly careful not to waken Susan. Taking a cup of hot coffee with him to the patio, he was surprised to find David fast asleep on one of the lounges he had carried up from the pool, and still dressed in the shirts and shorts he had been wearing. It was obvious to Brian that his son had never gotten to bed.

He tousled David's hair. "Hey, time to get up and get cleaned up, David." David stirred for a moment, opened and then closed his eyes.

"What time is it, Dad?" David asked.

"After eight," Brian responded, and spying the empty rum bottle, said. "You must have been on some binge last night, and was your mother your drinking partner?" David nodded.

Brian picked up the yellow legal pad that had fallen to the floor. "A Historical Novel of Barbados" by David McKenzie." He read aloud. "What is this all about, David?"

David, now fully awake, yawned, stretched and rose to his feet. "Thought it would be real cool to writer a novel about something I knew a lot about. More research will be required, but I love this island and so believe the book worthy, pertinent and hopefully of interest to a publisher."

"David, you may have a great idea but are you aware of the costs of publishing a book and how difficult it would be to even get it to an editor's desk. Someone I know wrote a do-it-yourself book, and after striking out too many times, self published at $200 a page." Brian handed the pad to David.

"I shall worry more about that after I get a few chapters down." David said. "I really just started last night. Actually early this morning."

"Your mother must have been down here drinking with you. The bedroom smelled like a rum factory, and she always complained how I smelled after a few stag parties." Brian laughed.

"Mom did have a few rums with me. We were discussing the potential of the book, actually." David said.

"She thought it a good idea?" Brian asked.

David smiled, recalling the entire conversation with his mother. "True, true. She thought it was a great idea, Dad." It was time to change the subject. "What's on the agenda for you guys, today?"

Before Brian could respond, Susan appeared dressed in a two-piece pink bathing suit, and announced that she was going for a sea bath. "Coffee, Susan?" Brian asked.

"I need a wake up swim. Any one care to join me?" When no one answered, she shrugged and ran off toward the beach.

David explained to Brian that he was going on a dive with Jessica later, but wondered what he might find for breakfast. Brian told him to shower and that he would cook some bacon and eggs.

When David returned to the kitchen, Brian had a plate of scrambled eggs bacon and toast waiting. Dressed in a tank top and bathing shorts, he sat down and ate a forkful of eggs. Brian advised that there was no orange juice, but he would pick some up at the market later.

"So, coffee or milk?" Brian asked.

"Milk will be fine. Got any toast?"

"Just ready to pop. Cream cheese or butter?"

"Cream cheese, please." David took another mouthful of eggs and shoved in a strip of crisp bacon. No breakfast for you?"

Brian peeled a ripe mango and cut slices from it. Placing them in a bowl, he added papaya still fresh from the fridge, a cut up banana fig and squeezed lime over the fruit. "Not having carbs and fat, since I am into healthy food now. I have to keep looking youthful like Mom."

"Really? Why? You having some kind of contest?" David had remembered Sophia's tale about the exploits of the Pirate Cruise captains.

Brian sat down and ate some of the fruit. "Oh, while you were in the shower, your dive instructor called and asked if you could meet him down at beach at old Miramar. He mentioned something about a problem with his car. Why don't you take Jessica down there in the Land Rover. Mom and I can manage without a car for a couple of hours." He put the empty dishes in the sink to soak.

"Sure. Does she know?" David asked.

"Does who know?" Brian responded.

"Jessica. Does she know that I am supposed to take her?" David persisted.

"She will as soon as you get your rear end over to her villa and tell her." Brian added some dish detergent to the sink and turned off the water. "It is already 9, and I think he said you were scheduled for 10, so you have an hour. Go find Jessica. I'll finish cleaning up."

David was about to knock, when Jessica emerged from the open sliding door. Her hair was still wet from showering. With only a towel loosely draped around her neck, she was naked.

David stood frozen in the doorway as she smiled and made no effort to collect a terrycloth robe that was draped over a patio lounge chair.

Jessica smiled broadly. "Good Morning, David. It's not time for our test is it?" David did not respond but continued to gawk. "Hey, I have three brothers, and we all used to swim nude in the creek at home. If it really bothers you, I'll put a robe on for you."

She picked up the robe that had been thrown onto the lounge, and slowly put it on. "I came over to tell you that I will be driving us down to our test." He said as Jessica allowed the robe to open a bit revealing the top of her breasts.

Jessica watched him and laughed. I cannot believe after seeing me in bikini and thong, that you are embarrassed. Have you never seen a completely naked woman?" She asked.

"I am serious about Sophia. I just left or am about to leave another relationship, so it makes me uncomfortable to be with you as you are." He stammered.

"Still don't get it David. You are fully dressed. I do believe you think I am seducing you." She paused and turned. "No matter. I'll put something on. It will be a bikini that leaves nothing to the imagination. Do you think that it might make the fish blush as well?"

David straightened up. "We have an hour, so meet me over at Blue Heron just before 10, or earlier if you choose."

"Great. Will do." Jessica said as she dropped the robe and moved back into the living room. David stood at the open door watching her every seductive move, unable to take his eyes from her tight buttocks. Then he remembered Sophia and beat a quick retreat to Blue Heron.

When he entered the kitchen, Brian and Susan were having coffee. "Was she awake?" Brian asked.

"Was who awake?" David responded.

"Jessica. You did go over to tell her that you would drive down for the test." Brian was testy.

"Right! Excuse me. Cannot dive without a bathing suit." David said as he took the steps to the upper floor two at a time and headed directly for his bathroom.

"Our son seems a bit frenetic." Susan observed. "What was that about?"

"Beats me." Brian answered. "You two had a drink fest?"

"You mean last night?" She asked.

"Last night, or early this morning. Whenever. What were you talking about?" He persisted. "I found an empty rum bottle and you smelled like a rum factory when you finally came to bed. Like what you always accused me of, Luv."

"David was just telling me about his plans for a book he plans to write about Barbados. He is very excited about it, and should be encouraged." Susan offered. "And we did do some heavy drinking."

"You see upset with me. Are you?" He asked.

No, darling. Nothing is wrong, unless there might be reason for me to b e upset." She looked at Brian who did not answer, as Susan kissed him on the cheek.

"I just thought he has been acting strangely. That's all." Brian said. "When I cam downstairs, he was sound asleep and the pad he was writing on was on the floor. What do you suspect he meant by Book Two? I neglected to ask him about that. He hasn't written Book One yet."

Susan reddened. "He only told me about writing a novel. Perhaps rum wrecked havoc with his mind and handwriting." She lied.

"Good enough. Are we meeting Geoffrey and Rachel today?" He asked.

"My lover getting a bit horny?" She asked.

"I am always horny around you." He answered.

"Ah, me and how many others?" She asked as she turned to leave. "Later, Luv. I need a shower and loads of makeup. She smiled as Jessica entered the kitchen area in a bikini that afforded the legal amount of cover by Barbados standards.

"Hello McKenzies." Jessica said.

"Hello yourself," Susan responded. "Got to shower. Brian will entertain you until David comes down. Have a good test. And you will join us for dinner tonight?"

"Cool. I would love to. Everyone has been so kind to me." She took a chair next to Brian. "I really appreciate your walking me back last night."

Brian blushed as Susan made a seductive move out of kitchen. "Jessica, one never knows who might be lurking in the bushes with bad thoughts." He said.

David came down and checked his watch. "It is five of ten and time to go."

Brian watched the two of them leave, becoming aroused when he saw what barely covered her bottom. If only he were David's age, he thought and how lucky for his son that he would have Jessica's back as her diving buddy.

Thirty-two

Barbados 1991

Jessica and David aced both the written and deep-water tests. A week had now passed and it was the morning of Geoffrey Townsand's birthday. Geoffrey was in quite a buoyant mood as he crossed Highway One from the Carlton Market car park, eager to join the group that had already assembled on the narrow beach. Jessica emerged from the sea, her long hair tied back in a bun, as David, Brian and Susan got their personal dive gear together.

"I am just so excited about this dive." Geoffrey called out. "What a grand birthday present for all of you to dive the Stavronikita with me."

Susan began to hum her musical version of Stavronikita when Brian playfully tossed water from his mask at her. David asked Jessica if she was nervous, and she responded that it was normal to be a bit concerned, being a novice, having never ever considered diving to the depths planned for the day.

Geoffrey inquired as to Edmund White's whereabouts. "Very odd for White to be late with the dive boat." He said as he scanned the horizon.

"Here he comes now." David called out as a boat painted blue and red began to turn toward the shore.

White anchored the dive boat a short distance off shore, so the divers would only have to carry their gear in thigh deep water. Bottles of air and weight belts were already aboard. Once their dive gear was stowed, David and Brian, who had assisted the women, hoisted themselves onto the boat as it rocked gently in the waves.

The dive boat was about thirty feet long and ten feet abeam. An awning covered most of it, hopefully to protect the divers from the sun. Benches had been secured on both the starboard and port sides, where the divers could sit and comfortably put on their gear. A young Bajan boy, whom White introduced as Winston, was at the helm. As the boat motored out toward a buoy marking the location of the wreck, Edmund White reviewed the rules, the need for a buddy system, and an absolute requirement to decompress at ten feet for ten minutes before surfacing.

They were given the choice of a slow free fall or to come down the anchor line attached to the buoy. When they reached their destination, it was time for last minute instructions.

The divers attached their regulators to the tanks, or bottles as Winston called them, and it was now time to put on their weight belts and vests.

Geoffrey and Brian each had octopuses attached to their regulators in case some one's equipment failed.

Edmund also carried two mini air tanks in his jacket. Since the only communication would be by sign language, this would be the final review before entering the water.

With their masks, snorkels and regulators in place, Brian elected to flip backwards into the water, while Susan chose to jump step. As they waited at the anchor line, Jessica and David back flipped into the water as if they had done it all their lives, and Geoffrey followed. Once Edmund was satisfied that every one was comfortably positioned, he entered the water. Winston would keep the dive boat near by, although there would be some drift with the tide. He would monitor their positions by observing their air bubbles as they rose to the surface.

David was the first to reach the deck of the rusting Russian freighter that had been sunk in the early 1970s, after a fire at sea. Jessica came down the anchor line, let go and floated down next to David.

She marveled at the wondrous world beneath the sea, where myriads of brightly colored fish swam around them seemingly unconcerned. They had both looked at a book depicting the sea life they might encounter, and were able to identify the sergeant majors, surgeon fish and yellow angels just to name a few.

Brian, Susan, Geoffrey and the dive master soon joined them on the deck, and the latter signaled that they follow him through a barnacle crusted passageway that lead to the port side of the ship.

He indicated that they should breathe easily and take in everything their eyes could see. Edmond had them check their gauges, and then motioned them to follow him over the side and into a large hole that had been blown out to scuttle the three hundred foot long vessel. He led them down into a cargo hold, and then out through the starboard side and returned to the deck.

Brian checked his gauge and noted that he had 1400 psi left. He had already used about a thousand psi and indicated to White that he was going to ascend. White looked at Jessica's gauge and seeing that she had about 1500 psi remaining motioned that she accompany Brian to the surface. Susan indicated that she had used little air and gave him a thumb's up. David did as well, but Geoffrey balked at ascending even with barely 1000 psi left in his tank.

Susan swam over to Geoffrey, slapped him on his ass, and pointed upward and indicated she would follow. White called David over to remain with him for more exploration since they had ample air remaining.

After hanging ten, Susan and Geoffrey finally broke through the surface of the sea, as the dive boat neared them with Jessica and Brian already safely aboard. Susan removed her weight belt first and handed it to Brian, and then Geoffrey did the same.

With snorkels in place, they removed their jackets and tanks, and handed them up to Brian and Winston, before attempting to climb up the ladder.

Geoffrey was upset that he had been ordered to ascend, believing he was capable of making that decision for himself.

Jessica was radiant. "Wasn't that just great?" She exclaimed.

"Could have been better." Geoffrey grumbled as Susan put her arms around him and wished him a happy birthday.

"You, Birthday Boy are an unmitigated asshole!" She said.

"Now, Now, this is a civilized island and we are a civilized people. On Barbados, that would be an unmitigated RASSHOLE!" He said with a smile. "He was correct. I need not take chances. It is after all, my birthday."

Brian and Winston watched as two sets of air bubbles came to the surface and then seemed to merge, while David and White held at ten feet. They breached the surface shortly thereafter, and after going through the same procedure as the others before them, climbed onto the boat. Edmond White immediately went over to Geoffrey who apologized, and thanked him for the dive and his justified concerns.

David told Jessica that he and White had descended close to the bottom at 120 feet, and then returned to the deck before they ascended. The two then compared notes as to what they had seen during the dive, which was only fifteen minutes in length but seemed much longer. They all toweled off and put on dry shirts, as Winston turned the dive boat toward the shore.

Since the McKenzies and Jessica had driven down in a taxi, they all piled into the Mercedes, complete with a shiny new perfectly fitting passenger window, and Geoffrey pulled out of the Carlton car park and headed north on Highway One.

"I am famished, and since the new rule is that the birthday person decides the plans for the day, I say it is my treat at Mullins for a late lunch. We can shower off there if you will. David, look under the seat back there. I believe you will find an unopened bottle of Cockspur. Let's start the party now." Geoffrey said with a broad grin.

"Wait," Susan advised. "What about Rachel?"

"Luv, you are so correct. Take my phone and give her a shout to meet us, please." He said. Susan was not certain he really meant for her to do that, but dialed the number, as the bottle of rum was passed around to the five who had just safely and successfully dived the Stavronikita.

Susan let the phone ring at least ten times. "No answer. I'll call again in a bit." She watched as the dinkey houses flew by, as Geoffrey pressed down on the accelerator giving the car more petrol, and began to sing. "Stavronikita, Stavronikita, Stavronikita….it's very good."

Thirty-three

Barbados 1991

That evening Geoffrey provided a fete in his honor for a minimum of 100 people. Besides the usual cast of characters, he had invited their postman, the barman from John Moore who served drinks, and all of the household help from both Blue Heron and Simonton. Of course Enid was there to cook enough fried chicken to satisfy everyone's hunger.

Susan, Jessica, Rachel and Sophia were dressed to kill wearing low cut gowns that showed most of their tan. Both Geoffrey and Brian wore loosely fitting white Tommy Bahamas shirts and dark trousers. David, to be different, wore a tee sporting a New York Yankee logo and dark jeans.

Sophia watched David dance with Jessica, envious of the attention her fiancé seemed to be giving to her, but Brian observing her discomfort, escorted her onto the dance floor where he amazed even Susan with his fluid movements. Purposely moving Sophia toward David and Jessica, they easily switched partners, the music having changed to something resembling a slow fox trot.

"Shouldn't you be dancing with your wife, Brian?" Jessica asked, as she put her arm around his neck.

"She's fine." He responded. "You look absolutely drop dead gorgeous, Brian said, as he felt a tap on his shoulder. Turning, he found Geoffrey waiting to dance with Jessica.

"Protocol, my handsome friend, I'd like a twirl around the floor as well," he said as they exchanged partners. Leaving Geoffrey, Susan smiled as she put both arms around her husband's neck and kissed him. "You know, Brian, vacations are great but we must get back to New York to earn money for the next one. I assume you have been keeping up with what is happening back in the States."

Brian frowned. "I was watching CNN this evening before we left for the party. We are still in the midst of a recession and who knows when things will get any better. The bad news is that we could have a democrat in the White House next year as a backlash against all of the economic woes." Brian danced bumps and grinds with Susan as HOT, HOT, HOT exploded through the speakers.

"Let's sit this one out, Brian." Susan finally said, as she removed her shoes. "Feet staring to hurt."

"One of your favorite songs and you want to sit it out?" He said.

"Haven't worn heels for three weeks, and I am feeling the pain. Go find another young, chickie to dance with." She said.

Brian sought out Rachel, who complained of being too tired to dance. "Sit with me Brian. We can at least talk. I am concerned about Geoffrey, his drinking and his escapades. We really could not afford this party. Tourism is slow. The Brits are staying on the continent, and little money is flowing into the business, so rentals are down."

Brian took her hand. "Look the U.S. economy has not been that great either, and Barbados has always done well with American tourists. Things will pick up soon. Have faith."

Despite Geoffrey's insistence that the party continue into the early dawn, most of the guests had already gone home by one a.m. Brian found Jessica in deep conversation with Sophia, and informed her that they was going back to Blue Heron, if she wished a ride. She told him that she would come back with David.

The McKenzies slept until ten the next morning, awakening to the smell of fresh coffee being brewed by Samuel Braithwaite. Susan went downstairs and was cautioned by him that the two "youngins" were still on the patio.

She was surprised to find both David and Jessica asleep in their clothes on lounge chairs. Susan gently roused Jessica by tapping the young woman on her shoulder.

"Jessica, It's morning. Time for breakfast." Susan said.

Jessica moaned and opened her eyes. "I think I had too much rum punch last night."

"Darling, I know you had too much rum punch last night." Susan replied. How about some coffee?"

"No, I had better get back to my place." She looked at Susan. "Look, David was a perfect gentleman. When we got back late, we both were so drunk, I couldn't walk and he said he wasn't about to carry me through the sand, so we parked here."

"Not a problem. You okay to walk back to your place or should I get Brian to help you?" Susan asked.

"I think I can make it on my own." She said as she got up.

"Why don't you shower and come back for some breakfast? We'll somehow, get my son here upstairs, and I still have to wake Brian." Susan said. Jessica found her pumps and made her way down the steps and through the sand. Susan watched until she was certain that she had safely reached the villa.

Brian was in the shower when the call from New York came. Susan told him to towel off in a hurry since his boss said he must speak to him immediately.

Brian spent about twenty minutes on the phone, advised that he was returning to New York on the next possible flight and hung up.

"Not very good news I assume." Susan said.

"We have to trim down the fat, as he said. The economy has tanked and affected our business adversely like every other business. Available credit has declined, oil prices have increased along with interest rates." He sat down on the edge of the bed.

"Are we the fat?" Susan asked. "At least, perhaps we can survive on what I earn. I believe things will get better."

"I'll find out when I find out. You don't have to go back yet." He said.

"No, my darling, I am coming with you. I have already started to pack. See what tickets are available even if we have to fly into Newark. How about some breakfast?"

David managed a smile as he entered the dining room. "I suppose you found Jessica on the patio." He said.

Susan pulled a chair for him. "Sit down and eat. No explanation necessary, but your father and I have something to talk with you about."

Brian and Susan explained their need to return home to New York. David was old enough to make his own choices, but the matter of money did come up. David explained that he would stay on the island, and that Geoffrey had offered him a job at the Fontabelle office at least for a while, and under the table. Brian suggested that he did not realize that Geoffrey could afford to pay him with tourism and rentals down.

They had just finished their second cup of coffee when Jessica came running in out of breath. Her hair was wet from a recent shower and she had put no make up on. "Just got a call from my, uh, boyfriend. His name is Justin." she sputtered, "and he asked me to marry him and I said yes!"

Susan got up from the table and hugged Jessica who began to cry. "That's great news, darling. You must be so happy."

"Yes, oh yes, I am thrilled. I want to go back to New Jersey today, but don't know if I can get a reservation." Jessica said excitedly.

"Tell you what, Brian has to make reservations for us, so he can try for you as well. Right Brian?" Susan said. Brian agreed to call the airline, as Susan sat Jessica down for some breakfast.

"Tell us about your young man," Susan said.

"Justin is at George Mason University and while initially a political science major, he is now just working towards his Masters in Business. We met actually on a blind date, and have only been able to see each other weekends, when he can drive the four hours up to New Jersey. I am living in Hoboken, and work in the city in the fashion industry. I went to F.I.T." She paused to put a forkful of scrambled eggs into her plate.

"Did you know he was going to propose?" David asked.

Jessica thought for a moment. "We have been going together, on and off for three years and I had an inkling it was going to happen. I was so unsure as to whether he was the one, so that's why I came to Barbados, alone. Oh, and the other good...No, great news is that he was headhunted by a big financial firm that wants him as soon as possible. I believe he said it was called Singer McCarthy and had its offices in the World Trade Center."

Brian came back with the news that he had secured three seats in first class for the American Airlines flight to JFK that afternoon. When he saw Jessica flinch, he assured her that he would pay for the ticket.

The Townsands were unhappy about the sudden departure, and were equally chagrined when Susan told them that they had no idea as to when they might return. Rachel said that they would look after David for as long as he wished to remain on the island, and suggested that it would be good for him to stay at Simonton instead of being alone at the villa.

The flight to New York was uneventful and Brian slept most of the way, while Jessica, excited as she was, talked with Susan for the entire trip. Brian arranged for a cab to take Jessica directly to Hoboken and asked that she call when she reached home. Jessica assured them that she would also call her parents as well.

The following morning, Brian got the bad news from the CEO. He still had his job, but many company perks had to be jettisoned, and among them Blue Heron in Barbados. As reluctant as he was to lose that great mirrored ceiling, he was more pragmatic about not being unemployed. Meghan called and told them that she had a new job, and a new boyfriend, and that she might bring him over for dinner so they could meet him. Late that evening Susan and Brian sat alone in the apartment trying to sort out their financial futures considering the terrible state of the economy.

"Luv," he asked. "When do you suppose we might return to Barbados? It is so much a part of our life, that I am going to miss."

Susan put her arms around Brian. "We can keep this apartment with what we both bring in, even if you have to take a cut. More important we have each other, so que sera, sera."

END OF PART ONE

PART TWO

Thirty-four

New York City 1994-1996

In 1994, the Feds Interest Reserve rate sat at 8.50%, a gallon of gasoline cost $1.09 and a dozen eggs cost 86 cents. You could see a movie for less than $5.00 and the average income was around $37,000. The bad news for Brian was that Major League Baseball was on strike, and he had no reason to go to Yankee Stadium.

Susan's performance at her firm had been impeccable and her billable hours had far exceeded those of the older members. After the senior partner had called her in to commend her performance, she hired two additional clerks, who would provide the time for research and the quality briefs she insisted upon. A major real estate firm gave her a significant retainer, requiring her to be at her desk more often than not. Brian's firm continued to flounder, despite the economic growth the country was experiencing, mainly because of an audit that again suggested questionable fraudulent practices on the part of the CFO. Brian was already in the process of rewriting his CV.

David returned to New York to pick up some of his things, and informed his parents that he and Sophia had put off marriage for a while, but planned to live together.

Geoffrey had found them a small apartment across from Mullins Beach. He was now working for Geoffrey and earning enough money to pay their expenses. Sophia was able to find employment in Bridgetown at Cave Shepard, a major department store on the island.

Susan and David, along with Meghan and her on and off beau attended Jessica and Justin's wedding at an exclusive New Jersey golf course, in Peapack, a horsy-set area frequented at one time by Jacqueline Kennedy. Justin worked in an office at Tower One, at the World Trade Center on the 76th floor for the company that had headhunted and employed him immediately after he earned his MBA. Actually it was Justin who suggested that Brian might be just the person, Singer McCarthy could be looking for, since their CFO had moved on.

Brian had four interviews with the firm, and when its CEO and stockholders were satisfied after two years of vetting, that he had no connection with a SEC investigation at his old firm, they made him an offer. In June of 1996, Brian McKenzie became the CFO of Singer McCarthy, and now occupied a posh corner office on the 75th floor of Tower One. From his leather chair, Brian had an amazing panoramic view of New York Harbor.

Jessica and Justin liked Hoboken enough to purchase two adjoining apartments, and turn them into a huge suite, that gave them a view of the World Trade Center and lower Manhattan.

It was comforting to her that if and when she became pregnant, she could look across the harbor and just feel his presence.

Brian, being ever the workhorse, put in long hours, leaving early in the morning and sometimes not returning home until ten in the evening. The weekends, he shared with Susan, and they made the most of that precious time biking in Central Park, jogging down 5th Avenue in the early morning hours and just spending time together. They missed Barbados, but their heavy schedules precluded any extended vacations.

They heard sporadically from Rachel and Geoffrey, but received news of what was happening on the island via phone calls with Sophia and David, who said he had almost completed the first book, and was also well into the second. Sophia's sister, Sara whom they oddly had never met, married a drummer in Toronto, and saw no reason to return to the island. One of the disturbing bits of news was that Geoffrey was drinking in excess, at least according to Rachel, who said she was concerned for his health. David explained that Geoffrey was not happy that Susan and Brian had not returned to celebrate his last three birthdays and to dive the Stavronikita, and that he expected them to be there at least to celebrate the Millennium if nothing else.

David also advised them, that although rentals had improved and new properties had become available, Geoffrey was not tending properly to business.

One evening while Brian was still at his office, Susan received a call from Geoffrey, who clearly had been drinking. "You cannot imagine how much I miss you two, particularly, you, Luv." He said. "When will you return to Barbados?"

"Geoffrey, are you all right?" She asked. There was no immediate reply. "Geoffrey, both of us miss being with you and Rachel. How is she?"

"Rachel is Rachel. She vexes me a lot and I suppose that I vex her equally as well." He responded. "You know David and Sophia are shacking up instead of getting married? Right. You know that?"

"Is this what is making you, uh…drink more than usual?" She stammered.

"We drink down here. The rum is good, and calms the nerves and the savage beast. Rachel shouldn't complain since when I drink, I can't get it up. She does not want me anyway. So she is safe along with all of the gorgeous tourists on the island. I don't recall the last time the two of us had sex."

"So, Geoffrey what is it that is really vexing you? It is not that we have not been back to the island. You cannot possibly be that upset about David and Sophia. Is business that bad on the island for you?" She asked.

"Business is what I make of it. I am sure that David has shared that with you. Right." He started to sob and then composed himself. "You know of our other daughter, who now calls herself Lady Sara. She lives in Toronto with a horrible bastard who abuses her. She met him singing with a band in Canada, married him and now is ashamed of what she has become, and refuses to leave. Rachel went up to see her. Sophia has called her so many times, but she will not leave him and come back home." Susan heard a few more sobs. "I want to kill the bloody bastard!"

"I wish I could help you. Perhaps Rachel is the one to deal with this. If she could encourage her to visit us in New York, it might be a minor, albeit temporary refuge for her. Put Rachel on the phone." Susan said.

"She is out doing her yoga thing." He said. "But I will tell her. I miss you and thank you for your concern. When will we see you?"

"Any chance of both you and Rachel coming to visit us?" She asked.

"Unlikely, I must tend to business, less I lose all of the confidence I have established. Take care. Love you." He said and hung up.

When Brian returned late that evening, she told him of her conversation with Geoffrey. "You want to bring his daughter here to us? We, I cannot afford any notoriety. The firm will not tolerate it. What if this abuser husband of hers decides to follow her here? No, Susan, please don't even consider it."

"Would you like me to warm up some dinner for you, Brian? She offered. If not I am going to bed to watch the news. I also have had a long day."

"Thanks, no. I had a quick meal at Windows on the World with a client. I'll just grab a drink and take a shower. Would you like a rum as well?" He asked.

"No, and I don't think you really need one either. One Geoffrey is enough." She said.

Brian shrugged and went over to the wet bar and poured himself three fingers of Extra Old Rum. He downed it with an ice chaser, licked his lips and went into the bedroom, where Susan was watching the local weather report.

"We are in for a big snow dump tomorrow. Neither of us may be able to get to work, at least on time if at all." She said. Susan watched as Brian undressed. We have been so busy, I don't remember you being so buff."

Brian smiled, standing naked obstructing her view of the television forecast. " It has been a long time since you noticed or cared. That weather girl sure has big tits for a small person."

"Make the shower quick before I change my mind, Luv." She said, as she heard the water running. Then she seductively removed her top and panties, and looked at the weather girl's profile as she turned toward the map. "Hey! Mine are as big as hers, you know."

Thirty-five

New York 1996

Snow began to fall in the early hours prior to dawn. By the time Brian's bedside alarm went off, at least eight inches had accumulated. Brian tried to peek through the blinds but with the windows frosted, and visibility at zero, he saw very little.

He nudged Susan, who had not responded to the alarm. "Almost seven Susan." He said. As she stretched and sat up, the covers fell away, revealing that she had neglected to put back on her nightwear. "Great," Brian said. "I'm always ready as you can see." Susan playfully tossed her pillow at him, got up from the bed and went into her bathroom.

By the time she was finished with her toilet, Brian had dressed and made coffee. "Toast?"

Susan buttered a piece of toast and took a sip of the hot coffee. "You are not planning to go to work are you?"

"Thought about it. How about you?" He responded.

"I have only a three block walk to my office, but you cannot possibly walk down to the Towers. It must be at least seventy long blocks." Susan said as she watched the weather forecast on TV. "Looks bad, Brian, DC already has a foot and New Jersey is getting pelted. Perhaps you shouldn't go. Take a hot shower, call the office and think it over."

Later, Brian came out of the bathroom toweling his hair. "That felt great. Who was that Bajan Captain who defined a perfect day as one that started with, a shower, a shave and a good fuck? Captain Patch, I think. His name was Patch because he wore that piece of leather over his right eye."

"You're wrong. The patch was over his left eye." Susan retorted. "And it wasn't Captain Patch who said it. It was Geoffrey's friend Richard, the one 'better known as' Foul mouth Dick. And what he never mentioned was a shower, and I doubt if he ever took a shower. It was a shave, a shit and a good fuck. You've already had one out of three, so go for the hat trick."

"Brian defiantly placed his hands on his hips. "Right eye my dear. The patch was definitely over the right eye, and it was Patch who said it. Why do you argue over something so unimportant?"

"You are wrong and I am correct, my Luv." Susan responded.

"Have it your way!" Brian said, as he marched back into his bathroom. When he emerged after his shave, Susan was dressed in a pants suit, and was pulling on her boots. "Where are my boots?" Brian asked.

"In the front closet where they always are." She said. "And take a warm hat and a scarf. Your winter jacket is on a chair in the dining room. If for some reason we must stay over at our offices, we should let each other know."

Brian kissed his wife and now adorned with his hat, scarf and boots, left the apartment. The lobby was empty. The daytime doorman had not even made it through the storm. When he existed the Dakota, he was met with a blast of cold air and deep snow, already up to the top of his boots. He looked around for a cab, but none were in sight. In fact, it appeared that no one else had ventured out into the storm. Brian managed to trudge through the deep snow for about five blocks and when he fell into a drift, after miscalculating where the curb was, he decided to return home and see how Susan had fared.

Upon reaching the Dakota, any evidence of someone entering or leaving had been covered with two or three more inches of snow. Rather than going back up stairs, he called the apartment from the house phone but received no answer.

Brian then decided to walk to Susan's office to see if she made it there safely. He found the building's doorman attempting to clear the walk of snow. Brian asked if he had seen Susan. The doorman explained that he had arrived not that long ago to find a locked entryway, and had seen no one when he arrived. Brian convinced him that he was Susan's husband and was allowed entry. He took the elevator up to the ninth floor and found Susan at her desk.

"Brian, what are you doing here?" She said obviously surprised. "I thought you'd at least have reached the Plaza Hotel by now."

"Could not make it very far through the snow, so I came back to make sure you were all right." He said.

Susan came around from here desk and kissed him. "That was very sweet of you. Stick around. I'm not certain how long it will be worth staying here. I checked the forecast and at least two and one half feet is expected. Thank you for worrying about me."

"It's my job to worry about you. I do love you, Susan." Brian answered.

Susan simply said. "I know."

The blizzard continued for a very long thirty-six hours during which time almost three feet of snow was dumped on the tri-state area.

Brian and Susan heard no more from Geoffrey Townsend regarding Sara. Susan, understanding her husband's angst as far as their involvement, said nothing more about it. She hoped that their friend's issues would resolve, but having had to deal, as an attorney in the past, with spousal abuse problems, she knew in her heart that it most likely would not.

Spring did not arrive too soon for the McKenzies who survived along with the rest of the North East, one of the most brutal winters in history. New Yorkers were happy to once again see the sidewalks free of snow and ice.

The McKenzies having entertained Meghan and her fiancé the previous evening by throwing a surprise dinner at the Palm, slept late the next morning. But it was Sunday and a day off from work was most welcome.

Susan and Brian were happy, for their daughter and Jay, their future son-in-law. Jay was a third year resident in Internal Medicine at the Bronx Municipal Hospital Center and Meghan was in her second year of medical school at Albert Einstein. David and Sophia called from Barbados to congratulate them.

Bright sunlight streamed through the bedroom window awakening Susan. Getting up from the bed, she opened the door that led to the small lanai overlooking Central Park.

"Hey, Brian, folks are up and around. Looks like a great day for a run through the park. What do you say?" She removed the pillow Brian had placed over his head to avoid the glare and kissed him on the forehead.

"Sure," he said. "You know I am always game for a run." Other than a rare visit to the gym, neither had had the time for exercise over the long winter.

Both dressed in generic shorts and tank tops, and laced up their barely used New Balance running shoes. Brian rummaged through his bureau and came up with his white baseball cap emblazoned with BARBADOS 1992 in bright red letters, and suggested that they take the stairs instead of the elevator, quickly reaching the main lobby.

They entered the park via its closest entrance from the Dakota, directly across from the Museum of Natural History.

"Okay," Brian said. "This is the plan. First some stretch exercises are in order, and then I suggest a leisurely jog down to the Ramble, cross in front of the boathouse and come back by Strawberry Fields. Then I shall spring for an elegant brunch at some posh restaurant that will put up with our attire and us."

"Then, perhaps a better choice would be the New Delhi. They would never know the difference." Susan said as she began her run. Oops, Damn. Not politically correct!"

"That is something better kept to ourselves, political correctness, you know." Brian said as he started to follow her. Running at a faster pace, he found himself unusually short of breath, but chalked it up to lack of exercise. Susan was now about fifty yards ahead, so he began to sprint in an attempt to catch up.

By the time he reached the Ramble, he had slowed down considerably. Susan had kept up her pace, and now was almost to the boathouse. When she realized Brian was not with her, she stopped and turned. He was sitting on one of the park benches.

Susan jogged back to the Ramble, and saw that his face was ashen. "You look awful. What's the matter?"

"Lack of exercise. Not used to the run." Brian was clearly out of breath. "I'll be fine after resting a bit."

"Need I call 911?" Susan asked taking a seat next to him.

"Give me a couple of minutes and I'll be okay." He replied.

"Hey, my Luv. When was your last checkup?" She asked.

"Not a factor." He said. "I'll rest for a moment and we can resume."

"Thank you for your reassurance," she said. "But I'm not buying it. I'll call Meghan when we get back to the apartment and get a recommendation for a good cardiologist. I am certain she knows someone at Jacobi Hospital or Montefiore."

"If you don't mind, I'd rather Mt Sinai. I have it on good authority, their physicians are superb." He said.

"My goodness, I married a medical snob." She exclaimed. "No matter, it will be done today."

Brian said he felt better, and that what ever it was had gone. They walked hand in hand, passing Strawberry Fields, the small quiet area dedicated to the memory of John Lennon, and then back to the Dakota with Brian feeling better.

Meghan, clearly concerned when Susan called her, said that Jay personally knew a cardiologist who taught at Einstein and had privileges at Mt. Sinai, and said she would have him call ahead to expedite an appointment. Brian, understanding that the battle was over before it began, relented and agreed to have a check up.

Susan insisted upon going with Brian for his checkup, despite his mild protestation. Jay was able to speak directly to the doctor providing what little information Meghan had shared. Brian's health insurance package was more than adequate so he was happy to pay the $50 copay the receptionist asked for after they entered the rather plush office and signed the registry.

He was handed a five-page insurance and medical history form that he reviewed and checked off everything applicable. For the most part, his history was significant, since it was fairly negative for personal and family illnesses. When he reached questions related to his sexual and urinary history, he left the boxes blank.

Brian sat in the examining room clad only in a T-shirt and boxer shorts for about ten minutes before the door opened, and an attractive young woman, whom he could not believe was more than thirty, entered the room. She shook his hand and introduced herself as Dr. Tyler Anderson, and noted that Brian seemed taken aback.

"It would appear that Jay never told you that I was a female cardiologist. Will that be a problem for you? Mr. McKenzie. Mr. McKenzie, I asked you a question."

Brian collected himself and took a deep breath. When he saw the name, it never occurred to him that even Susan knew that the cardiologist might be a female. Or did she?

"I am not averse to have my patients call me Tyler, since it is much less formal. Will that be acceptable to you Brian?" She asked smiling while taking a seat beside the examining table upon which Brian was perched.

Brian returned the smile. "Ready when you are Tyler, and I love your name."

"It is settled then," she said as she reviewed the information on his checklist. "So, no shortness of breath other than the present episode. Family history appears good with great longevity. You take no meds and some vitamins sparingly. How about exercise?"

"I used to run a lot. The times we spent in Barbados, I jogged swam and scuba dived. Also played a lot of tennis, but lately my work schedule has prevented me from doing much other than a rare visit to the gym." He said.

"Barbados. I have often wanted to go there." She said.

"You must. Everything is better in Barbados." He said. They both smiled.

Tyler Anderson returned to the checklist. "Hmmn, I see nothing checked relating to your sexual or urinary history. Or your date of birth. How come?"

Brian thought for a moment. "I really didn't think it was any of the receptionist's business. I was 46 in January. Will you send me a card? What else do you wish to know about me?"

"Frequency of urination or difficulty starting and sustaining a stream?" She asked. Brian responded to the negative.

"How about sex?" She asked.

"Is that an offer or just an inquiry?" Brian responded.

Tyler Anderson blushed and smiled. "Very funny. How often do you have sexual intercourse?"

"As often as possible," he responded.

"And are you monogamous?" She asked. She observed Brian's hesitation.

"Of course, Susan, my wife wouldn't have it any other way. We have been married a long time." He said.

"Let's get to the nitty gritty. Year of your birth?"

Brian said. "1950. I told you how old I was."

"Right. That would make your current age 46. All right, now Jay Hartstein is your daughter Meghan's fiancé. You also have a son I understand." She said.

"Yes, David. He currently lives in Barbados with friends. Both of them are well." He said.

She had Brian lie down and then took his pulse and blood pressure. He removed shirt and responded to the doctor's requests to breath or not breathe, as she listened with her stethoscope.

"Okay, now remove your boxers. Need to check your prostate." She said.

Brian looked at her without complying. "Thought you were a heart doctor." He said.

"Brian, I am really not personally interested in your genitalia, as much as you may or may not appreciate, but I plan to examine your abdomen, make certain you have no testicular masses, check for prostate enlargement and what ever else I might find upon rectal exam." She was emphatic.

Brian reluctantly removed his shorts, concerned that he might become aroused, and lay back on the table as she directed. Dr. Anderson examined his abdomen, put on a pair of latex gloves and proceeded to examine each of his testicles and then went on to unemotionally check his penis. "Turn on your side, Brian and raise up your right leg." She instructed. "Or would you rather step down on the floor and bend over?"

Brian opted for the former. When she was finished, she told him to dress except for his shirt, explaining that a technician would be in to do an ECG and draw some blood.

When the technician had finished, she told him to dress and meet the doctor in her private office for a consultation and instructions. He found Susan sitting with Dr. Anderson already deep in conversation.

"What are you two talking about?" He asked taking a seat next to his wife.

"Why, we are talking about you, Luv?" Susan responded.

"Brian," Tyler began. "First of all your blood pressure is a bit higher than I would like, so I plan to start you on some meds to improve that. Secondly, your prostate is a bit enlarged, so I did ordered a PSA as part of the blood panel already drawn. The draw will also examine your blood count, liver function and cholesterol. Now back to sex, that you seemed reluctant to discuss other than your lame attempt at being funny."

Brian was immediately concerned that Susan had shared their Bajan sexcapades with the good doctor. "Susan has confided in me that there are times that, despite the fact that sex is good, you can't sustain an erection. Now this could be just a result of hypertension or prostate hyperplasia, er, enlargement. With regard to your blood pressure, the higher number, the systolic, was 160 and your diastolic, the lower number was 96. I do not believe it was due to being half naked in my presence. The PSA will make certain that the hyperplasia of your prostate is just innocent enlargement. I must ask you to reduce the amount of alcohol you drink. I do not believe that moderate that you checked off is accurate; although I understand from Susan that consumption goes up for both of you while on holiday.

Brian seemed relieved that Susan had been reasonably discreet. "What now, Tyler?"

"All in all, you are in good physical shape. There will be a prescription waiting for you at the front desk along with your next appointment. Oh, your cardiogram was essentially normal, and you will get a call regarding your blood results. Expect a personal call from me to see how you are doing." She rose, shook hands with both Susan and Brian and led them out to the reception area.

Waiting for the elevator, Brian asked Susan what ever motivated her to tell Dr. Anderson about their sex life. "Because I knew you wouldn't." She answered. "I just noticed something lately, and you seemed to ignore it."

"I was more concerned about your telling her about Rachel and Geoffrey." He said.

"Gee, please don't leave out the drug dealer and his sexpot wife, Brian."

Brian shrugged. "I bet Geoffrey would find her hot."

"I trust you are referring to that tootsie and not your new cardiologist. Oh by the way, did she give you a hard on? Let's go home."

Thirty-six

New York 1996

After filling Brian's prescription at a nearby CVS, they went to a in vogue "noodle" restaurant on 58th St., for a light dinner. There were two messages on the answer phone when they returned to the apartment.

Meghan had called to see how Brian had made out with his doctor's appointment, and there was also a brief message from Geoffrey asking Brian to call him A.S.A.P.

Brian dialed the 246 area code and number Geoffrey had left, and the latter answered the phone with his deep Bajan voice. "Hello Mon. Thanks for ringing me back so soon. Are we on speakerphone? There seems to be an echo." He heard a button being hit, and the echo disappeared. "Better. Susan around?"

"No," Brian lied. "She's taking a bath." He looked at Susan, and placed his index finger on his lips.

"Cool! Brian, I have a little problem that I hope you can help me with." Geoffrey seemed anxious.

"Anything. You know that bro. What's up?" Brian asked.

"That is exactly the crux of the matter." Geoffrey responded. "There is a new drug, I need you to get for me if you can. Perhaps from Meghan. I hear from David that she is in training to be a medical doctor."

"True. True. But what does she have to do with any issues you may have?" Brian asked. "The drugs we have here, are available on the island, although from what I hear, our FDA drags their feet on new drugs. You would be more likely to find what you need on the island, since it is a member of the Commonwealth."

"Every one knows everything about everyone on this island. This is personal except for you, and I want it kept that way. Please do not embarrass me by telling Susan." Geoffrey pleaded.

"What's the name of this drug and what is it for?" Brian asked.

"Viagra and it is used for not being able to maintain a hard on." Geoffrey replied. "Bloody expensive, but damn the cost if it works as it is supposed to."

Brian was in no way ready to share his own personal issues with Geoffrey, but wanted to learn more about this Viagra. "How might it help your problem?" Susan turned her palms up and mouthed "What!" Brian waved her off and again put his index finger to his lips.

"From what I hear, it is amazing. Keeps you hard for hours. I have ED. They use it for something called erectile dysfunction. See if you can help me out." Geoffrey said. "Got to go, Rachel just walked in." Susan mouthed "Sara?"

"Hold on Geoffrey. You made no mention of Sara." Brian said.

"Apparently resolved," Geoffrey said. "She told the bastard off and plans to come to Barbados in a week or so. She has to tie up loose ends. Whatever that means. Ciao, my friend."

Brian hung up the phone and looked at Susan. "Seems that Geoffrey and I have more in common than sex with each other's wives. I am surprised that Tyler did not suggest I get this pill called Viagra that according to Geoffrey, counters this erectile dysfunction that I may have."

"Actually, we discussed it while waiting for you. She is not a urologist, but thought you should see one. I have her recommendation. She also said that elevated blood pressure as well as enlarged prostate could cause your problem to worsen. Now, what does Geoffrey want from us?" Susan asked.

"Not from us, but from Meghan or Jay. I could ask him to write a script for Geoffrey and enough so that I could share." Brian said.

"Not a great idea to medicate yourself." Susan said.

"I'll read the info that comes with the prescription or better, I'll go on line and check out its pros and cons. After all, you would like me harder for hours on end. Wouldn't you?" He asked.

"Tell you what. I'll go on line and collect the information for you. Do you have any idea what it costs?" She asked.

"Bloody expensive according to Geoffrey." Brian responded. "I'll call Jay and thank him for the referral to Tyler, and broach the Viagra subject for Geoffrey. It's not like it's a narcotic. Oh, regarding your question about Sara. She is returning to Barbados sans, as Geoffrey calls him, 'that bloody bastard'."

Susan sat at the laptop for about ten minutes, when she found what she was looking for. "Here it is Brian and it comes with warnings and disclaimers. You might go deaf. You might lose your sense of smell, and you might have an erection lasting for hours." She laughed.

"I'll read to you exactly how it is written. If your erection lasts more than four hours, you should go to an emergency room or call your doctor."

"Really," Brian said with a smile. "I would much rather just call out NEXT!" He ducked to avoid being hit with the latest issue of People Magazine.

Thirty-seven

New York and Barbados 1998-2000

Meghan McKenzie became the wife of Dr. Jay Hartstein on Sunday morning, April 12, 1998 at Temple Beth El, a conservative synagogue in Westfield, New Jersey. Despite her busy schedule as a first year resident in Pediatrics, she found the time to take lessons from the Rabbi who would convert her to Judaism, and ultimately marry them. Neither Jay nor his parents ever broached the subject. Meghan did it out of her love for her future husband. Jay had joined a multi-specialty medical group in Watchung, New Jersey, so he and his new wife were resigned to the fact that they would only see each other on the weekends she was not on call, at least for the time being.

Brian arranged to have the reception at Windows On The World, and paid for everything except the liquor that Jay's dad insisted was his obligation. There were about one hundred guests in attendance including Geoffrey Townsend who brought five cases of Barbados rum with him. David, served as best man, and Sophia was Meghan's choice to be one of her bridesmaids. Rachel could not attend since she found it necessary to remain in Barbados with Sara, whose drug and drinking issues still had not been resolved. Jessica and Justin were not able to make the ceremony, but did come to the reception.

Jessica told Meghan that she was trying to become pregnant.

Geoffrey forgave Brian and Susan for not attending any of his birthday bashes over the past several years having found a new lease on his sexual life, as a result of the miracle of modern medicine, Jay had obtained for him. Brian never thought that the drug was all that great, having moments when he believed he failed Susan, who seemed to be not at all enthusiastic about sex. He was glad Geoffrey had come to the wedding, even without Rachel, in hopes that his presence might invigorate Susan. This was not to be the case with David and Sophia staying at the apartment, so a menage was out of the question. The bad part was that Susan did not seem to be upset by her lack of interest in intimacy. Unfortunately, Geoffrey had to return to Barbados the Tuesday after the wedding. David convinced Sophia to stay for a week to see New York, much to the delight of his parents. Susan and Brian assured Geoffrey, before he left, that they would be staying with him and Rachel for the celebration of the Millennium.

New Years day 2000 would fall on a Saturday. While Susan expressed a desire to spend both Christmas and New Years on Barbados with the Townsends, Brian, convinced her that is was important to both of them, that they attend the office Christmas party.

They left from JFK on December 29, 1999 and landed at Grantley Adams where Sophia waited for them in Geoffrey's brand new Land Rover.

"I guess business on the island has improved, " Brian remarked as he loaded the luggage into the boot. Our flight was filled to capacity."

Sophia slowly eased the Rover from its parking place onto the highway. "So, tell me," Brian said. "Have there been many cane fires?"

Sophia looked at him. "What?" She asked.

"Ignore him," Susan said. "He has asked that question of every one who has ever picked us up at the airport all the years we have been coming to Barbados. Sophia, be a Hon and put the air on. It is great to be back here, but I got the usual blast of heat and humidity when we exited the plane and am starting to wilt."

"How are Jay and Meghan?" Sophia inquired.

"They are great, and were able to get away but only for the weekend. They will be arriving tomorrow." Brian said.

"Cool!" Sophia replied. "Has David said anything to you?"

"About what?" Susan asked.

"Well, let me be the first to inform you that you two are going to be grandparents. A little slip up on both our parts so I will be entering my third month." Sophia said not taking her eyes from the road.

"Your folks must be thrilled." Susan said.

"Mom knows, but Dad does not. He would be so vexed with us. So the solution is that David and I will be married in May, even with our little surprise showing. It is not what you Yanks might refer to a shotgun wedding, since David and I just moved up the time and nothing more."

"And you don't think Geoffrey is going to notice anything, and he can count you know." Brian said.

"Dad will be cool with everything, since he will want to control the entire wedding anyway." Sophia said, as she turned onto the top road, better known as highway number two. "We are going straight to Simonton, and since Mom has her car, she'll bring David and Dad back from Fontabelle." Sophia turned on the Rover's headlights. "It gets dark early. We still call it Tom's time." Former prime mister Tom Adams had instituted daylight saving's time back in the mid nineteen seventies.

Sophia's shortcuts were familiar to Brian, who had driven them not that many years ago. The cane was high and ripe, just waiting to be harvested. She drove past the old abandoned sugar cane factory and eventually made a right turn onto Highway One, near the estate where Sir Alec Guinness once vacationed. Simonton sat between the two highways, but the access was better from the Caribbean side. Susan and Brian watched, as the Rover passed the tall royal palms that had greeted so many McKenzies over so many years. As they drove up to the veranda, they were surprised to see Geoffrey and David waiting for them on the steps.

Geoffrey ran down to greet both of them, and David hugged his mother tightly. Susan smiled at him, and he understood that his and Sophia's secret had been shared.

"Rachel, Luv, our family has arrived from the states. Please be a dear and tray some ice. I have bottles of Extra Old, just begging to be consumed." Geoffrey called out as he went back into the house.

Rachel set the tray of glasses and ice down and embraced Susan and then Brian. "I am so glad you both are here to celebrate the Old Year, such as it has been." She said.

"That's right, you people celebrate it as Old Year, while we Yanks, as you say, celebrate New Years." Brian offered.

"Susan, what was that toast of yours?" Rachel asked.

Glasses were filled and passed around as Susan stood up from the chaise. "Hope I have not forgotten. Over the teeth, and past the gums, look out stomach, here it comes." With that, she downed the contents and followed it with an ice water chaser.

"You have too forgotten. That, my Luv, is sipping rum and not guzzling stuff like Cockspur. But I shall forgive you." Geoffrey said. "Sophia, no drink for you?"

"My stomach's a bit upset, Daddy, so I'll pass if you don't mind." She replied.

"Suit yourself but when I was your age or even a lot younger, your grandfather gave us rum for what ever ailed us."

"Sort of like the French with wine?" David said.

"Not exactly medicinal as wine, right? Right!" He answered his own question. "So I have not heard from Jay or Meghan." Geoffrey asked Brian.

"Not to worry, my Bajan friend. They will arrive Thursday."

"In that case, drinks around again for everyone. Sophia, are you certain?" Geoffrey asked. She said that she was, and excused herself, saying that she would check on the progress of dinner.

"So Brian, another fill?" Geoffrey asked as he collected Brian's empty glass.

"Perhaps later. I have been advised to cut down on my drinking and the warden here", he pointed at Susan, "is keeping count." Brian laughed.

"I told him that I would remove the cuffs Friday night for the celebration." Susan said. "How are we spending it? You were so secretive about the plans."

"Cuffs…cuffs. I comprehend now. Handcuffs. How clever you are Susan, and exceedingly beautiful as well." Susan blushed reminded of Geoffrey's sexual appraisal of her on his boat so many years ago.

Rachel took a seat next to Susan. "We have so much to catch up on. So many years since we all were together." She said taking Susan's hand.

"Right, Susan." Geoffrey said. " I have planned a perfect evening for all of us, and Jay and Meghan will arrive just in time."

Rachel looked at Susan and shrugged her shoulders. "A lot has happened since we last talked. You recall the Pirate Cruises? Well how could you possibly forget such debauchery? The owner wanted to expand and add a different venue, so he had this huge ship built, and asked if I might like to become a minor partner. I told him immediately that it would be a very minor role, but he accepted it. All of the partners are Bajan born and involved in some manner with tourism."

Susan clapped her hands like a young child might. "How exciting!" She exclaimed as a phone rang somewhere inside the house. Sophia came running with the news that Justin and Jessica would be coming down with Meghan and Jay, and it was Meghan who had called.

"That will not be a problem with all of these unexpected guests? Brian asked.

"Not at all, as far as we are concerned, the McKenzies will stay here at Simonton with us. David and Sophia have their own place, so we will find villa accommodations for them on the beach. You know that Blue Heron is being torn down to make room for condominiums. Some kind of progress." Geoffrey said.

"I don't suppose they can save those bedroom ceiling mirrors?" Brian asked.

"Too late, my friend. They are presently resting in what was once the old sugar boiling shack." Geoffrey said with a toothy, broad smile. "Oh, and about dinner. I had wished to take everyone out this evening, but Rachel talked me out of it."

"Right." Rachel interrupted. "I had better see what cook is doing. We are having pumpkin soup and codfish balls." She hesitated and looked at her husband. "Don't even say it Luv. Where was I? Right. The menu. Flying fish and lots of healthy local vegetables. Dessert will be that gorgeous warm chocolate pudding everybody loves, the recipe taken from the Cliff. Of course all the rum, whatever you wish to consume, plus I had Geoffrey spring for some cognac as well. I'll have a rum and coke."

The phone rang again. This time is was for Susan. She returned and sat down looking ashen. "Brian, refill the glasses and pour yourself a long one as well. Once everyone had a glass in there hand, Susan stood up. "You all must remember our friend Al. We introduced him to Barbados and it became his home away from home." There was a trace of a smile and then sadness.

"If you recall, he threw the wild parties at his villa on the beach. The phone call was from his daughter. My office must have told her how I could be reached. Al passed away Saturday morning in New Jersey. God bless you Al. If it feels good, do it, he used to say. Al, it just doesn't feel very good right now." Susan started to cry. One by one everyone came over and hugged her. Brian was the last and lingered the longest.

Susan stared absently past the magnificent royal palms to where the moonlight danced on the silent Caribbean Sea. She lifted her glass. "One more time for Al. Over the teeth and........" Brian finished what she was not able to continue.

Susan was not about to spoil the evening for everyone. She loved the people she was with. She loved Barbados and she loved Bajan food. All throughout dinner she managed to smile as they all reminisced about the good times they had over the years together. Susan had coffee and even a small cognac, but then excused herself. "You all don't mind if I retire?" She said and added. "Tomorrow is going to be a great day and we will all be together as a family."

Brian accompanied Susan up to their room and sat next to her on their bed. "You know, Al would not wish anything to spoil our holiday, here on his island as well as ours." He said, as she dabbed tears from her cheeks with a tissue.

"Brian, you wouldn't mind if we didn't tonight?" She said as she kissed him. "It is so sad that we have not spent any time with Al these past few years." She smiled. "It was just last year or the year before that he cooked dinner for us."

"We have a long day ahead of us, and certainly well into the New Year according to Geoffrey's schedule. Take a hot bath and get some sleep."

Susan gazed at an old map of Barbados that hung over the bureau. "He used to like that cove on the East Coast. I can't remember the name. Oh, we must be back in time for the funeral, which is scheduled for Wednesday. I'll clear my calendar. How about you?"

"I'll call the office tomorrow morning. At least one of the secretaries will be there." Brian said. He blew her a kiss and went back downstairs. When he returned hours later, he found Susan sound asleep. After quietly undressing, Brian slipped under the sheets and moved close to Susan, gently putting his hand on a shoulder that was still warm from the bath she taken earlier.

Thirty-eight

Barbados   MILLENIUM

Geoffrey assumed that he would be the first one downstairs, but was pleased to find Susan, her bathing suit, still damp from her swim in the pool. He took her face in his hands and kissed her lips gently. "You, Luv, look so much better, and obviously ready for a great weekend."

Susan smiled and moved over on the chaise to make room for him. "No one has said anything about Sara." She said. "Obviously she is not staying here at the house."

"Poor dearest Sara. Rachel cries at night wondering what we could have done wrong." Geoffrey waited for the lump in his throat to pass as Susan squeezed his hand. "We sent her to Antigua for rehabilitation. It is a closed sanitarium, where she is unable to leave the property on her own. Unfortunately, she has always found the worst of the worst here on the island. More drugs than alcohol. I am never certain how she paid for her habit. Actually, it is not something I choose to think about."

"We try to instill values in our children, but we are never always around to make certain they make the right choices." Susan said as Rachel came onto the patio.

"Okay, you two conspirators. Talking about me are you?" Rachel laughed. "Who would like some breakfast? I have eggs and good Canadian bacon. Coffee's just about perked."

Susan rose. "Geoffrey was filling me in about Sara. It is so sad." She said, hugging Rachel.

Rachel gently pulled away. "It is what it is, and we are making the best of it. I plan to fly over to Antigua next week to visit with her. Right, now about breakfast."

"I smell coffee," Brian said as he joined the others. "Tell me where I might find a tray and I'll bring some out to the patio." Rachel took his arm and led him back into the house. He returned shortly with cups of steaming hot coffee, cream and some good Barbadian sugar. "Rachel is making eggs and bacon for us, and David and Sophia are on their way."

"So Camp Director," Susan said to Geoffrey, "what's on the schedule for today?"

"We go to Mullins for as long as we wish, and then I thought we could drive over to the East Coast for drinks, and then to the airport to pick up the kids at four-ish. Best we take both the Rover and Rachel's Lexus." Geoffrey said as he burned his tongue, sipping the hot coffee.

David and Sophia arrived, dressed in shorts and tank tops, and joined the others for breakfast. They thought a morning at Mullins would be just fine. Rachel took Sophia aside and suggested that she not wear her bikini, and find a more appropriate non-revealing suit in her old room upstairs. She also asked when she and David planned to inform her father about their wedding plans. Sophia thought it would be just great to tell him when they kissed him Happy New Year on the boat.

Geoffrey finished the last of his breakfast. "Brian, I forgot to ask you about this Y2000 nonsense. Will the world come to an end as all of the clocks self-destruct? CNN keeps on predicting this will happen."

"I suggest you ignore this and most of what CNN has to say. They know they have a captive audience and will tell you anything they wish you to hear." Susan nodded in agreement. "Hopefully, the island, and the entire Caribbean will be soon exposed to more fair, honest, balanced, and truthful news in the near future."

"Right!" Rachel said. "We might be getting into politics. Let's not. I am ready for the beach! Leave the dishes for the housekeeper. Oh, and Samuel Braithwaite is now working here as well. He will be here later."

The Townsends and the McKenzies arrived at Mullins first, and moved six chaises close to the water, lest they burn the soles of their feet on the hot sand. David and Sophia arrived fifteen minutes later, Sophia having a problem with her choice of swimsuit. She opted for a two-piece suit Rachel had not worn for some time.

Geoffrey looked at his daughter incredulously. "Sophia, you have such a great figure. How come you are not showing it off with one your thong jobs?"

"I just did not like what I had, so I borrowed one of Mommy's." Sophia said. "Lets go for a swim David."

"Leave her be," Rachel said.

"If you say so love, but you and Susan are dressed more for Barbados, and have such great bodies to show off, and you certainly are doing that." Geoffrey said. "What do you think, Brian?"

Brian did not answer immediately, since he was watching a thirty or so woman walking topless into the water. "We have nude beaches now, Geoffrey? I'm sorry what were you saying?"

I was also commenting on the state of undress, which is good, of our wives compared to my overdressed daughter. That chick over there does have great tits though." Geoffrey said.

"Perhaps you should concentrate more on her than our daughter." Rachel said. "Come on Susan, let's give our men something to look at as we go for a swim."

Both Susan and Rachel took off their small covering skirts, revealing thongs that accentuated their swaying buttocks, as they made their way down to the sea. "This will definitely take my husband's mind from Sophia." Rachel said with a laugh.

Brian grinned proudly, as he watched his wife move towards the water's edge. "Not bad for a woman moving in on 48 years. Her body remains young. Sadly her passions have diminished."

"You are skylarking, Brian. Susan is older than I am. True. True?" Geoffrey said.

"My good Bajan friend. This must remain our secret. Right?" Geoffrey nodded in agreement, but the thought intrigued him.

By noon, the air had become extremely hot and unbearable with the sun hovering overhead. "Time to quit this place and run over to the East Coast. I need that breeze." Geoffrey said.

Brian swam out to the float where David and Sophia had spent most of the morning and informed them of their plans. He returned and told Geoffrey that they would meet everyone at the bar at Barclay's Park.

Geoffrey took the road that went past Cherry Hill, and parked on the side of the road, so they could admire the magnificent view of the Atlantic, as it swept in on the beaches of the East Coast of the Island. Far to the south they saw Three Boys Rock guarding Bathsheba.

At Barclay's Park, Geoffrey ordered three Banks for himself, Susan and Brian, while Rachel opted for her usual rum and coke. They took off their sandals and walked down to the water, where small brilliant colored shells, and black mussels had been washed upon the white sand. Brian and Susan sat in a pool of cool water trapped by rocks along the shore.

Rachel and Geoffrey walked further down the beach hand in hand, and Susan wondered how often that had ever happened.

"Rachel told me that the kids plan to tell Geoffrey about their wedding plans tomorrow night at mid-night." She said as she finished her now warm bottle of Banks.

"Kids are here!" Geoffrey shouted as he spied David and Sophia making their way down the rocks toward them.

"Daddy, David and I are hungry and we don't wish to eat here at the bar. Please can we go elsewhere?" Sophia said. "Perhaps the Kingsley Club?"

"Sadly, it is now closed. Well, there is a buffet at the Ocean Cliff or we could go to the Round House." Geoffrey said.

"I'm not a particular fan of buffets," Brian said, "and neither is Susan. You eat too much of the wrong things because it is unlimited. I say the Round House."

"Fine with us," Rachel said.

They were seated at a table out on the balcony where they had a view of the coast from Pico Tenerife down to Bathsheba. The continuous roar of the Atlantic, forced them speak a bit louder, but no one seemed to mind. Brian and Susan had hamburgers made supposedly with U.S. beef.

The waitress told them that the owner was from New Jersey. David and Sophia selected flying fish on a bun with fries and both Geoffrey and Rachel had Jamaican patties. They all had rum and cokes to wash their lunch down except for Sophia who preferred some soda water with lime.

After lunch and a few more drinks, it was decided that they would drive down to Bathsheba to do some shelling, since this way they would be closer to Grantley Adams. Jay and Meghan's flight was due in around three in the afternoon.

They reached the airport in plenty of time, and found out that two Air Canada Jumbos had landed with a full compliment of passengers. This meant that it would take a long time for customs and baggage issues to be resolved. From the second floor, through rather dirty windows, they saw Jay and Justin deplaning first with Meghan and Jessica following.

The four got on the customs line. Jay called out to Brian that the only luggage they had were carry-ons. Having nothing to declare, they were soon outside where everyone waited. After hugs and kisses, they divided up and Meghan, Jay and David rode with the Townsands in the Lexus, and Justin, Jessica and Sophia went in the Land Rover with Brian and Susan.

School was letting out by the time they reached Highway One, so they had frequent stops to deal with. Brian was able to pass a big blue bus he had been following, just missing an oncoming moke, and frightening the tourist at the wheel. David drove the Lexus, and decided to take a less traveled road that actually got him to Simonton some minutes before Brian.

"I was able to find a place for the four of you just next to David and Sophia's apartment. It has two large bedrooms each with a shower and you will be directly across from Mullins." Geoffrey said. "This way the six of you young people can have fun, without us older folk getting in your way. David can carry you there and then back to Simonton later, but for now we have arrived."

"You seemed not to have brought many clothes." Rachel said. "If you need something, I am sure we can help out."

"No worries," Jay remarked. "We really got a lot of stuff in these carry-ons. If you fold properly, the finest of duds will look just great. So as far as the party is concerned, we all will look elegant, particularly our gorgeous wives."

"Gentlemen and ladies, the bar at Simonton Great House, in the Parish of St. James, on beautiful Barbados, is open for business. Who asked if it is after five? It is always after five on Barbados." Geoffrey wheeled a movable bar onto the patio, and as almost on cue, Beautiful Barbados sung by the Merrymen filled the entire old house.

In order to placate her father, Sophia accepted a glass of red wine, but did not take more than a sip. Jay called Geoffrey aside and handed him a vial that contained at least 100 blue Viagra pills. When Geoffrey asked what he owed, Jay merely shrugged and said he had gotten them as samples from the urologist in his group. "Knock yourself out my friend," he said. "But please follow the instructions I have included."

Geoffrey thanked him profusely. "Don't worry about the cost of your accommodations since there are none. I also stocked your apartment with some great Barbados rum. Son, we all are going to have a bloody good time celebrating the Millennium. And that is true, true."

Geoffrey, ever the gracious host, kept the rum flowing and soon Jay and Justin had become expert at Barbados quickies. Jessica, having perfected the art a few years ago during her stay showed them how proficient she was.

Meghan was a good sport and went along, but expressed her preference for some white wine, or if she had rum it would be sugar cane brandy with soda.

Brian studied Jessica, who had matured beautifully. She told him that she had changed jobs, and now worked for a marketing firm that had moved their offices into Tower Two on the 56th floor. She was excited that she and Justin would be so close during the day.

Rachel looked at Geoffrey. "Oh, Lord!" Then she chip singed. "We have made no plans for dinner."

"We can drink dinner and then go to Enid's for a chaser." Geoffrey said.

"No," Meghan said. "I have taken care of that. I was able to get a table for ten at the Cliff. I told Jay so much about that hot chocolate pudding or what ever, he said we all had to go. And it is our treat. There will be no argument. Dinner is at eight, so we'll head back with David and Sophia, and we can shower and dress appropriately for the occasion."

Since dinner would cost the boys a small fortune in U.S. dollars David said he would pay his share. The service was elegant. Everyone chose a different entrée that they generously shared. Jay ordered cognac and coffee along with the warm chocolate pudding he heard so much about from Meghan and Jessica.

Susan suggested that if they were not too tired, that they stop at the Coach House for drinks, but insisted that Brian was buying and there would be no argument. The place was jumping as usual, but the group bellied up to the bar and came away with rum and cokes, all except Sophia who ordered a glass of white wine.

Meghan took her brother aside. "Okay David, what's up? Sophia had nothing to drink at dinner. I mean she ordered wine, took a sip and that was it."

"You must promise not to tell Geoffrey." He said. Mom and Dad and Rachel know that Sophia is pregnant. She believes that Geoffrey will be very vexed as she calls it. The plan is for us to tell Geoffrey that we plan to marry in May of this year, at midnight, and he'll be so excited being the wedding planner, he won't be so vexed when he finds out our little secret."

"I am so happy for you two. You both must be so excited." She said.

"We just have to figure out how to pay for the baby." David said.

"Come back to New York and let her deliver there. You could stay with us. We have lots of room." Meghan said.

"You know how much I appreciate that, but I will talk with Sophia. That's all I can promise. She is determined to have the baby on the island." David said.

"But what if there is a problem." She said.

"There will be no problems." He answered.

"I forgot to ask. How is your book coming along?"

"The first book is complete and needs editing. The second book which will hopefully be the lead for the first is almost finished." He responded.

"What's it about. The second book?" She asked.

He whispered in her ear. "Sex, sex, sex and more sex. You cannot imagine."

"I am not certain I wish to. When can I read it?"

"I have a copy at the apartment. I'll let you look at it, but only you." He said emphatically.

It was New Years Eve. Susan came down the long winding staircase in a very low cut red dress that rested just above her knees. Brian whistled as she reached the last step. "Hi! Beautiful."

"Hi, yourself," She answered. "Don't you look handsome?" Brian wore white pants and a checkered short sleeve shirt, and well-shined black loafers covered his sock-less feet. "Where are Rachel and Geoffrey?"

"On the patio," He replied, got to have drinks before we drink some more, you know."

Geoffrey handed Susan a glass of rum, and pointed to the glasses of ice water he had placed on the table. He smelled of the same Old Spice after-shave she remembered when they first had sex fourteen years ago.

Geoffrey wore a white, long sleeve shirt, three of whose top buttons remained undone, and black pants and short black boots. Rachel wore a white pants suit that unfortunately accentuated some of the weight she had gained around her hips.

"We shall meet the rest of our party at Deep Water Harbor where the boat is anchored. Sea's a bit rough so we shall remain in harbor all night. Right. We should be off."

As they drove south on Highway One, they noticed that parties at the Coach House and then the Cliff were already underway with laughter and loud calypso music. When they reached the end of Black Rock, Geoffrey turned the land Rover around the roundabout and onto Spring Garden Highway. Deep Water Harbor was a short ride ahead.

Brian was amazed at the size of the ship whose entry way was almost the width of its beam. Bright lights adorned the vessel and the Merrymen singing 'Hot,Hot,Hot' blasted from loudspeakers set along the length of the boat.

Members of the crew, wearing red and white horizontal striped shirts greeted them, suggesting that they move toward a strategically placed bar, almost the width of the boat itself.

Jay, Justin and Meghan were already on their third rum punch. Sophia excused herself saying that she had to use the head on the lower deck.

"Look at all of the stars, and the moon is so bright. You know, I believe 2000 will be a great year." Brian handed Susan a rum and coke. "I'd rather a sugar cane brandy and soda, if you don't mind, Brian." He just wondered if lately, he could get anything right.

"Not a problem. I can handle that." She watched him drink half of the glass she had turned down, and then he left to fetch what she wanted. Sophia joined her along the passageway that led to the stern, where dinner would be served.

"Sophia, darling. Is anything wrong?" Susan asked.

"No, but my body seems so out of control. I just cannot explain it. I hope it will be a good pregnancy. David will take me for a sonogram next week." Sophia said. "Here comes Daddy. I had better get a drink to hold for a prop." She kissed Geoffrey on his cheek as she passed him on her way back to David and the rest of their party at the bar.

"Ah!" He said. "Methinks I hear the strains of Beautiful Barbados. Fancy a dance with an old friend?"

They walked along the passageway to an area behind the bar, where a dance floor had been set up.

The Merrymen sang, and Susan and Geoffrey moved expertly to the song, she loved so much. Soon Brian and Rachel joined them, and in a matter of moments, all ten of them were swaying to the music. By ten p.m. the ship seemed packed with people, dancing, drinking and just having a good time. After a while, Brian and Susan left the dance floor, while Geoffrey danced with some of the local women he knew. Rachel seemed content to sit at the bar and drink.

A half hour before mid-night, party hats, bead necklaces that fluoresced and noise makers, were handed out to the revelers. Susan placed a black fedora on her head and began to move her hips Bajan style. Brian joined her and they seemed to just fit perfectly together. Geoffrey found Rachel and brought her to dance, and she forced a smile, while moving along with the rest. From the way Sophia danced with David, one would never have known she was pregnant.

The music stopped and the count down to the year 2000 began. At the stroke of mid-night, horns blew, everyone kissed everyone else, and Barbados said goodbye to the Old Year and welcomed in the year 2000.

Sophia kissed her father and whispered into his ear. "What great news. I shall tell the others. Sophia, I cannot wait to arrange the entire wedding for you and David. I will take care of everything." They all danced and partied well into the first day of the New Year. The Millennium had begun.

Thirty-nine

New York 2000

It had been five months since the McKenzie's celebrated the New Year in Barbados, and returned to the New York area to attend the funeral of their friend. Susan kept in touch with both David and Sophia regularly to see how they were faring. Rachel had been away from the island and Geoffrey, needing to spend more time with Sara in Antigua. David knew the sex of their baby, but Susan insisted it might be bad luck to tell, so they kept it to themselves. By the fourth month, Sophia could no longer hide the fact that she was expecting from her father, because of the growth of both her belly and her breasts. Surprisingly, Geoffrey took the news well. He had Rachel, Sara and the gala wedding to concern himself with after all.

David had to make plans for his required return to the States, since it had been six months since his last visit home, despite the fact he had concerns about leaving Sophia. Meghan arranged to take a few weeks off, and had planned to be in Barbados for the birth of Sophia's baby, whose due date was on or about June 14.

When Susan returned to the apartment, she was surprised to find David home and sound asleep on the couch.

He awoke when she kissed his forehead. "This is a surprise," she said.

"Rachel came home, so I made last minute plans to fly up for a few days." He said. "Sophia is fine. Just great in fact."

"So, Son, I must get a smashing dress for your wedding. Don't expect me to wear the one I wore at your sister's affair." Susan said. "I have heard nothing from the Bajan Wedding Planner, though." Susan remarked.

"I would assume you refer to my eventual father-in-law. Well, since her pregnancy is no longer a secret, and Geoffrey has accepted that fact without issue, we thought is best to wait till after the baby is born. Sophia wants to be her normal thin self, and wear a dress that will be both beautiful and fit well." David said.

"And Geoffrey is fine with this?" Susan asked.

"Both Geoffrey and Rachel thought it quite a better idea. Besides, Geoffrey has taken up golf, and spends more time than not on the new course at West Moreland. Bought new clubs and whatever. He wants to take me out but it is very expensive."

Susan laughed and chip singed. "I hope he is better at golf than he was at tennis. He was truly God awful."

"He did share that with me over a few rums at John Moore." David said.

"Speaking of John Moore," David. "There is a picture hanging over the bar of Captain Patch. Which eye was covered?" she asked.

David thought for a moment. "Actually, the picture was of Geoffrey's friend Foul Mouth Dick, pointing at some thing. But I have seen Patch in Bridgetown down by the Careenage. There is nothing wrong with either of his eyes. He alternates the patch just to drive folks crazy."

"Aha!" Susan exclaimed. "We were both right. Can't wait for your father to come home."

Brian arrived at about eight, thrilled that David had come home and suggested they all go out for dinner. David's choice of Angelo's on Mulberry Street, in Little Italy, was thought to be a great idea. Brian pulled into a parking garage around the corner from the restaurant, and found a long line of people, waiting to be admitted

"Damn!" Brian exclaimed.

"Not a problem, I learned this from a friend of mine. Follow me." David led Susan and Brian down a short flight of stairs along side the restaurant's entrance, and opened a door that led directly down into the main kitchen. The three maneuvered themselves past cooks roasting peppers, cooking pastas and assorted entrees, as they became enveloped in the smell of garlic and oregano. Three steps up led them to the main dining area, where David spoke to the maitre de. It took barely a few minutes for a table to be readied in the back room.

"I am amazed at your ingenuity," Brian said as he ordered a bottle of Chianti. "Okay, Son. I am paying, so you order the appetizers."

David eyed the vast array of choices and then made his selection, as the waiter, whose name was Solly, stood by waiting to memorize the order. Angelo's waiters never seemed to need to write anything down.

"We shall start with Spedini alla Romana, which is a fried mozzarella in a special sauce, and Vongole Oreganato, baked clams, and finish with Mozzarella di Bufala Affumicata alla Griglia, grilled smoked buffalo mozzarella with sun dried tomatoes and wild mushrooms." David translated. "They do not have this on any Bajan menu." The waiter stood waiting for the rest of the order smiling.

"Susan, Luv," Brian said. "What's your pleasure? I am going to have the veal Parmigiano."

"So many delicious choices," Susan said. "After all of these appetizers we ordered, I will have a linguini in a white clam sauce."

David looked at Brian. "Dad, I have not had a good steak in such a long time."

Brian smiled. "Forget the price, Son. Order the filet. It is good. This is a celebration of our grandchild and your wedding, and just having you home."

The food was phenomenal as usual, but all declined dessert. "Must we leave via the kitchen, David?" Susan asked.

David laughed, and as they started for the entrance, the maitre de kissed Susan on both cheeks, hugged Brian and shook hands with David.

David called Meghan and arranged to meet her for lunch at her hospital cafeteria the next day. Two days later he was back with Sophia in Barbados.

The following evening, Brian came home early carrying a pizza, much to Susan's delight, since she had little energy to cook. They watched television until ten p.m. and decided to retire.

When Brian came to bed after showering, he found Susan fast asleep. Crawling under the covers, he moved next to her and gently put his arm around Susan who was lying on her back. Just being next to her made him hard, so her placed a hand under her shirt and touched the nipple of her right breast. He was taken aback when she pushed his hand away, and turned on her side away from him. He decided to wait until the morning to bring it up.

When he awakened, Susan had already dressed, had her coffee and told him that she had an early appointment at the office, and afterwards had to go down to the courthouse. Brian thought over what had transpired, and realized it was not the first time she had rejected his advances in the past few months. Susan had become more moody lately, and he had attributed that to issues that all women ultimately had to deal with. She had made an appointment with her physician, but shared nothing about it with him.

That evening Brian was waiting for Susan when she returned to the apartment. "You are home early." She said. "I bought some French bread. Thought we would have a simple meal after that gastronomic orgy at Angelos. How about a salad?"

"Sounds good to me. Brian told her he had opened a bottle of Merlot that he believed had breathed sufficiently according to protocol.

"No, I really don't fancy any wine, Brian. She said wearily, finally taking off her coat and hanging it in the closet.

"Really? Okay, perhaps some Extra Old with ice water to follow?" He persisted.

"I really don't want any alcohol, Brian and perhaps you should not have any either. How come you are home so early?" She inquired sitting down on the settee.

"I had a late meeting uptown and it made no sense to go all he way back down to the Towers, so I came directly home." He said.

"Everything all right, Brian?" She asked.

"You mean as far as work?" He asked. "Work's fine. A bit hectic but tolerable."

"So, what else is bothering you?" She asked.

"We need to have a conversation." He said. "But first I'm going to have a rum." He started to go back to the kitchen.

"What happened to the Merlot?" She asked.

"I'll have that with my salad." He said.

"Are you and I having a problem?" She asked rising and blocking his entrance to the kitchen.

"Of course not, but there are always things to talk about." He lied, moving past her.

Susan returned to her seat and used the remote to turn on the television. Brian came back glass in hand and looked at her. " Perhaps this is an inconvenient time, and you would rather watch television instead."

She hit the mute button and the sound disappeared. "Okay, what's up?"

Brian took the remote from where she placed it on a table and hit the off button. "Best not to have any distractions." He said as he took a seat across from her and set the still full glass of rum down without drinking any.

"I guess I had better be direct. We are having a problem with intimacy. And beyond that, even a hug or a kiss seems troublesome. Any thoughts?" He asked. "Even on Barbados, you seemed distracted. Do you realize that during the four days we were there, we never had sex once?" He continued as Susan stared at him.

"Is that all that counts in a marriage? Sex?" She asked.

"I am afraid that whatever my answer, it will be taken wrong." Brian said, as he sipped some of the rum.

Susan thought for a moment. "Things change. We change. With women, their needs change, and not always in a way that men find satisfying. Some women are never sexually satisfied. Take this in the spirit I am offering it, and it is in no way accusatory." I'll take that rum you have in your hand." She downed it in one swallow and sat back.

"Admit it or not, you have had a problem for the past two years or more, whether due to prostate enlargement or elevated blood pressure, both of which, you know can effect sexual performance. You stimulate me to a point where I want it and then you peter out. Pun intended. This gets me frustrated to a point where avoiding intimacy is my way of dealing with it."

"Susan, I have Viagra but never know if it is worth taking, since I can't depend upon your interest. It is very frustrating for me as well."

"Brian, when the mood and the time is right we can try again. But not tonight." She said.

"What has happened to us, Susan? When will the time be right?" He asked.

"We, Brian, are getting older, and unfortunately, you are not the stud you once were and I am not the sexpot you thought I was or for that matter that I believed I was for one fleeting moment." She paused. "And if you think that Geoffrey could get me off now, remember that with all of his bluster, it's not there any more either. Rachel confided in me that Viagra or no Viagra, the salami is more of a pig without the blanket." She began to laugh.

"That's not very funny either." Brian said. "Hear me out just now. While I have no knowledge to confirm this, I believe that the male of the species has been directed genetically to procreate as long as feasible, and any interruption could set the stage for a disease, perhaps cancer to intervene. Therefore if a male is prevented from expelling sperm or coming, cancer of the prostate might be the unfortunate result."

"Brian, that is so far out, I doubt if there are any studies to substantiate that. However, if your concern is that great, jack off as often as you feel the urge. I am going into the kitchen and put together a salad. Might be best you drink as you may, because, my Luv, it ain't going to happen tonight. Why don't we just not dwell on it and que sera, sera."

Forty

New York Barbados 2000

When Susan returned home on the evening of June 10, she found four messages that had been left on the answer phone. The first two were for Brian, the third was a scam about them winning a cruise to the Bahamas, but the last was an urgent message from Meghan.

Meghan said was on her way back to Barbados on the next flight, direct or indirect, that would allow her to be present for the delivery of Sophia's baby. She completely understood her brother's angst. As good as the medical facilities had become on the island, they were not as good as what was available in New York, and Meghan was very concerned, since Sophia had been in labor for at least 10 hours. A last minute switch with understanding associates, willing to cover her services, allowed her to collect what she felt might be needed to resuscitate a new born, and without thinking that local Bajan rules might prevent her from providing her medical expertise, she was hell bent to make certain that her brother's child would have an uncompromised and uncomplicated birth.

Susan put a call through to David, but no one answered. She then called Rachel and Geoffrey, and got the same response.

She called the Queen Elizabeth Hospital, but the individuals with whom she was able to converse could not or would not give her any information whether or not Sophia was a patient in the maternity ward.

When Brian arrived home, she told him of Meghan's call. He called Jay but was put in touch with his answering service, which informed him that the doctor was not on call. Brian tried the home number and left a message. He found Samuel Braithwaite's number in his small black phone book, and dialed the 246 Barbados area code number and Samuel told him that Rachel and Geoffrey had not returned home from work before he left, and could possibly be at the hospital in Bridgetown. He said he knew a nurse there, and if he could not reach her, he would drive to Bridgetown and go to the hospital himself. Brian gave him the house number to call if he got any information at all, and Samuel assured him he would do so.

Susan was clearly agitated. "I could not get any answer from those fools at that hospital. I think we should pack a small bag and fly out."

"There are no planes leaving for Barbados now, so why don't we just wait for Samuel's call. I cannot imagine why Geoffrey or Rachel did not try to reach us, or even David for that matter. In any event I'll book two seats for tomorrow morning."

Brian put his arms around Susan in an attempt to comfort her, but she pulled away. "I was just trying to be nice," he said.

"I know." She responded coldly. "I just don't wish to be touched right now."

"How about some dinner? I'll order some sushi or rolls. Or would you rather some Chinese?" Brian asked. "This way one of us will be home if a call comes from Barbados."

"Order what you wish. I am really not hungry. When it comes, I'll pick what I want, if I want to." Susan said

Susan went into the bedroom and closed the door. Brian thought it would be best not to leave the apartment, so he called a nearby Chinese restaurant and ordered spare ribs, chicken with broccoli and some mixed fried rice. Brian knocked on the bedroom door, and there was no reply. When he entered the bedroom, he heard the sound of running water coming from Susan's bathroom.

Brian tried the knob and found the door locked from the inside. "Are you all right?" He called out.

"I'm taking a bath." Susan said curtly. "I am at least entitled to that, or do you think otherwise!"

"Why the locked door?" Brian asked. She did not respond. "I ordered Chinese food to be delivered, so I did not have to leave you alone

"What did you think I was going to do?" She asked. "I told you that I was taking a bath!"

The food arrived within thirty minutes. Brian called out to Susan, and her response was to begin without her. He went to the wet bar, poured himself two fingers of Mt. Gay and swigged it down. Then he poured another that followed the first. He made certain to wash, dry and replace the glass to its appropriate place, to avoid yet another argument.

His stomach growling, Brian opened the small white box that contained the spare ribs, plated a few, and added some hot mustard and duck sauce, he found in the bag. Susan still had not yet appeared.

He quickly finished all five ribs making certain to toss the bones in the garbage. Then he opened the two other boxes and spooned some of the rice and then the chicken onto his plate.

Susan appeared wearing a robe, her head covered with a towel. "You couldn't wait for me?" He just looked at her without replying. "She eyed what he had on his plate. "You get the same damn stuff all the time. Did you get ribs?"

"Yes, but they were getting cold, so I ate them." He responded defensively.

"You properly disposed of them?" She asked, as he nodded. Susan took a seat at the table, picked up a fork and sampled what he had on his plate. "Too much mustard on this," she said grimacing. "I definitely have had better Chinese food. Why did you choose this place?"

"Would you like your own plate so you can put whatever you wish on it?" He asked.

"I told you that I am not that hungry," She responded.

"Yes you did say that. Would you like something to drink perhaps as well?" He asked.

"Some Mt. Gay would be fine over ice." She answered.

Brian went to the bar without responding, and poured three fingers of dark rum over a spare amount of ice. Susan took the glass and drank half of it.

"Look, Susan, is this all about Sophia, and being left out of the loop? Or are you angry with me, or did something happen at the office that you would like to share?" He asked pouring rum into a glass.

She seemed to calm down after the rum. "Of course I am worried about Sophia. It is our grandchild after all." She said. "I don't think I am angry with you. Should I be?"

"Can't think of any reason." He said as the phone rang. Being the closest, he picked it up. "It's David," he said.

Susan stood and grabbed the phone from him. "David, what's going on? We could not reach any one."

David explained that Sophia had been in labor for a number of hours, and the baby was in the full breech position, and that the doctor was attempting to turn the baby while still in the womb.

He advised that Meghan had arrived and would be allowed in the delivery room to assist if needed. But as a last resort, Sophia might need a Caesarian section.

"Dad and I will take a morning flight to be with you. Why didn't Rachel and Geoffrey call us?" She asked.

"I decided it was my call," David said. "They are in the maternity waiting room and have been here for hours."

"You must let us know as soon as a decision is made regarding surgery or hopefully the baby will be born naturally." Susan pleaded.

After she cradled the phone and resumed her seat, Brian asked what David had told her. She repeated it verbatim, and asked for another glass of rum. "Don't you think you have had enough?" Brian asked.

"If you won't get it, I'll get it myself." She retorted.

Brian brought the bottle, two clean glasses and some ice and set them on the coffee table. He poured two substantial drinks, and then tried to make conversation, but Susan took the remote and turned on the television.

"I really wanted to talk to you about something that cannot wait, Susan."

"If it is more about sex. Hold off for a bit. I am more in need of some idiocy and that a-hole Liberal is on now." She said as she leaned her head back on a soft pillow and sipped her drink. "And clean your dish and utensils and put the uneaten food in the fridge." She changed the channel with the remote she clutched in her hand.

Brian knew better than to argue. More often than not, Susan would insist upon watching a program and immediately fall asleep. The moment Brian would change the channel provoked an argument and a claim she was watching.

Susan fell asleep on the couch, so Brian changed the channel to Monday night football and watched the Giants play wretchedly against the Green Bay Packers, who were ahead by six points in the second quarter. He did not see the end of the game and was awakened by the phone just before midnight. It was Meghan reporting that the obstetrician was able to successfully turn the baby, and deliver him vaginally. Meghan said she was called upon to suction her new nephew, and he responded immediately to a little oxygen and gentle smack on the rump. She told Brian she had cut the cord and he was now nestled at Sophia's breast.

"Hold on," Brian said. Let me wake your mother."

Susan, still groggy from the rum, took the phone and listened to her daughter. "I am so happy for them." She began to cry. "Have they chosen a name for our new grandson yet?" Meghan told her they were looking at a number of names, but had not as yet decided upon one. "We shall be down on the first flight out of JFK." Susan said. "Can someone pick us up at the airport?" Meghan told her that she was more than likely taking the plane they would come in on, so she would make certain someone would meet them at the airport.

With a sudden show of rare affection Susan hugged Brian and kissed him. "We had better go to bed. Oh, were you able to get seats?" She asked.

Brian was pleased for the moment to have the warm, comfortable Susan with him. "We have to be at the airport at 7 a.m. I was able to get the last two first class seats, arranged for a car service to pick us up at 6 a.m. I'll set the alarm." He held her tightly and for once, she made no attempt to pull away.

Forty-one

Barbados 2000

Geoffrey and Rachel met them at the baggage area. Meghan, who had already passed through outgoing customs, waved as she exited through the departure lounge and walked toward the aircraft being refueled for the trip back to New York. She held her right hand to her ear indicating they should call her later.

Susan insisted upon going directly to the Queen as Geoffrey sarcastically called the only hospital on the island now, ever since an excellent Catholic hospital in the parish of St. Lucy had been forced to close for lack of funding. Susan found the hospital dirty, rather smelly and made no bones about it. They took a slow moving elevator up to the Maternity floor where they found David and Sophia just enjoying the infant boy the new mother held to her breast.

"How long must you stay in this awful place?" Susan asked.

Brian looked at Geoffrey and Rachel, and shrugged his shoulders. "Can I hold him?" Brian asked, and Sophia took the little boy from her nipple and handed him to Brian.

"Be careful, you don't drop him, Brian." Susan warned.

"I believe I can hold my grandson here without both instructions and a pending calamity, although he just peed on me." Brian smiled. "But that's just fine." He added, as he handed the baby to Susan.

"He is beautiful," she said. "Whom does he look like?"

"He looks just like all of the other babies in the nursery." Sophia said. "David put him back in the crib for a bit. I am tired."

David took his son and placed him gently into the soft crib. "Mom, they will be here for just one more day."

Rachel hugged Susan. "We are grandparents together. Isn't that just great!" She said.

Geoffrey put his arms around Brian. "Bro, time to give the kids a break. What are your plans, David?"

"I am going to stay here until about nine. Then I'll come back to your house. Lonely, not having Sophia back at the apartment." He said and added. "I think it would be best that when she is discharged, Sophia stay at Simonton. This way you both can help her."

Brian agreed. "That sounds like a good idea."

The four new grandparents kissed David and Sophia, and left the Queen. Rachel sat in the back of the Land Rover with Susan and took her hand. "Are you feeling well? You look a bit peeked."

Geoffrey looked at the rear view mirror. "A few rums will perk her up. "I was so excited that I forgot to bring a camera."

"We left in such a hurry this morning, I didn't even think about that." Brian said.

"You would neglect something like that. Wouldn't you?" Susan said.

"No worries, I am sure David has already taken lots of pictures. Let us not be upset about stuff like that." Rachel advised.

When they returned to Simonton, Geoffrey brought the bags up to their room and found Brian waiting at the top of the staircase. "You startled me old man." Geoffrey said.

"I feel hundred years old, Geoffrey. I am sure you noticed that Susan is a bit irritable." Brian said.

"I saw that immediately and as well did Rachel. What's going on?" Geoffrey asked.

"We have been having some issues lately. Part of it might be her workload. I try to get home early enough to help out with dinner if we are eating in. No matter what I do, she finds fault, and it need not be anything of consequence."

"Look my friend, you are back in our island in the sun, where things just get better. That reminds me. Meghan brought down some Viagra from Jay. Might you have a need of some?" He asked with a smile.

"Things are not so well down there either. I try. She placates me and then becomes frustrated and her frustrations turn to anger. Apparently I haven't satisfied her. I offered to go down on her, so she at least can orgasm, but she refuses." Brian said. "She is completely turned off sexually."

"Been there Brian, so I know exactly how you feel. I know it's me, but Rachel is not well lubricated sometimes, and entering her becomes most difficult. I am even afraid to go Canadian chick hunting since, striking out would be most embarrassing. Sucks to get old." Geoffrey said. "I can't wait for the next generation of ED pill. This one is not working as advertised anymore."

The two went downstairs and found Susan and Rachel on the patio discussing names for their new grandchild. "How about Andrew?" Rachel asked.

"Sure," Geoffrey said. "Like in better known as Foul Mouth Andy? I think not. Okay, The bar at Simonton Great House is open. Who would like what?"

Susan looked at Brian and then to Geoffrey. "I prefer water actually." She said

"Sorry my Luv, you are still my Luv. Right!. We are fresh out of water. The pump failed last week." Susan forced a smile. "We must toast to little what's his name, and with good Barbados rum." Geoffrey returned with an unopened bottle of Mt. Gay, four tumblers and ice."

Brian poured Susan three fingers of the amber liquid. "Your turn, Susan, to do your thing for our new grandson."

Susan stood up and drained half of her glass. "All right," she said. "Now I am fortified and ready." They all raised their glasses as Susan began. "Will our grandson ever understand what I am about to say? Over the teeth and passed the gums, look out stomach here it comes."

They all laughed as Geoffrey refilled their glasses. Seeing Susan happy and animated, Brian hoped this was not a charade on her part. He desperately wanted the old funny, sweet Susan back. Geoffrey put on some slow music and asked Susan to dance.

He whispered something in her ear, and as she flipped her head back she laughed.

Brian read her lips as saying 'maybe'. He took Rachel's hand and led her down the patio steps towards the pool.

"Fancy a swim, do you Granddad?" She teased. Brian nuzzled her neck with his lips and she laughed. "That feels very good."

"No. Let's just stand here in the moonlight and talk." He replied.

"Fine. What would you like to speak about?" She responded.

"This must go no further. " He said. "Just between the two of us." Rachel nodded.

Brian paused to gather his thoughts. "Prior to our marriage, I had one, not very serious relationship, that I knew from the onset, would never be permanent. We were both very young, and first loves always give that false impression that they will last forever." Rachel listened and smiled.

"Susan told me that she had had a number of boyfriends, none of whom she allowed more than some perfunctory kissing. In the states, it is characterized somewhat like a baseball game. For example, a kiss would be getting to first base, and a home run would be the proverbial going all the way."

Brian held her hand. "Bloody wouldn't work with cricket, you know." Rachel said, laughing. "Sorry. Go on."

"It was very romantic those months before we got married," he continued. "And for the first few years as well."

Rachel thought for a moment. "We certainly were hitting home runs, as you say, before we married. How about you?"

"We had gone a weekend to the Hamptons, and just weren't able to control ourselves. It was unbelievably erotic." He said.

"Great sex?" Rachel asked.

"How would we have known? We really had nothing to compare it to, until we met you and Geoffrey. It was, however spontaneous in the beginning, and Susan seemed willing to try and do anything, except doing it 'doggy style' since she claimed it was too impersonal, and lacked intimacy. She made the rules and called it sex for sex sake." Brian said.

"Unfortunately," Rachel offered, "after a while you just lose the spontaneity, and sex becomes so mundane and scheduled around other things. Geoffrey and I certainly experienced this as well, and all or most married, or even unmarried couples living together find it to be true. However, the man is always poised and ready and the woman may not be. Being a good sport, she may just go along with it."

"Let me ask you this, Rachel. Must we make love to our women all of the time, or can we just plain fuck!" Brian asked, energized.

She squeezed his hand. "Oh, Brian, there must be time made for both love and pure animal erotic, no holds barred fucking. You and I did just that, you know. But we enjoyed each other to the fullest, didn't we. Alas, when a women grows older, has a child or two, they think less of the latter, while men like Geoffrey putting on a few years and pounds are just happy to be able to rise to the occasion."

"You know, Geoffrey and I are in many ways very much alike. We are easily frustrated when it comes to our wives." Brian said.

"How is your marriage, Brian?" She asked.

"It once felt so safe and familiar, but the honeymoon wore off a long time ago. Sex, as I said, had become boring and terribly routine. But then fourteen years ago, we came to Barbados, and there was Geoffrey, waiting on the dock. Everything changed for the better, but only for a while. That night, when Geoffrey asked if we switched, it threw both of us into a panic and scared out of our wits. We spoke at length that night, and ultimately what happened was both amazing and invigorating. Certainly for the best." Brian admitted.

"Why, Brian?" She asked.

"Susan changed. She became young again. She was seductive, challenging, and for the first time in a long time needing pure animal intimacy. More often than not, she was the initiator. Now, fast forward to the present. She has become morose and preoccupied. You know the old joke where the man is on top of the woman, who is on her back, albeit with her legs apart, instead of responding to his thrusts, comments that the ceiling needs painting. That's Susan." Brian looked at Rachel.

"And things got worse when I found it difficult to stay hard, so she feigned frustration and used it as an excuse to avoid sex and or physical contact for that matter." Brian was visibly upset.

"That is so sad." Rachel said. "I wonder if being thrust into the Grandma role will aggravate your situation."

"Wait, there is something else, I must tell you." Brian said. "When Geoffrey visited in New York and stayed at our apartment, something else happened."

"I know about the ménage de trois, Brian, and consider it a non-issue." She said.

"Okay, but I'm not certain it has not been an issue for Susan who could be harboring anger and guilt." He responded.

"I don't understand, Brian." Susan said.

"I have a feeling that she holds it against me that I allowed it to happen." Brian said remorsefully.

"Look, Brian. If Susan did not wish it to happen, it never would have. And Geoffrey would not have been such an eager participant if he felt it would create terrible discomfort for the two of you." Rachel responded. " Perhaps I might talk this out with Susan when the two of us are alone?"

"Brings me to another question, Rachel." Brian said. "When Susan and you were alone together below decks on the Lord Jim, did anything happen?" Rachel just smiled. "This is another concern of mine regarding Susan and sex that I have not yet sorted out."

Rachel looked back to the house. "They are going to wonder what we have been up to. We had better go back in. If the opportunity arises, would you like to…" She did not get to finish her thought

"I would only hope I can." Brian responded.

David brought Sophia and their son home from the hospital the next day, since she had convinced her doctor that she would be able get more rest, with two doting grandfathers and two grandmothers there to help.

Later that evening, after dinner and drinks, Susan went upstairs, showered and got into bed to await Brian. But when the door to the bedroom opened, it was Geoffrey, not Brian, who entered. Brian slept in Rachel's bed, but neither couple chose to be more intimate that night, happy just to be in each other's arms. Four days later, the McKenzies said a tearful goodbye to the Townsands, Sophia, David, and their new grandson, who had been given the name Richard Thomas McKenzie, and returned to New York.

Forty-two

New York September 2001

Susan returned to Barbados when Richard Thomas was six months old, and spent a week with the Townsands, and David and Sophia, who had moved permanently to Simonton. It was a good rest for Susan, who needed to be away from work and from Brian as well. She had found herself constantly sniping at him, and finding fault and disputing the most insignificant things. Brian on the other hand, now realized Susan to have become an authority on anything and everything with an argument just waiting to happen.

Brian had hoped that her trip to Barbados might serve as a cooling off period that would benefit them both. Susan returned from Barbados on the ninth of September, bringing with her frozen flying fish, two bottles of Mt. Gay rum and some Banks beer, that Geoffrey had secreted in her luggage. She talked endlessly at Customs, charming the agent who never questioned her about what she had in her bags. Her mood seemed good as she kissed Brian, and told him that she missed him. While he secretly hoped that perhaps something happened between her and Geoffrey, he had mixed feelings and was not about to bring that subject up.

Susan cooked some of the flying fish that they devoured with Bajan hot sauce and washed down with Banks beer. Later when they both were in bed, Susan turned to Brian and held and kissed him, but then rolled to her side, with her back to him. Brian could not fall asleep, but he was glad to have her home. He listened for a while to her quiet breathing, and then gently got out of bed and went out into the living room. He opened one of the bottles of rum that Susan had brought from Barbados, and had a few shots while watching re runs of earlier televised programs on Fox.

The next morning, on September 10th, Susan found him asleep on the couch. It was not until after she had showered and dressed, that she awakened him, telling him she was leaving for the office, and more than likely would not be home until nine in the evening. Brian said he would have some left over pizza in the fridge for dinner, and that he would see her later.

Early September had been more like late summer, with the temperatures hovering in the low seventies. Brian felt exceptionally healthy. His blood pressure had been under control, and with the help of Viagra, he could keep an erection long enough to masturbate himself to satisfaction. He had seen a physician on television who believed that men over forty who either have sexual relationships or masturbate frequently, will have less of a chance of getting prostate cancer.

Here was a justification, he was beginning to enjoy, although he longed for the real thing.

Brian met two and a half of Patch's criteria and then after showering, dressed and left the Dakota for his office at the World Trade Center. It was a short walk to the subway that brought him into the station below the Towers. It was already nine; so many people had been at their desks for at least a half hour. After a short executive meeting, Brian checked his calendar with his secretary, and began to answer some of the many messages left on his desk. He put a call through to Susan's office but was told she would be occupied until noon.

He had meetings first with the in house accountant, and then with the legal department, and by the time they ended it was time for lunch. A call from Justin came with an invitation to join him for lunch at Windows On The World. Justin met Brian as he entered the elevator on the 76th floor. The car rose smoothly to the 107th floor of the north Tower where the restaurant was located.

They were seated at a table near a window overlooking New York Harbor, and talked while eating chef salads and drinking iced tea. Justin told Brian that Jessica had taken a personal day and was going for a check up. "She thinks, she might be pregnant, but we have had our hopes dashed before."

Brian suggested that they schedule a dinner party at the Palm, and he would invite Meghan and Jay. Justin congratulated Brian on his becoming a grandfather, and apologized for not calling sooner. Brian said that Susan had just returned from Barbados and everything was fine there. They finished lunch that Justin insisted upon paying for, and went back to their respective offices.

Brian worked until six thirty but neglected to try to reach Susan again. He left the building just before seven, and it was almost dark by the time he came up the Subway steps. The apartment was empty when he arrived, so he warmed up the pizza, got into a pair of shorts and a tee, and poured himself some rum. Brian searched the channels and found the Monday night football game between the Giants and Broncos from Denver. He dozed off just as they started the third quarter, later waking to a recap of the game that Denver had won 31-20.

More disturbing was the fact that Susan had not yet returned home, and it was now almost midnight. He did not call Meghan lest he frightened her, so he poured himself another drink and waited. He heard a key in the lock at 12:30 a.m. Susan was surprised to see him up so late.

"I told you I would be late, Brian." She said.

"You said nine." He responded.

"Well, it was a tad later," she said.

"Two and a half hours is hardly a tad. I was worried." Brian said. " You might have called."

"You're right, I suppose, but one of the secretaries had a birthday, and invited everyone to join her down at the King Cole Bar, so I had to go." She said. "And since it's at the St. Regis on the East Side at 55th, trying to find a cab was a major chore…well you understand."

"So, what did you do?" He asked.

"Had a few drinks, talked and sang happy birthday. I am truly tired and need to shower. Tomorrow I have briefs to write, and will be spending the rest of the time defending clients in court, but that's what I do." As she walked past Brian, she kissed him on the top of his head and went into the bedroom. Brian found a late news and weather program and watched until it ended. The next morning was to be a beautiful day with not a cloud in the sky expected.

Brian awoke at 6:30 a.m. He could see Susan's reflection from her bathroom mirror, since she left the door open. She was just applying the finishing touches to her make up.

Brian went into his own bathroom, urinated and turned on the shower. The hot pellets of water from a designer Kohler fixture felt great on his skin, invigorating it. Susan pushed aside the shower curtain and told him that she had to leave early, and hopefully not be as late as the night before.

By the time Brian had toweled off, she was gone. At 7:30, the phone rang. It was the appointment secretary, who was always the first to arrive at work. She advised him that his first two appointments for the morning had been cancel and rescheduled. Brian thanked her and took the time to make scrambled eggs, which he ate with whole-wheat toast rounds he found in the fridge. Then he relaxed knowing that there was no rush to get to the office.

Jessica kissed her husband good morning. Justin told her that he was sorry she had to take a personal day off for naught, since the obstetrical office had to cancel yesterday's appointment. She was re-scheduled for today and was resigned to take another day off. "I will wave at you from our window, so you will know if you are going to be a Daddy." She said with a broad smile. She knew despite the fact that their Hoboken high rise faced the World Trade Towers, there was no way he could see her.

"Perhaps a smoke signal or better yet call me, Darling. Use the new cell phone I got you." He said as he finished the last of his coffee. "Got to make the ferry now. The next one will be crowded."

Jessica waked out onto the lanai, and felt the warmth of the morning sun. "Just look at that blue sky, Justin. There is not a cloud to be seen. What a beautiful day this is going to be. I just know it." Jessica had missed two periods and knew she had to be pregnant, but this had happened before. Her appointment was scheduled for 10:30 a.m. so she had plenty of time to enjoy the morning. Refilling her cup of decaffeinated coffee, she went out on the lanai, and stared at the New York Skyline, where the Twin Towers certainly commanded one's attention.

Meghan was still at work, having been on call for twelve hours with another twelve to go. She had been assigned to the Pediatric Emergency room at Jacobi, and was truly enjoying the assignment. Jay was still at home in Westfield getting ready to go to his Watchung office. The trip would take at least forty minutes from Westfield with the usually heavy morning traffic on Rte 22. He was looking for a home closer to work. Jay reached the office earlier than expected and used the time to review charts of patients due in that day.

The abusive and intrusive HMO's had reduced their reimbursements to the primary care physicians and were threatening to do the same for specialists. Adding to financial miseries physician were experiencing, was the fact that Medicare was about to cut their fees as well. Fortunately, there were still patients with traditional insurance or, well off enough to pay with cash. It was inevitable that their group would have to merge with another medical office, and was already speaking with one based at Overlook Hospital in Morristown.

Susan sat in the law library with two of the interns and one of the legal secretaries reviewing briefs, when her own personal secretary entered with coffee and doughnuts.

"It is a shame y'all have to be cooped up in this room. It is a simply gorgeous day outside with not a cloud. Just like back home in Norfolk, VA," She said with her distinct southern drawl.

They downed the doughnuts and finished the coffee at the same time and Susan collected all of the papers and placed them in a folder. "Great Job, people. You are all excused to go back to your regular jobs."

Susan went back to the spacious corner office that overlooked lower Broadway and downtown Manhattan.

She thought momentarily about how curt she had been with Brian the night before, but immediately dismissed it. The sky was really powder blue. She would try to make it up to him tonight.

At 8:00 a.m., Brian went down to the lobby newsstand for a New York Post. He had stopped buying the Times long ago, when it became their policy to put editorials on the front page instead of news. "Glorious day, Mr. McKenzie," the concierge called out. "Have a good one!" Brian returned to the apartment and turned on Fox & Friends.

At 8:46:30 am, American Airlines Flight 11 flew into the North Tower between the 93rd and 99th floors, carrying combustible fuel along with it. A fireball erupted and no one above the 93rd floor was able to evacuate. Justin was on his way up to his office when the aircraft impacted. He has just reached his floor, and as the elevator doors opened, he was greeted by heat and dense smoke. The stairwells, two floors above had disintegrated, so Justin made his way to the stairwell on his floor, helping people along the way. He prayed that he would survive what ever had happened.

Brian saw the first report that suggested it was a small plane that hit the Tower. He caught the express elevator that took him down to the lobby.

Even with the distance that the Dakota was from the Towers, he saw a gray plume of smoke spilling up into the blue sky. When he realized that trying to get a cab would be futile, he entered the park across from the Natural History Museum and began to run diagonally, in hopes that he would have a better chance of getting a taxi at its east entrance.

Brian wouldn't later regret that he had not decided to take the subway down to the Towers. So concerned about the people in the building, he neglected to call Susan.

Jessica had walked back into the apartment at approximately 8:40 am having the urge to urinate. She felt something strange in her abdomen. Something moved inside her.

She knew at that moment what it might be, and was about to call Justin when she heard an explosion from across the river. Returning to the lanai, she watched in horror, as the top of the North Tower erupted in flames, knowing that Justin was somewhere in that building. Taking the cell phone, she dialed his number. It seemed like an eternity before he answered, but it was very difficult to hear him because of the static. She thought he said he was trying to get down the stairs and was at the 60th floor, and he loved her. Then the phone went dead. She called the Dakota, but there was no answer at the apartment. The she called Susan.

Susan's secretary put her through, but Susan did not know where Brian was, and had not heard from him. Susan advised she stay near a phone at the apartment. Jessica told her that it was horrible to watch what was happening just across the river, and to be unable to do anything about it. She called her office in the South Tower and was informed that there were no problems there and people would be returning to their offices.

Susan sat with many of the office staff and partners, watching the news as the story began to unfold. It became evident that this was not an accident when they saw United Flight 175, also from Boston's Logan Airport crash into the South Tower between the 75th and 85th floors at 9:03:02. Susan knew that Jessica would normally have been at her desk at that time, at her office on the 83rd floor.

The impact severed communications with some television stations and radio towers located on the buildings, disrupting many television, radio and phone systems. Meghan was able to reach Susan by phone, asking about Brian. Susan cursed herself for how she has been treating him.

Her secretary told her she has a call from Barbados.

She heard Geoffrey's Bajan patois. "Saw the bloody news on CNN. Is everyone all right?" He asked frantically.

"Brian had to be at the office early for some appointments. I can't reach him and don't know if he is all right. He would be directly below impact." Susan began to cry. "Jessica called me. Justin went to work at his usual time and would be in the building. Wait, someone is trying to call me. Perhaps it is Brian." She spoke for a moment, and punched the hold button. "Geoffrey, that was Jessica, she reached Justin for a moment. He was trying to evacuate down a stairwell."

"I feel so terribly useless that I cannot be of any help. David, I do not believe knows what has happened. I shall have him call you. All the best from Rachel and Sophia." He did not know what else to say.

"You may not be able to reach us since the phones are screwed up. Damn these Muslim terrorists. Everyone believes they are responsible." Susan said before the line went dead.

She placed her head into her hands and sobbed. "My poor dear Brian. Are you safe?"

The bad news continued throughout the morning, as information was broadcast about the attack on the Pentagon, and the plane that crashed into a western Pennsylvania farm field.

Brian McKenzie finally reached the southernmost park exit across from the Plaza Hotel. Traffic on Broadway was at a standstill, as the NYPD prevented anything on wheels moving toward lower Manhattan. Realizing that he would have to walk or run the remainder of the way toward the Towers, he paused to rest on a bench just outside the park. He glanced at his watch. It was almost 9:40, and he looked for an unoccupied phone booth. He had to reach Susan. A man appeared finished with his call in a nearby kiosk, but when Brian approached to enter, he was informed that the lines were dead.

Continuing on foot, he made his way to Times Square where the News Banner told him what he already knew. Thinking that the best route would be Lexington Avenue and down to 6th, he walked and ran in that direction. Brian was partway down 6th Avenue, when he heard a roar, and saw an enormous plume of gray dust suddenly darken the sky. It was 9:54:04. The South Tower was in the process of collapse.

Brian got as far as Canal Street, but could go no further as ghost like figures, followed by something akin to a billowing dust storm, moved toward him. Unable to continue, Brian retreated northward. The zombie like forms of humanity continued to run for their lives, none able to respond to any of Brian's questions. He stood motionless for about 20 minutes, when he heard another roar perhaps louder than the first, which heralded the collapse of the North Tower. It was now 10:28:25.

Brian finally was able to grab the arm of someone willing to stop long enough to speak to him. Out of breath, covered with soot, the man gasped. "They are both gone. Both Towers have collapsed. So many lives lost. I don't know how many. There could have been 50,000 people in those buildings. I work around the corner on Broadway and was evacuated in time. I have to go find a phone to let my family know I am all right." Brian wished him luck and watched him disappear among the rest of humanity fleeing the area.

For an unexplained reason, Brian moved toward Mulberry Street, still a safe distance away from the center of the disaster.

Earlier, Justin and some of his associates had raced down the staircase as fast as they could, moving aside for police and firemen ascending to rescue others who might be trapped above.

He picked up a young woman wearing a cast on her left leg, flung her over his shoulder, and continued downward. He felt the building shudder and heard a noise from far above, but then all went momentarily quiet. When he finally existed the building, he saw emergency vehicles surrounding the area, and scores of police and firemen still entering both the South and North Towers. Justin handed the young woman over to an EMT, and was ordered to move away from the area. He had started his race for survival at two minutes to nine, and was able to safely exit the building thirty minutes later. He looked at his cell phone, saw that Jessica had tried to reach him again, but now there was no service. Moving quickly around the block to Broadway, he went to look for a friend who worked for a brokerage firm there, but found that the building had already been evacuated.

Desperate to find a working phone, he ran toward Canal Street. Justin turned as he heard a thundering noise behind him, and witnessed people trying to outrun the surge of gray dust smoke and debris, that tried to engulf them in southern Manhattan's stone and brick canyons.

He stood in awe of what was transpiring, and remained motionless until he heard the noise made by the collapse of the North Tower.

The once blue sky had been completely blotted out, and the area had become overwhelmingly dark, as the enormous bloat of dust blocked out the sun. It was imperative that he leave the area now.

Jessica watched in horror, from their apartment as first the South and then the North Towers disappeared from the Manhattan landscape. She put her hands on her abdomen, again feeling what she believed to be movement, and prayed that Justin was safe and out of harm's way. With communications lost, there was no way of knowing what was happening, and she had only television and some radio programs to rely upon for news.

Susan went along with others, to the top of her building, when the news of the collapse of the South Tower was aired. She was thankful that Jessica, who had not gone to work was safe, but trembled not knowing the fate of Brian, Justin and the potential 40,000 to 50,000 people who may have gone to work on this beautiful morning, unaware of what was about to change their lives, if they were among the fortunate allowed to live. She saw the gray dust rise into the sky, and spreading, almost blocking the view of New York harbor. She regretted every argument she had had with Brian over anything, and just wanted to be able to tell him that she loved him, desperately wishing to hold him in her arms.

Brian rested, exhausted, on the steps that led up to Angelo's, not knowing what do or where to go. He cursed the fact that he had left his cell phone at home in his rush to leave. Squinting down Mulberry toward Canal, he saw a figure approaching. Not until the man was very close, did he realize that it was Justin, his face and hair grayed by dust, but apparently uninjured. Brian jumped to his feet and hugged the young man, who related what he had been through and what he had seen.

"Thank God you are safe." Brian cried out. "Tell me anything you can, Justin."

Best he could, Justin went over what details he could remember, after hearing the explosion from the floors above, not knowing what had happened. He explained that he collected as many people from the office willing to go, and led them to safety down the only available stairwell, and out of the building well before its collapse. "I don't think we would have made it out of the North Tower after the collapse of the South."

They walked back up 6th Avenue where they were able to hail a cab moving north. Brian gave the driver Susan's office address.

Susan sat looking at her phone, waiting for it to ring. It all seemed so hopeless. Except for Pearl Harbor, no enemy had ever attacked the mainland of the United States, and now she felt so vulnerable. For her and so many of her generation, that was history, but this was reality. The Pentagon had been attacked and a passenger plane had crashed in Pennsylvania. For the moment, this was the only information available, but Susan expected more, but she was not certain more of what.

Susan's personal secretary interrupted her thoughts as she burst into her office. "Your husband is here!" She cried out with a broad grin. "He has been trying to reach you."

Susan rushed from behind her desk, and grasped Brian as he came through the open door. "Oh! Brian," she cried out. "I was so worried. I thought I had lost you." Susan held Brian with no indication that she would ever let go."

"I never got to work at the usually time." He was breathless. As it turned out I had no need to be there early. But it is my fortune, but damn it, the misfortune of so many people with whom I worked and all of the rest in those buildings. The phones were inoperable. I left my cell at the apartment. So I just ran down as near as I could and eventually Justin and I found each other.

Susan ran to Justin and embraced him. "I was just speaking to Jessica. We must call her. She is so worried."

Justin picked up the receiver and was relieved when he heard the dial tone. Jessica answered after the first ring, and was beside herself, thrilled to hear his voice. "Oh, my darling, are you all right?"

"I am fine Jessica. It must have been devastating for you" He said.

"I heard your voice and I am good." She said. "I never made it to the doctor but I really believe that you are going to be a Daddy. Please come home to me now Justin. I need you here so badly to make certain this is not just a dream."

Brian arranged for a car to take Justin back to the ferry, and across the Hudson back to Hoboken, but he did not know that thousands were attempting to escape lower Manhattan, making easy transport unavailable. When Justin reached the pier, he saw hundreds of small rescue boats crossing over to Manhattan. He would become one of thousands evacuated by boat captains who volunteered their vessels to help people in their attempt to escape.

Susan made an executive decision to have all of the personnel directly responsible to her to go home, without discussing it with any of the other partners.

"Brian, let's go home." She said. "We are of no help to anyone left in the buildings, and staying here is ludicrous." She sighed. "How many of the people you have worked along side of have survived? Do you know? At home we can at least make phone calls to the homes of your office staff and hope for the best."

When they finally got home, Brian made a number of calls, but reached only the husband of the woman that had called him early that morning, informing him that his morning appointments had been cancelled. He told Brian that he had not been able to connect with her, and was beside himself. Brian advised him to call as soon as he heard something. Susan offered to make lunch, but Brian declined, saying he had no appetite.

They remained glued to the television for hours, but were not consoled by the news, only for the fact that two thousand innocent people had lost their lives that morning, and not fifty thousand, had the terrorists acted one hour later.

The house phone rang. It was Rachel, calling from Barbados. "I never got down to the office, Rachel," Brian said. "And Justin is safe and more than likely back home with Jessica."

"Thank God you all are safe." She said. "The loss of life was terrible. We have not left the telee. I doubt if much of Barbados has."

"We don't yet know how many were lost here in New York or even the Pentagon. Sadly, we do know how many people were on that plane that crashed in Pennsylvania. Reports are still coming in about heroism performed by passengers who were able to reach family by cell phone before all communication was cut off."

"It must have been just awful. David wants to speak with you." Rachel said

"Dad," David said. "We are thankful you are all right. Did Justin make it out?"

"He did, David, and is with Jessica as we speak. More information is coming in. You probably are getting it on CNN. I cannot begin to tell you what I saw, or what Justin went through." Brian said, tears rolling down his cheeks.

There was a pause while David spoke with Rachel. "Dad, we have a problem here as well. Geoffrey became so distraught watching the Towers fall, he complained of chest pain. Despite his protests, we took him down to the Queen for evaluation."

"Geoffrey's at the Queen with chest pain." He shared with Susan. "David, would you suppose he might be willing come to New York? Jay certainly could provide better care."

"I doubt if he would leave the island." David said. "You know how stubborn he is, and we don't know if it is heart related anyhow. Let him be evaluated and we all can speak later."

Brian agreed and asked David to keep him appraised as to lab results, diagnosis and treatments offered to Geoffrey and he would relay them to Jay and Meghan. He then told Susan of the entire phone conversation.

"Should we go to Barbados and offer our support?" She asked.

Brian looked at his wife. "Susan, we have so many issues to deal with here, non the least of which are determining how many of my co-workers made it out of the building alive. How many of all of the people in both buildings are still with us? Geoffrey's illness will have to take second place. He is after all, among the living."

"But he is our friend!" She exclaimed.

"Right now we have thousands more whose fate remains unknown, to deal with." Brian said.

"Brian, you are right. That I cannot deny. I am so tired. Can we go to bed and watch the news from there?" She asked.

"Are you not hungry? I had breakfast and nothing more," He said.

"I can't think of food right now. Find something for yourself." She said.

Brian found some shrimp in the freezer. He boiled water, and tossed shrimp he had cleaned into the pot and then opened a bottle of Merlot and poured two glasses. While they "breathed" Brian mixed ketchup and white horseradish to make a sauce for the shrimp. Finally, when everything was ready, he placed the shrimp, sauce and the wine on a tray and brought it into the bedroom. Susan appeared to be asleep and in no way would be willing to be aroused for dinner or anything else, so he consumed all of the shrimp and drank both glasses of Merlot. He looked at his wife, sighed and went back to the living room where he slumped down onto the soft couch and turned on the TV.

Brian watched the replays of the aircraft striking the Towers, the hit on the Pentagon and the crash into the Pennsylvania field, as the media coverage of the events of the day seemed endless.

He turned away from the set when a video of people jumping to their deaths from the Towers was shown, wondering if he knew or had ever met any of these poor souls. Then the thought occurred to him that he was officially out of a job, since everything he had worked for, was now under tons of debris that was once the World Trade Towers. Brian wanted to call someone from work, but did not know how to begin or whom to choose. It was almost midnight, so he thought it would be best to wait until morning, understanding that there might never be a good time.

Then he saw Amos Mansfield, his COO being interviewed by a local newscast reporter. Trying to keep his composure, Amos asked that anyone who knew the whereabouts of any of the company personnel, get in touch with him and left a number. Brian dialed the number and it was busy. He tried a few more times with the same result, so he decided to wait until morning. As more information became available as to the identification of the terrorists, and what they had wrought on our country, it made him angrier. He poured another glass of Merlot and sat mesmerized as the disaster was played and replayed again and again.

Brian checked on Susan who was still fast asleep. He noticed a bottle of sleeping pills on her nightstand and wondered if she had taken any. He returned to the living room and his seat on the couch. Finally, around 4 a.m., he gave up the battle to stay awake and fell fast asleep.

Forty-three

New York Sept 12, 2001

Brian awoke abruptly to Susan's shaking him. "It's almost eight", She said, "And I have to be at my office by nine. What are your plans for the day, Brian?"

"My plans?" My office no longer exists, along with all of the people who never made it out of the buildings. I have to call Amos. He was on TV last night, but I thought it too late to make the call." He looked at his wife who had not yet changed out of her pajamas. "You should call Barbados and check on Geoffrey."

"Oh, can you do that? I have to shower and get dressed. It will be a long day for me." It seemed to Brian that everything was back to abnormal, despite what they both had gone through yesterday. He wondered if she was in a state of denial. The television was still showing the two planes crashing into the North and South Towers, people jumping from them, and then the massive emergency response from the fire and police departments, many of whose first responders died under the crush of the debris.

Work had already begun trying to find and pull survivors from the wreckage. Massive steel beams that once held the structures in place, stood twisted and broken. The work was difficult, but very rewarding, when another victim was pulled alive from the wreckage.

Susan dressed in a beige pants suit, white tailored shirt, with her hair pulled back in a ponytail. It was like nothing had happened. "I left you some bread you can toast, and there is coffee perking. Got to go." She said after kissing his forehead. Brian never took his eyes from the TV set, which continued to show the aircraft striking the towers over and over again, followed by the implosion of what was once the buildings that had comprised the World Trade Center, and all of the humanity that never would live to enjoy another morning.

President Bush had been informed of the tragedy, while reading to young students at a Florida elementary school. Keeping his composure, he gave instructions to his aides and remained with the children. On September 12, 2001, he met with his National Security Team, and was on his way to inspect damage incurred at the Pentagon. Not long thereafter, he spoke with the Mayor and Governor of New York. Late in the afternoon of September 14, President Bush addressed the workers at Ground Zero, reminding terrorists that the world would know what they had wrought, and suffer the consequences.

Brian had finally contacted his COO, and offered to attempt to reach as many survivors or family members as he could. With no office to return to, he based himself in the apartment, using the television as a source for a continuum of breaking news. Susan came and went each day, business as usual, and Brian did not know whether she was callous, or was resorting to some kind of reaction formation, to block the misery she was unable to express or deal with.

Geoffrey Townsand's so-called heart attack was dismissed as indigestion, but Rachel and David had their doubts. Stubborn to the core, Geoffrey refused to go to New York for another opinion. Rachel relented, since his pain had abated, and he appeared to be his normally aggressive self once more. Susan and Brian, so involved with what had happened as a result of the Islamic Terrorist attack on the World Trade Center, readily accepted what they heard from Barbados.

New York went through the process of ultimate recovery, dealing with the reality that no more people would be found alive in the rubble, which was systematically being removed to landfills in the five boroughs. Mayor Rudy Giuliani provided the needed assurances that he was in control, and in time, things would return to what most never again would accept as normal.

The United States had received a mortal blow, not experienced since Pearl Harbor on December 7, 1941. For the first time, the continent had been severely violated, and this was unacceptable. For the first time since called upon to build the tanks, the ships and provide an army in 1941, America was again up to the task, united except for those ignorant dissidents who accepted the ultimate insult, that took almost three thousand lives.

Susan arrived home unexpectedly early, and found Brian on the computer. "I am so tired, Brian. It appears that I have to book more hours to get us through this, now that you are unemployed."

"Actually, you are wrong." He said holding his arms out to her, but she made no attempt to move toward him. "I spoke with Amos this afternoon. He is setting up a fund for survivors of people we lost. The assets we had in the building can be replaced, but my friends and co-workers cannot. The firm's money is in a bank not anywhere near Ground Zero, so I will continue to draw a salary. He told me to take two weeks off while he finds another location. The uptown office is too small to accommodate the rest of us, and there were many, who fortunately survived." He paused and dropped his arms. "I will continue therefore to contribute as I have always done."

Susan finally came over to him and gave him a brief hug and perfunctory kiss on the cheek. "I didn't mean to say you wouldn't. Work is just getting me down."

"I was on the computer booking a flight to Barbados, and hope you might join me." He said.

"I can't leave work. I have too many court cases that I, alone, know more about than any one else. You will have to go without me." She said. "Let's eat dinner out. I don't feature washing dishes tonight, and you will have to pack a bag."

"Done. Flight leaves at 8 am. I arranged for a car service to JFK."

"Really?" She said with a smirk.

Forty-four

Barbados

Brian had called Geoffrey the moment he had made the decision to fly down to the island, and left a message on the answer phone, when no one picked up. His flight arrived on time and he rather enjoyed the feel of hot, humid air that greeted him as he deplaned. Fortunately, his aircraft was the only one on the tarmac, so he was able to claim his bag and move quickly through customs having nothing to declare.

He was both surprised and pleased to find Rachel waiting for him at the taxi stand. "I found your message and made it my business to pick you up, Brian. You have no idea how happy I am to have you back with me on the island."

Brian rolled his bag toward the car park. When they reached the car, Rachel took his carry on and tossed it into the boot. "Where's Geoffrey?" He asked.

"Geoffrey thought it time for him to visit Sara. He just needed to be with her." She said. "Relax, Brian. We have about an hour to kill, since I made a reservation for dinner at the Crane Hotel."

"So Rachel, how long will Geoffrey be away?" He asked.

"I don't expect him back until tomorrow, on the noon plane from Antigua, Brian. " She answered coyly.

After she had parked the Rover into a space at the Crane, Brian sat for a moment and stared at her. "There is something definitely different about you, Rachel. You look so vibrant and younger if I might say. Your hair is shorter, and I just don't know how to say it, you look just amazing."

"I have lost some weight that I needed desperately to lose. I have been walking, actually running, and enjoying every agonizing mile." She smiled. "No worries, It has affected nothing else about me. Absolutely, nothing else. That I can definitely assure you." Rachel smiled.

The hotel concierge informed them that dinner at any of their restaurants would not begin to be served until six, so Brian changed into shorts and a tee shirt, and the two of them took the long stairway down to the beach. Rachel playfully grabbed Brian's hand, and led him down to the water, where the surf was rapidly moving in to reclaim the sand.

"There is something about this island that says I am home." Brian said. "In reality, having been born here, I am home."

He looked at Rachel. "You are absolutely beautiful. You know, I need to kiss you."

Rachel placed her arms around his neck, and seemingly oblivious of her surroundings, pressed her lips hard against his. "I would have been sorely vexed if you didn't." She pulled away. "Why didn't Susan come down with you?"

"Please don't foul this moment." He said. "Things have not just been great back home."

"The disaster at the World Trade Center must have been devastating." She said.

"You have no idea. I needed this period of time to recoup. My concern is for all of those people who perished, and for their families not so fortunate as ours." He said.

By the time they made their way back up the stairs that would lead them to the hotel, it was 6 pm and the dining rooms were now open. Rachel had made an executive decision, and selected the new Zen Restaurant whose menu offered both Thai and Japanese food. They were escorted to a private booth, where they ordered hot sake, and asked for time to make a decision as to what they wanted for dinner.

"How about this," Brian suggested. "I could go for miso soup, a salad and this spicy Hanachi roll. What do you think?"

"Good choice," she said. "It is flying fish roe, cucumber, yellow tail with a dash of chili. Quite good. But we can share. I shall have the flying fish roe, salmon skin, cucumber, tempura prawns and crabmeat. That could be enough and we could order more if still hungry."

"Sounds good to me." Brian responded. "However, other cravings might yet have to be dealt with." Rachel clicked the small sake flask against his and smiled, knowingly.

They eased their way through dinner. "At some point we shall have to return to Simonton," She said. "You know that David, Sophia and Richard are waiting for us."

"I get it. Perhaps taking it a moment at a time would the best choice for all of us." He said.

They ate slowly, ordered another flask of sake and spent the next hour deep in conversation. When it became clear that their booth was in demand, Brian paid the bill with Barbadian money he had brought with him, and they walked out to the car park.

Rachel asked Brian if he might like to drive, but he explained that his island license had expired months ago.

Rachel got behind the wheel. "So, are you up for the Coach House?" She asked, Brian agreed, and she turned the Rover back toward the road that would pass Grantley Adams and return them to the highway. With the absence of traffic, they made good time reaching Highway One and soon were pulling into the Coach House car park.

"Any concerns about being just with me?" He asked.

"None what so ever," she said. "We have been seen here together before. Besides, the Bajan gossip hens will make any thing up they have not seen anyway. It will be cool. No worries."

The Coach House was already filled with local people just off from work, so they bellied up to the bar, passing pleasantries with friends. Brian ordered rum and cokes for both of them, and they found a place to sit in the recently refurbished lounge.

"So. Here's to us," Rachel said lifting her glass.

"This is where is all began, didn't it?" Brian said, checking out the new surroundings.

"I don't regret anything, Brian. Do you or Susan? Geoffrey certainly has none."

Brian smiled. "Do you recall how nervous I was that first time, Rachel? But, you certainly put me at ease immediately."

"At ease?" She laughed. "I remember you quickly rising to the occasion."

"Tell me something, Rachel. Were you all that comfortable? Was it strictly Geoffrey's idea? You know Susan and I had never done anything like that before." He asked.

"Honestly, while I was attracted to you, I didn't know if I would allow it to go anywhere." She said and then drained half of her glass.

"Keep that thought," he said rising. "I'll get two more drinks."

"Brian, be a Luv and bring some Extra Old this time. I don't need any more sugar from the cola." She said.

Brian returned with two glasses and a bottle of dark rum. "We are on the honor system to pay for what we drink." At one time, you started to tell me about what happened when you and Geoffrey went to Canada for holiday." Brian said as he filled her glass half way.

"Let me back track a bit further." She said, taking a sip, and moving along side of him. "I worked as a teller at a division of Barclay's in a small town outside of Toronto called Beeton. After being to Toronto, Beeton became most boring with all of the houses looking alike, all made of the same brick, and with little to do for entertainment other than hitting the two bars in town. The Friday night highlight at one was women's mud wrestling." She fisted him in the shoulder when he asked if she was ever a participant. "The other biggie was a yearly corn roast when the crop came in. That was my life, Brian, until I made a decision to take a holiday in Barbados."

She paused for a moment to listen to the music of a steel drum band, that had just set up for the evening's entertainment. "I came to the island, at the young age of twenty three, having never been out of Canada, mind you, was talked into taking one of the Pirate Cruises, and there I met Geoffrey who swept me of my feet. He was young, so handsome with his mustache and goatee. I did not return to Canada, but moved in with him, just loving every sensuous moment. For the first week, we spent more time in bed than not, you know."

We were married here and had two children. I knew that Bajan men believed not having at least one affair, a denial of manhood, but having never refused Geoffrey, I never ever thought he might stray."

We made a contract that gave him some leeway, but while the girls were young, I would have none of it." She smiled. "It worked out well. He always had a good job. Always came home at night." She finished her drink and refilled her glass and paused to reflect.

"Then one year, we took a holiday in Canada. It was my first time back. We stayed at a hotel near York in Toronto, and had the good fortune to bring a nanny for the girls. There was, however, a darker secret that Geoffrey had kept to himself. The third night in Toronto, Geoffrey told me that he had met some people, and we had been invited to a party in one of the hotel suites. He said they were young, beautiful and liked to have fun. What he did not tell me was that he knew one of the couples from the Pirate Adventure Cruise, and they were into switch parties and group sex. I became suspicious when I found an unopened package of Trojans in his night bag, when I was looking for Tylenol. Since I had my tubes tied after my last pregnancy, we never used condoms any more. But, I decided not to ask."

Brian took her hand. "Look you appear troubled by all of this. If you'd rather not continue on, it's okay." He said.

"Actually, I have told only one person, other than you about what occurred and that was Susan, but not in the detail I plan to give you. This is good catharsis for me Brian. If you have the patience, let me go on. Be a Luv and fill my glass."

Rachel took a drink, touched a napkin to her lips and continued. "I really wasn't a big drinker then. Perhaps I would have a Cosmo or such, and had not yet taken a fancy to rum drinks. An occasional martini, if it was flavored, but that was it. The nanny was with the girls in their room, since it was already nine, and Geoffrey was just itching to go to this party. I noticed that he had put his night bag away. Anyway, the party was in a penthouse suite, and when we arrived we were introduced as the new kids in town. Everybody seemed very chummy with everyone else. The liquor flowed and the island music seemed to warm everyone to what ever was planned for the evening. A couple on the couch had begun to disrobe while everyone else watched. Geoffrey came over, kissed me and told me that he loved me. Then he told me it was switch party. At first I had no idea what he was talking about, until this very good looking man came over, took my hand and led me to cushions that covered the floor. I looked to Geoffrey for help, but he was chatting up a young blonde woman. Christian, the man who began taking my clothes off, said, that she was his wife and it was all right, and that we did not have to do any thing if I chose not to. He seemed very kind and asked me if I would like a drink to calm me down. Christian brought me a glass of rum, taught me how to down it quickly, and follow it with some ice water. He said that every one in the room was clean and that all of the men had been with each of the women at previous parties, and that everyone enjoyed each other."

Rachel smiled nervously. "Geoffrey, along with just about everyone else was now naked. I allowed my self to be undressed, and then I lay back on a cushion as Christian began to make love to me. He was amazingly kind and gentle."

"That must have been terrifying for you." Brian said.

"The rum removed all inhibitions. The lights were dimmed, but I could see that all of the men were young and handsome and the women were quite beautiful. I remember hearing Donna Summer softly singing, Love Me Love Me Baby, as Christian picked me up in his arms and then placed me amid a tangle of legs, breasts, penises and wet vaginas with expectations of immediate and exquisite gratification. I did not look for Christian again, nor did I need to know what Geoffrey was doing. I willingly became an ardent participant in something akin to a feeding frenzy, but this was so sexually charged that I tasted everything, offered up every part of myself, and just wanted to orgasm over and over again. I don't even recall how many different men or even women that I had sex with that night. It turned out to be extraordinarily exciting, and even thought about doing it again. I was exhausted by the time we returned to our rooms and went directly to the children to make sure they were all right. When Geoffrey told me that another party had been scheduled for the following evening, I refused to go and told him he wasn't going either, and that we were returning to Barbados."

"Geoffrey asked me if I enjoyed the experience, and had to admit that I had. I did not ask him how many women he had fucked. My greatest concern was that neither of us would catch a disease."

Brian tried to contain his own arousal. "Would you do it again?" He asked.

"It was so spontaneous, that is could never be replicated. I never once felt dirty. No! A group that large is potentially dangerous." She said. "I think it started out with ten couples."

Rachel became teary-eyed. "Geoffrey realized that I meant what I said, but complained that it was in all Bajan men's blood to seek a bit on the side. I told him that if I wasn't enough for him, perhaps he should leave. But, I could not do that to the girls and suffer the embarrassment of divorce. Geoffrey suggested a compromise. If we met a young couple that came down to Barbados for holiday, and if we were mutually attracted to each other, we might consider switching. I said nothing, but then we met you and Susan. That was one of the best decisions I had ever made."

Forty-five

Barbados 2001

Brian noting that they had consumed a half of a liter of rum capped the bottle. "We collectively have had enough to drink, Luv."

"Actually, Brian, you have had much less to drink than I. Clearly I have had the most and am exceedingly drunk." Her words had begun to slur. "Were you trying to get me drunk for the purpose of taking advantage of me?"

Brian just smiled. "License or no license, give me the keys. I am driving us home."

They reached Simonton without difficulty around midnight. David had locked the front door, but left the porch lights on. Rachel unlocked the door and offered to make some coffee, but Brian thought it would be best to call it a night. Now somewhat sober, she showed him to his room next to the master bedroom she shared with Geoffrey. David and Sophia's rooms were in the other wing, now secured for the night. Brian kissed Rachel and told her that he would see her in the morning.

"If you think your evening is over, you have another think coming. Either you come to me or I come to you." She said as she left him standing in the hall.

Brian unpacked what clothes he would need for the morning. He heard water running in a nearby shower as he got under the covers. He momentarily thought about what Rachel had said and turned over on his side ready for sleep. Around two in the morning, he felt someone slip under the sheets and lie next to him. The last time he and Rachel had shared a bed, they just held each other the entire night. He turned to find her wide-awake, lying quite naked next to him. Placing her hands between his legs, she asked, "Downed some Viagra did you? Oh, Brian, I need to have you so badly."

Brian kissed her breasts one at a time, slowly sucking each nipple, and putting a hand between her legs, found her wet and receptive. "No, Luv, no Viagra, just you." He groaned, as she moved down to take him in her mouth. It was a moment of triumph for Brian to know that there had been nothing physically wrong with him. He allowed Rachel to move on top of him when she was ready, and as she easily pulled him inside of her, he responded to her downward thrusts, awaiting their mutual and ultimate expression of sexual gratification. Afterwards, they held each other, finally falling into a deep sleep.

When he awoke the next morning, he was alone, but still was able to smell the scent Rachel had left behind on his pillow. He thought of Susan, momentarily, but dismissed any idea of having done anything wrong. After all, she had screwed Geoffrey while he was away in Boston. He wondered if it was possible to love two women at the same time, and then realized that physically he had already done that. He was not yet prepared to love two women emotionally, but was getting close to doing so. He tried to rationalize his current situation. He had a commitment to a wife who rejected him sexually. He had no commitment to a lover, who was completely undemanding and receptive. Then there was Geoffrey. If Susan were here on the island, she might outright reject Geoffrey, as she had rejected her husband. He had to convince Susan to come to Barbados. He wondered if the four of them hooked up again, all might be right with their world. Either Susan or Geoffrey might be the problem. Which one or even both could be his problem.

Sophia found Rachel in the kitchen, making breakfast and seemingly happier than she had seen her mother in a long time. "Well, you are one chipper Barbadian, aren't you Mommy?" She said. "Can I help with anything?" Rachel asked her to set the table, and told her she was making ham and eggs. "I can readily smell that. You know we stayed up as long as we could last night, but you two never showed up. Richard Thomas really wanted to see his grandfather, you know."

"I am so sorry, Sophia. I hope Richard Thomas will not be terribly vexed with his grandmother, but I had made dinner reservations at the Crane, not knowing if Brian's plane would be on time. We had sushi rolls and whatever and stopped at the Coach House on the way back. There was so much to catch up on, so we talked for hours."

"David is changing Richard's diaper and will be down shortly. How is Susan?" Sophia asked.

"According to Brian, she had too many suits pending to come down with him." Rachel said as she heated the fry pan for the eggs.

"So, grandpa Brian will be here with us alone to enjoy his grandson." Sophia said.

"Of course, but you must understand what Brian has just gone through with the terrorist attack, and loss of lives, many of whom were his friends and co-workers. He needs some R&R." Rachel said as she cracked the eggs.

"And might you be the source of his R&R, Mommy," Sophia asked as David appeared with the baby in his arms.

Rachel took Sophia aside. "Leave it alone, Sophia. We are doing what is best for everyone. I don't know what you know, or what you think you know. Your father is expected on the morning flight from Antigua. Hopefully, Sara is under control. We all are doing the best we can for everyone. Don't read any more into it than that."

Sophia chip singed, took Richard from David and kissed him. "David, warm up some cereal for the baby if you will, and then go wake your Dad up."

Brian appeared in the doorway, dressed in a tank top and shorts. "No need. I am up and am going for a run. How about you David?" He embraced his son and kissed his cheek.

Sophia gave Brian a kiss. "Sorry but David must take care of the baby. Parents do have responsibility you know."

"Well, let me feed my grandson if I can. Look how big he has grown." Brian said, taking the cereal bowl from David. "I'll feed him and then take my run."

David looked at Sophia. "Well since that is now under control, why don't we take a stroll on the beach." Half way down toward the water, David turned to Sophia. "You are upset over something. What? If I may ask?"

"Okay!" she responded. "Your father and my mother came home quite late last night and who knows what they were doing."

"Jesus, Sophia, they are adults. We both know the history. What are you accusing them of?"

"My father is off the island." She said.

"Sorry, but I can't buy that. He is no prince, since we both know he was fucking my mother." David responded.

"Don't be so gross. I need to ask you this. Am I enough for you sexually, or might you need something on the side? After all Bajan men must have all of their needs fulfilled."

"Might I remind you that I am not Bajan born," he responded.

"You once told me that you were attracted to Jessica. If the opportunity arose, would you consider switching with them?" She asked.

"Why are we having this dumb conversation? All right, if you might consider having sex with Justin. Would you? Are you attracted to him?" He responded.

They returned to the plantation house. "We had better go in and see how your Dad is faring with Richard." She said.

"No! You never answered my question." He said.

Sophia took David's hand and pulled him up the patio steps. "Ask me again if and when they ever come back to the island."

"Wait! Are you suggesting that something like that might be inevitable?" He asked. "Like this is Barbados?"

"I am telling you nothing more than, what's that Doris Day song? Oh, yes, que sera, sera." She said. Brian appeared with the baby. "So Grandpa Brian, did Richard finish his breakfast? We certainly are ready for ours, aren't we David?"

After the breakfast dishes were washed, Rachel told the others that she had to go down to the office and tend to business in Geoffrey's absence. David and Sophia said they were planning to go to the East Coat for the day, but Brian said he would accompany Rachel to Fontabelle after he made a call to Susan.

He let the phone ring at least five times, but the answer phone never picked up. Assuming that she had already left for the office, Brian gave up, decided to forego the run, and changed into clothes more appropriate to spend the day with Rachel, who had planned to stay at the office, until she had to meet Geoffrey's flight due in at noon.

Rachel stopped at the Holetown Police station so Brian could get a current license. When they returned to the car, she sat in the passenger seat and asked Brian to drive. "You do recall that we drive on the left? Right?"

Brian got behind the steering wheel. "All right now! Right. Left. Which is it Luv?" He asked jokingly.

Rachel laughed. "Just drive, you idiot."

They had just passed Payne's Bay when Rachel asked him to pull over to a sandy spot on the beach side. "Do you think me horrid for what I told you about what we did in Toronto?" She asked.

Brian took her hand. "Unlikely and I believe I will suffer a perpetual hard on just remembering everything you told me."

Rachel laughed. "I love you Brian. I love Geoffrey as well, but in a different way. Is it possible that the four of us could carry on this way forever?"

"I would wish for nothing more, but I can't speak for Susan. I just don't understand her anymore. Perhaps if we can get her down here she might loosen up, and revert back to the Susan we all loved to make love to."

Rachel looked at him, but did not respond. She wondered if Susan had shared their private moments with him. "Do you suppose if we told Susan about Toronto, she might find it invigorating?"

Brian pulled back onto the road, remembering to cross over to the left side. "Perhaps if Geoffrey told the story as good as you did. Right now, I had better watch where I am driving."

Rachel put a hand between his legs and smiled. "No time for skylarking now. Got to clean up a desk full of paper work at the office, and be spit spot to pick up Geoffrey at noon."

While Rachel pored over invoices piled high on the desk, Brian put a call through to Susan, who answered the phone herself. "Hi, Brian, how's Barbados? Done anything interesting?"

"Good to talk to you also." He said. "How come you answered the phone?"

"Secretary took a few sick days and I have not found a temp. So. How are the children and our grandson?" She asked.

"Richard is adorable. Sophia and David are just great. I drove down to Fontabelle with Rachel, and we will pick Geoffrey up at Grantley at noon."

"Geoffrey was away? So, you were alone with Rachel." She said.

"Correct. Geoffrey was in Antigua to see Sara. Look I really, no we really would like you to come down even for just a few days. I might even have a surprise for you." He said as Rachel chip singed.

"I love surprises. What is it? Not this week, Brian. Perhaps if you are still there next week, I might be able to, but definitely not this week." She was emphatic.

"Surprise will have to wait, then." He said.

"Can I speak with Rachel?" Susan asked. Brian gave her the phone. Rachel listened to what ever was being said to her and then said, "Of course." She handed the phone back to Brian who talked for a moment and then said goodbye.

"What did she say?" He asked.

"She asked if I got laid last night." She said has she rifled through more papers.

"Are you crazy? She knows that Geoffrey was off the island so that leaves me, right?" Brian was upset.

"Not necessarily, you know. After all this is Barbados." Rachel laughed, came around the desk and hugged him. "She asked me if I would take good care of you and I said of course. Geoffrey's plane should be landing shortly, so we had better be off."

Brian picked up a Phillips screw from the floor. "Hey, wanna screw?"

"Rachel looked surprised. "You will have to ask Geoffrey." She responded.

"Are you serious?" He asked.

"Absolutely not. Skylarking, you know."

Forty-six

Barbados 2001

They watched Geoffrey deplane from their vantage point in the second floor airport lounge. Despite the fact that Grantley Adams was a relatively new facility, the floors were dirty and the windows seemed not to have been recently cleaned. Geoffrey carried only one shoulder bag, as he moved quickly down the long walkway provided for incoming passengers. Finally, spotting Rachel and Brian, he waved and went directly to the customs' line designated for Barbadian citizens.

Geoffrey met them outside at the taxi queue. "It is fantastic to see you Brian. Hope you are planning an extended stay with us."

Rachel kissed her husband. "How is Sara faring, Geoffrey?"

"Well a bit better every day, but she has a long way to go. Honestly, I don't like the facility, and would like to bring her back here. Actually thought of doing it today, but knew I had better discuss it with you first. She really wants to come home."

"Car is just over there, Geoffrey. We can discuss this later." Rachel said as the three walked toward the space in which she had parked

"Susan did not accompany you, Brian. Did she." He said. "Pity, I so would like to have seen her again. It has been too long. Well, any one fancy a stop at John Moore's on the way?"

"No, Geoffrey, we are going directly home. You can party later. And, I cleaned up and paid some of the delinquent bills I found on your desk, and sent out invoices for payments owed us. When are you going to put your business cap on?" She asked as she opened the rear door and got in. "Brian, please sit in front."

"Have never worn a cap Luv, and do not plan to do so." He said, as he got behind the wheel. "So, do we have a negative vote for John Moore?" He asked, moving the car onto the main road.

"Home Geoffrey, you may drink later if you wish. Right Brian." Brian smiled, but said nothing.

Nearing the Great House, Geoffrey drove up the long roadway flanked by the Royal palms. "Forgot to ask, Brian. Did Jay happen to provide you with any blue pills for me?" Geoffrey braked at the front steps, where Sophia waited with the baby.

"Geoffrey, the pills are a crutch and don't work. Leave it alone. What you really need is a little bit of Susan perhaps." Rachel offered as Brian blushed, not knowing whether or not to be angry.

"You really are still so vexed with me, aren't you?" Geoffrey said, exiting the car.

"Hey Mon, leave it alone for a while. Let me get the drinks. Why don't you two go out on the patio?" Brian said.

"Daddy, your grandson wants you to say hello to him." Sophia said.

Geoffrey took the little boy in his arms and kissed him. "Grandpa will play with you later." He thought for a moment. "You have two grandpas. How will you call us? I have an idea. I shall be Grandpa Geoffrey and you Brian will be Pop Pop Brian. Keep on saying that to reinforce it, Sophia. Where is David?"

"He went to the stable to feed the horses." Sophia said.

"You now have horses?" Brian asked, as Geoffrey nodded. "Susan loves to ride. Well she did. Who knows now?"

"We have four, two male Arabians, a female palomino and a quarter horse. All young and just adore being out running. I had Richard on one with me last week." Geoffrey said. "And if Susan chooses to ride, she will just love the palomino."

"Tell me you are skylarking." Rachel said.

"No, Luv. True. True. He loved it." Geoffrey said, handing the baby back to Sophia. "Right, Brian to the drinks. We can all have them on the patio. It must be after five somewhere in the world."

"Sophia, why don't we feed Richard his lunch, and let the two Grandpas have time to themselves. I'll check on David out in the stable." Rachel said as she picked the baby up.

"It must have been just terrible." Geoffrey said. "The videos more than likely do no justice to what happened."

"You cannot imagine," Brian responded, and went on to tell him about his run through the park, and ultimately finding Justin in a sea of grey ash. So, how are you my Man?"

"This affair about Sara has been devastating. I hate having her imprisoned such as it is, but Rachel will give me a bad time. I know it's best for her." Geoffrey said as he poured some Mt. Gay into two glasses.

"How about you?" Brian asked.

"You are referring to the sex thing. It has gotten worse. Rachel has lost patience with me, so I got her one of those electric rubber dildos that look and feel like the real thing. I have never seen her use it." He said.

"I offered to get one for Susan, but she said she would throw it out. She really has made no effort to deal with our issues. I know now it is not all my problem." Brian realized he might have said more than he should have."

"How do you know that for sure," Geoffrey said, taking a substantial swig. When Brian did not answer immediately, Geoffrey laughed. "It's cool, my brother. When we were driving back from the airport, I looked at Rachel in the rear view mirror and she mouthed the words, 'yes we did'. Almost feels like payback. It's cool."

"I appreciate that Geoffrey. How are we going to get Susan down here? She really needs to get out of New York and that office." Brian said.

"I shall write her a letter. I am very good at that, you know, and send it out priority mail on the last plane to New York this evening. She should get it by tomorrow. I'll mark it FOR HER EYES ONLY under threat of whatever."

Rachel brought sandwiches and a pitcher of limeade and placed it on the table, as David, still wearing his riding boots joined them. "Off the patio," Rachel ordered, "with those muck covered boots, and be sure to wash your hands."

David backed down onto the grass, bowed deeply and laughed. "Yes Mistress. Right away, Mistress. I shall return cleaned up. Save me something to eat, and Dad, I have news regarding my book."

"Soils my floors often enough. But he is a wonderful husband and father. Mistress indeed!" She laughed, and went to make more sandwiches.

David returned wearing a clean shirt, khaki shorts and sandals. While munching a tuna fish sandwich, he told Brian about his book. "Yes, a London publisher has allowed one of their editors to look at a book proposal I sent, but I have yet to hear anything back. With money so tight, I may not, but one can only hope."

"Explain the book proposal." Brian said.

"Easy enough. They are smart enough to know a book's plusses and minuses from an outline of each chapter, a synopsis, and what the author might be willing to agree to regarding, marketing stuff, and retrieval from store shelves if that be needed." David explained.

"Retrieval. That would be a minus I suppose." Brian said.

"Only partially correct. The royalty is determined by how many books are ultimately sold, but depending upon how the contract is worded regarding disposal of books not sold, it might be reduced."

"I have no idea what I may be offered up front if the book is accepted. I really have my eyes on the historical novel for its potential sales appeal. However, I would not discount a movie made of the proposal London now has, since it is prurient enough to wet a lot of people's sexual appetites. 'Lady Chatterley's Lover' was always a good seller."

Geoffrey finished the rum and wiped his lips. "David, there is no way any of us might be assumed the protagonists in this novel of yours, is there?" He asked as Brian nodded.

"Sophia knows what she knows, and has read it cover to cover. She believes that no one on the island could draw the connection." He took another bite of sandwich. "I gave parts of the book to Meghan to read when she was down here. She never questioned me, so I doubt if that is an issue."

"She has never questioned Susan or myself about it, so hopefully it's a dead issue. But she is pretty smart." Brian said.

"Neither Sophia nor I are about to say anything. I just suggest it be left alone. But you four have given me lots of stuff to work with." Brian glared at him. "I'm kidding. I'm kidding." He said.

"We are trying to get your mother down here. She has got to get away from the office for a few days." Brian said.

"I agree." David said. "It must be difficult living in the city after what happened. What's with your job? Your office is gone."

"As well as too many of the people I worked with. We are developing another office up town. Actually it will be an expansion of what we have there currently. I'm still okay financially."

"I was thinking," David said. "If the books go off in a big way, I'd like to start a fund for the families of people lost in the buildings."

"That is very generous of you, but they will need money now as well as for educating the children of those who died." Brian said.

"Excellent point." Geoffrey added. "Let's drink to that, and then I have an important letter to write."

Bajan Properties Ltd.
Fontabelle, St. Michael, Barbados

Geoffrey Townsand   President

Rachel Townsand Vice President

246-6969

Dearest Susan,

I aware of your concerns regarding someone in your office seeing this before you do, but I decided that leaving it as a phone message at your apartment would be as inappropriate. I miss you terribly and think of all the times we were together constantly. Fresh in my mind is that last time we made love in New York too many years ago. Please find a way to clear your calendar and spend time with me/us. What happened in New York continues to send a shock wave around the world. Our small island country feels for the lost people, their friends and families and the people of the U.S. as a result of the terrible tragedy at the Trade Towers.

I have just come back from Antigua visiting Sara who is showing some signs of improvement. It appears that she is following the program, and hopefully will be able soon to return to us clean and healthy.

Our grandson Richard Thomas is a joy, and is staring to say a few intelligible words. I will correct that by teaching him pure Bajan and how to chip sing. Brian is fine and certainly in need of being here, and away from the turmoil at home. Rachel still works with me, and just loves helping Sophia with the baby. David has just about completed both books and there is some interest in the second and spicier of the two at a London publishing house. I/we love and miss you. Please find a way to come down. I am longing to pick you up at Grantley Adams very soon. My "attack" was attributed to indigestion.

Luv you,

Geoffrey

Forty-seven

New York-Barbados

Having overslept, Susan did not reach her office until ten. Fortunately, her first appointment rescheduled for the following day. By 11:30, the only other client on her calendar had failed to appear, and her stomach repeatedly reminded her that she had not had time for breakfast. Susan called the young woman who had been sent by the Temp Agency, and asked her to find a menu for a deli located around the corner. While waiting, she looked out the windows that faced lower Manhattan, and saw the grey haze that continued to hover over what was once the World Trade Center.

The temp brought in the menu, along with a FedEx that had just been delivered. "This just came Mrs. McKenzie and with strict instructions it was for your eyes only." She said as Susan took the large envelope from her.

When she saw that it was from Barbados and Geoffrey, Susan smiled. "Do me a favor, and call in an order for a pastrami on rye with Russian dressing, and get something for yourself as well. See if any one still here would like something. Oh, and put up a fresh pot of coffee."

Susan opened the envelope, and read the letter three times. She suddenly felt renewed and relaxed for the first time in a long time. Susan put the letter back into its envelope, locked it in a desk drawer and picked up the phone. The she dialed the number of one of the minor partners. "Maury, it's Susan, I need a favor from you."

It was almost four in the afternoon when the phone rang at Townsand and Townsand. "Hello," he answered, Geoffrey Townsand here. How can I be of service?"

"Good afternoon, Mr. Townsand. I believe I need to be serviced." He immediately recognized Susan's sultry voice.

"Luv, it's you." He said.

"Are you alone?" She asked.

"For the moment, Rachel went out to fetch fresh ink cartridges for the printer. I expect her back shortly." He said. "You received my letter?"

"As you requested, I have rearranged my schedule, actually a bit more than that, but we can discuss it when I arrive." She said.

"Fantastic!" He exclaimed. "Tell me when you shall arrive and I will be there."

"You cannot believe what an uplift your letter was. I am so looking forward to seeing you. I have so much to discuss with you."

"I'm glad. When might I expect you?" Geoffrey asked.

"I am booked on the Monday afternoon BWI flight, due to arrive at 4:15. Just you Geoffrey, just you." She pleaded.

"I shall find some way to have Brian occupy Rachel." He said.

"If I had to make an educated guess that should not present a problem." Susan said.

"Susan, what are you suggesting? Something I may not be privy to?" He said, stifling a laugh.

"Oh and I forgot to mention, I have always had a fondness for Hebrew National." She said.

"Is that some kind of an American code word?" He asked.

"Your job to figure it out." She said knowing that Brian would lead him in the right direction if asked to."

On the way back to Simonton, Rachel noted Geoffrey to be on a high. "Luv, did you happen to book at least 50% of our rentals while I was out? You are in an extraordinary great mood." She said.

"Sadly no, but it's Friday, and I have planned a great evening for the three of us." He said.

"Really, and what are David and Sophia's plans for the evening? She asked.

"They are having dinner with the Weatherheads and are taking Richard with them." He said.

"Really, you are a fountain of information, but you are not telling me everything, are you." She said.

"True, True, Luv. I thought a marvelous dinner at Olives in Holetown, a brief jaunt to the Coach House, and then back home for an orgiastic, Olympic, ménage de trois." He said.

"And you have passed this by Brian for his approval?" She asked.

"Not needed, but you can veto the plan if you are so inclined." He responded.

"I shall dress appropriately, and look forward to any and everything you have planned. See if you can bypass some of this school bus traffic." Rachel said.

Later, Brian complimented Rachel on how beautiful she looked, as she joined them on the patio. He wore a dress shirt and dark trousers, while Geoffrey chose an all white ensemble. After parking the car across the road from the Holetown restaurant, the three walked hand in hand into the main entrance. They chose to eat in the garden area on the first floor, and were immediately seated. Geoffrey ordered rum and cokes. Brian thought he was in an exceptionally good mood. "What's up Geoffrey? You look like the proverbial cat that swallowed the canary."

"Personally, I would prefer the pulled pork with garlic mashed potatoes and sautéed cristophine." He said. Both Brian and Rachel opted for the grilled chicken and fried plantain with local vegetables. Geoffrey ordered a bottle of 1999 Merlot from California.

After coffee and brandy, Geoffrey suggested that they could bar hop or return to Simonton, perhaps for a swim. "It has become quite warm, what say you all?"

"We can go home, have drinks and decide how the rest of the evening will proceed." Brian suggested.

"What a grand idea," Rachel said. "I vote with Brian."

"Outnumbered, I readily agree with the majority." Geoffrey said laughing as he steered the Lexus in the direction of Simonton.

Sophia had left a note that they planned to stay over in St. George with the Weatherheads, and that she had made the decision to give the housekeeper the evening off. Rachel wondered if her daughter had just given them carte blanche.

"I shall bring a cart of drinks down to the pool." Geoffrey called out. "Any suggestions? And any one wearing a swim suit shall be designated a pussy."

Brian and Rachel were already in the pool when Geoffrey joined them. "I plan to swim some laps and burn off dinner." Brian said.

"Really," Rachel said as she reached between his legs. "I can suggest a better way to do a calorie burn."

"Music," Geoffrey said as he climbed up and out of the water. "We need music." He went into the house and soon, songs from the Merrymen's recent Canadian tour came over the speakers.

He returned to find Brian and Rachel at opposite ends of the pool. "Let's do a few quickies, and then go upstairs. We all know what we want. No need to provide further entertainment for the neighbors."

Rachel lay between her two lovers. "You cannot imagine how powerful I feel holding both your cocks in my hands." She murmured. Both Geoffrey and Brian thought it was déjà vu.

"Actually we can both well imagine your sense of strength." Geoffrey said. "I have a secret I feel I should share with you. Susan is arriving in a day or so. Please do not let on that I told you, and look slightly surprised when she arrives."

The smell of brewed coffee wafted up to the bedroom where Rachel and Brian lay, exhausted from the sexual exercises performed the night before. "Geoffrey, Luv, is I assume, preparing breakfast. He has been most generous, but the two of you could not have satisfied me more. You both were amazingly creative. If you need anything I might drop in the suggestion box, please advise. And as to Geoffrey's query regarding the strength of my holdings last night, you cannot imagine."

"Don't sell yourself short my dear. I am not certain what, if anything was omitted." Brian said.

Geoffrey had scrambled eggs and crisp bacon on the table, when Brian and Rachel came into the kitchen. "Smells great," Brian said. "What are the plans for today?"

Geoffrey smiled. "We have the Bajan Mist at our disposal today, at least until three. Then I propose we run over to the east coast, and then back here for a quick dinner." He began to hum portions of Beautiful Barbados.

"Be real Geoffrey. The kids will be back today, so discretion is the name of the game." Rachel advised. "And more of this strange humming. You have a secret you are just dying to share. Right?"

"I have already let the cat out. I know that Susan will arrive on the late Monday flight." He blurted out. "To keep our secret, I shall pick her up and remember, you two shall be so surprised."

By eleven in the morning, they were sunning on the deck of the catamaran, as Geoffrey expertly steered out of Deep Water Harbor toward Carlisle Bay. When Rachel excused herself to use the head, Geoffrey called Brian up to the helm. "Got to ask you something. Susan said she favored something called Hebrew Nations something. I don't recall and she laughed at me."

Brian stifled his laughter with his hand, almost choking on the rum he had just swallowed.

"I am not amused." Geoffrey said. "What's so funny?"

"After that first night when we switched, I pestered Susan to make a comparison. Well, perhaps I wanted to know which of us was the better lover. She finally although reluctantly agreed, and said that your cock was as big as a salami, and she feared that you would never get it into her. Obviously to her delight, it turned out not to be an issue."

"Let me understand this now. She compared me to something one might order in one of your New York delis? I certainly hope I was as you Yanks say an Extra Large." Geoffrey laughed.

"That is something she will have to define, my friend." Brian said.

Rachel appeared on deck, and announced that she planned to sun on the mesh stretched over the bow. Releasing the ties that held her bra, she let it drop, slipped out of her bikini bottoms and crawled up onto the platform where she spread eagled. "Any one wish to join me Brian?" She asked.

Geoffrey steered the craft into the wind. "Go Brian and be her knight errant. And please by all means prevent our figurehead from getting sunburned."

Brian dropped his trunks and crawled up along side of Rachel who pulled him on top of her. "Don't wish to burn you know." With his ass to windward, he entered her easily, as Geoffrey watched with amusement. "I believe I shall steer out toward that cruise boat. People seem to have cameras at the ready."

Forty-eight

Barbados 2001

Geoffrey had called American Airlines a number of times, and was assured that Susan's flight might arrive on schedule. Nevertheless, he left Fontabelle early, and sat in the airport arrivals car park with the air conditioning running on high. Temperatures at noon were reported to be at 86' with no let up in sight for the next few days. He thought to himself that Susan would pick the hottest day of the year to return to the island. He entered the terminal and found her in the baggage area, where a porter had already collected her three large bags from the carousel.

They embraced while the porter stood by scratching his head. "So good to be back Geoffrey. You know how much I love this island." She said.

"Love me as much, Luv." He watched as the porter loaded the bags onto a cart. "You have enough luggage here, never to return to the States." Geoffrey gave the porter some Barbadian currency and told him to go to customs, where the agent greeted and waved him through. The porter loaded the bags in the boot of the Rover and wished Susan a good holiday.

Susan thanked Geoffrey for providing a cool car for the trip home. "Projected to be the hottest few days Barbados has experienced in many a year." He said as Susan leaned over and kissed him."

"I am so glad to be back home." She said, as Geoffrey pushed the CD play button. "Oh, my, 'Baby Count On Me'. How appropriate. Shall we stop for our usual pre-drink drink?" She asked, laughing.

"I planned ahead, my Darling. Reach behind the seat, and you shall find a bottle of Mt. Gay and two, forgive me, plastic glasses." Susan poured, as Geoffrey turned the car out onto the highway.

"How is Brian?" She asked.

"Brian is doing just fine and he misses you terribly." He said.

"And Rachel, Sophia, David and my sweet grandson?" She asked.

"Fantastic, all of them. You don't know how good it is too have you back. You are still Bajan, no matter how long you have been away." He said. "And you, Susan. How have you been? You look absolutely gorgeous."

"Do I now, Geoffrey? I thought Bajans use the word gorgeous to describe something exceptionally good to eat." She smiled and poured a half glass of rum that they shared."

"As I recall the menu and our history, fantastic buffet is more appropriate." He said as he went around the last roundabout. "Susan you really look radiant."

"Actually, Geoffrey, I felt something stirring in me the moment we landed. Something that I have sadly not felt for too long a time."

"How long can you stay with us, Susan?" He asked as he turned the car past Barbados Telephone and onto the Upper Road."

"You saw the luggage I brought with me. I am considering taking a sabbatical, and briefly alluded to that before I left the office this morning. Right now all of my cases are covered. I really think I am burned out."

"She watched fields of uncut cane rush by. "So, have I missed anything, Geoffrey?" She asked.

"In what respect love?" He responded.

"You know exactly what I am talking about." She said curtly. She relaxed and finished the last of the rum. "Oh, Geoffrey, I have acted very poorly towards my husband. I am sure he has told you that I have become, well frigid. He has been able to perform, hasn't he?"

"I have heard no reports from Rachel to the contrary." He said.

"Then the fault has been mine. No matter. Everything will just have to work out. Geoffrey, pull into the car park. There is something we must talk about before we get home. Has Brian said terrible things about me?"

"We are now just parked at Super Center. Planning to do some last minute shopping are you?" He asked. "What is it that you believe Brian might have said about you?"

"That I have been awful towards him, and he deserved none of my anger. I cannot remember the last time he and I had real sex or any actually. Now I understand that his inability to satisfy was due to me and not all his fault." She said.

"And your solution is?" He asked.

"I have no solution that will make things whole again. I just feel so unfulfilled. I feel that I have been prevented from being the person I really wish to be. Was Brian obstructive? Perhaps, but in a way, any husband would try, to keep a marriage together. The four of us have had quite a relationship, loving and amazingly sexual. We have often congratulated ourselves that our marriages have survived. But have they, really Geoffrey? I believe there is an undercurrent that makes our relationship shaky." Susan waited for him to respond.

"This is what I would propose. Let's try to resume where we all left off, and let the chips fall where they may." Geoffrey said. "Time to go home and face the music. The clear message is that the four of us really love each other. Perhaps we cannot draw on the gymnastics we all were capable of when we were younger, but I would still like give it a go." He turned on the ignition and pulled out onto Highway One.

"There is much more that I must speak with you about." She said. " But, in time. In time."

When he turned up the roadway leading to Simonton, they saw Sophia and Richard walking toward them. "Stop Geoffrey!" Susan got out of the car and picked Richard up in her arms. "I have so missed you my Love." She said and then hugged Sophia. "Where are my big men?"

"David and Brian went down for a sea bath. They should be back very soon." Sophia said as she warmly returned Susan's embrace.

"Rachel," he called out, "Company is here. I'll carry Susan's bags upstairs. Break open the bar for a very special reunion."

Sophia thought her mother's embrace of Susan lingered more than one might expect. "I'll get the drinks. Any one not wanting rum? We have scotch, vodka and just about everything else." She said dismissing what she thought she had just witnessed.

Rachel went upstairs with Susan. Geoffrey left them alone, after he deposited her bags in their room. Susan stepped back and looked at Rachel. "You look so much younger, darling, and you have lost weight."

"I lost some weight with exercise, cut down on the rum, and I feel great." Rachel said.

"I could use a major makeover," Susan said, removing her blouse and undoing her bra. "And I have got to get out of these clothes." Susan removed her skirt and folded it over a chair.

"Let me help you unpack, and get your things into the bureau. I am pleased that you are planning on an extended stay." Rachel said. "And if I may make a suggestion, you need to get laid."

Susan smiled. "It was such a confusing few days. I know that I have over packed. Hey, regarding your analysis, any suggestions?"

Brian came in and observing Susan in her state of undress, said, "Okay, am I interrupting something?"

Susan kicked off her heels and walked barefoot and bare breasted to her husband. "I would like a kiss, Luv. I missed you too, you know."

"I just knew that Barbados would be the answer." Brian said as Geoffrey entered.

"Hey, looks like I am overdressed." Geoffrey said. "Uh, and Sophia's on her way up to change Richard. I have drinks on the patio and something called bruschetta."

Susan changed into shorts and a cotton tea shirt, left her bra back in the room, and went downstairs to join Rachel and Geoffrey, while Brian took a quick shower. David used the outside shower to wash off the sea salt, and was toweling off when he met Susan in the living room.

He kissed his mother and told her how happy he was that she was able to get away. Checking out her outfit, he laughed. "Geoffrey organizing a wet, tee-shirt contest?"

Susan walked past him and on to the patio.

"Okay. Dinner plans. What do you say we try out the new Mango by The Sea?" He asked while pouring Susan a glass of Extra Old.

"Golly, I haven't been there since it was just the plain old Mango Café." Susan remarked. "Let's wait for Brian."

Since they had no baby sitter, Sophia and David said they would stay home and watch a video David rented from Chubby DeFreitas.

Later in the evening, when they entered the Speightstown restaurant, they saw a beautiful canopied dining room overlooking the sea, and with tables set in classical English service, with myriads of utensils. Geoffrey complimented the owner on the changes that had been made as the four were seated.

"I remember this place being a cheap date." Brian said as he scanned the menu. "From what I can see, not any more."

"Unimportant, after all the Mango By The Sea should be honored to have Brian and Susan dining here. Not quite Mike's but quite an ambitious menu from what I can see."

There were so many specialty drinks listed, Susan and Rachel had difficulty choosing, but ultimately both ordered Mango daiquiris. "So, Brian will you have a sissy drink as well?" Geoffrey asked. Brian ordered a rum and coke and Geoffrey opted for a sugar cane brandy and soda.

Geoffrey noticed that Susan and Rachel looked exceedingly luscious, and realized neither were wearing bras. Susan wore a smart looking beige camisole over white slacks, and Rachel had chosen a black linen top that complimented black slacks. Both women were radiant.

"You both look gorgeous," Geoffrey said as he felt Susan's heel hit his crotch."

"The choices are elegant, as are the prices, Geoffrey. Don't you think?" Rachel said.

"True. True Luv. No worries." Geoffrey responded as he raised his glass. "To our family. We are family once again. So good to have everyone home." Glasses clinked.

"No, I am not doing it." Susan laughed, as the others looked at her. "This place is much too elegant for an 'over the teeth toast.'" She looked at her menu again, and asked Rachel if she might like to share a goat cheese and vegetable appetizer.

Rachel thought it a good idea, since it had been her first choice. Brian and Geoffrey said they needed some meat, so they agreed to share the racks of baby back ribs. Susan told the waiter they needed more time to make their dinner selections.

All found their appetizers, "gorgeous", as they say, and finally made their entrée decisions. Susan had decided upon lemon grass chicken with a light coconut cream sauce, Rachel picked ocean crepes filled with shrimp and fish, and both of the men finally chose giant Tiger prawns.

Geoffrey called the wine steward over. "Bet he cannot fill this order," he said. "Would you happen to have a bottle of One World Orange Street Ruby Cabernet/Merlot." He was embarrassed when the steward asked if he preferred the 1999 or 2000 vintage.

Rachel looked at her husband. "Where did you ever find that name, and remember it?"

"It was in a trade paper we received at the office," he said. "Never thought he would have known what it was. Ah, here comes our dinner, and the wine as well. Enjoy."

"Is this a local wine?" Susan asked.

"No, the best Barbados can do is rum and beer. Grapes require a cooler climate, you know. Actually, it comes from South Africa, and I find it quite nice." He said after sampling it. The others agreed.

Despite the delicious sounding names on the dessert menu, none were ordered. Susan and Rachel had tea with milk and sugar.

The men sipped Courvoisier as they looked with admiration, at their two beautiful women across the table.

After dinner, Geoffrey asked for suggestions how they might spend the rest of the evening. Susan said she preferred to return to Simonton, where they might just sit and talk.

They found Sophia and David cuddled on the den couch in their pajamas, watching television. Sophia volunteered that his choice of movie proved to be a disaster. "I guess there was just too much sex," he said. "Or hopefully, not enough." Susan looked at Brian as if to say 'your DNA'.

"I plan to change into something more comfortable." Susan said.

"Gracious, you are halfway there." Brian said ducking a pillow thrown by Susan.

"Meet you all down by the pool." Susan said. " I am off to change.

Susan changed back into the shorts she had worn earlier. Brian put on a Pirate Adventure tee and bathing trunks. "Going for a swim, Luv?"

"Actually have not decided." He said. "And yourself?"

"Something, I would like to discuss with Geoffrey, if you don't mind, of course." She said. Brian said okay.

Forty-nine

Barbados 2001

When Brian came back, he found Rachel alone on the patio. She pulled him down next to her on the chaise and cradled his head in her arms. "Susan and Geoffrey have gone down to the beach. We have the time to ourselves. Brian, do you love me?"

"Of course I do, but you must understand that I love my wife as well." He said. "How can we find a way, any way that might allow the four of us to prove that the relationship the four of us have can continue to grow?"

"Just tell me that you love me. That is what matters right now. I have no idea how Geoffrey and Susan feel, Brian, and that scares me." She said.

Susan and Geoffrey made their way down to a beach that was being reclaimed by the dark sea. She allowed the warm water to wash over her toes. "I love Barbados, Geoffrey. I love you and I love Brian and Rachel, emotionally and physically, but I must love all of you without any sense of regret, and that is so confusing right now. And how do we justify our feelings and emotions with our children. They must understand, accept and not hate us."

Geoffrey put his arms around her. "What do you wish of me? I will do any thing to make you happy." He said.

"At one time, you asked me to join you for a holiday. My immediate instincts were to assume Cannes or such. You had thoughts about developing a small resort that might cater to basic needs of people, far beyond those prurient offered by Club what ever. I regret that I dismissed what you believed in. If you might still want me, take me with you, and I will stay for whatever period of time it might require. When I told Brian of your invitation five years ago, he rejected it as inappropriate. If the four of us can ever find away to live as one unit, I must make this move, sadly, that both Rachel, Brian and others might find extremely painful."

"I find it interesting that you chose the word might, regarding Rachel and Brian's acceptance." Geoffrey said.

"I have to assume that it will always be a matter of choice." Susan said.

"Choice, I shall remember that." Geoffrey said. "Let's go back up to the house. Rachel and Brian will be wondering where we are. I have a list of rental properties in the Grenadines in my office. I'll check them out tomorrow. Don't say anything to anybody about this yet."

The patio was empty when they returned, so Geoffrey turned off the lights and secured the doors. Susan found Brian asleep when she came to their room. After taking a shower, she toweled off, slipped under the sheets and moved next to Brian. He woke up feeling her hand between his legs. Turning, he found himself facing Susan's bare breasts.

"I need you to suck my nipples," She said as she placed his hand on her crotch. In no time she moaned and pulled his hand away.

"You came, I assume." Brian said.

"Of course. Take off your bottoms and I'll give you some relief." She took a **tissue** from the bed stand and massaged him until he ejaculated. "You were harder than usual." Susan kissed him and turned on her side away from him. "Good night."

Rachel was in the kitchen brewing coffee when she heard a car engine start. When she looked out the window she saw Geoffrey unlocking the main gate. "Where are you going so early?" She called out.

"Trust me, my Luv, I could be making a decision today that might change our lives. I will be back as soon as I can." He yelled, as he steered the Rover toward the main road.

Susan appeared in the kitchen as Rachel began to pour coffee. "Trouble", she asked. "Were you and Geoffrey arguing?"

"No Geoffrey said he would join us later and suggested he meet us at Mullins," she lied. Wear your least, if not best and I shall do the same. I am making some eggs with bacon. Give Brian a call to come down."

"Sadness does not become you, Rachel. You mean so much to me." Susan said.

"I need more than that, Susan. Tell me that you love me." Rachel implored."

Susan took Rachel's face in her hands and kissed her. "Rachel, I love you more than it might be possible for two people to love each other."

Brian parked the Lexus along the road by Mullins, since the small car park was full. The beach bar had a new look as a rustic dining room had been built on the north side where the showers had once been. Rachel, Sophia and Susan went for lounges, while Brian walked Richard down to the water.

David had some project he was working on and said he might join them later.

When Susan and Rachel took off their shorts, both were wearing thongs. Not to be outdone by the others, Sophia, who had slimmed down, wore a brief top and thong as well. Many eyes followed the three as they walked to the edge of the water where they joined Brian and the baby.

"Wow!" He said. "I wondered why the three of you had just garnered the attention of every man on the beach. You guys look simply amazing."

"Don't go too deep with Richard. We are going out to the float." Rachel said. "Need to get rid of these tan lines." Then all three women dived into the water, surfaced and moved gracefully toward their objective.

After twenty minutes, Richard became bored with his pail and shovel, so Brian took him up to the bar for a soda. He found Geoffrey there, and the two ordered Banks beer.

Brian observed the broad smile on his friend's face. "You look awfully pleased with yourself. What's up?"

"I am trying to finalize a real estate deal, I had been mulling over for a few years. I shall tell you about it later, if and when it's signed, sealed and delivered." Geoffrey said.

"Why not tell me now?" Brian asked.

"Need it to be absolutely solid, Brian. I want nothing to jinx the deal, if there even might be a deal." Geoffrey said. "Another beer?"

Brian shrugged his shoulders. "If you say so. Okay to both. When will you know?"

"It's still up in the air and I need a firm commitment from a potential partner. Where are our women?" He asked

"All three are on the float. Here take your grandson for a bit, so I can go for a swim." Brian said as he handed Richard to Geoffrey.

Later as the four adults and Richard sat at the restaurant, they took turns bringing the baby up from under the table, where he continued to gravitate. Since Geoffrey never mentioned anything about his business deal, Brian chose not to bring it up.

They stayed until three, and then returned to Simonton, where they found David doing laps in the pool. Sophia handed Richard to Rachel, and ran to join her husband.

"You look fantastic in that thong. Absolutely phenomenal." He said.

"You like the new me?" She asked.

"What else don't I know?" He asked.

Sophia kissed David, and then began to swim laps, while he wondered if he was missing something very important.

Everyone was happy to have dinner at home, so Susan and Rachel cooked pasta with chicken and local vegetables. They had after dinner drinks, and David and Sophia announced that they were tired and planned to go to bed, now that the baby was asleep.

Geoffrey suggested that they move up to the master bedroom to watch television. After a tense period, Susan said. "Let's drop the bullshit. We all know what we want. Everyone just get naked and Geoffrey we do not need any effen games."

Susan reluctantly agreed to watch what Geoffrey called blue movies, but after fifteen minutes, Brian shut the TV down. "I'd rather do it than watch it." He said. Brian and Rachel left Geoffrey and Susan at foreplay, and went to the room across the hall.

Later, Geoffrey rolled to his back and looked at his watch. "Luv, you seem insatiable but I am exhausted and spent. I do not believe I have anything left in the tank, literally and figuratively."

Susan tried to mount him. "You cannot imagine how long I have waited to orgasm repeatedly. I actually forgot what the feeling would be like to just cum over and over. One more time, and I promise to leave you alone."

"We must talk. I have exciting news. I placed a bid on property on Cariacou." He said.

Susan kissed him and rolled off. "Tell me everything." She said.

"What do you remember of my plans?" He asked, as he got off the bed to pick up some papers from his desk.

"As I recall, you wanted take me on holiday for nefarious purpose." Susan said laughing.

"This is what I envision." He said as he spread the papers out on the bed. "A resort for adults, not like Sandals or the other poshy expensive places, but primitive, back to nature. There would be buildings on stilts in case any water came up the beach. Very tropical housing with palm fronds and stuff like that, and a place where guests might purchase provisions and such."

"Restaurant?" She asked.

"No Cariacou has quite built up now. More than enough hotels and restaurants. This will be a place for adults to lose their inhibitions, and just enjoy each other's company. No television, mind you, but lots of books. I plan to stock a library. A restaurant might actually cramp their style, so to speak." He added.

"Is this a nudist colony?" She asked.

"Depends upon the choices our guests might make. I certainly plan to be naked as a jaybird each day, unless I have to leave the premises. How about you?"

"I would give it serious consideration, since the thought of doing it is excites me." She said. "How big is this property. Will it be easy to develop? And most important, what is going to cost?"

"The local government is terribly corrupt. I have some money for a down payment on construction, and I'll hire all local people. The property totals about eighty acres with almost thirty acres of beachfront. The rest is palm forest, most of which I would leave intact. A man, who recently passed, owned it and his daughter wishes to dispose of the property, and move to London. I am flying down the next day or so to meet with her and her attorney."

"I'm going with you." She said. "We had better speak with Brian and Rachel, now."

"It's quite late. What if they are in the middle of…you know?" He said.

"This is much too important to wait," she said as she threw a robe around her self and opened the bedroom door.

Brian and Rachel were still awake, lying in bed talking when Susan and Geoffrey entered. "We have to something to tell you." Susan said.

Geoffrey outlined his plans for the resort and explained that he and Susan would be flying down to Cariacou as early as possible. "Susan, of course, as my barrister."

Brian was not pleased with any of it. "How well have you thought this out?" He asked.

"I have been working on this concept for years." He went on to describe the physical layout, and how he would meet construction costs.

"Whose are these people who would want to come down to Cariacou?" Rachel asked.

"Well to do young people, stock brokers and lawyers, most of whom in need of getting away from it all. Each house would rent for $5000 U.S. per week. I envision healthy young men and women, eager to just have fun. I plan for 24 houses. You do the math."

"What will there be for them to do?" Rachel asked. "These people are constantly on the go."

"That is exactly the point. They can do absolutely nothing. They can relate to themselves, and others in the resort. Some might seek out each other for the same satisfaction we have enjoyed. Of course, we will have separate accommodations on our own fifteen or more acres of beach and palm forest." Geoffrey added.

"So, you plan to be a high class pimp, Geoffrey? And who exactly are the WE that will be living on the fifteen acres adjoining your fun palace?" Brian asked.

Susan ignored her husband's first reference. "I plan to take that holiday with Geoffrey that I turned down five years ago. We will build it together, Brian. You can market it from New York, and Rachel from here on Barbados. There could be boating trips through the Grenadines with people staying a week at our resort. It would be opened 365 days every year. Miles might even be interested in promoting it through Pirate Adventures." Susan said. Geoffrey thought that to be an excellent point.

"What about your work? What about me? What do you plan to tell Meghan and David?" Brian asked.

Susan sighed and bundled her robe tightly around her. "I have always resented that you would not allow me to go years ago, and my unhappiness has been building, Brian. I have already indicated to my partners, that I planned to take a sabbatical. The firm owes me for many billing hours that will provide some money to help the project." She thought for a moment. "Brian, while I love you, I have been brutal towards you. I believe that some time away from each other will be a good thing. David will understand for obvious reasons and Meghan will have to know the truth."

"It was never a matter of giving my permission." Brian said. "It was something that I did not expect my wife to do."

"Rachel pulled the covers up to her neck. "If you go through with this Geoffrey, I am going to Antigua to be with Sara." Rachel said. "I could not stay in Barbados and endure the stares and cackles. David was going to tell you tomorrow but he received a letter from London. Both of his books will be published, and there is interest in obtaining movie rights. So the children will be financially secure."

"And just when do you plan to come home, Susan" Brian asked, angrily.

"That will depend upon when we meet our objective." She said. "I will call you often as I can, and write to tell you how everything coming along."

Geoffrey was able to find air accommodations to Cariacou for a late morning flight, so Brian and Rachel drove them to the airport. On the trip back to Simonton, Rachel began to sob. My whole life has been turned upside down, Brian."

"Come back to New York with me," He pleaded.

"Geoffrey signed Simonton over to me. I am gifting it to David and Sophia. I'll pack what I need, and I plan to go to Antigua tomorrow." She said.

"I wish you would reconsider coming with me." Brian said as the car approached the Great House. "We need each other more than ever right now."

"I have lived here for all of my married life, and will miss it and the island terribly. Most of all, I will miss you and David, Sophia and Richard. Sara is still troubled and I need to be with her. I will still love Geoffrey despite his foolishness. Come. We have to tell the children."

Rachel left Barbados the next day, and Brian was back in the apartment in New York three days later. For the next two months, he heard nothing from Susan. The work overload in the new office kept him sufficiently occupied. The terrible events of 9/11 remained on everyone's mind, and troops were sent into Afghanistan.

"It was late afternoon and he was preparing to leave the office when Susan called. "How are you Luv?" She asked as if nothing had happened.

She went on to tell him that construction was going well with the seed money she was able to contribute. "You will just love it here." She said. "We have our own home and beach, and we sea bathe whenever we wish."

"Geoffrey is well? I gather?" Brian asked without emotion.

"He is just great. Like a little kid in his own tropical play ground. How is Rachel?"

"Rachel moved to Antigua as she said she would. I received a brief note three weeks ago, but have not spoken with her. I am concerned about her." He said.

"We have heard nothing either." She gave him a phone number. "It's a new cell phone. Please call me if you hear any thing."

"How about I call you just to talk with you. I love you Susan." He said.

"I know." She said. "Please call."

When Brian returned to the apartment, he found the answering machine flashing. It was so good to hear Rachel's voice. She wanted to come to see him if he still wanted her.

He dialed the number she had left. "Of course I want you, he said before Hello."

Rachel told him that Sara had met a young man assigned to help the new people, as they were admitted to the facility. She said that Sara had progressed so well, she would be allowed to live outside the hospital, but required to return for therapy. She would live with Noah and his family until they found a place of their own.

"So I am happy for them both. I want to come see you. I can be on the afternoon plane to Newark if that's not too much trouble." She said.

"Trouble? If the only flight you could get were to D.C., I would drive down there. Oh, and I heard from Susan. She is very excited about what they have accomplished."

"I bet they are." She said tersely. "Geoffrey has called twice. In fact I just got off the phone with him. He was happy for Sara."

They spoke for a half hour more, and Brian took down her flight information. He called the concierge downstairs and arranged for a car to take him to Newark, late the following afternoon.

Then he dialed the number Susan had given him and got her voice mail. He left a message that Rachel had called and would be staying with him at the apartment.

Brian had not been on the Turnpike for years, but it appeared that none of the sordid scenery had changed for the better. He went into the terminal at Newark, leaving the driver to be harassed by the airport Gestapo, and found Rachel, looking splendid, waiting for her bags at the carousel. They hugged and kissed and she seemed not to wish to let go. Brian carried her luggage out to the curb, and was fortunate to spot the car and driver coming around for the third time. They finally returned to the apartment, enjoyed a long, lingering kiss in the elevator, and he moved her luggage directly into the bedroom he had shared with Susan. "Find some empty drawers and put your stuff in, Luv. Wash up if need be, then I'll get us some drinks."

Rachel walked around the spacious apartment to get her bearings. She found Brian in the kitchen, seasoning two large steak filets. "Fancy garlic mashed? I left our drinks in the living room."

After dinner, they sipped cognac and sat on the couch talking. "What do we do if Susan and Geoffrey want us to join them for some reason." Rachel inquired.

Brian kissed her. "We go. It's as simple as that. They may have something. We could give it a chance." He said.

"I have given my husband so many chances, you know. If the situation might arise, I'll think about it, but promise nothing. Brian, how long may I stay here with you?" She asked.

"Forever," he said, and taking her hand led her into the bedroom, where they undressed. It does not appear that there will be a demand for your side of the bed." He admired how beautiful she was standing naked, so casually, in front of him. "Do you realize that we have never showered together?"

"Now is as good a time as ever." She said, taking his hand.

They made love in the shower, dried each other off with warm towels, and crawled under the covers. At three in the morning, he woke her up and pulled her on top of him."

The next morning, he received a call from Meghan. "I have been so busy with work and moving, I lost touch with every one. I got a bizarre letter from Mom that she was still somewhere in the Grenadines building a resort with Geoffrey. What's up Father?"

He went on to explain as much as he knew about the resort, and then told her that Rachel was staying with him at the apartment. "On Mom's side of the bed?" She asked.

"Oh, my God. The book. David's book. It's all about the four of you! Jay suspected something, when he read the proofs David sent. And now I understand, Hollywood may be calling. How exciting my mother and father could soon be on the big screen screwing their heads off with my brother's in-laws."

"I understand your anger, and we have a great deal of explaining to do to you and Jay. It may seem bizarre to you, but the four of us took a chance and liked it." He explained why Rachel was in New York, and asked that Meghan not be angry with her. Meghan agreed to have lunch with them on the weekend.

Almost two years from the day that Susan and Geoffrey had left for Cariacou, letters arrived at the apartment addressed to both Rachel and Brian. In them, were requests that they both come for an extended stay. It took a day and a half to convince Rachel just to go and see what it was like. Brian called Susan's cell phone and left a message that they would leave for Cariacou in two weeks.

Fifty

Barbados 2004

David, holding four year old Richard, tightly in his arms, rode the beautiful Arabian, he had given the name, Simonton's Future, up the hill toward the overgrown cemetery. He had purchased the horse from Clyde Harris, who had ridden him last at the Wednesday afternoon polo matches on Holder's Hill.

The small cemetery was still sheltered by the Tamarind tree that had watched over the burial site of the many Barbadians who had called the historic plantation home.

David dismounted, and carefully placed his son on the ground. After tethering Future to a nearby tree, he smiled. "Okay, Richard today is clean up day. The people buried here deserve better than to have their only remembrance blurred by all of this vegetation. The young boy smiled, and ran to the top of the hill that led down to the beach.

"Daddy, I wish to take a sea bath. Can we please?" Richard said. He had picked up some of the singsong Bajan cadence from some of his friends.

"Deal, Richard but only when we finish what we came here to do." David gave him a high-five to seal the deal. "Start pulling weeds. You are a very strong boy." David said as he showed his son how to grasp the foliage at its base and pull.

It took well over an hour to remove the growth from the old stones, that were the only markers giving evidence to the existence of the strong men and women, who had dedicated their lives to Barbados. Richard pulled a large clump of grass exposing a stone whose markings he was able to make out.

"Daddy, look!" The small boy called out. "I have found you." David looked carefully at the ancient stone. Richard was correct. Cleaning it off, he saw the name 'David McKenzie' carved into the gravestone.

"I don't know how to explain, son, other than to say that someone by that name once lived here at Simonton. We owe him so much. I read about him in some of Grandpa Geoffrey's books. One day, when you are a bit older, I will tell you about him. Let's clear a few more stones and then we can go for a swim in the sea. How would you like to ride a jet ski?" Richard clapped his hands. David laughed and chip singed. "If we do, it must be our secret from Mommy, Right?"

The little boy clapped again, and tried to chip sing. "True, True."

"Ah, chip singing is an art." David said, as he squeezed Richard's lips together. "Now try sucking in as if on a straw like so." The little boy did the best he could. "That was super. That was the best one yet."

Later in the day, Sophia told David that Richard had informed her of his great day, "And did he tell you that we cleared most of the grave sites on the hill?"

"Actually, he was very proud of finding someone with your name." Sophia said.

"Great," David said. "Anything else?"

"No, Luv, am I missing something?" She asked.

"Nothing I can think of." He said.

"Oh, and I saw the two of you on a jet ski. Have we heard anything from our parents?" She asked.

"Actually, yes. My Dad called this morning when you were at market. Your mother has been staying with him in New York. They plan to join my mother and your father in Cariacou. Their venture got off the ground quickly, and has started to turn a profit."

"What exactly is this thing they are doing?" She asked. "Sounds to me like an excuse to shack up."

"Sounds like a nudist colony to me?" He said.

"Exactly. I wouldn't put it past my father to think up something like that." Sophia said. "Are they happy?"

"From what I understand, extremely." He responded.

Sophia pursed her lips. "And, David, our life is becoming a bore. We wake up each morning, spend the day at the beach, eat dinner, watch television and go to sleep." She said.

"You forget the great sex, and the fact that I am trying grow sugar cane again. I really believe in that. I also see the value of growing vegetables on the island, and developing a canning industry, rather than bringing foods back in from outside at greater cost. The hotels and restaurants would be supportive. There is so much that we import that can be grown and developed right here so much more cheaply." David said.

"David, you are talking business. I want some fun. I just need to spend an evening out with friends, having a few drinks." Sophia said. "We have Anya to stay over with Richard, so let's just go out and have a good time."

"Then. Let's dress up instead of jeans and tees." He said.

David pulled into the last available space at the Coach House car park. "We are here, my Luv, let's find some old friends. Perhaps we'll make new friends."

Sophia, immediately found a group of people she knew from lower school. "David, be a Luv and do get me a rum and coke." She said as she moved away.

David was able to squeeze to the end of the long bar where one of the barmen recognized him. He felt her presence, and inhaled the exotic perfume worn by a woman who had just pressed against him. "How does one get a drink here?" A sultry voice asked.

"Not necessarily a problem, Luv. I can help with that. What is your pleasure?" He asked.

"What would you suggest?" She answered.

"Barbados has the best rums in the world. I would suggest a sipping rum we call Extra Old." He said as he ordered two glasses. "Now, as a member of the Commonwealth in excellent standing, mind you, I must know your name and everything pertinent about you."

She extended her hand. "I do not believe a word of it, but I like you. You sound more American to me. Are you a local?" She asked, taking a glass of the dark liquid from David.

"I am from New York, but am more Bajan than you. You like my choice of drink." David observed. "I am David and you are?"

"Rebecca Leigh Morrison, and my husband, Denis and I are on holiday to celebrate my birthday, which just happens to be today." She cooed.

"Fantastic! It is an ancient Barbadian dictum," he said. "That a maiden, while in celebration of her birthday, must reveal her age, or submit to a kiss to the person willing to buy her libation." David said.

"You are absolutely making that up." She said laughing.

"Do you dare chance the inevitable?" He asked.

"Never," she said, moving closer, allowing her tongue to explore his lips, and then lingering for a moment. "If it is required that I submit my age hourly, I duly refuse," she said as she reached her hand behind his neck pulling him toward her, so her breasts pressed firmly against his linen shirt. "I am going to love Barbados. So, are you going to ask me, again how old I am today?"

David ordered two more rums and asked the barman to run a tab. "Rebecca Luv, I would so like you to meet my wife and some of our friends. They are just over there." He said. " Now, this fellow Denis. Where is he?"

"He's a big boy and can take care of himself. I am certain that he'll find us." Rebecca said, taking his arm.

David introduced Rebecca to Sophia, Andy, Steven, and the women they all just met. Steven was doing his usual imitation of a vagina, by placing two fingers over his mouth while sticking his tongue through them. "That is lewd and I love it, Sophia said as her friends laughed. "I hope this display of Bajan humor has not vexed you, Rebecca."

"Vexed, oh, no, not at all. You will find that I am a very good sport. I see that Denis is about to join us," Rebecca said as she saw him approach.

Denis, at better than six feet and gym trim, was immediately welcomed by Sophia. "Our spouses have already met." Immediately taken by his good looks, Sophia offered to buy him a drink. Without waiting for any further introductions, he allowed her to lead him back to the crowded bar.

After they endured the local Bajan patois, and even Andy's failed attempt at downing a second yard of ale, the four found an empty booth under the stars, well away from the front entrance.

"So, where are you staying on our island?" David asked.

"We supposedly were housed at the Ocean Bluff Resort, but they overbooked, and our travel agent will hear from me," Denis said. Our bags are still there. We took a cab, and asked him to drop us at the best bar. "It seems so desolate over there."

"Actually, the East Coast is rather beautiful. Not much to do at night, well I guess that all depends." Sophia said as she finished her drink. I'll get you another. How about you two?" Denis asked.

Sophia and David found out that Rebecca and Denis were from Hartford, Connecticut, and he worked as an adjuster at an insurance company, while she did reporting for a Fox News affiliate. They had been married eight years and had no children. Denis returned with three glasses of Extra Old and a Banks beer for himself.

David said that the Banks beer was an excellent choice and brewed right on the island. "Might I be presumptive and suggest the following. Rather than having to drive all the way back to your hotel where you do not have a room, stay with us for the night."

Sophia said. "Grand idea, David." Denis watched her drain her glass and marveled that she did not seem at all drunk And have either of you been instructed on how to do a Barbadian quickie?"

"I'm game for anything." He said. "Teach me. Rebecca seems to be in good hands." He said as he watched his wife walk with David to inspect a beautifully carved old carriage that sat on flat stones near the car park.

Later, as the four young people began to enjoy their chance meeting, David, again suggested that it was too late to drive back to the East Coast, and there were no cabs in the car park. "Besides, you might have to sleep out on the beach."

"We have an estate in St James, just a short distance away, actually. We have more than enough room. Stay with us, and if you don't like our accommodations, which incidentally are free, I will take you tomorrow to collect your bags and anywhere else you wish. There is no obligation whatsoever. I am certain we have duds that will fit you for tonight."

"Free is good, Denis." Rebecca said. "We can't turn down free" Denis needed little prodding to agree to David's proposal. David paid his bar tab, and taking Sophia's arm led them to the Mercedes. Rebecca did not hesitate when David opened the passenger door for her, and asked her to get in. Sophia gently pulled Denis in next to her in the back seat.

As David drove from the Coach House onto the quiet highway, Rebecca moved closer and whispered in his ear. "Do you switch? Denis may need a bit of prodding, but it's clear he likes Sophia." David smiled. He was pleased with Sophia's choice for an evening out.

When they arrived at Simonton Great House, Sophia led Rebecca up the stairs to the upper floor, to show her where they would stay for the night. "Your home is lovely," Rebecca said. "And where is your room?"

Sophia opened the door into the master bedroom and both women entered. When the room was illuminated, Rebecca gasped, as she saw that the walls and ceilings were mirrored. "I can see myself at every possible angle," she said.

Sophia laughed. "That would be the general idea." She said. "Daddy brought the mirrors from another home, that was torn down to make room for condominiums. David remembered they were in storage and had them installed."

Rebecca washed up in the bathroom Sophia indicated would be hers, and changed into a top and shorts that Sophia had left on the bed for her. Rebecca opened one of the bureau drawers and found one of Susan's new thongs. She smiled wondering what David or Denis might say if she dared to wear it.

Sophia found Rebecca waiting at the top of the stairs, and led her back down to the first floor and back out to the patio, where their husbands sat talking. David poured four glasses of rum and they toasted to their new friendship.

"Denis", Rebecca said. You must come up and see the master bedroom. It is all mirrored from floor to ceiling."

"In some ways a gift from both of our fathers." David said.

"Sounds like a veritable play ground for adults." Denis remarked clicking his glass with Sophia's." I can't wait." Rebecca smiled knowing he was hooked. David was not absolutely certain where this all was leading, but wondered if there might be enough material for a new book.

Fifty-one

Cariacou 2005

Rachel and Brian landed at the airport in Cariacou, collected their luggage, and looked around for Geoffrey and Susan. A man approached, carrying a small sign upon was written the words 'Master Brian'.

"You are the persons described to me. Welcome to Cariacou." He said. "I am to take you to Choices." He loaded their bags into a van and smiled. "Please get in, and I shall carry you there. It will take about 30 minutes and is quite isolated you know."

The island had grown up a bit, since they were last there. They saw what appeared to be a hotel in the distance, but not much else to suggest development of the tourist trade. Their driver introduced himself as Michael, and said he worked for Choices, a small resort that catered to couples wishing to enjoy each other to the fullest as 'Mr. Geoffrey says'. "That would be man and lady. We have enough of the other folk in the Grenadines."

Brian thought best not to comment on what Michael had just said. "We have been here before when we sailed from St. Vincent to Grenada, a while back and moored in the harbor overnight. We stopped at an artist's shop. Canute Caliste, his name was."

"Oh, Mr. Canute passed a while back. His paintings are quite valuable now." He said.

"Damn!" Brian said. "Always a bridesmaid."

"Sorry," Michael responded. "Did not quite get that."

"Ignore him." Rachel said, taking Brian's hand. How far are we from...Choices?"

"The resort is just down the hill now, and ahead to the beach. We are on Choices property as I speak." Michael said.

They reached a pink, stucco coated visitor center at the base of the hill. A sign over the concierge desk indicated that they had arrived at 'CHOICES, A Resort Catering to Uninhibited Adults'. Driving around the building, Michael steered to a narrow road, passing about two-dozen frond covered buildings, each securely set on a system of poles, that elevated them above the sand. Each structure sat upon a little more than a quarter of an acre, providing some semblance of privacy. Almost at the entrance was another building, whose sign indicated it, was where provisions might be purchased.

"We are full," Michael volunteered, and we have been, since the doors opened. Now most of the guests are down at the beach swimming, fishing or doing some boating you know." Michael said. "Please do not be offended if some are all unclothed. I am so used to it, that I pay them no mind. Choices." He drove on to a locked gate that opened from a remote attached to the visor. Once they had passed through, they found themselves on an isolated tract of beach. Michael maneuvered the Rover toward a large frond-thatched structure, also supported by stilts, and perhaps one hundred yards away from the sea.

"I shall unload your bags now, and then go back to the resort, where I am the manager. I trust that you shall enjoy your stay on Cariacou to its fullest." Afterwards, he waved and drove the van back toward the gate.

Susan was the first to greet them. She was nude and seemed quite comfortable. Geoffrey came up from the beach with fish he had just caught. He was naked as well. Rachel marveled at the total bronze tans both sported. It was momentarily a bit awkward, until Brian made an observation. "This is silly. I have seen my wife naked. As a matter a fact, we all have been naked doing more with each other than standing around gawking." Brian quickly disrobed and tossed everything he had worn onto the sand, and Rachel followed suit without missing a beat.

Brian looked at Susan. "You look absolutely radiant." He said. "So very different."

"Different? Yes very different and giddily happy." She said as she embraced Brian and then Rachel. "You too will soon have no tan lines, Rachel." No one is watching us. So no concerns, since we own all of the land upon which we stand. No one cares what we do, and we have no prurient interests with regard to our guests at Choices Resort. How they interact is their choice. Actually, we seldom see them. Michael is very efficient you know. We do dress sparingly if we must go into town however, and that's a drag."

"Susan, I find it hard to believe that you would agree to give up, well, things for this back to nature existence." Brian said.

"Brian, believe it or not, I have become, thanks to Geoffrey, completely free of inhibitions." Susan said. "As we wrote in our letters, Geoffrey and I want you to join us and remain here. We can fly to Barbados or New York, as we might desire, with the understanding that it is here we belong and will return. If you believe that the choices we have made will lead to complete happiness, we ask you both to consider this."

Geoffrey brought out a bottle of rum from the house. "I received letters from David and Sophia, and Meghan. They would like to visit with us. Jay, on the other hand, felt that he might not be within his comfort zone. On the other hand both Justin and Jessica thought what we were doing to be simply amazing, as she put it, and look forward to visit. They shall all be welcome."

Susan took the bottle from Geoffrey and opened it. She went through her normal toast to rum as every one took their turns taking a drink.

Later that evening, as the cook fires turned to embers, Brian, Susan, Geoffrey and Rachel, lay naked together on the moonlight, drenched beach.

"We belong to each other and hide nothing from each other. You noticed that there are no doors even on the toilets. You must admit, Brian that for me that is a significant concession. Geoffrey and I have found that sex is greater when spontaneous, and there are times that we might fulfill our fantasies in the sand, the palm forest or the surf. We invite you to become part of our life. There are times we make love, and other times we allow the animal in us to take over. Both have become so pleasurable, and we hope you both will share these times with us. Geoffrey and I have denied each other nothing." Susan reached for Brian's hand.

"There is a book in the bedroom called the Karma Sutra. We want you to join us in experimenting with many of the amazing sexual positions defined in it. I love you Brian, and I love Geoffrey and Rachel equally as well. What has led us all here is a chance decision we made in the car park of the Coach House in 1986. It has turned out to be a good one. Look at it this way, now the two of you gents will be blessed with having a perpetual hard-on."

Brian lay back on the cool sand and stared at the star filled sky. "We were concerned about the stability of our marriage, after that first night. Then we continued to experiment, taking our sexual experience almost to the nth degree, and congratulated ourselves that we, as a couple were still together, and that our children would somehow understand. Over these past nineteen years, we have learned a great deal about each other and, and I about myself." He took Susan's hand and kissed it. "What would have happened if Rachel and I had decided not to come here?"

Susan leaned over and kissed Brian. "I would have never let that happen."

Rachel put her mouth onto Susan's right nipple, slowly running her tongue around it. "Okay, Susan and I have worked out a reasonable schedule. Monday, Tuesday, Thursday, Saturday and Sunday, all day and night, we are yours in every conceivable way. Be advised that on Wednesday and Friday afternoons, the two of us will fully participate in and enjoy, a very private, and different kind of love.

LUV BAJAN STYLE is a work of fiction. The names of people in the novel do not exist in the context depicted and are for the most part, a product of my imagination. The names of places, such as the bars, restaurants, beaches and hotels, however exist or once existed. The Law firms and enterprises run by the Townsands are not real, nor does the Pirate Adventure Cruise exist as such. The Merrymen are a real Barbadian band that entertained for over twenty years all over the world. The islands that make up the Grenadines do exist. We did once cruise the islands on a ship called The Lord Jim, but not the one depicted in the novel. Canute Caliste, a local artist, lived on Cariacou and painted primitive landscapes. Alas, he is no longer with us. Sadly, the adult club. Choices Resorts does not now and never (sic) has existed on Cariacou. Barbados and its amazing people will always have a special place in my heart and mind.

The following books will soon be made available:

A LONG BEAT TO WINDWARD: multi-generational Historical Novel About Barbados

GODPLAYERS: Murder In Health Management Org.

AN INSURABLE DEATH: Murder and Recourse Insurance

THE KENYAN LEGACY

CHOICES

A TROPICAL RESORT FOR UNINHBITED ADULTS

CARIACOU ISLAND THE GRENADINES

Just picture yourself spending a week, living in thatch rooved huts built up on stilts, with acres of cocoanut forests and beach surrounding you. Each unit contains one bedroom, a bathroom and small kitchen/dining room. The cool nightly breeze from the sea makes air-conditioning unnecessary and while there is no TV or Wi-Fi on the grounds of the resort, you will find all of the usual hotel type amenities a short walk away. Guests may purchase assorted liquor and food supplies at a store located on the grounds.

Where else can young couples find space away from their big city lives, and spend a week unabashed, undressed and totally uninhibited? The resort provides fishing and scuba gear, along with water scooters as part of your vacation package

We are now completely booked into April 2007, but we can put you on our waiting list which is strongly advised.

For more information call 866-REAL-LOVE
OR visit our website at www.choices.com

22581527R00355

Made in the USA
Lexington, KY
04 May 2013